'Creole began to tell us what the blues were ~~~~~~ about anything very new. He and the boys up there were keeping it new, at the risk of ruin, destruction, madness and death, in order to find new ways to make us listen. For, while the tale of how we suffer and how we are delighted, and how we may triumph is never new, it always must be heard. There isn't any other tale to tell, it's the only light we've got in all this darkness' – 'Sonny's Blues'

Jazz is more than music, more than a look, an attitude – it's a way of life. HOT AND COOL takes the reader deep into this world of hot music and cool people with contemporary short stories by some of the world's most celebrated writers.

The eclectic spirit of the great Charlie Parker is brought to life in Julio Cortázar's 'The Pursuer'; the revolutionary exuberance of jazz is examined in Amiri Baraka's 'The Screamers'; the black and white art worlds collide in Langston Hughes' 'The Blues I'm Playing'; the drug addiction that plagues the world jazz was born in is explored in James Baldwin's classic 'Sonny's Blues'.

With stories by Eudora Welty, Peter De Vries, Maya Angelou, Donald Barthelme and others also included, HOT AND COOL is a stunning collection that carries all the power and colour of the music itself.

MARCELA BRETON is a jazz and literary critic whose work has appeared in numerous magazines and periodicals, including *Jazz Times*, *Coda*, *Americas*, *El Taller Literario* and *GCN*. She holds a master's degree in Library and Information Science from the University of Texas and lives in Bethel, Connecticut.

HOT AND COOL
Jazz Short Stories

HOT AND COOL
Jazz Short Stories

Edited by
MARCELA BRETON

BLOOMSBURY

First published in Great Britain 1991
Copyright © 1990 by Marcela Breton

This paperback edition published 1991

Bloomsbury Publishing Ltd,
2 Soho Square, London W1V 5DE

The moral right of the author has been
asserted

A CIP catalogue record for this book is
available from the British Library

ISBN 0 7475 0815 1

Printed in Great Britain by Clays Ltd, St Ives Plc

This book is dedicated to Nancy
(with the laughing face),
and to Dexter Gordon,
master raconteur on the tenor saxophone.

CONTENTS

"When Lester came out he played very melodic. . . . He was always telling a story and Bird did the same thing. That kind of musical philosophy is what I try to do because telling a story is, I think, where it's at."

DEXTER GORDON

". . . literature is forever blowing a horn, singing about youth when youth is irretrievably gone, singing about your homeland . . ."

JOSEF SKVORECKY

INTRODUCTION

THERE IS HEIGHTENED interest and expectation when two art forms intersect and create out of their meeting new visions of beauty, truth, and emotion. We wish to believe that the arts are related and while we can accept that the muses lead separate lives, it is pleasing now and again to see them in sisterly rapport. Those paintings variously titled "The Reader" or "Woman with a Book" captivate by the promise they hold out of enlarging and expressing, through a different vernacular, the unique nature of the reading experience. When Marcel Proust describes the "little phrase" of Vinteuil's sonata in *Remembrance of Things Past,* we hold our breath and prick up our ears, as it were, in the hope that he will further articulate the particular feelings music arouses. The conjunction of music with other art forms has relevance to the jazz listener in works such as Henri Matisse's *Jazz,* the movies *Round Midnight* and *Bird,* Dorothy Baker's novel *Young Man with a Horn* the poetry of Langston Hughes and Ted Joans, and Jack Gelber's play *The Connection.* A further illustration of the relationship between music and literature has been the latter's borrowing of certain musical forms and structures. Proust compared his great novel to a symphony and referred to *Swann's Way* as the opening movement. Other examples of literary works that employ the characteristics of musical composition include Aldous Huxley's *Point Counter Point* and T. S. Eliot's *Four Quartets*.

This anthology of jazz stories was conceived with the idea that the exploration of the jazz theme in a short story would seduce the music lover and the reader of short fiction by bringing together two artistic streams and thereby deepening the reservoir of "beauty-truths," to borrow Aldous Huxley's famous phrase. The jazz devotee will find the pleasures of the music authenticated by their translation into prose fiction. We read stories, in part, to find our thoughts and experiences mirrored, and thereby verified, by the author. The language of music appeals to our emotions; it stimulates impressions that exhilarate, sadden, or make pensive. Prose acts on the intellect first and subsequently traces a route to the emotions. Words pertain to the topography of the mind, while the sounds of music, particularly popular music, belong to the geography of the heart. Jazz, however, appeals to us viscerally and intellectually. These stories articulate its dual nature, while also decoding and extending the musical idiom so as to illuminate the visage of jazz in unexpected ways. The lover of literature will traverse the same road as the jazz fan but in an opposite direction. He will seek out the music as a substantiation of what he has read in the stories. He will want the words translated into the sounds. These short stories serve as a link between the worlds of music and literature; a bridge permitting a steady flow of traffic between the two regions.

Music and literature have features in common. They are alike in their power to disinter the past, to resuscitate forgotten scenes and memories. In James Baldwin's "Sonny's Blues," the narrator relives whole segments of the past when he goes to hear his brother play jazz. These episodes of pain and grief are evoked and momentarily transcended through the agency of jazz. The music reconnects the narrator with his past while simultaneously liberating him of its oppressive burden; in feeling fully, he is somehow freed. "I saw my mother's face again, and felt, for the first time, how the stones of the road she had walked on must have bruised her feet. I saw the moonlit road where my father's brother died. And it brought something else back to me, and carried me past it; I saw my little girl again and felt Isabel's tears again, and I felt my own tears begin to rise. And I was yet aware that this was only a moment, that the world waited outside, as hungry as a tiger, and that trouble stretched above us, longer than the sky."

The short story is a particularly appropriate vehicle for the jazz theme. The jazz musician has always viewed his role as that of a storyteller. In fact, to refer to the jazz musician as a teller of tales has become a truism. The great Lester Young acknowledged the influence of the saxophonist Frankie Trumbauer and spoke of how "Trumbauer always told a little story." The alto saxophonist Art Pepper defined the best jazz musicians as being the "best storytellers" and likened their accomplishments to that of the adroit conversationalist who is able to "paint the best word picture." The noted jazz critic Leonard Feather, in analyzing the artistry of the drummer Elvin Jones, wrote that "Jones's storytelling . . . reminds me that his main achievement is the creation of a circle of sound. . . ." Kid Jones, the percussionist in Ann Petry's "Solo on the Drums" makes of his instrument a lyrical mouthpiece with which he tells of past joys and present anguishes. "He made the big drum rumble and reverberate. He went a little mad on the big drum. Again and again he filled the theater with a sound like thunder. The sound seemed to come not from the drums but from deep inside himself; it was a sound that was being wrenched out of him—a violent, raging, roaring sound. As it issued from him he thought, This is the story of my love, this is the story of my hate, this is all there is left of me."

Feather's term "a circle of sound" can be modified and easily applied to the structure of the short story: a circle of language. The staple of the jazz repertoire is the 32-bar song, a loosely structured composition with a defined opening and closing in which the middle portion is given over to improvisation. The principle of circularity is integral to the short story where within the limits imposed by the beginning and ending the writer is allowed a degree of extemporization. The late Julio Cortazar, a practitioner of both forms, wrote: "My experience tells me that in a sense a short story like the ones I have been describing does not have a prose structure. . . . I have been struck by the degree to which the effectiveness and the meaning of the story depend on those values that give poetry, like jazz, its specific character: tension, rhyme, internal rhythms, the unexpected within the parameters of the anticipated, that fatal liberty that cannot be altered without an irrevocable loss." In these stories we find language that mimics the rhythmic cadences of music and acquires the improvisatory beauty of the best jazz. Donald Barthelme's "The King of Jazz" gives us the "unexpected within the parameters of the anticipated" in prose that is richly inventive and melodic. "You mean that sound that sounds like the cutting edge of life? That sounds like polar bears crossing Arctic ice pans? That sounds like a herd of musk ox in full flight? That sounds like male walruses diving to the bottom of the sea? That sounds like fumaroles smoking on the slopes of Mt. Katmai? That sounds like the wild turkey walking through the deep, soft forest? That sounds like beavers chewing trees in an Appalachian marsh? That sounds like an oyster fungus growing on an open aspen trunk? That sounds like a mule deer wandering a montane of the

Sierra Nevada? That sounds like prairie dogs kissing?"
Barthelme's stream-of-consciousness writing is very much
like the jazz musician's improvised solo.

The stories collected here cover the entire range of the
jazz experience: the musical styles such as the blues,
boogie-woogie, swing and bebop as well as the social and
psychological factors that have shaped the jazz musician.
These nonmusical factors have included racism, drugs,
mental illness, low pay and poor working conditions. The
universality of jazz, its appeal to diverse foreign cultures
is shown in stories that are variously set in France,
Eastern Europe, and Mexico, and by the presence of
writers such as the Argentine Julio Cortazar and the
Czechoslovakian Josef Skvorecky.

Many of these stories explore the rich traditions of the
black race. The American black experience is the well-
spring of jazz music, and these stories express that reality in its joyous as well as suffering dimensions. In Eudora
Welty's "Powerhouse," we meet a "person of joy, a fanatic," the great Powerhouse, a pianist in the style of
Albert Ammons and Meade Lux Lewis who lives as in-
tensely as he plays. He approaches every facet of his life
with the same gusto and appetite. In Leroi Jones' "The
Screamers," a honking saxophonist of the Illinois Jacquet-
Gene Ammons school of tenors, and his sidemen, lead a
trail of nightclub patrons into the streets. The spilling
into the streets by the black musicians and their audience is meant to signify a symbolic recapture of the city
by its oppressed minority. The cacophonous sound and
the weaving disruption of traffic is a prefigurement of
the revolution. "We screamed and screamed at the clear
image of ourselves as we should always be. Ecstatic,
completed, involved in a secret communal expression. It
would be the form of the sweetest revolution, to hucklebuck
into the fallen capital, and let the oppressors lindy hop
out." Toni Cade Bambara's "Medley" celebrates the humor and originality of speech indigenous to black cul-

ture. "Medley," "The Screamers," and "Powerhouse" evoke and salute what LeRoi Jones has referred to as the "black cults of emotion."

Racism and poverty are the suffering side of the black experience. The beauty and longevity of jazz are a tribute to the indomitability of the black race, its persistent pursuit of artistic dreams in the face of daunting circumstances. The sounds of jazz are the speech of the disenfranchised and the marginal. Jazz is arguably the most significant artistic movement of the twentieth century and it is the black American's unique contribution to universal culture. These two facts taken together serve to enfeeble and ultimately disarm the bigot.

In J. F. Powers' "He Don't Plant Cotton," we have the near-archetypal tale of a jazz trio menaced by a group of white, drunken Southern men. Although abused and harassed the trio gains a moral victory in the end. In Maya Angelou's "The Reunion," Miss Philomena Jenkins, a black jazz pianist, understands that she has risen above her former white employer by the fact of her constant struggle to express her identity in musical terms. Her talent is a richer patrimony than any economic or social status. In C. W. Smith's "The Plantation Club," there is no moral or spiritual gain. A bebop musician and the two white boys who idolize him are arrested for smoking marijuana. The black saxophonist is put in jail while the white boys are released to their parents. The ending of "The Plantation Club" is bitterly ironic.

Langston Hughes was a master ironist and a writer who celebrated jazz in poetry, fiction, and essays. Although he has been called the greatest black American writer, his genius remains underappreciated. The stories in his collection *The Ways of White Folks* are perfect examples of the form. In "The Blues I'm Playing," Hughes brilliantly examines the divisions that separate blacks and whites by focussing on the relationship between the wealthy Manhattan socialite, Mrs. Ellsworth, and her protégée Oceola Jones, a virtuoso black pianist.

Humor is the key ingredient in Donald Barthelme's "The King of Jazz" and Peter De Vries's "Jam Today." Barthleme satirizes an established jazz ritual, the cutting contest. The De Vries story pits a lover of swing music against the adherents of bop and creates humor out of this clash in tastes.

Julio Cortazar's "The Pursuer," is based on incidents in the life of Charlie Parker. Cortazar took the factual details of Parker's troubled life and sifted and transformed them into a moving work of fiction. "The Pursuer" also offers a portrait of the jazz critic and of the symbiotic and oftentimes fractious relationship he maintains with the musician. Bruno, the critic, is a man who worries that his biography of Johnny, the Parker character, will be rendered null and void by Johnny's future actions. "To be honest, what does his life matter to me? The only thing that bothers me is that if he continues to let himself go on living as he has been . . . he'll end up by making lies out of the conclusions I've reached in my book. He might let it drop somewhere that my statements are wrong, that his music's something else."

The expatriate scene has been a significant offshoot of jazz for as long as black musicians have gone abroad in search of greater income, artistic freedom, respect, and esteem. France has welcomed many of these musicians, and in Richard Yates' "A Really Good Jazz Piano" and Terry Southern's "You're Too Hip, Baby" the settings are the Riviera and Paris. The Yates story shows that the bogeyman of bigotry knows no boundaries and that he takes possession of the well-educated sophisticate as much as of the ignorant red-neck. Southern's story is an ironic look at the essential hollowness of those who would view jazz and its musicians as mere notches in the belt of hipness.

In Josef Skvorecky's "Eine Kleine Jazzmusik," set in

Eastern Europe, and Willard Marsh's "Mending Wall,"
set in Mexico, we read about prejudice against Jews and
Hispanics, respectively. Skvorecky's story examines the
dangers of playing jazz in a pro-Nazi environment where
hatred of "nigger jazz" is as virulent as anti-Semitism. In
"Mending Wall," a group of pre-law Anglo students show
their contempt for their Latin "friend" by using his prized
jazz record collection as an instrument of torture.

Jazz stories operate under the same imperative as other
short fiction: to dramatize human situations and emotions through strong characterization and powerful prose.
In addition, they seek to duplicate, or at the very least
suggest, the sounds of jazz. Clearly, this is an ambitious
aim, since no art form can fully usurp the properties of
another. All of these stories, in small or large measure,
essay the challenge of describing the music. They do so
by using the full arsenal of poetic, rhythmic and meta-
phoric language at their disposal. To their credit these
writers are judicious in their efforts. They are conscious
of their status as guests in the house of music and at no
moment do they try to settle in as permanent residents.
They tend to keep their descriptions brief and to use
oblique or indirect methods to depict jazz music. Al Young,
in his story "Chicken Hawk's Dream," communicates the
discipline imposed on the jazz instrumentalist by showing us his counterpart, the dreamer who lives in a drug-
induced haze. " 'Dreamed I was walking round New York,
you know, walkin round all the places where Bird walked
and seen all the shit he seen and all thru this dream I'm
playing the background music to my own dream, dig,
and it's on alto sax, man, and I'm cooking away something terrible and what surprise me is I can do the
fingerin and all that jive—I can blow that horn, I know I
can blow it in real life, I *know* I can!' " The story fuses
the world of music, dreams, and drugs, and reveals the
stark contrast between the stillborn fantasies of the drug

user and the musician's mature wrestling with his instrument.

The metaphor is the flower of prose fiction. It can be likened to the quote in jazz music. Metaphor and musical quote serve to embellish and adorn the surrounding context and are most effective when most natural and spontaneous. A strained metaphor or a planned quote do little but draw attention to themselves. Fiction lacking in metaphors is like a barren plain. The musician who quotes aptly seduces by his sheer exuberance and by his mastery of musical history. Metaphor and musical quote are the stamps of the artist's individuality and originality.

Martin Gardner's "The Devil and the Trombone" cleverly juxtaposes an organ-playing angel and a trombone-playing devil to define the ecstatic and melancholy nature of jazz music. When the angel plays, the narrator writes that "a great peace settled over my soul. The world was good. Life was good. . . . All that seemed black and horrible was a necessary prelude to some greater goodness." Upon hearing the devil blow on the trombone a set of contrary feelings are stirred up. "And now my soul was troubled with a great unrest. All that we call good in life . . . was nothing but an illusion. Sickness and sin were the realities." The angel and the devil begin to jam and in their musical give and take they mirror the contradictory nature of life. "All the frenzied fullness and complexity of the modern world, with its curious mixture of good and evil, rose up before me." Jazz reflects the paradox of life and is at one and the same time joyous and sad.

In Terry Southern's "You're Too Hip, Baby" the metaphor is first a castle, then a cathedral, and finally a tapestry to indicate what jazz sounds like when one is stoned on hash.

Rudolph Fisher's "Common Meter" very nearly succeeds in duplicating the sounds of jazz. The story deals with those famous battle of the bands contests that flourished in the 1930s. The story hums with vibrancy and authenticity. The dialogue is ribald and humorous, and the descriptions of the musicians and their music transports us to that dance hall and induces us to join in the chorus of clapping by which audiences expressed their approval of a particular orchestra. "He had chosen the parent of blues songs, the old St. Louis Blues, and he adduced every device that had ever adorned that classic. Clarinets wailed, saxophones moaned, trumpets wept wretchedly, trombones laughed bitterly, even the great bass horn sobbed dismally from the depths. . . . Soon dancers closed their eyes, forgot their jostling neighbors, lost themselves bodily in the easy sway of that slow, fateful measure, vaguely aware that some quality hitherto lost had at last been found." In "Common Meter" the author orchestrates the elements of dialogue, humor, sensuality, and musical description to create a story that takes us back to a particular epoch of jazz history. For those of us born too late to have been participants or witnesses of these musical jousting contests, a story like "Common Meter" is the next best thing. When we listen to a recording of a famed carving contest, such as Dexter Gordon and Wardell Gray's "The Chase," we hear in the background the swelling roar of the crowd as the sax players take them to higher and higher musical plateaus. Rudolph Fisher adds to that roar by giving us the expressions and movements of that jubilant audience, by showing us how they flirt and argue with one another, how they interact with the musicians, in short, by providing the total range of gestures, reactions, and relations that typified these celebrated musical competitions.

Jazz stories can never eclipse the music. That is not their intention. The story a jazz musician narrates on his instrument is complete in itself. These prose tales at their best offer elaboration and coloration without replacing or distracting from the music. The story told by a musician is a shimmering orb that may glow more luminously in a finely crafted short story and, vice versa, these prose fictions acquire greater meaning and profundity in our renewed contact with the music. When this kind of artistic exchange occurs, fiction and jazz become fellow actors in the drama, as James Baldwin writes in "Sonny's Blues," of "how we suffer, and how we are delighted."

—Marcela Breton
Bethel, Connecticut

COMMON METER

THE ARCADIA, ON HARLEM'S Lenox Avenue, is "The World's Largest and Finest Ballroom—Admission Eighty-Five Cents." Jazz is its holy spirit, which moves it continuously from nine till two every night. Observe above the brilliant entrance this legend in white fire:

TWO—ORCHESTRAS—TWO

Below this in red:

FESS BAXTER'S FIREMEN

Alongside in blue:

BUS WILLIAMS' BLUE DEVILS

Still lower in gold:

HEAR THEM OUTPLAY EACH OTHER

So much outside. Inside, a blazing lobby, flanked by marble stairways. Upstairs, an enormous dance hall the length of a city block. Low ceilings blushing pink with rows of inverted dome lights. A broad dancing area, bounded on three sides by a wide soft-carpeted promenade, on the fourth by an ample platform accommodating the two orchestras.

People. Flesh. A fly-thick jam of dancers on the floor, grimly jostling each other; a milling herd of thirsty-eyed

boys, moving slowly, searchingly over the carpeted promenade; a congregation of languid girls, lounging in rows
of easy chairs here and there, bodies and faces uncon-
cerned, dark eyes furtively alert. A restless multitude of
empty, romance-hungry lives.

Bus Williams' jolly round brown face beamed down on
the crowd as he directed his popular hit—"She's Still My
Baby":

> You take her out to walk
> And give her baby-talk,
> But talk or walk, walk or talk—
>   She's still my baby!

But the cheese-colored countenance of Fessenden Baxter, his professional rival, who with his orchestra occupied the adjacent half of the platform, was totally oblivious
to "She's Still My Baby."

Baxter had just caught sight of a girl, and catching
sight of girls was one of his special accomplishments.
Unbelief, wonder, amazement registered in turn on his
blunt, bright features. He passed a hand over his straightened brown hair and bent to Perry Parker, his trumpetist.

"P.P., do you see what I see, or is it only the gin?"

"Both of us had the gin," said P.P., "so both of us sees
the same thing."

"Judas Priest! Look at that figure, boy!"

"Never was no good at figures," said P.P.

"I've got to get me an armful of that baby."

"Lay off, papa," advised P.P.

"What do you mean, lay off?"

"Lay off. You and your boy got enough to fight over
already, ain't you?"

"My boy?"

"Your boy, Bus."

"You mean that's Bus Williams' folks?"

"No lie. Miss Jean Ambrose, lord. The newest hostess.
Bus got her the job."

Fess Baxter's eyes followed the girl. "Oh, he got her the job, did he?—Well, I'm going to fix it so she won't need any job. Woman like that's got no business working anywhere."

"Gin," murmured P.P.

"Gin hell," said Baxter. "Gunpowder wouldn't make a mama look as good as that."

"Gunpowder wouldn't make you look so damn good, either."

"You hold the cat's tail," suggested Baxter.

"I'm tryin' to save yours," said P.P.

"Save your breath for that horn."

"Maybe," P.P. insisted, "she ain't so possible as she looks."

"Huh. They can all be taught."

"I've seen some that couldn't."

"Oh you have?—Well, P.P., my boy, remember, that's you."

Beyond the brass rail that limited the rectangular dance area at one lateral extreme there were many small round tables and clusters of chairs. Bus Williams and the youngest hostess occupied one of these tables while Fess Baxter's Firemen strutted their stuff.

Bus ignored the tall glass before him, apparently endeavoring to drain the girl's beauty with his eyes; a useless effort, since it lessened neither her loveliness nor his thirst. Indeed the more he looked the less able was he to stop looking. Oblivious, the girl was engrossed in the crowd. Her amber skin grew clearer and the roses imprisoned in it brighter as her merry black eyes danced over the jostling company.

"Think you'll like it?" he asked.

"Like it?" She was a child of Harlem and she spoke its language. "Boy, I'm having the time of my life. Imagine getting paid for this!"

"You ought to get a bonus for beauty."

"Nice time to think of that—after I'm hired."

"You look like a full course dinner—and I'm starved."

"Hold the personalities, papa."

"No stuff. Wish I could raise a loan on you. Baby—what a roll I'd tote."

"Thanks. Try that big farmer over there hootin' it with Sister Full-bosom. Boy, what a side-show they'd make!"

"Yeah. But what I'm lookin' for is a leadin' lady."

"Yeah? I got a picture of any lady leadin' you anywhere."

"You could, Jean."

"Be yourself, brother."

"I ain't bein' nobody else."

"Well, be somebody else, then."

"Remember the orphanage?"

"Time, papa. Stay out of my past."

"Sure—if you let me into your future."

"Speaking of the orphanage—?"

"You wouldn't know it now. They got new buildings all over the place."

"Somehow that fails to thrill me."

"You always were a knock-out, even in those days. You had the prettiest hair of any of the girls out there—and the sassiest hip-switch."

"Look at Fred and Adele Astaire over there. How long they been doing blackface?"

"I used to watch you even then. Know what I used to say?"

"Yeah. 'Toot-a-toot-toot' on a bugle."

"That ain't all. I used to say to myself, 'Boy, when that sister grows up, I'm going to—'."

Her eyes grew suddenly onyx and stopped him like an abruptly reversed traffic signal.

"What's the matter?" he said.

She smiled and began nibbling the straw in her glass.

"What's the matter, Jean?"

"Nothing, Innocence. Nothing. Your boy plays a devilish one-step, doesn't he?"

"Say. You think I'm jivin', don't you?"

"No, darling. I think you're selling insurance."

"Think I'm gettin' previous, just because I got you the job."

"Funny, I never have much luck with jobs."

"Well, I don't care what you think, I'm going to say it."

"Let's dance."

"I used to say to myself, 'When that kid grows up, I'm going to ask her to marry me.' "

She called his bluff. "Well, I'm grown up."

"Marry me, will you, Jean?"

Her eyes relented a little in admiration of his audacity. Rarely did a sober aspirant have the courage to mention marriage.

"You're good, Bus. I mean, you're good."

"Every guy ain't a wolf, you know, Jean."

"No. Some are just ordinary meat-hounds."

From the change in his face she saw the depth of the thrust, saw pain where she had anticipated chagrin.

"Let's dance," she suggested again, a little more gently.

They had hardly begun when the number ended, and Fess Baxter stood before them, an ingratiating grin on his Swiss-cheese-colored face.

"Your turn, young fellow," he said to Bus.

"Thoughtful of you, reminding me," said Bus. "This is Mr. Baxter, Miss Ambrose."

"It's always been one of my ambitions," said Baxter, "to dance with a sure-enough angel."

"Just what I'd like to see you doin'," grinned Bus.

"Start up your stuff and watch us," said Baxter. "Step on it, brother. You're holding up traffic."

"Hope you get pinched for speedin'," said Bus, departing.

The Blue Devils were in good form tonight, were really "bearing down" on their blues. Bus, their leader, however, was only going through the motions, waving his baton idly. His eyes followed Jean and Baxter, and it was nothing to his credit that the jazz maintained its spirit. Occasionally he lost the pair: a brace of young wild birds double-timed through the forest, miraculously avoiding the trees; an extremely ardent couple, welded together, did a decidedly localized mess-around; that gigantic black farmer whom Jean had pointed out sashayed into the line of vision, swung about, backed off, being fancy. . . .

Abruptly, as if someone had caught and held his right arm, Bus' baton halted above his head. His men kept on playing under the impulse of their own momentum, but Bus was a creature apart. Slowly his baton drooped, like the crest of a proud bird, beaten. His eyes died on their object and all his features sagged. On the floor forty feet away, amid the surrounding clot of dancers, Jean and Baxter had stopped moving and were standing perfectly still. The girl had clasped her partner close around the shoulders with both arms. Her face was buried in his chest.

Baxter, who was facing the platform, looked up and saw Bus staring. He drew the girl closer, grinned, and shut one eye.

They stood so a moment or an hour till Bus dragged his eyes away. Automatically he resumed beating time. Every moment or so his baton wavered, slowed, and hurried to catch up. The blues were very low-down, the nakedest of jazz, a series of periodic wails against a background of steady, slow rhythm, each pounding pulse descending inevitably, like leaden strokes of fate. Bus found himself singing the words of this grief-stricken lamentation:

> Trouble—trouble has followed me all my days,
> Trouble—trouble has followed my all my days—
> Seems like trouble's gonna follow me always.

The mob demanded an encore, a mob that knew its blues and liked them blue. Bus complied. Each refrain became bluer as it was caught up by a different voice:

the wailing clarinet, the weeping C sax, the moaning B-flat sax, the trombone, and Bus' own plaintive tenor:

> Baby—baby—my baby's gone away.
> Baby—baby—my baby's gone away—
> Seems like baby—my baby's gone to stay.

Presently the thing beat itself out, and Bus turned to acknowledge applause. He broke a bow off in half. Directly before the platform stood Jean alone, looking up at him.

He jumped down. "Dance?"

"No. Listen. You know what I said at the table?"

"At the table?"

"About—wolves?"

"Oh—that—?"

"Yeah. I didn't mean anything personal. Honest, I didn't." Her eyes besought his. "You didn't think I meant anything personal, did you?"

" 'Course not," he laughed. "I know now you didn't mean anything." He laughed again. "Neither one of us meant anything."

With a wry little smile, he watched her slip off through the crowd.

From his side of the platform Bus overheard Fess Baxter talking to Perry Parker. Baxter had a custom of talking while he conducted, the jazz serving to blanket his words. The blanket was not quite heavy enough tonight.

"P.P., old pooter, she fell."

Parker was resting while the C sax took the lead. "She did?"

"No lie. She says, 'You don't leave me any time for cash customers.' "

"Yeah?"

"Yeah. And I says, 'I'm a cash customer, baby. Just name your price.' "

Instantly Bus was across the platform and at him, clutched him by the collar, bent him back over the edge of the platform; and it was clear from the look in Bus's eyes that he wasn't just being playful.

"Name her!"

"Hey—what the hell you doin'!"

"Name her or I'll drop you and jump in your face. I swear to—"

"Nellie!" gurgled Fessenden Baxter.

"Nellie who—damn it?"

"Nellie—Gray!"

"All right then!"

Baxter found himself again erect with dizzy suddenness. The music had stopped, for the players had momentarily lost their breath. Baxter swore and impelled his men into action, surreptitiously adjusting his ruffled plumage.

The crowd had an idea what it was all about and many good-naturedly derided the victim as they passed:

" 'Smatter, Fess? Goin' for toe-dancin'?"

"Nice back-dive, papa, but this ain't no swimmin' pool."

Curry, the large, bald, yellow manager, also had an idea what it was all about and lost no time accosting Bus.

"Tryin' to start somethin'?"

"No. Tryin' to stop somethin'."

"Well, if you gonna stop it with your hands, stop it outside. I ain't got no permit for prize fights in here— 'Course, if you guys can't get on together I can maybe struggle along without one of y' till I find somebody."

Bus said nothing.

"Listen. You birds fight it out with them jazz sticks, y' hear? Them's your weapons. Nex' Monday night's the jazz contest. You'll find out who's the best man next Monday night. Might win more'n a lovin' cup. And y' might lose more. Get me?"

He stood looking sleekly sarcastic a moment, then went to give Baxter like counsel.

*   *   *

Rumor spread through the Arcadia's regulars as night succeeded night.

A pair of buddies retired to the men's room to share a half-pint of gin. One said to the other between gulps:

"Lord today! Ain't them two roosters bearin' down on the jazz!"

"No lie. They mussa had some this same licker."

"Licker hell. Ain't you heard 'bout it?"

" 'Bout what?"

"They fightin', Oscar, fightin'."

"Gimme that bottle 'fo' you swaller it. Fightin'? What you mean, fightin'?"

"Fightin' over that new mama."

"The honey-dew?"

"Right. They can't use knives and they can't use knucks. And so they got to fight it out with jazz."

"Yeah? Hell of a way to fight."

"That's the only way they'd be any fight. Bus Williams'd knock that yaller boy's can off in a scrap."

"I know it. Y'oughta seen him grab him las' night."

"I did. They tell me she promised it to the one 'at wins this cup nex' Monday night."

"Yeah? Wisht I knowed some music."

"Sho-nuff sheba all right. I got a long shout with her last night, papa, an' she's got ever'thing!"

"Too damn easy on the eyes. Women like that ain't no good 'cep'n to start trouble."

"She sho' could start it for me. I'd 'a' been dancin' with her yet, but my two bitses give out. Spent two hard-earned bucks dancin' with her, too."

"Shuh! Might as well th'ow yo' money in the street. What you git dancin' with them hostesses?"

"You right there, brother. All I got out o' that one was two dollars worth o' disappointment."

Two girl friends, lounging in adjacent easy chairs, discussed the situation.

"I can't see what she's got so much more'n anybody else."

"Me neither. I could look a lot better'n that if I didn't have to work all day."

"No lie. Scrubbin' floors never made no bathin' beauties."

"I heard Fess Baxter jivin' her while they was dancin'. He's got a line, no stuff."

"He'd never catch me with it."

"No, dearie. He's got two good eyes too, y'know."

"Maybe that's why he couldn't see you flaggin' 'im."

"Be yourself, sister. He says to her, 'Baby, when the boss hands me that cup—' "

"Hates hisself, don't he?"

" 'When the boss hands me that cup,' he says, 'I'm gonna put it right in your arms.' "

"Yeah. And I suppose he goes with the cup."

"So she laughs and says, 'Think you can beat him?' So he says, 'Beat him? Huh, that bozo couldn't play a hand organ.' "

"He don't mean her no good though, this Baxter."

"How do you know?"

"A kack like that never means a woman no good. The other one ast her to step off with him."

"What!"

"Etta Pipp heard him. They was drinkin' and she was at the next table."

"Well, ain't that somethin'! Ast her to step off with him! What'd she say?"

"Etta couldn't hear no more."

"Jus' goes to show ya. What chance has a honest workin' girl got?"

Bus confided in Tappen, his drummer.

"Tap," he said, "ain't it funny how a woman always seems to fall for a wolf?"

"No lie," Tap agreed. "When a guy gets too deep, he's long-gone."

"How do you account for it, Tap?"

"I don't. I jes' play 'em light. When I feel it gettin' heavy—boy, I run like hell."

"Tap, what would you do if you fell for a girl and saw her neckin' another guy?"

"I wouldn't fall," said Tappen, "so I wouldn't have to do nothin'."

"Well, but s'posin' you did?"

"Well, if she was my girl, I'd knock the can off both of 'em."

"S'posin' she wasn't your girl?"

"Well, if she wasn't my girl, it wouldn't be none of my business."

"Yeah, but a guy kind o' hates to see an old friend gettin' jived."

"Stay out, papa. Only way to protect yourself."

"S'posin' you didn't want to protect yourself? S'posin' you wanted to protect the woman?"

"Hmph! Who ever heard of a woman needin' protection?"

"Ladies and gentlemen!" sang Curry to the tense crowd that gorged the Arcadia. "Tonight is the night of the only contest of its kind in recorded history! On my left, Mr. Bus Williams, chief of the Blue Devils. On my right, Mr. Fessenden Baxter, leader of the Firemen. On this stand, the solid gold loving-cup. The winner will claim the jazz championship of the world!"

"And the sweet mama, too, how 'bout it?" called a wag.

"Each outfit will play three numbers: a one-step, a fox-trot, and a blues number. With this stop watch which you see in my hand, I will time your applause after each number. The leader receiving the longest total applause wins the loving-cup!"

"Yeah—and some lovin'-up wid it!"

"I will now toss a coin to see who plays the first number!"

"Toss it out here!"

"Bus Williams's Blue Devils, ladies and gentlemen, will play the first number!"

Bus's philosophy of jazz held tone to be merely the vehicle of rhythm. He spent much time devising new rhythmic patterns with which to vary his presentations. Accordingly he depended largely on Tappen, his master percussionist, who knew every rhythmic monkeyshine with which to delight a gaping throng.

Bus had conceived the present piece as a chase, in which an agile clarinet eluded impetuous and turbulent traps. The other instruments were to be observers, chorusing their excitement while they urged the principals on.

From the moment the piece started something was obviously wrong. The clarinet was elusive enough, but its agility was without purpose. Nothing pursued it. People stopped dancing in the middle of the number and turned puzzled faces toward the platform. The trap drummer was going through the motions faithfully but to no avail. He traps were voiceless, emitted mere shadows of sound. He was a deaf mute making a speech.

Brief, perfunctory, disappointed applause rose and fell at the number's end. Curry announced its duration:

"Fifteen seconds flat!"

Fess Baxter, with great gusto, leaped to his post.

"The Firemen will play their first number!"

Bus was consulting Tappen.

"For the love o' Pete, Tap—?"

"Love o' hell. Look a' here."

Bus looked—first at the trap drum, then at the bass; snapped them with a finger, thumped them with his knuckles. There was almost no sound; each drum-sheet was dead, lax instead of taut, and the cause was immediately clear: each bore a short curved knife cut following its edge a brief distance, a wound unnoticeable at a glance, but fatal to the instrument.

Bus looked at Tappen, Tappen looked at Bus.

"The cream-colored son of a buzzard!"

Fess Baxter, gleeful and oblivious, was directing a whirlwind number, sweeping the crowd about the floor at an exciting, exhausting pace, distorting, expanding, etherealizing their emotions with swift-changing dissonances. Contrary to Bus Williams's philosophy, Baxter considered rhythm a mere rack upon which to hang his tonal tricks. The present piece was dizzy with sudden disharmonies, unexpected twists of phrase, successive false resolutions. Incidentally, however, there was nothing wrong with Baxter's drums.

Boiling over, Bus would have started for him, but Tappen grabbed his coat.

"Hold it, papa. That's a sure way to lose. Maybe we can choke him yet."

"Yeah—?"

"I'll play the wood. And I still got cymbals and sandpaper."

"Yeah—and a triangle. Hell of a lot o' good they are."

"Can't quit," said Tappen.

"Well," said Bus.

Baxter's number ended in a furor.

"Three minutes and twenty seconds!" bellowed Curry as the applause eventually died out.

Bus began his second number, a fox-trot. In the midst of it he saw Jean dancing, beseeching him with bewildered dismay in her eyes, a look that at once crushed and crazed him. Tappen rapped on the rim of his trap drum, tapped his triangle, stamped the pedal that clapped the cymbals, but the result was a toneless and hollow clatter, a weightless noise that bounced back from the multitude instead of penetrating into it. The players also, distracted by the loss, were operating far below par, and not all their leader's frantic false enthusiasm could compensate for the gaping absence of bass. The very spine had been ripped out of their music, and Tappen's desperate efforts were but the hopeless flutterings of a stricken, limp, pulseless heart.

"Forty-five seconds!" Curry announced. "Making a total so far of one minute flat for the Blue Devils! The Firemen will now play their second number!"

The Firemen's fox-trot was Baxter's rearrangement of Burleigh's "Jean, My Jean," and Baxter, riding his present advantage hard, stressed all that he had put into it of tonal ingenuity. The thing was delirious with strange harmonies, iridescent with odd color-changes, and its very flamboyance, its musical fine-writing and conceits delighted the dancers.

But it failed to delight Jean Ambrose, whom by its title it was intended to flatter. She rushed to Bus.

"What is it?" she was a-quiver.

"Drums gone. Somebody cut the pigskin the last minute."

"What? Somebody? Who?"

"Cut 'em with a knife close to the rim."

"Cut? He cut—? Oh, Bus!"

She flashed Baxter a look that would have crumpled his assurance had he seen it. "Can't you— Listen." She was at once wild and calm. "It's the bass. You got to have—I know! Make 'em stamp their feet! Your boys, I mean. That'll do it. All of 'em. Turn the blues into a shout."

"Yeah? Gee. Maybe—"

"Try it! You've got to win this thing."

An uproar that seemed endless greeted Baxter's version of "Jean." The girl, back out on the floor, managed to smile as Baxter acknowledged the acclaim by gesturing toward her.

"The present score, ladies and gentlemen, is—for the Blue Devils, one minute even; for the Firemen, six minutes and thirty seconds! The Devils will now play their last number!" Curry's intonation of "last" moved the mob to laughter.

Into that laughter Bus grimly led his men like a captain leading his command into fire. He had chosen the parent of blues songs, the old St. Louis Blues, and he adduced every device that had ever adorned that classic. Clarinets wailed, saxophones moaned, trumpets wept

wretchedly, trombones laughed bitterly, even the great
bass horn sobbed dismally from the depths. And so perfectly did the misery in the music express the actual
despair of the situation that the crowd was caught from
the start. Soon dancers closed their eyes, forgot their
jostling neighbors, lost themselves bodily in the easy
sway of that slow, fateful measure, vaguely aware that
some quality hitherto lost had at last been found. They
were too wholly absorbed to note just how that quality
had been found: that every player softly dropped his heel
where each bass-drum beat would have come, giving
each major impulse a body and breadth that no drum
could have achieved. Zoom-zoom-zoom-zoom. It was not a
mere sound; it was a vibrant throb that took hold of the
crowd and rocked it.

They had been rocked thus before, this multitude. Two
hundred years ago they had swayed to that same slow
fateful measure, lifting their lamentation to heaven,
pounding the earth with their feet, seeking the mercy of
a new God through the medium of an old rhythm, zoom-
zoom. They had rocked so a thousand years ago in a city
whose walls were jungle, forfending the wrath of a terrible black God who spoke in storm and pestilence, had
swayed and wailed to that same slow period, beaten on a
wild boar's skin stretched over the end of a hollow tree
trunk. Zoom-zoom-zoom-zoom. Not a sound but an emotion that laid hold on their bodies and swung them into
the past. Blues—low-down blues indeed—blues that
reached their souls' depths.

But slowly the color changed. Each player allowed his
heel to drop less and less softly. Solo parts faded out, and
the orchestra began to gather power as a whole. The
rhythm persisted, the unfaltering common meter of blues,
but the blueness itself, the sorrow, the despair, began to
give way to hope. Ere long hope came to the verge of
realization—mounted it—rose above it. The deep and
regular impulses now vibrated like nearing thunder, a

mighty, inescapable, all-embracing dominance, stressed by the contrast of wind-tone; an all-pervading atmosphere through which soared wild-winged birds. Rapturously, rhapsodically, the number rose to madness and at the height of its madness, burst into sudden silence.

Illusion broke. Dancers awoke, dropped to reality with a jolt. Suddenly the crowd appreciated that Bus Williams had returned to form, had put on a comeback, had struck off a masterpiece. And the crowd showed its appreciation. It applauded its palms sore.

Curry's suspense-ridden announcement ended:

"Total—for the Blue Devils, seven minutes and forty seconds! For the Firemen, six minutes and thirty seconds! Maybe that wasn't the Devils' last number after all! The Firemen will play their last number!"

It was needless for Baxter to attempt the depths and heights just attained by Bus Williams's Blue Devils. His speed, his subordination of rhythm to tone, his exotic coloring, all were useless in a low-down blues song. The crowd moreover, had nestled upon the broad, sustaining bosom of a shout. Nothing else warmed them. The end of Baxter's last piece left them chilled and unsatisfied.

But if Baxter realized that he was beaten, his attitude failed to reveal it. Even when the major volume of applause died out in a few seconds, he maintained his self-assured grin. The reason was soon apparent: although the audience as a whole had stopped applauding, two small groups of assiduous handclappers, one at either extreme of the dancing area, kept up a diminutive, violent clatter.

Again Bus and Tappen exchanged sardonic stares.

"Damn' if he ain't paid somebody to clap!"

Only the threatening hisses and boos of the majority terminated this clatter, whereupon Curry summed up:

"For Bus Williams's Blue Devils—seven minutes and forty seconds! For Fess Baxter's Firemen—eight minutes flat!"

He presented Baxter the loving-cup amid a hubbub of murmurs, handclaps, shouts, and hisses that drowned whatever he said. Then the hubbub hushed. Baxter was assisting Jean Ambrose to the platform. With a bow and a flourish he handed the girl the cup.

She held it for a moment in both arms, uncertain, hesitant. But there was nothing uncertain or hesitant in the mob's reaction. Feeble applause was overwhelmed in a deluge of disapprobation. Cries of "Crooked!" "Don't take it!" "Crown the cheat!" "He stole it!" stood out. Tappen put his finger in the slit in his trap drum, ripped it to a gash, held up the mutilated instrument, and cried, "Look what he done to my traps!" A few hardboiled ruffians close to the platform moved menacingly toward the victor. "Grab 'im! Knock his can off!"

Jean's uncertainty abruptly vanished. She wheeled with the trophy in close embrace and sailed across the platform toward the defeated Bus Williams. She smiled into his astonished face and thrust the cup into his arms.

"Hot damn, mama! That's the time!" cried a jubilant voice from the floor, and instantly the gathering storm of menace broke into a cloudburst of delight. That romance-hungry multitude saw Bus Williams throw his baton into the air and gather the girl and the loving-cup into his arms. And they went utterly wild—laughed, shouted, yelled and whistled till the walls of the Arcadia bulged.

Jazz emerged as the mad noise subsided: Bus Williams's Blue Devils playing "She's Still My Baby."

EUDORA WELTY

POWERHOUSE

POWERHOUSE IS PLAYING!

He's here on tour from the city—"Powerhouse and His Keyboard"—"Powerhouse and His Tasmanians"—think of the things he calls himself! There's no one in the world like him. You can't tell what he is. "Nigger man"?—he looks more Asiatic, monkey, Jewish, Babylonian, Peruvian, fanatic, devil. He has pale gray eyes, heavy lids, maybe horny like a lizard's, but big glowing eyes when they're open. He has African feet of the greatest size, stomping, both together, on each side of the pedals. He's not coal black—beverage colored—looks like a preacher when his mouth is shut, but then it opens—vast and obscene. And his mouth is going every minute: like a monkey's when it looks for something. Improvising, coming on a light and childish melody—*smooch*—he loves it with his mouth.

Is it possible that he could be this! When you have him there performing for you, that's what you feel. You know people on a stage—and people of a darker race—so likely to be marvelous, frightening.

This is a white dance. Powerhouse is not a show-off like the Harlem boys, not drunk, not crazy—he's in a

trance; he's a person of joy, a fanatic. He listens as much
as he performs, a look of hideous, powerful rapture on
his face. Big arched eyebrows that never stop traveling,
like a Jew's—wandering-Jew eyebrows. When he plays
he beats down piano and seat and wears them away. He is
in motion every moment—what could be more obscene?
There he is with his great head, fat stomach, and little
round piston legs, and long yellow-sectioned strong big
fingers, at rest about the size of bananas. Of course you
know how he sounds—you've heard him on records—but
still you need to see him. He's going all the time, like
skating around the skating rink or rowing a boat. It
makes everybody crowd around, here in this shadowless
steel-trussed hall with the roselike posters of Nelson
Eddy and the testimonial for the mind-reading horse in
handwriting magnified five hundred times. Then all quietly he lays his finger on a key with the promise and
serenity of a sibyl touching the book.

Powerhouse is so monstrous he sends everybody into
oblivion. When any group, any performers, come to town,
don't people always come out and hover near, leaning
inward about them, to learn what it is? What is it?
Listen. Remember how it was with the acrobats. Watch
them carefully, hear the least word, especially what they
say to one another, in another language—don't let them
escape you; it's the only time for hallucination, the last
time. They can't stay. They'll be somewhere else this
time tomorrow.

Powerhouse has as much as possible done by signals.
Everybody, laughing as if to hide a weakness, will sooner
or later hand him up a written request. Powerhouse
reads each one, studying with a secret face: that is the
face which looks like a mask—anybody's; there is a moment when he makes a decision. Then a light slides
under his eyelids, and he says, "92!" or some combination

of figures—never a name. Before a number the band is all frantic, misbehaving, pushing, like children in a schoolroom, and he is the teacher getting silence. His hands over the keys, he says sternly, "You-all ready? You-all ready to do some serious walking?"—waits—then, STAMP. Quiet. STAMP, for the second time. This is absolute. Then a set of rhythmic kicks against the floor to communicate the tempo. Then, O Lord! say the distended eyes from beyond the boundary of the trumpets, Hello and goodbye, and they are all down the first note like a waterfall.

This note marks the end of any known discipline. Powerhouse seems to abandon them all—he himself seems lost—down in the song, yelling up like somebody in a whirlpool—not guiding them—hailing them only. But he knows, really. He cries out, but he must know exactly. "Mercy! ... What I say! ... Yeah!" And then drifting, listening—"Where that skin beater?"—wanting drums, and starting up and pouring it out in the greatest delight and brutality. On the sweet pieces such a leer for everybody! He looks down so benevolently upon all our faces and whispers the lyrics to us. And if you could hear him at this moment on "Marie, the Dawn Is Breaking"! He's going up the keyboard with a few fingers in some very derogatory triplet-routine, he gets higher and higher, and then he looks over the end of the piano, as if over a cliff. But not in a show-off way—the song makes him do it.

He loves the way they all play, too—all those next to him. The far section of the band is all studious, wearing glasses, every one—they don't count. Only those playing around Powerhouse are the real ones. He has a bass fiddler from Vicksburg, black as pitch, named Valentine, who plays with his eyes shut and talking to himself, very young: Powerhouse has to keep encouraging him. "Go on, go on, give it up, bring it on out there!" When you heard him like that on records, did you know he was really pleading?

He calls Valentine out to take a solo.

"What you going to play?" Powerhouse looks out kindly from behind the piano; he opens his mouth and shows his tongue, listening.

Valentine looks down, drawing against his instrument, and says without a lip movement, " 'Honeysuckle Rose.' "

He has a clarinet player named Little Brother, and loves to listen to anything he does. He'll smile and say, "Beautiful!" Little Brother takes a step forward when he plays and stands at the very front, with the whites of his eyes like fishes swimming. Once when he played a low note, Powerhouse muttered in a dirty praise, "He went clear downstairs to get that one!"

After a long time, he holds up the number of fingers to tell the band how many choruses still to go—usually five. He keeps his directions down to signals.

It's a bad night outside. It's a white dance, and nobody dances, except a few straggling jitterbugs and two elderly couples. Everybody just stands around the band and watches Powerhouse. Sometimes they steal glances at one another, as if to say, Of course, you know how it is with *them*—Negroes—band leaders—they would play the same way, giving all they've got, for an audience of one. . . . When somebody, no matter who, gives everything, it makes people feel ashamed for him.

Late at night they play the one waltz they will ever consent to play—by request, "Pagan Love Song." Powerhouse's head rolls and sinks like a weight between his waving shoulders. He groans, and his fingers drag into the keys heavily, holding on to the notes, retrieving. It is a sad song.

"You know what happened to me?" says Powerhouse.

Valentine hums a response, dreaming at the bass.

"I got a telegram my wife is dead," says Powerhouse, with wandering fingers.

"Uh-huh?"

His mouth gathers and forms a barbarous O while his fingers walk up straight, unwillingly, three octaves.

"Gypsy? Why how come her to die? Didn't you just phone her up in the night last night long distance?"

"Telegram say—here the words: "your wife is dead." He puts 4/4 over the 3/4.

"Not but four words?" This is the drummer, an unpopular boy named Scoot, a disbelieving maniac.

Powerhouse is shaking his vast cheeks. "What the hell was she trying to do? What was she up to?"

"What name has it got signed, if you got a telegram?" Scoot is spitting away with those wire brushes.

Little Brother, the clarinet player, who cannot now speak, glares and tilts back.

"Uranus Knockwood is the name signed." Powerhouse lifts his eyes open. "Ever heard of him?" A bubble shoots out on his lip like a plate on a counter.

Valentine is beating slowly on with his palm and scratching the strings with his long blue nails. He is fond of a waltz, Powerhouse interrupts him.

"I don't know him. Don't know who he is." Valentine shakes his head with the closed eyes.

"Say it again."

"Uranus Knockwood."

"That ain't Lenox Avenue."

"It ain't Broadway."

"Ain't ever seen it wrote out in any print, even for horse racing."

"Hell, that's on a star, boy, ain't it?" Crash of the cymbals.

"What the hell was she up to?" Powerhouse shudders. "Tell me, tell me, tell me." He makes triplets, and begins a new chorus. He holds three fingers up.

"You say you got a telegram." This is Valentine, patient and sleepy, beginning again.

Powerhouse is elaborate. "Yas, the time I go out, go way downstairs along a long cor-ri-dor to where they puts us: coming back along the cor-ri-dor: steps out and hands me a telegram: your wife is dead."

"Gypsy?" The drummer like a spider over his drums.

"Aaaaaaaaa!" shouts Powerhouse, flinging out both powerful arms for three whole beats to flex his muscles, then kneading a dough of bass notes. His eyes glitter. He plays the piano like a drum sometimes—why not?

"Gypsy? Such a dancer?"

"Why you don't hear it straight from your agent? Why it ain't come from headquarters? What you been doing, getting telegrams in the *corridor*, signed nobody?"

They all laugh. End of that chorus.

"What time is it?" Powerhouse calls. "What the hell place is this? Where is my watch and chain?"

"I hang it on you," whimpers Valentine. "It still there."

There it rides on Powerhouse's great stomach, down where he can never see it.

"Sure did hear some clock striking twelve while ago. Must be *midnight*."

"It going to be intermission," Powerhouse declares, lifting up his finger with the signet ring.

He draws the chorus to an end. He pulls a big Northern hotel towel out of the deep pocket in his vast, special-cut tux pants and pushes his forehead into it.

"If she went and killed herself!" he says with a hidden face. "If she up and jumped out that window!" He gets to his feet turning vaguely, wearing the towel on his head.

"Ha, ha!"

"Sheik, sheik!"

"She wouldn't do that." Little Brother sets down his

clarinet like a precious vase, and speaks. He still looks like an East Indian queen, implacable, divine, and full of snakes. "You ain't going to expect people doing what they says over long distance."

"Come on!" roars Powerhouse. He is already at the back door, he has pulled it wide open, and with a wild, gathered-up face is smelling the terrible night.

Powerhouse, Valentine, Scoot and Little Brother step outside into the drenching rain.

"Well, they emptying buckets," says Powerhouse in a mollified voice. On the streets he holds his hands out and turns up the blanched palms like sieves.

A hundred dark, ragged, silent, delighted Negroes have come around from under the eaves of the hall, and follow wherever they go.

"Watch out Little Brother don't shrink," says Powerhouse. "You just the right size now, clarinet don't suck you in. You got a dry throat, Little Brother, you in the desert?" He reaches into the pocket and pulls out a paper of mints. "Now hold 'em in your mouth—don't chew 'em. I don't carry around nothing without limit."

"Go in that joint and have beer," says Scoot, who walks ahead.

"Beer? Beer? You know what beer is? What do you say is beer? What's beer? Where I been?"

"Down yonder where it say World Café—that do?" They are in Negrotown now.

Valentine patters over and holds open a screen door warped like a seashell, bitter in the wet, and they walk in, stained darker with the rain and leaving footprints. Inside, sheltered by dry smells stand like screens around a table covered with a red-checkered cloth, in the center of which flies hang onto an obelisk-shaped ketchup bottle. The midnight walls are checkered again with admonishing "Not Responsible" signs and black-figured, smoky calendars. It is a waiting, silent, limp room. There is a burned-out-looking nickelodeon and right beside it a long-necked wall instrument labeled "Business Phone, Don't Keep Talking." Circled phone numbers are written up everywhere. There is a worn-out peacock feather hanging by a thread to an old, thin, pink, exposed light bulb, where it slowly turns around and around, whoever breathes.

A waitress watches.

"Come here, living statue, and get all this big order of beer we fixing to give."

"Never seen you before anywhere." The waitress moves and comes forward and slowly shows little gold leaves and tendrils over her teeth. She shoves up her shoulders and breasts. "How I going to know who you might be? Robbers? Coming in out of the black of night right at midnight, setting down so big at my table?"

"Boogers," says Powerhouse, his eyes opening lazily as in a cave.

The girl screams delicately with pleasure. O Lord, she likes talk and scares.

"Where you going to find enough beer to put out on this here table?"

She runs to the kitchen with bent elbows and sliding steps.

"Here's a million nickels," says Powerhouse, pulling his hand out of his pocket and sprinkling coins out, all but the last one, which he makes vanish like a magician.

Valentine and Scoot take the money over to the nickelodeon, which looks as battered as a slot machine, and read all the names of the records out loud.

"Whose 'Tuxedo Junction'?" asks Powerhouse.

"You know whose."

"Nickelodeon, I request you please to play 'Empty Bed Blues' and let Bessie Smith sing."

Silence: they hold it like a measure.

"Bring me all those nickels on back here," says Powerhouse. "Look at that! What you tell me the name of this place?"

"White dance, week night, raining, Alligator, Mississippi, long ways from home."

"Uh-huh."

"Sent for You Yesterday and Here You Come Today" plays.

The waitress, setting the tray of beer down on a back table, comes up taut and apprehensive as a hen. "Says in the kitchen, back there putting their eyes to little hole peeping out, that you is Mr. Powerhouse. . . . They knows from a picture they seen."

"They seeing right tonight, that is him," says Little Brother.

"You him?"

"That is him in the flesh," says Scoot.

"Does you wish to touch him?" says Valentine. "Because he don't bite."

"You passing through?"

"Now you got everything right."

She waits like a drop, hands languishing together in front.

"Little-Bit, ain't you going to bring the beer?"

She brings it, and goes behind the cash register and smiles, turning different ways. The little fillet of gold in her mouth is gleaming.

"The Mississippi River's here," she says once.

Now all the watching Negroes press in gently and bright-eyed through the door, as many as can get in. One is a little boy in a straw sombrero which has been coated with aluminum paint all over.

Powerhouse, Valentine, Scoot and Little Brother drink beer, and their eyelids come together like curtains. The wall and the rain and the humble beautiful waitress waiting on them and the other Negroes watching enclose them.

"Listen!" whispers Powerhouse, looking into the ketchup bottle and slowly spreading his performer's hands over the damp, wrinkling cloth with the red squares. "Listen how it is. My wife gets missing me. Gypsy. She goes to the window. She looks out and sees you know what. Street. Sign saying Hotel. People walking. Somebody looks up. Old man. She looks down, out the window. Well? . . . *Ssssst! Plooey!* What she do? Jump out and bust her brains all over the world."

He opens his eyes.

"That's it," agrees Valentine. "You gets a telegram."

"Sure she misses you," Little Brother adds.

"No, it's nighttime." How softly he tells them! "Sure. It's the night time. She say, What do I hear? Footsteps walking up the hall? That him? Footsteps go on off. It's not me. I'm in Alligator, Mississippi, she's crazy. Shaking all over. Listens till her ears and all grow out like old music-box horns but still she can't hear a thing. She says, All right! I'll jump out the window then. Got on her nightgown. I know that nightgown, and her thinking there. Says, Ho hum, all right, and jumps out the window. Is she mad at me! Is she crazy! She don't leave *nothing* behind her!"

"Ya! Ha!"

"Brains and insides everywhere, Lord, Lord."

All the watching Negroes stir in their delight, and to their higher delight he says affectionately, "Listen! Rats in here."

"That must be the way, boss."

"Only, naw, Powerhouse, that ain't true. That sound too *bad*."

"Does? I even know who finds her," cries Powerhouse. "That no-good pussyfooted crooning creeper, that creeper that follow around after me, coming up like weeds behind me, following around after me everything I do and messing around on the trail I leave. Bets my numbers, sings my songs, get close to my agent like a Betsy-bug; when I going out he just coming in. I got him now! I got my eye on him."

"Know who he is?"

"Why, it's that old Uranus Knockwood!"

"Ya! Ha!"

"Yeah, and he coming now, he going to find Gypsy. There he is, coming around that corner, and Gypsy kadoodling down, oh-oh, watch out! *Sssssst! Plooey!* See, there she is in her little old nightgown, and her insides and brains all scattered round."

A sigh fills the room.

"Hush about her brains. Hush about her insides."

"Ya! Ha! You talking about her brains and insides— old Uranus Knockwood," says Powerhouse, "Look down and say Jesus! He say, Look here what I'm walking round in!"

They all burst into halloos of laughter. Powerhouse's face looks like a big hot iron stove.

"Why, he picks her up and carries her off!" he says.

"Ya! Ha!"

"Carries her *back* around the corner. . . ."

"Oh, Powerhouse!"

"You know him."

"Uranus Knockwood!"

"Yeahhh!"

"He take our wives when we gone!"

"He come in when we goes out!"

"Uh-huh!"

"He go out when we comes in!"

"Yeahhh!"

"He standing behind the door!"

"Old Uranus Knockwood."

"You know him."

"Middle-size man."

"Wears a hat."

"That's him."

Everybody in the room moans with pleasure. The little boy in the fine silver hat opens a paper and divides out a jelly roll among his followers.

And out of the breathless ring somebody moves forward like a slave, leading a great logy Negro with bursting eyes, and says, "This here is Sugar-Stick Thompson, that dove down to the bottom of July Creek and pulled up all those drownded white people fall out of a boat. Last summer, pulled up fourteen."

"Hello," says Powerhouse, turning and looking around at them all with his great daring face until they nearly suffocate.

Sugar-Stick, their instrument, cannot speak; he can only look back at the others.

"Can't even swim. Done it by holding his breath," says the fellow with the hero.

Powerhouse looks at him seekingly.

"I his half brother," the fellow puts in.

They step back.

"Gypsy say," Powerhouse rumbles gently again, looking at *them*, " 'What is the use? I'm gonna jump out so far—so far. . . .' *Sssssst—!*"

"Don't, boss, don't do it again," says Little Brother.

"It's awful," says the waitress. "I hates that Mr. Knockwoods. All that the truth?"

"Want to see the telegram I got from him?" Powerhouse's hand goes to the vast pocket.

"Now wait, now wait, boss." They all watch him.

"It must be the real truth," says the waitress, sucking in her lower lip, her luminous eyes turning sadly, seeking the windows.

"No, babe, it ain't the truth." His eyebrows fly up, and he begins to whisper to her out of his vast oven mouth. His hand stays in his pocket. "Truth is something worse, I ain't said what, yet. It's something hasn't come to me, but I ain't saying it won't. And when it does, then want me to tell you?" He sniffs all at once, his eyes come open and turn up, almost too far. He is dreamily smiling.

"Don't, boss, don't, Powerhouse!"

"Oh!" the waitress screams.

"Go on git out of here!" bellows Powerhouse, taking his hand out of his pocket and clapping after her red dress.

The ring of watchers breaks and falls away.

"*Look* at that! Intermission is up," says Powerhouse.

He folds money under a glass, and after they go out, Valentine leans back in and drops a nickel in the nickelodeon behind them, and it lights up and begins to play "The Goona Goo." The feather dangles still.

"Take a telegram!" Powerhouse shouts suddenly up into the rain over the street. "Take a answer. Now what was that name?"

They get a little tired.

"Uranus Knockwood."

"You ought to know."

"Yas? Spell it to me."

They spell it all the ways it could be spelled. It puts them in a wonderful humor.

"Here's the answer. I got it right here. 'What in the hell you talking about? Don't make any difference: I gotcha.' Name signed: Powerhouse."

"That going to reach him, Powerhouse?" Valentine speaks in a maternal voice.

"Yas, yas."

All hushing, following him up the dark street at a distance, like old rained-on black ghosts, the Negroes are afraid they will die laughing.

Powerhouse throws back his vast head into the steaming rain, and a look of hopeful desire seems to blow somehow like a vapor from his own dilated nostrils over his face and bring a mist to his eyes.

"Reach him and come out the other side."

"That's it, Powerhouse, that's it. You got him now."

Powerhouse lets out a long sigh.

"But ain't you going back there to call up Gypsy long distance, the way you did last night in that other place? I seen a telephone.... Just to see if she there at home?"

There is a measure of silence. That is one crazy drummer that's going to get his neck broken some day.

"No," growls Powerhouse. "No! How many thousand times tonight I got to say No?"

He holds up his arm in the rain.

"You sure-enough unroll your voice some night, it about reach up yonder to her," says Little Brother, dismayed.

They go on up the street, shaking the rain off and on them like birds.

Back in the dance hall, they play "San" (#99). The jitterbugs start up like windmills stationed over the floor, and in their orbits—one circle, another, a long stretch and a zigzag—dance the elderly couples with old smoothness, undisturbed and stately.

When Powerhouse first came back from intermission, no doubt full of beer, they said, he got the band tuned up again in his own way. He didn't strike the piano keys for pitch—he simply opened his mouth and gave falsetto howls—in A, D and so on—they tuned by him. Then he took hold of the piano, as if he saw it for the first time in his life, and tested it for strength, hit it down in the bass, played an octave with his elbow, lifted the top, looked inside, and leaned against it with all his might. He sat down and played it for a few minutes with outrageous force and got it under his power—a bass deep and coarse as a sea net—then produced something glimmering and fragile, and smiled. And who could ever remember any of the things he says? They are just inspired remarks that roll out of his mouth like smoke.

They've requested "Somebody Loves Me," and he's already done twelve or fourteen choruses, piling them up nobody knows how, and it will be a wonder if he ever gets through. Now and then he calls and shouts, " 'Somebody loves me! Somebody loves me, I wonder who!' " His mouth gets to be nothing but a volcano. "I wonder who!"

"Maybe . . ." He uses all his right hand on a trill.

"Maybe . . ." He pulls back his spread fingers, and looks out upon the place where he is. A vast, impersonal and yet furious grimace transfigures his wet face.

". . . Maybe it's you!"

MARTIN GARDNER

THE DEVIL AND THE TROMBONE

THE UNIVERSITY'S CHAPEL WAS dark when I walked by it, but I could hear faintly the sound of an organ playing inside. I glanced at my wristwatch. It was almost midnight.

"Strange," I thought, "that someone would be playing at this hour."

I was on my way home from a meeting of the campus Philosophical Society. As an assistant professor of political science, and co-author of a textbook on international relations, I had been asked to chairman a symposium on "Right and Wrong in International Law." It had been a technical, tangled discussion, and my brain was tired. Partly to rest my mind, partly out of curiosity, I pulled open the heavy chapel door and entered.

The church was pitch black inside except for a dim glow of light behind the pulpit where the organ console was concealed. The Gothic walls and windows reverberated with low, sonorous chords.

I struck a match so I could find my way to a seat in the rear, where I settled into a comfortable position and listened. The chords were unlike any chords I had ever heard.

It wasn't long until my curiosity got the upper hand. I stood up and felt my way slowly down the central aisle. Then I stopped suddenly and caught my breath.

The light was coming not from the bulb above the music rack, but from the organist himself. He was young and handsome, and he was wearing a white robe. Two enormous wings extended from his shoulders and were folded close to the body. The wings radiated a hazy luminescence.

He glanced over, saw me standing there, and took his hands from the keys. The chapel was instantly silent.

"You startled me," he said, smiling crookedly. "How did you get in?"

I pointed down the aisle. "Through the . . . the front entrance," I stammered.

He frowned and shook his head in self-reproach. "My fault," he said. "I thought the door was locked."

I didn't say anything.

"It's not often I get a chance to play one of these things," he went on, adjusting several stops. "I'm horribly out of practice. But here's something that might interest you."

His fingers began to move gracefully over the keyboards, and the somber chapel suddenly became alive with melody.

And while he played, a great peace settled over my soul. The world was good. Life was good. Death was good. All that seemed black and horrible was a necessary prelude to some greater goodness. Every episode of history was part of the Will of God. I thought of the German prison camps, of the bombing of Hiroshima, of the atomic wars yet to come. They, too, were good.

Then from the deep purple shadows behind the organ, a tall figure with pointed ears emerged. He wore no clothing. Dark reddish hair covered his swarthy arms, chest, and legs. In his left hand, gleaming like silver, was a slide trombone.

He put the instrument to his lips and blew a low, outrageous note like the sound of a Bronx cheer. At the same moment the organist lifted his hands from the keys.

The dark man played alone, beating a foot slowly on the stone floor and improvising in a relaxed New Orleans style. The melodic line was filled with sweeping glissandos.

And now my soul was troubled with a great unrest. All that we call good in life, I saw clearly, was nothing but an illusion. Sickness and sin were the realities. The brief moments of peace and harmony—for a person, nation, or the world—only added pathos to a final tragedy. At the end of human history loomed the blankness of a Great Destruction.

Then the slender hands of the organist returned to the ivory keys, and the two players began to jam. They were improvising independently, but their separate efforts blended into a rich texture of counterpoint and polyrhythm.

All the frenzied fullness and complexity of the modern world, with its curious mixture of good and evil, rose up before me. I felt neither peace nor anxiety, but a strange excitement and exultation. There were journeys to be made, with real goals to reach, real dangers to avoid. There were battles to be fought!

A sinewy tail crept from the back of the dark man. The cloven scarlet tip crawled into the bell of the slide-horn, serving as a mute. The organist looked at me and grinned.

"Authentic tail gate," he commented.

The jamming continued. One by one the age-old problems of political philosophy found clear and simple answers. Right and wrong were easy to define. International dilemmas melted away. I saw the good and bad of every nation. I knew exactly what our foreign policy should be.

The organist's hands and sandaled feet were dancing wildly now, and the dark stranger was bending back, the trombone pointed upward in defiance, playing loud and wicked smears. My head felt as though it had expanded to the bursting point. I understood the meaning of life. I knew why the world had been created. I was about to penetrate the ultimate mystery—the mystery of God's own existence—when the players stopped abruptly.

The chapel was as quiet as a tomb. My hands were shaking and cold trickles of perspiration ran down my face. There was a dull ache above each temple.

"It's a good thing we stopped," the dark man said huskily. "Another note and your brain would have cracked."

"You'd better go back to your seat," said the man in white, "and wake yourself up."

In dazed obedience I stumbled back along the aisle, sat down again, and closed my eyes. When I opened them, the soft glow in front had disappeared. I walked to the console, fired a match, and waved it about in the blackness. Not a soul was in sight. I placed my hand on the leather cushion. It was cold. There were no feathers on the floor.

My wife was reading in a chair when I got home.

"Sam," she called to me (I had gone to the bathroom to take some aspirin), "I'm worried about Joey. He disobeyed several times tonight, and he refused to go to bed until an hour after bedtime. Do you think we should start punishing him?"

I washed down a couple of tablets with a glass of water. "My dear," I said, drying my lips on a towel, "I haven't the faintest idea."

PETER DE VRIES

JAM TODAY

MUSIC IS A FIELD in which I can't seem to keep up with the van. I no sooner cultivate a taste for Milhaud, Schoenberg, and Poulenc than I find the intellectuals talking about Bunk Johnson, Baby Dodds, and Cow Cow Davenport. I got into a jam by attending a jam recently—one of these phonograph-record jams, or platter parties, to which each guest brings his or her favorite hot or blues recording. The level and tone of any such congregation depend on how many collector's items turn up. A Westport couple my wife and I know, whom I shall call Chittenden, invited us to this one, a Saturday night affair.

My wife left the choice of our "ticket of admission" to me, and I settled on a Benny Goodman swing version of "Sweet Sue," simply because it happened to be my favorite at the time. I had no doubts about the acceptability of the arrangement, which is by Goodman himself—though the platter qua platter is certainly no collector's item— and since I was fond of the record, I jotted my name on the envelope it was in, to make sure nobody would go off with it by mistake after the party.

We arrived about ten o'clock, and, going into the living room, I deposited my offering on a table near the door. The phonograph had not yet been turned on, but the evening was well under way, with one large group trying to get a definition of "gut bucket." I eased over toward another, smaller knot and sat down beside a tall brunette, a student from Bennington who kept running her fingers backward down through her hair. The people around her were arguing about who the greatest trombonist of our day is. "Who do you say?" the girl asked, turning to me.

God knows the only trombonist with whose methods and repertory I can lay claim to any familiarity is Homer Rodeheaver, the playing evangelist. I used to go with other Calvinist youths to hear him in Orchestra Hall, in Chicago, and I remember a little joke Rodeheaver used to pull about his instrument. He would work it up and down a few times and then say, "This is a Methodist trombone—it backslides." I dined out on that in my old Dutch Reformed days, but one look at this girl from Bennington told me not to try any funny stuff. "That's a hard question for me to answer," I said thoughtfully.

I was safe for the moment, but real embarrassment presently pounced like a cat. The two or three groups in the room merged into one, like batter on a griddle, when Chittenden began airing his views on true jazz. "You can safely rule out 98 percent of what's played," he said. Several nodded. "But the lowest point of all is probably swing. I mean there are people who seriously think that's jazz."

"Excuse me," I said to the girl.

Grinning deceptively and from time to time bobbing my head at what Chittenden was saying, I edged my way around the room toward the table where my record was. I backed up to it and stood there casually, feeling around behind me with one hand till my fingers found the disc. I slipped quickly into the vestibule and opened the door of the closet where my overcoat was hanging. Holding the record in both hands, and pushing it deep in among the wraps so as to muffle the sound, I broke it into five or six pieces, shoved them into a pocket of my overcoat, envelope and all. I wasn't a moment too soon. As I sauntered back into the living room, the Chittendens were calling for the tickets of admission.

I heard some pretty esoteric things that night: Johnny Dodds' Washboard Band, Bessie Jackson, the Chicago Bucktown Five, the Dixieland Jug Blowers—items spanning the quarter century and more that one must go back in order to stay abreast. Chittenden had a Jelly Roll Morton on which he had taken out a floater policy with the Equitable Insurance people. Of course, the records were all acoustical; that is, they were made in the days when performers sang or played into a large megaphone. Such waxes are hard to listen to—a factor that tends to screen out non-connoisseurs, whose ears have been spoiled by listening to high-fidelity electrical recordings. As collector's item followed collector's item, I reflected on the humiliation I had been narrowly spared; mine would have been the only electrical recording there.

"Where is yours, by the way?" Chittenden asked.

"I forgot it," I said, trying, I hoped inconspicuously, to semaphore "will explain later" to my wife.

On edge from all the strain, I said loudly and nervously, "Let's dance." People looked at me, surprised to have encountered a notion as heretical as that at the Chittendens'. At Eddie Condon's, perhaps the "purest" of the places devoted to jazz, they haven't even *got* a floor.

The conversation became brisk and technical, and I dropped a remark that contained the word "colophony." I was sure at the time that it referred to modern counterpoint, but when I looked it up in the dictionary later, at home, I discovered it just means rosin. I resent this to some extent; rosin is a pretty flat thing for a word like "colophony" to mean. There was a sharp skirmish over what constitutes a true "dirty growl," and then the discussion settled on the relative styles of certain performers. As the haze thickened and the heat rose and the din grew, little was discernible to me but the sound of celebrated names. The girl from Bennington, still ceaselessly bathing her fingers in her hair, looked at me inquiringly after making an assertion I didn't get exactly, and I said, "Peanuts Hucko," which was the first thing that came to my mind.

"What?" she asked, bending an ear toward me.

"Peanuts Hucko," I said, raising my voice.

She nodded consideringly. Emboldened, I said, "Slow Drag Pavageau," a reference I had picked up from another group earlier in the evening, and then threw in a few more names as they occurred to me from hearsay or reading. "Pinetop Smith, Mutt Carey, Big Eye Louis Nelson," I said to the girl and occasionally to other people. "Jimmy and Mama Yancey."

But all conversation must end. At last the party broke up and everyone spilled through the doorway on a bright tide of exclamation and farewell. Chittenden, who was going to drive some guests to their train, had got into his wraps, too. My wife started to inquire after our missing platter. "Shh!" I said, trying to steer her away from Chittenden, who was nearby, and as we walked out to the driveway I explained that someone had sat on it and that I didn't want to make him feel too bad. From the cool, sweet cisterns of the midnight air my spirit drank repose, unaware that the payeroo was still to come.

I have said that I slipped the remnants of "Sweet Sue" into a pocket of my overcoat. That, as I fumbled hastily among the dangling sleeves, was what I *thought* I had done. Thrusting a hand into the pocket now, I felt nothing—nothing, that is, but a sick swoop. Who had acquired the remains of the record? I was not left to wonder long. A light clacking sound on my left was followed by a puzzled murmur from Chittenden, who was fishing fragments out of his pocket and peering at them.

"What—in the world—is *this*?" he asked, examining the shards in the moonlight.

"Good night, all!" I said, bundling my wife into our car. I climbed in behind the wheel and was off in a spatter of mud.

We rocked down Bayberry Lane in silence for some time.

"Why so quiet?" my wife asked, at last. "Sad about the record?"

"Yes, I am. I'd give anything if we hadn't brought that one," I said, remembering just then that the envelope with my name on it was in Chittenden's pocket, too.

ANN PETRY

SOLO ON THE DRUMS

THE ORCHESTRA HAD A week's engagement at the Randlert Theater at Broadway and Forty-second Street. His name was picked out in lights on the marquee. The name of the orchestra and then his name underneath by itself.

There had been a time when he would have been excited by it. And stopped to let his mind and his eyes linger over it lovingly. Kid Jones. The name—*his* name— up there in lights that danced and winked in the brassy sunlight. And at night his name glittered up there on the marquee as though it had been sprinkled with diamonds. The people who pushed their way through the crowded street looked up at it and recognized it and smiled.

He used to eat it up. But not today. Not after what had happened this morning. He just looked at the sign with his name on it. There it was. Then he noticed that the sun had come out, and he shrugged and went on inside the theater to put on one of the cream-colored suits and get his music together.

After he had finished changing his clothes, he glanced in the long mirror in his dressing room. He hadn't changed any. Same face. No fatter and no thinner. No gray hair.

Nothing. He frowned. Because he felt that the things that were eating him up inside ought to show. But they didn't.

When it was time to go out on the stage, he took his place behind the drums, not talking, just sitting there. The orchestra started playing softly. He made a mental note of the fact that the boys were working together as smoothly as though each one had been oiled.

The long gray curtains parted. One moment they were closed. And then they were open. Silently. Almost like magic. The high-powered spots flooded the stage with light. He could see specks of dust gliding down the wide beams of light. Under the bands of light the great space out front was all shadow. Faces slowly emerged out of it—disembodied heads and shoulders that slanted up and back, almost to the roof.

He hits the drums lightly. Regularly. A soft, barely discernible rhythm. A background. A repeated emphasis for the horns and the piano. The man with the trumpet stood up and the first notes came out sweet and clear and high.

Kid Jones kept up the drum accompaniment. Slow. Careful. Soft. And he felt his left eyebrow lift itself and start to twitch as the man played the trumpet. It happened whenever he heard the trumpet. The notes crept up, higher, higher, higher. So high that his stomach sucked in against itself. Then a little lower and stronger. A sound sustained. The rhythm of it beating against his ears until he was filled with it and sighing with it.

He wanted to cover his ears with his hands because he kept hearing a voice that whispered the same thing over and over again. The voice was trapped somewhere under the roof—caught and held there by the trumpet. "I'm leaving I'm leaving I'm leaving."

The sound took him straight back to the rain, the rain that had come with the morning. He could see the beginning of the day—raw and cold. He was at home. But he was warm because he was close to her, holding her in his arms. The rain and the wind cried softly outside the window.

And now—well, he felt as though he were floating up and up and up on that long blue note of the trumpet. He half closed his eyes and rode up on it. It had stopped being music. It was that whispering voice, making him shiver. Hating it and not being able to do anything about it. "I'm leaving it's the guy who plays the piano I'm in love with him and I'm leaving now today." Rain in the streets. Heat gone. Food gone. Everything gone because a woman's gone. It's everything you ever wanted, he thought. It's everything you never got. Everything you ever had, everything you ever lost. It's all there in the trumpet—pain and hate and trouble and peace and quiet and love.

The last note stayed up in the ceiling. Hanging on and on. The man with the trumpet had stopped playing, but Kid Jones could still hear that last note. In his ears. In his mind.

The spotlight shifted and landed on Kid Jones—the man behind the drums. The long beam of white light struck the top of his head and turned him into a pattern of light and shadow. Because of the cream-colored suit and shirt, his body seemed to be encased in light. But there was a shadow over his face so that his features blended and disappeared. His hairline receded so far back that he looked like a man with a face that never ended. A man with a high, long face and dark, dark skin.

He caressed the drums with the brushes in his hands. They responded with a whisper of sound. The rhythm came over but it had to be listened for. It stayed that way for a long time. Low, insidious, repeated. Then he made the big bass drum growl and pick up the same rhythm.

The Marquis of Brund, pianist with the band, turned to the piano. The drums and the piano talked the same rhythm. The piano high. A little more insistent than the drums. The Marquis was turned sideways on the piano bench. His left foot tapped out the rhythm. His cream-colored suit sharply outlined the bulkiness of his body against the dark gleam of the piano. The drummer and the pianist were silhouetted in two separate brilliant shafts of light. The drums slowly dominated the piano.

The rhythm changed. It was faster. Kid Jones looked out over the crowded theater as he hit the drums. He began to feel as though he were the drums and the drums were he.

The theater throbbed with the excitement of the drums. A man, sitting near the front, shivered and his head jerked to the rhythm. A sailor put his arm around the girl sitting beside him, took his hand and held her face still and pressed his mouth close over hers. Close. Close. Close. Until their faces seemed to melt together. Her hat fell off and neither of them moved. His hand dug deep into her shoulder and still they didn't move.

A kid sneaked in through a side door and slid into an aisle seat. His mouth was wide open and he clutched his cap with both hands, tight and hard against his chest as he listened.

The drummer forgot he was in the theater. There was only him and the drums and they were far away. Long gone. He was holding Lulu, Helen, Susie, Mamie close in his arms. And all of them—all those girls blended into that one girl who was his wife. The one who said, "I'm leaving." She had said it over and over again, this morning, while rain dripped down the windowpanes.

When he hit the drums again it was with the thought that he was fighting with the piano player. He was choking the Marquis of Brund. He was putting a knife in clean between his ribs. He was slitting his throat with a long straight blade. Take my woman. Take your life.

The drums leaped with the fury that was in him. The

men in the band turned their heads toward him—a faint astonishment showed in their faces.

He ignored them. The drums took him away from them, took him back, and back, and back, in time and space. He built up an illusion. He was sending out the news. Grandma died. The foreigner in the litter has an old disease and will not recover. The man from across the big water is sleeping with the chief's daughter. Kill. Kill. Kill. The war goes well with the men with the bad smell and the loud laugh. It goes badly with the chiefs with the round heads and the peacock's walk.

It is cool in the deep track in the forest. Cool and quiet. The trees talk softly. They speak of the dance tonight. The young girl from across the lake will be there. Her waist is slender and her thighs are rounded. Then the words he wanted to forget were all around Kid Jones again. "I'm leaving I'm leaving I'm leaving."

He couldn't help himself. He stopped hitting the drums and stared at the Marquis of Brund—a long malevolent look, filled with hate.

There was a restless, uneasy movement in the theater. He remembered where he was. He started playing again. The horn played a phrase. Soft and short. The drums answered. The horn said the same thing all over again. The drums repeated it. The next time it was more intricate. The phrase was turned around, it went back and forth and up and down. And the drums said it over, exactly the same.

He knew a moment of panic. This was where he had to solo again and he wasn't sure he could do it. He touched the drums lightly. They quivered and answered him.

And then it was almost as though the drums were talking about his own life. The woman in Chicago who hated him. The girl with the round, soft body who had been his wife and who had walked out on him, this morning, in the rain. The old woman who was his mother, the same woman who lived in Chicago, and who hated

him because he looked like his father, his father who had
seduced her and left her, years ago.

He forgot the theater, forgot everything but the drums.
He was welded to the drums, sucked inside them. All of
him. His pulse beat. His heart beat. He had become part
of the drums. They had become part of him.

He made the big drum rumble and reverberate. He
went a little mad on the big drum. Again and again he
filled the theater with a sound like thunder. The sound
seemed to come not from the drums but from deep inside
himself; it was a sound that was being wrenched out of
him—a violent, raging, roaring sound. As it issued from
him he thought, This is the story of my love, this is the
story of my hate, this is all there is left of me. And
the sound echoed and reechoed far up under the roof of the
theater.

When he finally stopped playing, he was trembling; his
body was wet with sweat. He was surprised to see that
the drums were sitting there in front of him. He hadn't
become part of them. He was still himself. Kid Jones.
Master of the drums. Greatest drummer in the world.
Selling himself a little piece at a time. Every afternoon.
Twice every evening. Only this time he had topped all
his other performances. This time, playing like this after
what had happened in the morning, he had sold all of
himself—not just a little piece.

Someone kicked his foot. "Bow, you ape. Whassamatter
with you?"

He bowed from the waist and the spotlight slid away
from him, down his pants legs. The light landed on the
Marquis of Brund, the piano player. The Marquis' skin
glistened like a piece of black seaweed. Then the light
was back on Kid Jones.

He felt hot and he thought, I stink of sweat. The
talcum he had dabbed on his face after he shaved felt
like a constricting layer of cement. A thin layer but

definitely cement. No air could get through to his skin. He reached for his handkerchief and felt the powder and the sweat mix as he mopped his face.

Then he bowed again. And again. Like a—like one of those things you pull the string and it jerks, goes through the motion of dancing. Pull it again and it kicks. Yeah, he thought, you were hot all right. The go-go gals ate you up and you haven't any place to go. Since this morning you haven't had anyplace to go. "I'm leaving it's the guy who plays the piano I'm in love with the Marquis of Brund he plays such sweet piano I'm leaving leaving leaving—"

He stared at the Marquis of Brund for a long moment. Then he stood up and bowed again. And again.

LANGSTON HUGHES

THE BLUES I'M PLAYING

OCEOLA JONES, PIANIST, STUDIED under Philippe in Paris. Mrs. Dora Ellsworth paid her bills. The bills included a little apartment on the Left Bank and a grand piano. Twice a year Mrs. Ellsworth came over from New York and spent part of her time with Oceola in the little apartment. The rest of her time abroad she usually spent at Biarritz or Juan les Pins, where she would see the new canvases of Antonio Bas, young Spanish painter who also enjoyed the patronage of Mrs. Ellsworth. Bas and Oceola, the woman thought, both had genius. And whether they had genius or not, she loved them, and took good care of them.

Poor dear lady, she had no children of her own. Her husband was dead. And she had no interest in life now save art, and the young people who created art. She was very rich, and it gave her pleasure to share her richness with beauty. Except that she was sometimes confused as to where beauty lay—in the youngsters or in what they made, in the creators or the creation. Mrs. Ellsworth had been known to help charming young people who wrote terrible poems, blue-eyed young men who painted awful pictures. And she once turned down a garlic-smelling soprano-singing girl who, a few years later, had all the critics in New York at her feet. The girl was so sallow. And she really needed a bath, or at least a mouthwash, on the day when Mrs. Ellsworth went to hear her sing at an East Side settlement house. Mrs. Ellsworth had sent a small check and let it go at that—since, however, living to regret bitterly her lack of musical acumen in the face of garlic.

About Oceola, though, there had been no doubt. The Negro girl had been highly recommended to her by Ormond Hunter, the music critic, who often went to Harlem to hear the church concerts there, and had thus listened twice to Oceola's playing.

"A most amazing tone," he had told Mrs. Ellsworth, knowing her interest in the young and unusual. "A flare for the piano such as I have seldom encountered. All she needs is training— finish, polish, a repertoire."

"Where is she?" asked Mrs. Ellsworth at once. "I will hear her play."

By the hardest, Oceola was found. By the hardest, an appointment was made for her to come to East 63rd Street and play for Mrs. Ellsworth. Oceola had said she was busy every day. It seemed that she had pupils, rehearsed a church choir, and played almost nightly for colored house parties or dances. She made quite a good deal of money. She wasn't tremendously interested, it seemed, in going way downtown to play for some elderly lady she had never heard of, even if the request did come from the white critic, Ormond Hunter, via the pastor of the church whose choir she rehearsed and to which Mr. Hunter's maid belonged.

It was finally arranged, however. And one afternoon, promptly on time, black Miss Oceola Jones rang the doorbell of white Mrs. Dora Ellsworth's gray stone house just off Madison. A butler who actually wore brass buttons opened the door, and she was shown upstairs to the music room. (The butler had been warned of her coming.) Ormond Hunter was already there, and they shook hands. In a moment, Mrs. Ellsworth came in, a tall stately gray-haired lady in black with a scarf that sort of floated behind her. She was tremendously intrigued at meeting Oceola, never having had before amongst all her artists a black one. And she was greatly impressed that Ormond Hunter should have recommended the girl. She began right away, treating her as a protegée; that is, she began asking her a great many questions she would not dare ask anyone else at first meeting, except a protegée. She asked her how old she was and where her mother and father were and how she made her living and whose music she liked best to play and was she married and would she take one lump or two in her tea, with lemon or cream?

After tea, Oceola played. She played the Rachmaninoff *Prelude in C Sharp Minor*. She played from the Liszt *Études*. She played the *St. Louis Blues*. She played Ravel's *Pavanne pour une Enfante Défunte*. And then she said she had to go. She was playing that night for a dance in Brooklyn for the benefit of the Urban League.

Mrs. Ellsworth and Ormond Hunter breathed, "How lovely!"

Mrs. Ellsworth said, "I am quite overcome, my dear. You play so beautifully." She went on further to say, "You must let me help you. Who is your teacher?"

"I have none now," Oceola replied. "I teach pupils myself. Don't have time anymore to study—nor money either."

"But you must have time," said Mrs. Ellsworth, "and money, also. Come back to see me on Tuesday. We will arrange it, my dear."

And when the girl had gone, she turned to Ormond Hunter for advice on piano teachers to instruct those who already had genius, and need only to be developed.

II

Then began one of the most interesting periods in Mrs. Ellsworth's whole experience in aiding the arts. The period of Oceola. For the Negro girl, as time went on, began to occupy a greater and greater place in Mrs. Ellsworth's interests, to take up more and more of her time, and to use up more and more of her money. Not that Oceola ever asked for money, but Mrs. Ellsworth herself seemed to keep thinking of so much more Oceola needed.

At first it was hard to get Oceola to need anything. Mrs. Ellsworth had the feeling that the girl mistrusted her generosity, and Oceola did—for she had never met anybody interested in pure art before. Just to be given things for *art's sake* seemed suspicious to Oceola.

That first Tuesday, when the colored girl came back at Mrs. Ellsworth's request, she answered the white woman's questions with a why-look in her eyes.

"Don't think I'm being personal, dear," said Mrs. Ellsworth, "but I must know your background in order to help you. Now, tell me . . ."

Oceola wondered why on earth the woman wanted to help her. However, since Mrs. Ellsworth seemed interested in her life's history, she brought it forth so as not to hinder the progress of the afternoon, for she wanted to get back to Harlem by six o'clock.

Born in Mobile in 1903. Yes, m'am, she was older than she looked. Papa had a band, that is her stepfather. Used to play for all the lodge turnouts, picnics, dances, barbecues. You could get the best roast pig in the world in Mobile. Her mother used to play the organ in church, and when the deacons bought a piano after the big revival, her mama played that, too. Oceola played by ear for a long while until her mother taught her notes. Oceola played an organ, also, and a cornet.

"My, my," said Mrs. Ellsworth.

"Yes, m'am," said Oceola. She had played and practiced on lots of instruments in the South before her
stepfather died. She always went to band rehearsals with
him.

"And where was your father, dear?" asked Mrs. Ellsworth.

"My stepfather had the band," replied Oceola. Her
mother left off playing in the church to go with him
traveling in Billy Kersands' Minstrels. He had the
biggest mouth in the world, Kersands did, and used
to let Oceola put both her hands in it at a time and
stretch it. Well, she and her mama and steppapa settled
down in Houston. Sometimes her parents had jobs and
sometimes they didn't. Often they were hungry, but
Oceola went to school and had a regular piano teacher,
an old German woman, who gave her what technique she
had today.

"A fine old teacher," said Oceola. "She used to teach
me half the time for nothing. God bless her."

"Yes," said Mrs. Ellsworth. "She gave you an excellent
foundation."

"Sure did. But my steppapa died, got cut, and after
that Mama didn't have no more use for Houston so we
moved to St. Louis. Mama got a job playing for the
movies in a Market Street theater, and I played for a
church choir, and saved some money and went to Wilber-
force. Studied piano there, too. Played for all the college
dances. Graduated. Came to New York and heard Rachmaninoff and was crazy about him. Then Mama died, so
I'm keeping the little flat myself. One room is rented
out."

"Is she nice?" asked Mrs. Ellsworth, "your roomer?"

"It's not a she," said Oceola. "He's a man. I hate women
roomers."

"Oh!" said Mrs. Ellsworth. "I should think all roomers
would be terrible."

"He's right nice," said Oceola. "Name's Pete Williams."

"What does he do?" asked Mrs. Ellsworth.

"A Pullman porter," replied Oceola, "but he's saving money to go to Med school. He's a smart fellow."

But it turned out later that he wasn't paying Oceola any rent.

That afternoon, when Mrs. Ellsworth announced that she had made her an appointment with one of the best piano teachers in New York, the black girl seemed pleased. She recognized the name. But how, she wondered, would she find time for study, with her pupils and her choir, and all. When Mrs. Ellsworth said that she would cover her *entire* living expenses, Oceola's eyes were full of that why-look, as though she didn't believe it.

"I have faith in your art, dear," said Mrs. Ellsworth, at parting. But to prove it quickly, she sat down that very evening and sent Oceola the first monthly check so that she would no longer have to take in pupils or drill choirs or play at house parties. And so Oceola would have faith in art, too.

That night Mrs. Ellsworth called up Ormond Hunter and told him what she had done. And she asked if Mr. Hunter's maid knew Oceola, and if she supposed that that man rooming with her was anything to her. Ormond Hunter said he would inquire.

Before going to bed, Mrs. Ellsworth told her housekeeper to order a book called "Nigger Heaven" on the morrow, and also anything else Brentano's had about Harlem. She made a mental note that she must go up there sometime, for she had never yet seen that dark section of New York; and now that she had a Negro protégée, she really ought to know something about it. Mrs. Ellsworth couldn't recall ever having known a single Negro before in her whole life, so she found Oceola fascinating. And just as black as she herself was white.

Mrs. Ellsworth began to think in bed about what gowns would look best on Oceola. Her protegée would have to be well-dressed. She wondered, too, what sort of a place the girl lived in. And who that man was who lived with her. She began to think that really Oceola ought to have a place to herself. It didn't seem quite respectable. . . .

When she woke up in the morning, she called her car and went by her dressmaker's. She asked the good woman what kind of colors looked well with black; not black fabrics, but a black skin.

"I have a little friend to fit out," she said.

"A *black* friend?" said the dressmaker.

"A black friend," said Mrs. Ellsworth.

III

Some days later Ormond Hunter reported on what his maid knew about Oceola. It seemed that the two belonged to the same church, and although the maid did not know Oceola very well, she knew what everybody said about her in the church. Yes, indeedy! Oceola were a right nice girl, for sure, but it certainly were a shame she were giving all her money to that man what stayed with her and what she was practically putting through college so he could be a doctor.

"Why," gasped Mrs. Ellsworth, "the poor child is being preyed upon."

"It seems to me so," said Ormond Hunter.

"I must get her out of Harlem," said Mrs. Ellsworth, "at once. I believe it's worse than Chinatown."

"She might be in a more artistic atmosphere," agreed Ormond Hunter. "And with her career launched, she probably won't want that man anyhow."

"She won't need him," said Mrs. Ellsworth. "She will have her art."

But Mrs. Ellsworth decided that in order to increase the rapprochement between art and Oceola, something should be done now, at once. She asked the girl to come down to see her the next day, and when it was time to go home, the white woman said, "I have a half-hour before dinner. I'll drive you up. You know I've never been to Harlem."

"All right," said Oceola. "That's nice of you."

But she didn't suggest the white lady's coming in, when they drew up before a rather sad-looking apartment house in 134th Street. Mrs. Ellsworth had to ask could she come in.

"I live on the fifth floor," said Oceola, "and there isn't any elevator."

"It doesn't matter, dear," said the white woman, for she meant to see the inside of this girl's life, elevator or no elevator.

The apartment was just as she thought it would be. After all, she had read Thomas Burke on Limehouse. And here was just one more of those holes in the wall, even if it was five stories high. The windows looked down on slums. There were only four rooms, small as maids' rooms, all of them. An upright piano almost filled the parlor. Oceola slept in the dining room. The roomer slept in the bed-chamber beyond the kitchen.

"Where is he, darling?"

"He runs on the road all summer," said the girl. "He's in and out."

"But how do you breathe in here?" asked Mrs. Ellsworth. "It's so small. You must have more space for your soul, dear. And for a grand piano. Now, in the Village . . ."

"I do right well here," said Oceola.

"But in the Village where so many nice artists live we can get . . ."

"But I don't want to move yet. I promised my roomer he could stay till fall."

"Why till fall?"

"He's going to Meharry then."

"To marry?"

"Meharry, yes m'am. That's a colored Medicine school in Nashville."

"Colored? Is it good?"

"Well, it's cheap," said Oceola. "After he goes, I don't mind moving."

"But I wanted to see you settled before I go away for the summer."

"When you come back is all right. I can do till then."

"Art is long," reminded Mrs. Ellsworth, "and time is fleeting, my dear."

"Yes, m'am," said Oceola, "but I gets nervous if I start worrying about time."

So Mrs. Ellsworth went off to Bar Harbor for the season, and left the man with Oceola.

IV

That was some years ago. Eventually art and Mrs. Ellsworth triumphed. Oceola moved out of Harlem. She lived in Gay Street west of Washington Square where she met Genevieve Taggard, and Ernestine Evans, and two or three sculptors, and a cat painter who was also a protegée of Mrs. Ellsworth. She spent her days practicing, playing for friends of her patron, going to concerts, and reading books about music. She no longer had pupils or rehearsed the choir, but she still loved to play for Harlem house parties—for nothing—now that she no longer needed the money, out of sheer love of jazz. This rather disturbed Mrs. Ellsworth, who still believed in art of the old school, portraits that really and truly looked like people, poems about nature, music that had soul in it, not syncopation. And she felt the dignity of art. Was it in keeping with genius, she wondered, for Oceola to have a studio full of white and colored people every Saturday night (some of them actually drinking gin *from bottles*) and dancing to the most tomtom-like music she had ever heard coming out of a grand piano? She wished he could lift Oceola up bodily and take her away from all that, for art's sake.

So in the spring, Mrs. Ellsworth organized weekends in the upstate mountains where she had a little lodge and where Oceola could look from the high places at the stars, and fill her soul with the vastness of the eternal, and forget about jazz. Mrs. Ellsworth really began to hate jazz—especially on a grand piano.

If there were a lot of guests at the lodge, as there sometimes were, Mrs. Ellsworth might share the bed with Oceola. Then she would read aloud Tennyson or Browning before turning out the light, aware all the time of the electric strength of that brown-black body beside her, and of the deep drowsy voice asking what the poems were about. And then Mrs. Ellsworth would feel very motherly toward this dark girl whom she had taken under her wing on the wonderful road of art, to nurture and love until she became a great interpreter of the piano. At such times the elderly white woman was glad her late husband's money, so well invested, furnished her with a large surplus to devote to the needs of her protégées, especially to Oceola, the blackest—and most interesting of all.

Why the most interesting?

Mrs. Ellsworth didn't know, unless it was that Oceola really was talented, terribly alive, and that she looked like nothing Mrs. Ellsworth had ever been near before. Such a rich velvet black, and such a hard young body! The teacher of the piano raved about her strength.

"She can stand a great career," the teacher said. "She has everything for it."

"Yes," agreed Mrs. Ellsworth, thinking, however, of the Pullman porter at Meharry, "but she must learn to sublimate her soul."

So for two years then, Oceola lived abroad at Mrs. Ellsworth's expense. She studied with Philippe, had the little apartment on the Left Bank, and learned about Debussy's African background. She met many black Algerian and French West Indian students, too, and listened to their interminable arguments, ranging from Garvey to Picasso to Spengler to Jean Cocteau, and thought they all must be crazy. Why did they or anybody argue so much about life or art? Oceola merely lived—and loved it. Only the Marxian students seemed sound to her for they, at least, wanted people to have enough to eat. That was important, Oceola thought, remembering, as she did, her own sometimes hungry years. But the rest of the controversies, as far as she could fathom, were based on air.

Oceola hated most artists, too, and the word *art* in French or English. If you wanted to play the piano or paint pictures or write books, go ahead! But why talk so much about it? Montparnasse was worse in that respect than the Village. And as for the cultured Negroes who were always saying art would break down color lines, art could save the race and prevent lynchings! "Bunk!" said Oceola. "My ma and pa were both artists when it came to making music, and the white folks ran them out of town for being dressed up in Alabama. And look at the Jews! Every other artist in the world's a Jew, and still folks hate them."

She thought of Mrs. Ellsworth (dear soul in New York), who never made uncomplimentary remarks about Negroes, but frequently did about Jews. Of little Menuhin she would say, for instance, "He's a *genius*—not a Jew," hating to admit his ancestry.

In Paris, Oceola especially loved the West Indian ballrooms where the black colonials danced the beguin. And she liked the entertainers at Bricktop's. Sometimes late at night there, Oceola would take the piano and beat out a blues for Brick and the assembled guests. In her playing of Negro folk music, Oceola never doctored it up, or filled it full of classical runs, or fancy falsities. In the blues she made the bass note throb like tomtoms, the trebles cry like little flutes, so deep in the earth and so high in the sky that they understood everything. And when the nightclub crowd would get up and dance to her blues, and Bricktop would yell, "Hey! Hey!" Oceola felt as happy as if she were performing a Chopin étude for the nicely gloved Oh's and Ah'ers in a Crillon salon.

Music, to Oceola, demanded movement and expression, dancing and living to go with it. She liked to teach, when she had the choir, the singing of those rhythmical Negro spirituals that possessed the power to pull colored folks out of their seats in the amen corner and make them prance and shout in the aisles for Jesus. She never liked those fashionable colored churches where shouting and movement were discouraged and looked down upon, and where new England hymns instead of spirituals were sung. Oceola's background was too well-grounded in Mobile, and Billy Kersands' Minstrels, and the Sanctified churches where religion was a joy, to stare mystically over the top of a grand piano like white folks and imagine that Beethoven had nothing to do with life, or that Schubert's love songs were only sublimations.

Whenever Mrs. Ellsworth came to Paris, she and Oceola spent hours listening to symphonies and string quartettes and pianists. Oceola enjoyed concerts, but seldom felt, like her patron, that she was floating on clouds of bliss. Mrs. Ellsworth insisted, however, that Oceola's spirit was too moved for words at such times—therefore she understood why the dear child kept quiet. Mrs. Ellsworth herself was often too moved for words, but never by pieces like Ravel's *Bolero* (which Oceola played on the phonograph as a dance record) or any of the compositions of *les Six*.

What Oceola really enjoyed most with Mrs. Ellsworth
was not going to concerts, but going for trips on the little
river boats in the Seine; or riding out to old chateaux in
her patron's hired Renault; or to Versailles, and listening to the aging white lady talk about the romantic
history of France, the wars and uprising, the loves and
intrigues of princes and kings and queens, about guillo-
tines and lace handkerchiefs, snuff boxes and daggers.
For Mrs. Ellsworth had loved France as a girl, and had
made a study of its life and lore. Once she used to sing
simple little French songs rather well, too. And she always regretted that her husband never understood the
lovely words—or even tried to understand them.

Oceola learned the accompaniments for all the songs
Mrs. Ellsworth knew and sometimes they tried them
over together. The middle-aged white woman loved to
sing when the colored girl played, and she even tried
spirituals. Often, when she stayed at the little Paris
apartment, Oceola would go into the kitchen and cook
something good for late supper, maybe an oyster soup, or
fried apples and bacon. And sometimes Oceola had pigs'
feet.

"There's nothing quite so good as a pig's foot," said
Oceola, "after playing all day."

"Then you must have pigs' feet," agreed Mrs. Ellsworth.

And all this while Oceola's development at the piano
blossomed into perfection. Her tone became a singing
wonder and her interpretations warm and individual.
She gave a concert in Paris, one in Brussels and another
in Berlin. She got the press notices all pianists crave.
She had her picture in lots of European papers. And she
came home to New York a year after the stock market
crashed and nobody had any money—except folks like
Mrs. Ellsworth who had so much it would be hard to ever
lose it all.

Oceola's one-time Pullman porter, now a coming doctor, was graduating from Meharry that spring. Mrs. Ellsworth saw her dark protégée go South to attend his graduation with tears in her eyes. She thought that by now music would be enough, after all those years under the best teachers, but alas, Oceola was not yet sublimated, even by Philippe. She wanted to see Pete.

Oceola returned North to prepare for her New York concert in the fall. She wrote Mrs. Ellsworth at Bar Harbor that her doctor boyfriend was putting in one more summer on the railroad, then in the autumn he would intern at Atlanta. And Oceola said that he had asked her to marry him. Lord, she was happy!

It was a long time before she heard from Mrs. Ellsworth. When the letter came, it was full of long paragraphs about the beautiful music Oceola had within her power to give the world. Instead, she wanted to marry and be burdened with children! Oh, my dear, my dear!

Oceola, when she read it, thought she had done pretty well knowing Pete this long and not having children. But she wrote back that she didn't see why children and music couldn't go together. Anyway, during the present Depression, it was pretty hard for a beginning artist like herself to book a concert tour—so she might just as well be married awhile. Pete, on his last run in from St. Louis, had suggested that they have the wedding Christmas in the South. "And he's impatient, at that. He needs me."

This time Mrs. Ellsworth didn't answer by letter at all. She was back in town in late September. In November, Oceola played at Town Hall. The critics were kind, but they didn't go wild. Mrs. Ellsworth swore it was because of Pete's influence on her protegée.

"But he was in Atlanta," Oceola said.

"His spirit was here," Mrs. Ellsworth insisted. "All the time you were playing on that stage, he was here, the monster! Taking you out of yourself, taking you away from the piano."

"Why, he wasn't," said Oceola. "He was watching an operation in Atlanta."

But from then on, things didn't go well between her and her patron. The white lady grew distinctly cold when she received Oceola in her beautiful drawing room among the jade vases and amber cups worth thousands of dollars. When Oceola would have to wait there for Mrs. Ellsworth, she was afraid to move for fear she might knock something over—that would take ten years of a Harlemite's wages to replace, if broken.

Over the teacups, the aging Mrs. Ellsworth did not talk any longer about the concert tour she had once thought she might finance for Oceola, if no recognized bureau took it up. Instead, she spoke of that something she believed Oceola's fingers had lost since her return from Europe. And she wondered why anyone insisted on living in Harlem.

"I've been away from my own people so long," said the girl, "I want to live right in the middle of them again."

Why, Mrs. Ellsworth wondered further, did Oceola, at her last concert in a Harlem church, not stick to the classical items listed on the program. Why did she insert one of her own variations on the spirituals, a syncopated variation from the Sanctified church, that made an old colored lady rise up and cry out from her pew, "Glory to God this evenin'! Yes! Hallelujah! Whooo-oo!" right at the concert? Which seemed most undignified to Mrs. Ellsworth, and unworthy of the teachings of Philippe. And furthermore, why was Pete coming up to New York for Thanksgiving? And who had sent him the money to come?

"Me," said Oceola. "He doesn't make anything interning."

"Well," said Mrs. Ellsworth, "I don't think much of him." But Oceola didn't seem to care what Mrs. Ellsworth thought, for she made no defense.

Thanksgiving evening, in bed, together in a Harlem apartment, Pete and Oceola talked about their wedding to come. They would have a big one in a church with lots of music. And Pete would give her a ring. And she would have on a white dress, light and fluffy, not silk. "I hate silk," she said. "I hate expensive things." (She thought of her mother being buried in a cotton dress, for they were all broke when she died. Mother would have been glad about her marriage.) "Pete," Oceola said, hugging him in the dark, "let's live in Atlanta, where there are lots of colored people, like us."

"What about Mrs. Ellsworth?" Pete asked. "She coming down to Atlanta for our wedding?"

"I don't know," said Oceola.

"I hope not, 'cause if she stops at one of them big hotels, I won't have you going to the back door to see her. That's one thing I hate about the South—where there're white people, you have to go to the back door."

"Maybe she can stay with us," said Oceola. "I wouldn't mind."

"I'll be damned," said Pete. "You want to get lynched?"

But it happened that Mrs. Ellsworth didn't care to attend the wedding, anyway. When she saw how love had triumphed over art, she decided she could no longer influence Oceola's life. The period of Oceola was over. She would send checks, occasionally, if the girl needed them, besides, of course, something beautiful for the wedding, but that would be all. These things she told her the week after Thanksgiving.

"And Oceola, my dear, I've decided to spend the whole winter in Europe. I sail on December eighteenth. Christmas—while you are marrying—I shall be in Paris with my precious Antonio Bas. In January, he has an exhibition of oils in Madrid. And in the spring, a new young poet is going over whom I want to visit Florence, to really know Florence. A charming white-haired boy from Omaha whose soul has been crushed in the West. I want

to try to help him. He, my dear, is one of the few people
who live for their art—and nothing else. . . . Ah, such a
beautiful life! . . . You will come and play for me once
before I sail?"

"Yes, Mrs. Ellsworth," said Oceola, genuinely sorry
that the end had come. Why did white folks think you
could live on nothing but art? Strange! Too strange! Too
strange!

V

The Persian vases in the music room were filled with
long-stemmed lilies that night when Oceola Jones came
down from Harlem for the last time to play for Mrs. Dora
Ellsworth. Mrs. Ellsworth had on a gown of black velvet
and a collar of pearls about her neck. She was very kind
and gentle to Oceola, as one would be to a child who has
done a great wrong but doesn't know any better. But to
the black girl from Harlem, she looked very cold and
white, and her grand piano seemed like the biggest and
heaviest in the world—as Oceola sat down to play it with
the technique for which Mrs. Ellsworth had paid.

As the rich and aging white woman listened to the
great roll of Beethoven sonatas and to the sea and moonlight of the Chopin nocturnes, as she watched the swaying
dark strong shoulders of Oceola Jones, she began to reproach the girl aloud for running away from art and
music, for burying herself in Atlanta and love—love for a
man unworthy of lacing her boot straps, as Mrs. Ellsworth put it.

"You could shake the stars with your music, Oceola.
Depression or no Depression, I could make you great.
And yet you propose to dig a grave for yourself. Art is
bigger than love."

"I believe you, Mrs. Ellsworth," said Oceola, not turning away from the piano. "But being married won't keep
me from making tours, or being an artist."

"Yes, it will," said Mrs. Ellsworth. "He'll take all the music out of you."

"No, he won't," said Oceola.

"You don't know, child," said Mrs. Ellsworth, "what men are like."

"Yes, I do," said Oceola simply. And her fingers began to wander slowly up and down the keyboard, flowing into the soft and lazy syncopation of a Negro blues, a blues that deepened and grew into rollicking jazz, then into an earth-throbbing rhythm that shook the lilies in the Persian vases of Mrs. Ellsworth's music room. Louder than the voice of the white woman who cried that Oceola was deserting beauty, deserting her real self, deserting her hope in life, the flood of wild syncopation filled the house, then sank into the slow and singing blues with which it had begun.

The girl at the piano heard the white woman saying, "Is this what I spent thousands of dollars to teach you?"

"No," said Oceola simply. "This is mine. . . . Listen! . . . How sad and gay it is. Blue and happy—laughing and crying. . . . How white like you and black like me. . . . How much like a man. . . . And how like a woman. . . . Warm as Pete's mouth. . . . These are the blues . . . . I'm playing."

Mrs. Ellsworth sat very still in her chair looking at the lilies trembling delicately in the priceless Persian vases, while Oceola made the bass notes throb like tomtoms deep in the earth.

O, if I could holler

sang the blues,

Like a mountain jack,
I'd go up on de mountain

sang the blues,

> *And call my baby back.*

"And I," said Mrs. Ellsworth rising from her chair, "would stand looking at the stars."

J. F. POWERS

HE DON'T PLANT COTTON

SPRING ENTERED THE BLACK belt in ashes, dust, and drabness, without benefit of the saving green. The seasons were known only by the thermometer and the clothing of the people. There were only a few nights in the whole year when the air itself told you. Perhaps a night in April or May might escape the plague of smells, achieve a little of the enchantment, be the diminished echo of spring happening ardently in the suburbs, but it was all over in a night and the streets were filled with summer, as a hollow mouth with bad breath, and even the rain could not wash it away. And winter . . .

The beginning snow swirled in from the lake, dusting the streets with white. Baby squinted down the lonesome tracks. The wind twisted snow into his eyes, the flakes as sharp as sand, grinding, and his eyeballs were coated with cold tears. Baby worked his hands in his overcoat pockets to make heat. He saw a woman cross the street to catch the Big Red, which was coming now, but the woman refused stiffly to run for it. The wind went off hooting down the tracks ahead. Baby got on. The conductor held out one hand for the fare and yanked a cord twice with the other, prodding the red monster into motion.

Baby sat down inside. A cold breeze swept the floor, rattling old transfers and gum wrappers. Baby placed his feet uneasily on the heater to make the meager warmth funnel up his pants' legs. The dark flesh beneath the tuxedo was chilled to chalky gray at the joints. He listened to the wheels bump over the breaks in the track, and the warmth from the heater rose higher on his legs. He became warm and forgetful of the weather, except as scenery. The streets were paved evenly with snow twinkling soft and clean and white under the lights, and velvet red and green from the neon signs.

New York may be all right, he hummed to himself, but Beale Street's paved with gold. That's a lie, he thought; I been down on Beale. And Chicago, same way. All my life playing jobs in Chicago, and I still got to ride the Big Red. And that's no lie. Jobs were getting harder and harder to find. What they wanted was Mickey Mouse sound effects, singing strings, electric guitars, neon violins, even organs and accordions and harmonica teams. Hard to find a spot to play in, and when you did it was always a white place with drunken advertising men wanting to hear "a old song"—"My Wild Irish Rose" or "I Love You Truly." So you played it, of course, and plenty of schmaltz. And the college kids who wanted swing—any slick popular song. So you played that, too. And always you wanted to play the music you were born to, blue or fast, music that had no name. You managed somehow to play that, too, when there was a lull or the place was empty and you had to stay until 4 A.M. anyway.

Baby got off the streetcar and walked the same two blocks he saw every night except Tuesday. The wind had died down almost entirely and the snow whirled in big flakes end over end. Padding along, Baby told himself he liked winter better than summer. Then he came to the place, said, "How's it, Chief?" to the doorman, an Indian passing for Negro, when down three steps, and forgot all about winter and summer. It was always the same here. It was not so much a place of temperatures as a place of lights and shades and chromium, pastel mirrors, the smell of beer, rum, whisky, smoke—a stale blend of odors and shadows, darkness and music. It was a place of only one climate and that was it.

Baby's overcoat, hat, and scarf went into a closet and settled familiarly on hooks. His old tuxedo walked over to the traps. Its black hands rubbed together briskly, driving out the chill. One hand fumbled in the dark at the base of the big drum, and a second later a watery blue light winked on dully and flooded the drumhead, staring like a blind blue eye. Immediately the tuxedo sat down and worked its feet with a slight rasping noise into the floor. The fingers thumped testingly on the hide, tightened the snare. They knew, like the ears, when it was right. Gingerly, as always, the right foot sought the big drum's pedal. The tuxedo was not ready yet. It had to fidget and massage its seat around on the chair, stretch out its arms, and hug the whole outfit a fraction of an inch this way and that. Then the eyes glanced at the piano player, signaling ready. The drumsticks paused a moment tensely, slid into the beat, barely heard, accenting perfectly the shower of piano notes. Everything worked together for two choruses. Then the piano player tapered his solo gently, so that at a certain point Baby knew it was his. He brought the number to a lifeless close, run down. Too early in the evening.

"Dodo," Baby said to the piano player, "Libby come in yet?"

Dodo sent a black hand up, slow as smoke, toward the ceiling. "Upstairs," he said, letting the hand fall to the keyboard with a faint, far-off chord. It stirred there, gently worming music from the battered upright. Notes drew nearer, riding on ships and camels through a world of sand and water, till they came forthright from the

piano, taking on patterns, as the other black hand came
to life on the bass keys, dear to Dodo. Baby picked up his
sticks, recognizing the number. He called it "Dodo's
Blues," though he knew Dodo called it nothing. Every
night about this time, when there was no crowd and
Dodo hadn't yet put on the white coat he wore servicing
the bar, they would play it. Baby half closed his eyes.
With pleasure he watched Dodo through the clouds of
rhythm he felt shimmering up like heat from his drums.
Baby's eyes were open only enough to frame Dodo like a
picture; everything else was out. It was a picture of
many dimensions; music was only one of them.

Here was a man, midgety, hunchbacked, black, and
proud—mostly all black and music. A little man who,
when he was fixing to play, had to look around for a
couple of three-inch telephone directories. Piling them on
top of the piano bench, he sat down, with all their names
and streets and numbers and exchanges under him. He
had very little of thighs and stomach—mostly just back,
which threw a round shadow on the wall. When he leaned
farther away from the piano, so the light slanted through
his hands, his shadow revealed him walking on his hands
down the keyboard, dancing on the tips of fingery toes.
Sometimes it seemed to Baby through half-closed eyes,
when Dodo's body was bobbing on the wall and his hands
were feet dancing on the keyboard, as though the dim
light shaped him into a gigantic, happy spider. When he
became a spider you could forget he was a man, hunchbacked, runtish, black; and he, too, could forget perhaps
that he had to be careful and proud. Perhaps he could be
happy always if his back and size and color and pride
were not always standing in the way. The piano made
him whole. The piano taught him to find himself and
jump clean over the moon. When he played, his feet
never touched the pedals.

People were beginning to fill the place. They finished
off the number, Baby smiling his admiration, Dodo scru-
pulously expressionless.

"For a young man . . ." Baby said.

Dodo got down off the telephone directories and threw them under the piano at the bass end, beyond the blue glow of the big drum. He had seen Libby come down the steps from the dressing room—a red dress, a gardenia. Dodo went behind the bar and put on his white service coat. Libby sat down at the piano.

Helplessly attracted, several men came over from the bar and leaned on the piano. They stared, burdening Libby's body with calculations. Singly at first and then, gathering unity, together. Libby sang a popular song. The men went back to the bar to get their drinks, which they brought over and set on top of the upright. Libby sang the words about lost love, and the men licked their lips vacantly. At the end of the song they clapped fiercely. Libby ignored them with a smile.

"Say, that was just fine," one man said. "Where you from anyhow?"

With a little grin Libby acknowledged Baby. Baby, beaming his veteran admiration of a fine young woman, nodded.

"Where you from? Huh?"

"New Orleans."

"Well, you don't say!" the man blurted out joyfully. "We're from down South, too . . . Mississippi, matter of fact!"

Icily, Libby smiled her appreciation of this coincidence. She looked at Baby, who was also registering appropriately. Just think of that! Small world! And welcome to our city!

"Well, what do you know!" crowed the gentleman from Mississippi. "So you're from down South!" He was greatly pleased and already very drunk. He eyed his friends, four or five of them, distributing his discovery equally among them.

"You never know," he explained. Then he appeared to suffer a pang of doubt. He turned quickly to Libby again, as though to make sure she was still there. His eyes jellied blearily and in them an idea was born.

"I know," he said. "Sing . . . sing—sing 'Ol' Man River' for the boys. They all'd sure like that."

Without responding, Libby looked down at her hands, smiling. She measured chords between her thumbs and little fingers, working her amusement into the keys. Baby stared at the mottled hide of his snare drum, at the big one's rim worn down from playing "Dixieland." The gentleman from Mississippi got worried.

"Aw, sing it," he pleaded. So Libby sang a chorus. The gentlemen from Mississippi were overwhelmed. They loved the song, they loved the South, the dear old Southland. Land of cotton, cinnamon seed, and sandy bottom. Look away! Look away! They loved themselves. Look away! Look away! There was the tiniest touch of satire in Libby's voice, a slightly overripe fervor. Baby caught it and behind the bar Dodo caught it, but the gentlemen did not. Dodo had put down the martini glass he was polishing and look away! look away!—good.

At the bridge of the second chorus, Libby nodded "Take it!" to Baby. He stood up, staggering from the heat of the fields, clenching his black, toilworn fists. In profound anguish, he hollered, giving the white folks his all, really knocking himself out.

> *Tote dat barge*
> *Lift dat bale*
> *Git a little drunk—*

Baby grimaced in torment and did his best to look like ol' Uncle Tom out snatchin' cotton.

Behind the bar, unnoticed, Dodo's sad black face had turned beatific. "—And you land in jail!" Dodo could not see the other faces, the big white ones, but he could imagine them, the heads fixed and tilted. It was too dark in the place, and he could make out only blurrily the

outlines of the necks. Ordinarily he was capable only of
hating them. Now he had risen to great unfamiliar heights
and was actually enjoying them. Surprised at this capacity in himself, yet proud he could feel this way, he was
confused. He went further and started to pity them. But
his memory stood up outraged at his forgetfulness and
said, Kill that pity dead. Then he remembered he was
really alone in the place. It was different with Libby and
Baby, though they were black, too. He did not understand why. Say their skin was thicker—only that was
not why. Probably this was not the first time they had
jived white folks to death and them none the wiser. Dodo
was not like that; he had to wait a long time for his
kicks. From his heart no pity went out for the white
men. He kept it all to himself, where it was needed. But
he had to smile inside of him with Libby and Baby. Only
more. Look at that fool, Baby! Jam up!

> Bend yo' knees
> An' bow yo' head
> An' pull dat rope
> Until yo're dead.

Baby sat down with a thud, exhausted. The gentlemen
from Mississippi brayed their pleasure. My, it was good
to see that black boy all sweatin' and perspirin' that way.
They clapped furiously, called for drinks, gobbled . . .
"And bring some for the darkies!"
Baby swallowed some of his drink. He looked at the
beaten rim of the big drum, then at the sticks. He took
out his pocketknife and scraped the rough, splintery places
smooth. He glanced at Libby and ventured the kind of
smile he felt and knew she did. He finished his drink.
The gentlemen from Mississippi hung around the piano,
getting drunker, shouting in one another's faces. Nervously Libby lighted a cigarette. A college boy tried to
make conversation with her while his honey-haired girl
assumed an attitude of genuine concern.

"Can you play 'Hot Lips'?" He was the real American Boy.

"Don't know it," Libby lied. She wished she didn't.

"Can you play 'Sugar Blues'?" Right back.

"Don't know it."

One of the Mississipi gentlemen, who had been hanging back, crowded up to the piano, making his move. He drained his drink and pushed closer to the piano so as to brush Libby's left hand with the front of his trousers. Libby moved her hand, sounding a chord that Baby caught. The gentleman, grinning lewdly, tried to follow her hand up the keyboard.

"That's all right," he snickered. "Play lots of bass, honey."

The first gentleman from Mississippi, drink in hand, stumbled over from the bar. He told Libby to play that "Ol' Man River" song some more. Libby hesitated. Then she lit into it, improvising all around it, and it was a pleasure for Baby, but the first gentleman from Mississippi was not happy. He said if that was the best she could do she had better try singing. Libby sang only one chorus. The gentlemen from Mississippi, though they applauded, were not gratified. There was an air of petulance among them. They remembered another time they heard the song, but it was not clear now what had made it different and better. They saw Baby all right, but they did not remember that he was the one who had sung before, the good one that toted their bars, lifted their bales, and landed drunk in their jails. Something was wrong, but they saw no remedy. Each gentleman suspected the fault was personal, what with him drinking so heavy and all.

Dodo, behind the bar, had not enjoyed the song the last time, hating the coercion the white men worked on Libby and Baby, and feared his advantage was slipping away. In a minute he would be hating them to pieces again.

"Can you play 'Tiger Rag'?" The American Boy was back.

"No." Libby made a face and then managed to turn it into a smile for him. He held his drink up for the world to see on the night before the big game.

The honey-haired girl wrenched her face into a winning smile and hit the jackpot. "Can you play 'St. Louis Blues'?"

"How you want it?" Libby said. She put out her cigarette. "Blues, rhumba . . . what kind a way?"

"Oh, play it low down. The way *you people* play it." So Libby would understand, she executed a ponderous wink, narrowed her eyes, and made them glitter wantonly behind the lashes. "*You* know," she said.

Libby knew. She played "St. Louis," losing herself in it with Baby. She left the college boy and the honey-haired girl behind. She forgot she knew. She gazed at Baby with her eyes dreamy, unseeing, blind with the blue drum, her head nodding in that wonderful, graceful way. Baby saw his old tuxedo in the mirror, its body shimmying on the chair, and he was pleased. The drums, beating figures, rocked with a steady roll. They were playing "Little Rock Getaway" now, the fine, young-woman music.

And Libby was pleased, watching Baby. And then, somehow, he vanished for her into the blue drum. The sticks still danced at an oblique angle on the snare, but there were no hands to them and Libby could not see Baby on the chair. She could only feel him somewhere in the blue glow. Abandoning herself, she lost herself in the piano. Now, still without seeing him, she could feel him with a clarity and warmth beyond vision. Miniature bell notes, mostly blue, blossomed ecstatically, perished *affettuso*, weaving themselves down into the dark beauty of the lower keys, because it was closer to the drum, and multiplied. They came back to "St. Louis" again.

"Stop." The first gentleman from Mississippi touched Libby on the arm. "When I do that to you, that means 'Stop,' " he said. Libby chorded easily. "Some of the boys like to hear that 'Ol' Man River' some more." He straightened up, turning to the other gentlemen, his smile assuring them it would not be long now.

"Kick off," Baby sighed.

But Libby broke into "St. Louis" again. Baby, with a little whoop, came clambering after, his sticks slicing into the drum rim, a staccato "Dixieland."

The first gentleman frowned, touching Libby's arm, "Remember what that means? Means 'Ol' Man River,'" he said calmly, as though correcting a slight error. "Toot sweet. Know what that means? That's French. Means right now." No harm done, however. Just that his friends here, a bunch of boys from down South, were dying to hear that song again—up to him to see that they got satisfaction—knew there would be no trouble about it.

"We'll play it for you later on," Libby said quickly. "We got some other requests besides yours. How many you got now, Baby?"

Baby held up eight fingers, very prompt.

"Coming up," he said.

The first gentleman was undecided. "Well ..." he drawled. Libby began a popular song. The first gentleman faced his friends. His eyes more or less met theirs and found no agreement. The boys looked kind of impatient, like a bunch of boys out for a little fun and not doing so well. He turned to Libby again.

"We just gotta have that 'Ol' Man River' some more. Boys all got their hearts set on it," he said. "Right away! Toot sweet! Toot—away!" There he'd gone and made a joke, and the boys all laughed and repeated it to each other. Libby played on, as though she had not heard. The first gentleman took hold of her arm. She gazed steadily up into his bleary eyes.

"Not now. Later."

"No, you don't. You gotta play it right now. For a bunch of boys from down South. They all got a hankerin' to hear that 'Ol' Man River' some more."

"So you best play it," another gentleman said, leaning

down hard on the old upright piano. "On account of I'm
gonna take and give ear. We kinda like how that old
song sounds up North. Whatcha all need. The drummer
will sing," he said, and looked at Baby. Baby looked
back, unsmiling.

Libby chorded lightly, waiting for the gentlemen from
Mississippi to get tired. They could not see how it was
with her and Baby—never.

"You ain't gonna play?"

Baby's eyes strained hard in their sockets.

"We ain't comin'," Libby said.

Baby's eyes relaxed and he knew the worst part was
over. They felt the same way about it. They had made up
their minds. The rest was easy. Baby was even a little
glad it had happened. A feeling was growing within him
that he had wanted to do this for a long time—for years
and years, in a hundred different places he had played.

Secretly majestic, Baby sat at his drums, the goal of
countless uplifted eyes—beseeching him. For it seemed
that hordes of white people were far below him, making
their little commotions and noises, asking favors of him,
like Lord, please bring the rain, or Lord, please take it
away. Lord Baby. Waves of warm exhilaration washed
into him, endearing him to himself. No, he smiled, I am
sorry, no favors today. Yes, Lord, they all said, if that's
the way it is, so be it.

But somebody objected. The manager's voice barked,
far below, scarcely audible to Baby in his new eminence.
". . . honoring requests," he heard, and ". . . trouble with
the local," and ". . . wanting to get a sweet-swing trio in
this place a long time now." And the manager, strangely
small, an excited, pale pygmy, explaining to the gentlemen from Mississippi, also small, how it was, "That's all
I can do in the circumstances," and them saying, "Well, I
guess so; well, I guess so all right; don't pay to pamper
'em, to give 'em an inch."

Baby noticed Libby had got up from the piano and put

on her coat, the long dress hanging out at the bottom, red.

"I won't change," she said, and handed Baby the canvas cover for the snare drum.

"Huh?" Baby said foggily. He set about taking his traps apart. Dodo, not wearing his white service coat, came over to help.

"You don't have to," Baby said.

Chief, freezing outside in his long, fancy maroon coat, opened the door for them. "You all through, Baby?"

"Yeah, Chief. You told that right."

They walked down the street toward the car line. Baby, going first, plowed a path for Libby and Dodo in the snow. Window sills, parked cars, and trees were padded with it. The wind was dead and buried. Baby bore the big drum on his shoulder and felt the sticks pressing tight and upright in his vest pockets, two on each side. Libby had her purse and street clothes rolled up under her arm. Dodo carried the snare drum.

Softly as snow, Libby laughed, "That's all I can do in the circumstances," she said.

"I got your old circumstances," Baby said.

Then they were silent, tramping in the snow.

At the corner they waited in a store entrance for a south-bound streetcar. Libby raised a foot now and then, shuddering with cold. Dead still, Dodo breathed down inside the collar of his overcoat, retarding his breath, frowning at the little smoke trickling out, as though it were the only thing left in the world to remind him he was alive. Baby talked of taking a cab and finally did go out into the street to hail one approaching. It slowed up, pulled over to the curb, hesitated . . . and lurched away, with Baby's hand reaching for the door. Baby watched the cab speed down the snowy street, following it for a few steps, speechless. There was nothing to do. Without looking, he saw Libby and Dodo shivering in the store entrance. They had seen the cab come and go. They had not moved an inch. They waited unfooled, as before, for the Big Red.

"What's wrong with you, Baby?" Libby called out. A tiny moment of silence, and she was laughing, gradually louder, mellow octaves of it, mounting, pluming . . .

Like her piano, it seemed to Baby—that fine, young-woman laughter.

"Why you laugh so much, woman?" he inquired plaintively from the street. Then he moved to join them, a few steps only, dallying at the curb to temper the abruptness of his retreat. Like her piano on "Little Rock"—that fine, young-woman laughter.

JAMES BALDWIN

SONNY'S BLUES

I READ ABOUT IT IN the paper, in the subway, on my way to work. I read it, and I couldn't believe it, and I read it again. Then perhaps I just stared at it, at the newsprint spelling out his name, spelling out the story. I stared at it in the swinging lights of the subway car, and in the faces and bodies of the people, and in my own face, trapped in the darkness which roared outside.

It was not to be believed, and I kept telling myself that as I walked from the subway station to the high school. And at the same time I couldn't doubt it. I was scared, scared for Sonny. He became real to me again. A great block of ice got settled in my belly, and kept melting there slowly all day long, while I taught my classes algebra. It was a special kind of ice. It kept melting, sending trickles of water all up and down my veins, but it never got less. Sometimes it hardened and seemed to expand until I felt my guts were going to come spilling out or that I was going to choke or scream. This would always be at a moment when I was remembering some specific thing Sonny had once said or done.

When he was about as old as the boys in my classes his face had been bright and open, there was a lot of copper in it; and he'd had wonderfully direct brown eyes, and great gentleness and privacy. I wondered what he looked like now. He had been picked up, the evening before, in a raid on an apartment downtown, for peddling and using heroin.

I couldn't believe it: but what I mean by that is that I couldn't find any room for it anywhere inside me. I had kept it outside me for a long time. I hadn't wanted to know. I had had suspicions, but I didn't name them, I kept putting them away. I told myself that Sonny was wild, but he wasn't crazy. And he'd always been a good boy, he hadn't ever turned hard or evil or disrespectful, the way kids can, so quick, so quick, especially in Harlem. I didn't want to believe that I'd ever see my brother going down, coming to nothing, all that light in his face gone out, in the condition I'd already seen so many others. Yet it had happened and here I was, talking about algebra to a lot of boys who might, every one of them for all I knew, be popping off needles every time they went to the head. Maybe it did more for them than algebra could.

I was sure that the first time Sonny had ever had horse, he couldn't have been much older than these boys were now. These boys, now, were living as we'd been living then; they were growing up with a rush and their heads bumped abruptly against the low ceiling of their actual possibilities. They were filled with rage. All they really knew were two darknesses, the darkness of their lives, which was now closing in on them, and the darkness of the movies, which had blinded them to that other darkness, and in which they now, vindictively, dreamed, at once more together than they were at any other time, and more alone.

When the last bell rang, the last class ended, I let out my breath. It seemed I'd been holding it for all that time.

My clothes were wet—I may have looked as though I'd been sitting in a steam bath, all dressed up, all afternoon. I sat alone in the classroom a long time. I listened to the boys outside, downstairs, shouting and cursing and laughing. Their laughter struck me for perhaps the first time. It was not the joyous laughter which—God knows why—one associates with children. It was mocking and insular, its intent was to denigrate. It was disenchanted, and in this, also, lay the authority of their curses. Perhaps I was listening to them because I was thinking about my brother and in them I heard my brother. And myself.

One boy was whistling a tune, at once very complicated and very simple, it seemed to be pouring out of him as though he were a bird, and it sounded very cool and moving through all that harsh, bright air, only just holding its own through all those other sounds.

I stood up and walked over to the window and looked down into the courtyard. It was the beginning of the spring and the sap was rising in the boys. A teacher passed through them every now and again, quickly, as though he or she couldn't wait to get out of that courtyard, to get those boys out of their sight and off their minds. I started collecting my stuff. I thought I'd better get home and talk to Isabel.

The courtyard was almost deserted by the time I got downstairs. I saw this boy standing in the shadow of a doorway, looking just like Sonny. I almost called his name. Then I saw that it wasn't Sonny, but somebody we used to know, a boy from around our block. He'd been Sonny's friend. He'd never been mine, having been too young for me, and, anyway, I'd never liked him. And now, even though he was a grown-up man, he still hung around that block, still spent hours on the street corner, was always high and raggy. I used to run into him from time to time and he'd often work around to asking me for a quarter or fifty cents. He always had some real good excuse, too, and I always gave it to him, I don't know why.

But now, abruptly, I hated him. I couldn't stand the way he looked at me, partly like a dog, partly like a cunning child. I wanted to ask him what the hell he was doing in the school courtyard.

He sort of shuffled over to me, and he said, "I see you got the papers. So you already know about it."

"You mean about Sonny? Yes, I already know about it. How come they didn't get you?"

He grinned. It made him repulsive and it also brought to mind what he'd looked like as a kid. "I wasn't there. I stay away from them people."

"Good for you." I offered him a cigarette and I watched him through the smoke. "You come all the way down here just to tell me about Sonny?"

"That's right." He was sort of shaking his head and his eyes looked strange, as though they were about to cross. The bright sun deadened his damp dark-brown skin and it made his eyes look yellow and showed up the dirt in his conked hair. He smelled funky. I moved a little away from him and I said, "Well, thanks, but I already know about it and I got to get home."

"I'll walk you a little ways," he said. We started walking. There were a couple of kids still loitering in the courtyard and one of them said good night to me and looked strangely at the boy beside me.

"What're you going to do?" he asked me. "I mean, about Sonny?"

"Look, I haven't seen Sonny for over a year. I'm not sure I'm going to do anything. Anyway, what the hell can I do?"

"That's right," he said quickly, "ain't nothing you can do. Can't much help old Sonny no more, I guess."

It was what I was thinking and so it seemed to me he had no right to say it.

"I'm surprised at Sonny, though," he went on—he had

a funny way of talking, he looked straight ahead as though he were talking to himself—"I thought Sonny was a smart boy, I thought he was too smart to get hung."

"I guess he thought so too," I said sharply, "and that's how he got hung. And how about you? You're pretty goddamn smart, I bet."

Then he looked directly at me, just for a minute. "I ain't smart," he said. "If I was smart, I'd have reached for a pistol a long time ago."

"Look. Don't tell me your sad story, if it was up to me, I'd give you one." Then I felt guilty—guilty, probably, for never having supposed that the poor bastard had a story of his own, much less a sad one, and I asked, quickly, "What's going to happen to him now?"

He didn't answer this. He was off by himself some place. "Funny thing," he said, and from his tone we might have been discussing the quickest way to get to Brooklyn, "when I saw the papers this morning, the first thing I asked myself was if I had anything to do with it. I felt sort of responsible."

I began to listen more carefully. The subway station was on the corner, just before us, and I stopped. He stopped, too. We were in front of a bar and he ducked slightly, peering in, but whoever he was looking for didn't seem to be there. The juke box was blasting away with something black and bouncy and I half watched the barmaid as she danced her way from the juke box to her place behind the bar. And I watched her face as she laughingly responded to something someone said to her, still keeping time to the music. When she smiled one saw the little girl, one sensed the doomed, still-struggling woman beneath the battered face of the semi-whore.

"I never give Sonny nothing," the boy said finally, "but a long time ago I come to school high and Sonny asked me how it felt." He paused, I couldn't bear to watch him; I watched the barmaid, and I listened to the music which seemed to be causing the pavement to shake. "I told him it felt great." The music stopped, the barmaid paused and watched the juke box until the music began again. "It did."

All this was carrying me some place I didn't want to go. I certainly didn't want to know how it felt. It filled everything, the people, the houses, the music, the dark, quicksilver barmaid, with menace; and this menace was their reality.

"What's going to happen to him now?" I asked again.

"They'll send him away some place and they'll try to cure him." He shook his head. "Maybe he'll even think he's kicked the habit. Then they'll let him loose"—he gestured, throwing his cigarette into the gutter. "That's all."

"What do you mean, 'that's all'?"

But I knew what he meant.

"I mean, that's all." He turned his head and looked at me, pulling down the corners of his mouth. "Don't you know what I mean?" he asked, softly.

"How the hell would I know what you mean?" I almost whispered it, I don't know why.

"That's right," he said to the air, "how would he know what I mean?" He turned toward me again, patient and calm, and yet I somehow felt him shaking, shaking as though he were going to fall apart. I felt that ice in my guts again, the dread I'd felt all afternoon; and again I watched the barmaid, moving about the bar, washing glasses, singing. "Listen. They'll let him out and then it'll just start all over again. That's what I mean."

"You mean—they'll let him out. And then he'll just start working his way back in again. You mean he'll never kick the habit? Is that what you mean?"

"That's right," he said cheerfully. "You see what I mean."

"Tell me," I said at last, "why does he want to die? He must want to die, he's killing himself, why does he want to die?"

He looked at me in surprise. He licked his lips. "He don't want to die. He wants to live. Don't nobody want to die, ever."

Then I wanted to ask him—too many things. He could not have answered, or if he had, I could not have borne the answers. I started walking. "Well, I guess it's none of my business."

"It's going to be rough on old Sonny," he said. We reached the subway station. "This is your station?" he asked. I nodded. I took one step down. "Damn!" he said, suddenly. I looked up at him. He grinned again. "Damn, if I didn't leave all my money home. You ain't got a dollar on you, have you? Just for a couple of days, is all."

All at once something inside gave and threatened to come pouring out of me. I didn't hate him anymore. I felt that in another moment I'd start crying like a child.

"Sure," I said. "Don't sweat." I looked in my wallet and didn't have a dollar; I only had a five. "Here," I said. "That hold you?"

He didn't look at it—he didn't want to look at it. A terrible, closed look came over his face, as though he were keeping the number on the bill a secret from him and me. "Thanks," he said, and now he was dying to see me go. "Don't worry about Sonny. Maybe I'll write him or something."

"Sure," I said. "You do that. So long."

"Be seeing you," he said. I went on down the steps.

And I didn't write Sonny or send him anything for a long time. When I finally did, it was just after my little girl died, he wrote me back a letter which made me feel like a bastard.

Here's what he said:

Dear brother,
    You don't know how much I needed to hear from you. I wanted to write you many a time but I dug how

much I must have hurt you and so I didn't write. But now I feel like a man who's been trying to climb out of some deep, real deep and funky hole and just saw the sun up there, outside. I got to get outside.

I can't tell you much about how I got here. I mean I don't know how to tell you. I guess I was afraid of something or I was trying to escape from something and you know I have never been very strong in the head (smile). I'm glad Mama and Daddy are dead and can't see what's happened to their son and I swear if I'd known what I was doing I would never have hurt you so, you and a lot of other fine people who were nice to me and who believed in me.

I don't want you to think it had anything to do with me being a musician. It's more than that. Or maybe less than that. I can't get anything straight in my head down here and I try not to think about what's going to happen to me when I get outside again. Sometime I think I'm going to flip and never get outside and sometime I think I'll come straight back. I tell you one thing, though, I'd rather blow my brains out than go through this again. But that's what they all say, so they tell me. If I tell you when I'm coming to New York and if you could meet me, I sure would appreciate it. Give my love to Isabel and the kids and I was sure sorry to hear about little Gracie. I wish I could be like Mama and say the Lord's will be done, but I don't know it seems to me that trouble is the one thing that never does get stopped and I don't know what good it does to blame it on the Lord. But maybe it does some good if you believe it.

Your brother, Sonny

Then I kept in constant touch with him and I sent him whatever I could and I went to meet him when he came back to New York. When I saw him many things I thought I had forgotten came flooding back to me. This was because I had begun, finally, to wonder about Sonny, about the life that Sonny lived inside. This life, whatever it was, had made him older and thinner and it had deepened the distant stillness in which he had always moved. He looked very unlike my baby brother. Yet, when he smiled, when we shook hands, the baby brother I'd never known looked out from the depths of his private life, like an animal waiting to be coaxed into the light.

"How you been keeping?" he asked me.

"All right. And you?"

"Just fine." He was smiling all over his face. "It's good to see you again."

"It's good to see you."

The seven years' difference in our ages lay between us like a chasm: I wondered if these years would ever operate between us as a bridge. I was remembering, and it made it hard to catch my breath, that I had been there when he was born; and I had heard the first words he had ever spoken. When he started to walk, he walked from our mother straight to me. I caught him just before he fell when he took the first steps he ever took in this world.

"How's Isabel?"

"Just fine. She's dying to see you."

"And the boys?"

"They're fine, too. They're anxious to see their uncle."

"Oh, come on. You know they don't remember me."

"Are you kidding? Of course they remember you."

He grinned again. We got into a taxi. We had a lot to say to each other, far too much to know how to begin.

As the taxi began to move, I asked, "You still want to go to India?"

He laughed. "You still remember that. Hell, no. This place is Indian enough for me."

"It used to belong to them," I said.

And he laughed again. "They damn sure knew what they were doing when they got rid of it."

Years ago, when he was around fourteen, he'd been all hipped on the idea of going to India. He read books about people sitting on rocks, naked, in all kinds of weather, but mostly bad, naturally, and walking barefoot through hot coals and arriving at wisdom. I used to say that it sounded to me as though they were getting away from wisdom as fast as they could. I think he sort of looked down on me for that.

"Do you mind," he asked, "if we have the driver drive alongside the park? On the West Side—I haven't seen the city in so long."

"Of course not," I said. I was afraid that I might sound as though I were humoring him, but I hoped he wouldn't take it that way.

So we drove along, between the green of the park and the stony, lifeless elegance of hotels and apartment buildings, toward the vivid, killing streets of our childhood. These streets hadn't changed, though housing projects jutted up out of them now like rocks in the middle of a boiling sea. Most of the houses in which we had grown up had vanished, as had the stores from which we had stolen, the basements in which we had first tried sex, the rooftops from which we had hurled tin cans and bricks. But houses exactly like the houses of our past yet dominated the landscape, boys exactly like the boys we once had been found themselves smothering in these houses, came down into the streets for light and air and found themselves encircled by disaster. Some escaped the trap, most didn't. Those who got out always left something of themselves behind, as some animals amputate a leg and leave it in the trap. It might be said, perhaps, that I had escaped; after all, I was a school teacher. Or that Sonny had, he hadn't lived in Harlem for years. Yet, as the cab moved uptown through streets which seemed, with a rush, to darken with dark people, and as I covertly studied Sonny's face, it came to me that what we both were seeking through our separate cab windows was that part

of ourselves which had been left behind. It's always at
the hour of trouble and confrontation that the missing
member aches.

We hit 110th Street and started rolling up Lenox Avenue. And I'd known this avenue all my life, but it seemed
to me again, as it had seemed on the day I'd first heard
about Sonny's trouble, filled with a hidden menace which
was its very breath of life.

"We almost there," said Sonny.

"Almost." We were both too nervous to say anything
more.

We live in a housing project. It hasn't been up long. A
few days after it was up it seemed uninhabitably new;
now, of course, it's already run-down. It looks like a
parody of the good, clean, faceless life—God knows the
people who live in it do their best to make it a parody.
The beat-looking grass lying around isn't enough to make
their lives green, the hedges will never hold out the
streets, and they know it. The big windows fool no one; they
aren't big enough to make space out of no space. They
don't bother with the windows, they watch the TV screen
instead. The playground is most popular with the children who don't play at jacks, or skip rope, or roller skate,
or swing, and they can be found in it after dark. We
moved in partly because it's not too far from where I
teach, and partly for the kids; but it's really just like the
houses in which Sonny and I grew up. The same things
happen, they'll have the same things to remember. The
moment Sonny and I started into the house I had the feeling that I was simply bringing him back into the danger
he had almost died trying to escape.

Sonny had never been talkative. So I don't know why I
was sure he'd be dying to talk to me when supper was
over the first night. Everything went fine, the oldest boy
remembered him, and the youngest boy liked him, and
Sonny had remembered to bring something for each of
them; and Isabel, who is really much nicer than I am,

more open and giving, had gone to a lot of trouble about dinner and was genuinely glad to see him. And she's always been able to tease Sonny in a way that I haven't. It was nice to see her face so vivid again and to hear her laugh and watch her make Sonny laugh. She wasn't, or, anyway, she didn't seem to be, at all uneasy or embarrassed. She chatted as though there were no subject which had to be avoided and she got Sonny past his first, faint stiffness. And thank God she was there, for I was filled with that icy dread again. Everything I did seemed awkward to me, and everything I said sounded freighted with hidden meaning. I was trying to remember everything I'd heard about dope addiction and I couldn't help watching Sonny for signs. I wasn't doing it out of malice. I was trying to find out something about my brother. I was dying to hear him tell me he was safe.

"Safe!" my father grunted, whenever Mama suggested trying to move to a neighborhood which might be safer for children. "Safe, hell! Ain't no place safe for kids, nor nobody."

He always went on like this, but he wasn't ever really as bad as he sounded; not even on weekends, when he got drunk. As a matter of fact, he was always on the lookout for "something a little better," but he died before he found it. He died suddenly, during a drunken weekend in the middle of the war, when Sonny was fifteen. He and Sonny hadn't ever got on too well. And this was partly because Sonny was the apple of his father's eye. It was because he loved Sonny so much and was frightened for him that he was always fighting with him. It doesn't do any good to fight with Sonny. Sonny just moves back, inside himself, where he can't be reached. But the principal reason that they never hit it off is that they were so much alike. Daddy was big and rough and loud-talking, just the opposite of Sonny, but they both had—that same privacy.

Mama tried to tell me something about this, just after Daddy died. I was home on leave from the Army.

This was the last time I ever saw my mother alive. Just the same, this picture gets all mixed up in my mind with pictures I had of her when she was younger. The way I always see her is the way she used to be on a Sunday afternoon, say, when the old folks were talking after the big Sunday dinner. I always see her wearing pale blue. She'd be sitting on the sofa. And my father would be sitting in the easy chair, not far from her. And the living room would be full of church folks and relatives. There they sit, in chairs all around the living room, and the night is creeping up outside, but nobody knows it yet. You can see the darkness growing against the windowpanes and you hear the street noises every now and again, or maybe the jangling beat of a tambourine from one of the churches close by, but it's real quiet in the room. For a moment nobody's talking, but every face looks darkening, like the sky outside. And my mother rocks a little from the waist, and my father's eyes are closed. Everyone is looking at something a child can't see. For a minute they've forgotten the children. Maybe a kid is lying on the rug, half asleep. Maybe somebody's got a kid in his lap and is absent-mindedly stroking the kid's head. Maybe there's a kid, quiet and big-eyed, curled up in a big chair in the corner. The silence, the darkness coming, and the darkness in the faces frightens the child obscurely. He hopes that the hand which strokes his forehead will never stop—will never die. He hopes that there will never come a time when the old folks won't be sitting around the living room, talking about where they've come from, and what they've seen, and what's happened to them and their kinfolk.

But something deep and watchful in the child knows that this is bound to end, is already ending. In a moment someone will get up and turn on the light. Then the old folks will remember the children and they won't talk any more that day. And when light fills the room, the child is filled with darkness. He knows that every time this happens he's moved just a little closer to that darkness outside. The darkness outside is what the old folks have been talking about. It's what they've come from. It's what they endure. The child knows that they won't talk any more because if he knows too much about what's happened to them, he'll know too much too soon, about what's going to happen to him.

The last time I talked to my mother, I remember I was restless. I wanted to get out and see Isabel. We weren't married then and we had a lot to straighten out between us.

There Mama sat, in black, by the window. She was humming an old church song—Lord, you brought me from a long ways off. Sonny was out somewhere. Mama kept watching the streets.

"I don't know," she said, "if I'll ever see you again, after you go off from here. But I hope you'll remember the things I tried to teach you."

"Don't talk like that," I said, and smiled. "You'll be here a long time yet."

She smiled, too, but she said nothing. She was quiet for a long time. And I said, "Mama, don't you worry about nothing. I'll be writing all the time, and you be getting the checks . . ."

"I want to talk to you about your brother," she said, suddenly. "If anything happens to me he ain't going to have nobody to look out for him."

"Mama," I said, "ain't nothing going to happen to you or Sonny. Sonny's all right. He's a good boy and he's got good sense."

"It ain't a question of his being a good boy," Mama said, "nor of his having good sense. It ain't only the bad ones, nor yet the dumb ones that gets sucked under." She stopped, looking at me. "Your Daddy once had a brother," she said, and she smiled in a way that made me feel she was in pain. "You didn't never know that, did you?"

"No," I said, "I never knew that," and I watched her face.

"Oh, yes," she said, "your Daddy had a brother." She looked out of the window again. "I know you never saw your Daddy cry. But I did—many a time, through all these years."

I asked her, "What happened to his brother? How come nobody's ever talked about him?"

This was the first time I ever saw my mother look old.

"His brother got killed," she said, "when he was just a little younger than you are now. I knew him. He was a fine boy. He was maybe a little full of the devil, but he didn't mean nobody no harm."

Then she stopped and the room was silent, exactly as it had sometimes been on those Sunday afternoons. Mama kept looking out into the streets.

"He used to have a job in the mill," she said, "and, like all young folks, he just liked to perform on Saturday nights. Saturday nights, him and your father would drift around to different places, go to dances and things like that, or just sit around with people they knew, and your father's brother would sing, he had a fine voice, and play along with himself on his guitar. Well, this particular Saturday night, him and your father was coming home from some place, and they were both a little drunk and there was a moon that night, it was bright like day. Your father's brother was feeling kind of good, and he was whistling to himself, and he had his guitar slung over his shoulder. They was coming down a hill and beneath them was a road that turned off from the highway. Well, your father's brother, being always kind of frisky, decided to run down this hill, and he did, with that guitar banging and clanging behind him, and he ran across the road, and he was making water behind a tree. And your father was sort of amused at him and he was still coming down the hill, kind of slow. Then he heard a car motor and that same minute his brother stepped from behind the tree, into the road, in the moonlight. And he started to cross the road. And your father started to run down the hill, he says he don't know why. This car was full of white men. They was all drunk, and when they seen your father's brother they let out a great whoop and holler and they aimed the car straight at him. They was having fun, they just wanted to scare him, the way they do sometimes, you know. But they was drunk. And I guess the boy, being drunk, too, and scared, kind of lost his head. By the time he jumped it was too late. Your father says he heard his brother scream when the car rolled over him, and he heard the wood of that guitar when it give, and he heard them strings go flying, and he heard them white men shouting, and the car kept on a-going and it ain't stopped till this day. And, time your father got down the hill, his brother weren't nothing but blood and pulp."

Tears were gleaming on my mother's face. There wasn't anything I could say.

"He never mentioned it," she said, "because I never let him mention it before you children. Your Daddy was like a crazy man that night and for many a night thereafter. He says he never in his life seen anything as dark as that road after the lights of the car had gone away. Weren't nothing, weren't nobody on that road, just your Daddy and his brother and that busted guitar. Oh, yes. Your Daddy never did really get right again. Till the day he died he weren't sure but that every white man he saw was the man that killed his brother."

She stopped and took out her handkerchief and dried her eyes and looked at me.

"I ain't telling you all this," she said, "to make you scared or bitter or to make you hate nobody. I'm telling you this because you got a brother. And the world ain't changed."

I guess I didn't want to believe this. I guess she saw this in my face. She turned away from me, toward the window again, searching those streets.

"But I praise my Redeemer," she said at last, "that He called your Daddy home before me. I ain't saying it to throw no flowers at myself, but, I declare, it keeps me from feeling too cast down to know I helped your father get safely through this world. Your father always acted like he was the roughest, strongest man on earth. And everybody took him to be like that. But if he hadn't had me there—to see his tears!"

She was crying again. Still, I couldn't move. I said, "Lord, Lord, Mama, I didn't know it was like that."

"Oh, honey," she said, "there's a lot that you don't know. But you are going to find it out." She stood up from the window and came over to me. "You got to hold on to your brother," she said, "and don't let him fall, no matter what it looks like is happening to him and no matter how evil you gets with him. You going to be evil with him many a time. But don't you forget what I told you, you hear?"

"I won't forget," I said. "Don't worry, I won't forget. I won't let nothing happen to Sonny."

My mother smiled as though she were amused at something she saw in my face. Then, "You may not be able to stop nothing from happening. But you got to let him know you's there."

Two days later I was married, and then I was gone. And I had a lot of things on my mind and I pretty well forgot my promise to Mama until I got shipped home on a special furlough for her funeral.

And, after the funeral, with just Sonny and me alone in the empty kitchen, I tried to find out something about him.

"What do you want to do?" I asked him.

"I'm going to be a musician," he said.

For he had graduated, in the time I had been away, from dancing to the juke box to finding out who was playing what, and what they were doing with it, and he had bought himself a set of drums.

"You mean, you want to be a drummer?" I somehow had the feeling that being a drummer might be all right for other people but not for my brother Sonny.

"I don't think," he said, looking at me very gravely, "that I'll ever be a good drummer. But I think I can play a piano."

I frowned. I'd never played the role of the older brother quite so seriously before, had scarcely ever, in fact, asked Sonny a damn thing. I sensed myself in the presence of something I didn't really know how to handle, didn't understand. So I made my frown a little deeper as I asked: "What kind of musician do you want to be?"

He grinned. "How many kinds do you think there are?"

"Be serious," I said.

He laughed, throwing his head back, and then looked at me. "I am serious."

"Well, then, for Christ's sake, stop kidding around and answer a serious question. I mean, do you want to be a concert pianist, you want to play classical music and all that, or—or what?" Long before I finished he was laughing again. "For Christ's sake, Sonny!"

He sobered, but with difficulty. "I'm sorry. But you sound so—scared!" and he was off again.

"Well, you may think it's funny now, baby, but it's not going to be so funny when you have to make your living at it, let me tell you that." I was furious because I knew he was laughing at me and I didn't know why.

"No," he said, very sober now, and afraid, perhaps, that he'd hurt me, "I don't want to be a classical pianist. That isn't what interests me. I mean"—he paused, looking hard at me, as though his eyes would help me to understand, and then gestured helplessly, as though perhaps his hand would help—"I mean, I'll have a lot of studying to do, and I'll have to study everything, but, I mean, I want to play with—jazz musicians." He stopped. "I want to play jazz," he said.

Well, the word had never before sounded as heavy, as real, as it sounded that afternoon in Sonny's mouth. I just looked at him and I was probably frowning a real frown by this time. I simply couldn't see why on earth he'd want to spend his time hanging around nightclubs, clowning around on bandstands, while people pushed each other around a dance floor. It seemed—beneath him, somehow. I had never thought about it before, had never been forced to, but I suppose I had always put jazz musicians in a class with what Daddy called "good-time people."

"Are you serious?"

"Hell, yes, I'm serious."

He looked more helpless than ever, and annoyed, and deeply hurt.

I suggested, helpfully: "You mean—like Louis Armstrong?"

His face closed as though I'd struck him. "No. I'm not talking about none of that old-time, down home crap."

"Well, look, Sonny, I'm sorry, don't get mad. I just don't altogether get it, that's all. Name somebody—you know, a jazz musician you admire."

"Bird."

"Who?"

"Bird! Charlie Parker! Don't they teach you nothing in the goddamn Army?"

I lit a cigarette. I was surprised and then a little amused to discover that I was trembling. "I've been out of touch," I said. "You'll have to be patient with me. Now. Who's this Parker character?"

"He's just one of the greatest jazz musicians alive," said Sonny, sullenly, his hands in his pockets, his back to me. "Maybe the greatest," he added bitterly, "that's probably why you never heard of him."

"All right," I said, "I'm ignorant. I'm sorry. I'll go out and buy all the cat's records right away, all right?"

"It don't," said Sonny, with dignity, "make any differ-

ence to me. I don't care what you listen to. Don't do me
no favors."

I was beginning to realize that I'd never seen him so
upset before. With another part of my mind I was thinking that this would probably turn out to be one of those
things kids go through and that I shouldn't make it seem
important by pushing it too hard. Still, I didn't think it
would do any harm to ask: "Doesn't all this take a lot of
time? Can you make a living at it?"

He turned back to me and half leaned, half sat, on the
kitchen table. "Everything takes time," he said, "and—
well, yes, sure, I can make a living at it. But what I don't
seem to be able to make you understand is that it's the
only thing I want to do."

"Well, Sonny," I said gently, "you know people can't
always do exactly what they want to do—"

"No, I don't know that," said Sonny, surprising me, "I
think people ought to do what they want to do, what else
are they alive for?"

"You getting to be a big boy," I said desperately, "it's
time you started thinking about your future."

"I'm thinking about my future," said Sonny, grimly. "I
think about it all the time."

I gave up. I decided, if he didn't change his mind, that
we could always talk about it later. "In the meantime," I
said, "you got to finish school." We had already decided
that he'd have to move in with Isabel and her folks. I
knew this wasn't the ideal arrangement, because Isabel's
folks are inclined to be dicty and they hadn't especially
wanted Isabel to marry me. But I didn't know what else
to do. "And we have to get you fixed up at Isabel's."

There was a long silence. He moved from the kitchen
table to the window. "That's a terrible idea. You know it
yourself."

"Do you have a better idea?"

He just walked up and down the kitchen for a minute.
He was as tall as I was. He had started to shave. I
suddenly had the feeling that I didn't know him at all.

He stopped at the kitchen table and picked up my cigarettes. Looking at me with a kind of mocking, amused defiance, he put one between his lips. "You mind?"

"You smoking already?"

He lit the cigarette and nodded, watching me through the smoke. "I just wanted to see if I'd have the courage to smoke in front of you." He grinned and blew a great cloud of smoke to the ceiling. "It was easy." He looked at my face. "Come on, now. I bet you was smoking at my age, tell the truth."

I didn't say anything but the truth was on my face, and he laughed. But now there was something very strained in his laugh. "Sure. And I bet that ain't all you was doing."

He was frightening me a little. "Cut the crap," I said. "We already decided that you was going to go and live at Isabel's. Now what's got into you all of a sudden?"

"You decided it," he pointed out. "I didn't decide nothing." He stopped in front of me, leaning against the stove, arms loosely folded. "Look, brother. I don't want to stay in Harlem no more, I really don't." He was very earnest. He looked at me, then over toward the kitchen window. There was something in his eyes I'd never seen before, some thoughtfulness, some worry all his own. He rubbed the muscle of one arm. "It's time I was getting out of here."

"Where do you want to go, Sonny?"

"I want to join the Army. Or the Navy, I don't care. If I say I'm old enough, they'll believe me."

Then I got mad. It was because I was so scared. "You must be crazy. You goddamn fool, what the hell do you want to go and join the Army for?"

"I just told you. To get out of Harlem."

"Sonny, you haven't even finished school. And if you really want to be a musician, how do you expect to study if you're in the Army?"

He looked at me, trapped, and in anguish. "There's

ways. I might be able to work out some kind of deal. Anyway, I'll have the G.I. Bill when I come out."

"If you come out." We stared at each other. "Sonny, please. Be reasonable. I know the setup is far from perfect. But we got to do the best we can."

"I ain't learning nothing in school," he said. "Even when I go." He turned away from me and opened the window and threw his cigarette out into the narrow alley. I watched his back. "At least, I ain't learning nothing you'd want me to learn." He slammed the window so hard I thought the glass would fly out, and turned back to me. "And I'm sick of the stink of these garbage cans!"

"Sonny," I said, "I know how you feel. But if you don't finish school now, you're going to be sorry later that you didn't." I grabbed him by the shoulders. "And you only got another year. It ain't so bad. And I'll come back and I swear I'll help you do whatever you want to do. Just try to put up with it till I come back. Will you please do that? For me?"

He didn't answer and he wouldn't look at me.

"Sonny. You hear me?"

He pulled away. "I hear you. But you never hear anything I say."

I didn't know what to say to that. He looked out of the window and then back at me. "O.K.," he said, and sighed. "I'll try."

Then I said, trying to cheer him up a little, "They got a piano at Isabel's. You can practice on it."

And as a matter of fact, it did cheer him up for a minute. "That's right," he said to himself. "I forgot that." His face relaxed a little. But the worry, the thoughtfulness, played on it still, the way shadows play on a face which is staring into the fire.

But I thought I'd never hear the end of that piano. At first, Isabel would write me, saying how nice it was that

Sonny was so serious about his music and how, as soon
as he came in from school, or wherever he had been
when he was supposed to be at school, he went straight
to that piano and stayed there until suppertime. And,
after supper, he went back to that piano and stayed there
until everybody went to bed. He was at that piano all
day Saturday and all day Sunday. Then he bought a
record player and started playing records. He'd play one
record over and over again, all day long sometimes, and
he'd improvise along with it on the piano. Or he'd play
one section of the record, one chord, one change, one
progression, then he'd do it on the piano. Then back to
the record. Then back to the piano.

Well, I really don't know how they stood it. Isabel
finally confessed that it wasn't like living with a person
at all, it was like living with sound. And the sound didn't
make any sense to her, didn't make any sense to any of
them—naturally. They began, in a way, to be afflicted by
this presence that was living in their home. It was as
though Sonny were some sort of god, or monster. He
moved in an atmosphere which wasn't like theirs at all.
They fed him and he ate, he washed himself, he walked
in and out of their door; he certainly wasn't nasty or
unpleasant or rude. Sonny isn't any of those things; but
it was as though he were all wrapped up in some cloud,
some fire, some vision all his own; and there wasn't any
way to reach him.

At the same time, he wasn't really a man yet, he was
still a child, and they had to watch out for him in all
kinds of ways. They certainly couldn't throw him out.
Neither did they dare to make a great scene about that
piano because even they dimly sensed, as I sensed, from
so many thousands of miles away, that Sonny was at
that piano playing for his life.

But he hadn't been going to school. One day a letter
came from the school board and Isabel's mother got it—
there had, apparently, been other letters, but Sonny had

torn them up. This day when Sonny came in, Isabel's
mother showed him the letter and asked where he'd been
spending his time. And she finally got it out of him that
he'd been down in Greenwich Village, with musicians
and other characters, in a white girl's apartment. And
this scared her and she started to scream at him, and
what came up, once she began—though she denies it to
this day—was what sacrifices they were making to give
Sonny a decent home and how little he appreciated it.

Sonny didn't play the piano that day. By evening,
Isabel's mother had calmed down but then there was the
old man to deal with, and Isabel herself. Isabel says she
did her best to be calm, but she broke down and started
crying. She says she just watched Sonny's face. She could
tell, by watching him, what was happening with him.
And what was happening was that they penetrated his
cloud, they had reached him. Even if their fingers had
been a thousand times more gentle than human fingers
ever are, he could hardly help feeling that they had
stripped him naked and were spitting on that nakedness.
For he also had to see that his presence, that music,
which was life or death to him, had been torture for them
and that they had endured it, not at all for his sake, but
only for mine. And Sonny couldn't take that. He can take
it a little better today than he could then, but he's still
not very good at it and, frankly, I don't know anybody
who is.

The silence of the next few days must have been louder
than the sound of all the music ever played since time
began. One morning, before she went to work, Isabel was
in his room for something and she suddenly realized that
all of his records were gone. And she knew for certain
that he was gone. And he was. He went as far as the
Navy would carry him. He finally sent me a postcard
from some place in Greece, and that was the first I knew
that Sonny was still alive. I didn't see him any more
until we were both back in New York and the war had
long been over.

He was a man by then, of course, but I wasn't willing
to see it. He came by the house from time to time, but we
fought almost every time we met. I didn't like the way he
carried himself, loose and dreamlike all the time, and I
didn't like his friends, and his music seemed to be merely
an excuse for the life he led. It sounded just that weird
and disordered.

Then we had a fight, a pretty awful fight, and I didn't
see him for months. By and by I looked him up, where he
was living, in a furnished room in the Village, and I
tried to make it up. But there were lots of other people in
the room and Sonny just lay on his bed, and he wouldn't
come downstairs with me, and he treated these other
people as though they were his family and I weren't. So I
got mad and then he got mad, and then I told him that
he might just as well be dead as live the way he was
living. Then he stood up and told me not to worry about
him anymore in life, that he was dead as far as I was
concerned. Then he pushed me to the door and the other
people looked on as though nothing were happening, and
he slammed the door behind me. I stood in the hallway,
staring at the door. I heard somebody laugh in the room
and then the tears came to my eyes. I started down the
steps, whistling to keep from crying, I kept whistling to
myself, You going to need me, baby, one of these cold,
rainy days.

I read about Sonny's trouble in the spring. Little Grace
died in the fall. She was a beautiful little girl. But she
only lived a little over two years. She died of polio and
she suffered. She had a slight fever for a couple of days,
but it didn't seem like anything and we just kept her in
bed. And we would certainly have called the doctor, but
the fever dropped, she seemed to be all right. So we
thought it had just been a cold. Then, one day, she was
up, playing, Isabel was in the kitchen fixing lunch for
the two boys when they'd come in from school, and she

heard Grace fall down in the living room. When you have a lot of children you don't always start running when one of them falls, unless they start screaming or something. And, this time, Grace was quiet. Yet Isabel says that when she heard the thump and then that silence, something happened in her to make her afraid. And she ran to the living room and there was little Grace on the floor, all twisted up, and the reason she hadn't screamed was that she couldn't get her breath. And when she did scream, it was the worst sound, Isabel says, that she'd ever heard in all her life, and she still hears it sometimes in her dreams. Isabel will sometimes wake me up with a low, moaning, strangled sound, and I have to be quick to awaken her and hold her to me, and where Isabel is weeping against me seems a mortal wound.

I think I may have written Sonny the very day that little Grace was buried. I was sitting in the living room in the dark, by myself, and I suddenly thought of Sonny. My trouble made his real.

One Saturday afternoon, when Sonny had been living with us, or, anyway, been in our house, for nearly two weeks, I found myself wandering aimlessly about the living room, drinking from a can of beer, and trying to work up the courage to search Sonny's room. He was out, he was usually out whenever I was home, and Isabel had taken the children to see their grandparents. Suddenly I was standing still in front of the living room window, watching Seventh Avenue. The idea of searching Sonny's room made me still. I scarcely dared to admit to myself what I'd be searching for. I didn't know what I'd do if I found it. Or if I didn't.

On the sidewalk across from me, near the entrance to a barbecue joint, some people were holding an old-fashioned revival meeting. The barbecue cook, wearing a dirty white apron, his conked hair reddish and metallic in the pale sun, and a cigarette between his lips, stood in the doorway, watching them. Kids and older people paused

in their errands and stood there, along with some older
men and a couple of very tough-looking women who
watched everything that happened on the avenue, as
though they owned it, or were maybe owned by it. Well,
they were watching this, too. The revival was being
carried on by three sisters in black, and a brother. All
they had were their voices and their Bibles and a tambourine. The brother was testifying, and while he testi-
fied two of the sisters stood together, seeming to say,
Amen, and the third sister walked around with the tambourine outstretched and a couple of people dropped coins
into it. Then the brother's testimony ended and the sister
who had been taking up the collection dumped the coins
into her palm and transferred them to the pocket of her
long black robe. Then she raised both hands, striking the
tambourine against the air, and then against one hand,
and she started to sing. And the two other sisters and the
brother joined in.

It was strange, suddenly, to watch, though I had been
seeing these street meetings all my life. So, of course,
had everybody else down there. Yet, they paused and
watched and listened and I stood still at the window.
" 'Tis the old ship of Zion," they sang, and the sister with
the tambourine kept a steady, jangling beat, "it has
rescued many a thousand!" Not a soul under the sound of
their voices was hearing this song for the first time, not
one of them had been rescued. Nor had they seen much
in the way of rescue work being done around them.
Neither did they especially believe in the holiness of
the three sisters and the brother, they knew too much
about them, knew where they lived, and how. The woman
with the tambourine, whose voice dominated the air,
whose face was bright with joy, was divided by very little
from the woman who stood watching her, a cigarette
between her heavy, chapped lips, her hair a cuckoo's
nest, her face scarred and swollen from many beatings,
and her black eyes glittering like coal. Perhaps they both

knew this, which was why, when, at the rare times they
addressed each other, they addressed each other as "sister." As the singing filled the air, the watching, listening
faces underwent a change, the eyes focusing on something within; the music seemed to soothe a poison out of
them; and time seemed, nearly, to fall away from the
sullen, belligerent, battered faces, as though they were
fleeing back to their first condition, while dreaming of
their last. The barbecue cook half shook his head and
smiled, and dropped his cigarette and disappeared into
his joint. A man fumbled in his pockets for change and
stood holding it in his hand impatiently, as though he
had just remembered a pressing appointment further up
the avenue. He looked furious. Then I saw Sonny, standing on the edge of the crowd. He was carrying a wide,
flat notebook with a green cover, and it made him look,
from where I was standing, almost like a schoolboy. The
coppery sun brought out the copper in his skin; he was
very faintly smiling, standing very still. Then the singing stopped, the tambourine turned into a collection plate
again. The furious man dropped in his coins and vanished; so did a couple of the women, and Sonny dropped
some change in the plate, looking directly at the woman
with a little smile. He started across the avenue, toward
the house. He has a slow, loping walk, something like
the way Harlem hipsters walk, only he's imposed on this
his own half-beat. I had never really noticed it before.

I stayed at the window, both relieved and apprehensive. As Sonny disappeared from my sight, they began
singing again. And they were still singing when his key
turned in the lock.

"Hey," he said.

"Hey, yourself. You want some beer?"

"No. Well, maybe." But he came up to the window and
stood beside me, looking out. "What a warm voice," he said.

They were singing, "If I Could Only Hear My Mother
Pray Again!"

"Yes," I said, "and she can sure beat that tambourine."

"But what a terrible song," he said, and laughed. He dropped his notebook on the sofa and disappeared into the kitchen. "Where's Isabel and the kids?"

"I think they went to see their grandparents. You hungry?"

"No." He came back into the living room with his can of beer. "You want to come some place with me tonight?"

I sensed, I don't know how, that I couldn't possibly say no. "Sure. Where?"

He sat down on the sofa and picked up his notebook and started leafing through it. "I'm going to sit in with some fellows in a joint in the Village."

"You mean, you're going to play, tonight?"

"That's right." He took a swallow of his beer and moved back to the window. He gave me a sidelong look. "If you can stand it."

"I'll try," I said.

He smiled to himself and we both watched as the meeting across the way broke up. The three sisters and the brother, heads bowed, were singing, "God be with you 'till we meet again." The faces around them were very quiet. Then the song ended. The small crowd dispersed. We watched the three women and the lone man walk slowly up the avenue.

"When she was singing before," said Sonny, abruptly, "her voice reminded me for a minute of what heroin feels like sometimes—when it's in your veins. It makes you feel sort of warm and cool at the same time. And distant. And—and sure." He sipped his beer, very deliberately not looking at me. I watched his face. "It makes you feel—in control. Sometimes you've got to have that feeling."

"Do you?" I sat down slowly in the easy chair.

"Sometimes." He went to the sofa and picked up his notebook again. "Some people do."

"In order," I asked, "to play?" And my voice was very ugly, full of contempt and anger.

"Well"—he looked at me with great, troubled eyes, as though, in fact, he hoped his eyes would tell me things he could never otherwise say—"they think so. And if they think so . . . !"

"And what do you think?" I asked.

He sat on the sofa and put his can of beer on the floor. "I don't know," he said, and I couldn't be sure if he were answering my question or pursuing his thoughts. His face didn't tell me. "It's not so much to play. It's to stand it, to be able to make it at all. On any level." He frowned and smiled: "In order to keep from shaking to pieces."

"But these friends of yours," I said, "they seem to shake themselves to pieces pretty goddamn fast."

"Maybe." He played with the notebook. And something told me that I should curb my tongue, that Sonny was doing his best to talk, that I should listen. "But of course you only know the ones that've gone to pieces. Some don't—or at least they haven't yet, and that's just about all any of us can say." He paused. "And then there are some who just live, really, in hell, and they know it and they see what's happening and they go right on. I don't know." He sighed, dropped the notebook, folded his arms. "Some guys, you can tell from the way they play, they on something all the time. And you can see that, well, it makes something real for them. But of course," he picked up his beer from the floor and sipped it and put the can down again, "they want to, too, you've got to see that. Even some of them that say they don't—some, not all."

"And what about you?" I asked—I couldn't help it. "What about you? Do you want to?"

He stood up and walked to the window and remained silent for a long time. Then he sighed. "Me," he said. Then: "While I was downstairs before, on my way here, listening to that woman sing, it struck me all of a sudden how much suffering she must have had to go through—to sing like that. It's repulsive to think you have to suffer that much."

I said: "But there's no way not to suffer—is there, Sonny?"

"I believe not," he said, and smiled, "but that's never stopped anyone from trying." He looked at me. "Has it?" I realized, with this mocking look, that there stood between us, forever, beyond the power of time or forgiveness, the fact that I had held silence—so long! when he had needed human speech to help him. He turned back to the window. "No, there's no way not to suffer. But you try all kinds of ways to keep from drowning in it, to keep on top of it, and to make it seem—well, like you. Like you did something, all right, and now you're suffering for it. You know?" I said nothing. "Well, you know," he said, impatiently, "why do people suffer? Maybe it's better to do something, to give it a reason, any reason."

"But we just agreed," I said, "that there's no way not to suffer. Isn't it better, then, just to—take it?"

"But nobody just takes it," Sonny cried, "that's what I'm telling you! Everybody tries not to. You're just hung up on the way some people try—it's not your way!"

The hair on my face began to itch, my face felt wet. "That's not true," I said, "that's not true. I don't give a damn what other people do, I don't even care how they suffer. I just care how you suffer." And he looked at me. "Please believe me," I said, "I don't want to see you—die—trying not to suffer."

"I won't," he said, flatly, "die trying not to suffer. At least, not any faster than anybody else."

"But there's no need," I said, trying to laugh, "is there? in killing yourself."

I wanted to say more, but I couldn't. I wanted to talk about will power and how life could be—well, beautiful. I wanted to say that it was all within; but was it? or, rather, wasn't that exactly the trouble? And I wanted to promise that I would never fail him again. But it would all have sounded—empty words and lies.

So I made the promise to myself and prayed that I would keep it.

"It's terrible sometimes, inside," he said, "that's what's the trouble. You walk these streets, black and funky and cold, and there's not really a living ass to talk to, and there's nothing shaking, and there's no way of getting it out—that storm inside. You can't talk it and you can't make love with it, and when you finally try to get with it and play it, you realize nobody's listening. So you've got to listen. You got to find a way to listen."

And then he walked away from the window and sat on the sofa again, as though all the wind had suddenly been knocked out of him. "Sometimes you'll do anything to play, even cut your mother's throat." He laughed and looked at me. "Or your brother's." Then he sobered. "Or your own." Then: "Don't worry. I'm all right now and I think I'll be all right. But I can't forget—where I've been. I don't mean just the physical place I've been, I mean where I've been. And, what I've been."

"What have you been, Sonny?" I asked.

He smiled—but sat sideways on the sofa, his elbow resting on the back, his fingers playing with his mouth and chin, not looking at me. "I've been something I didn't recognize, didn't know I could be. Didn't know anybody could be." He stopped, looking inward, looking helplessly young, looking old. "I'm not talking about it now because I feel guilty or anything like that—maybe it would be better if I did. I don't know. Anyway, I can't really talk about it. Not to you, not to anybody." And now he turned and faced me. "Sometimes, you know, and it was actually when I was most out of the world, I felt that I was in it, that I was with it, really, and I could play or I didn't really have to play, it just came out of me, it was there. And I don't know how I played, thinking about it now, but I know that I did awful things, those times, some-times, to people. Or it wasn't that I did anything to them—it was that they weren't real." He picked up the beer can; it was empty; he rolled it between his palms: "And other times—well, I needed a fix. I needed to find a place to lean, I needed to clear a space to listen—and I couldn't find it, and I—went crazy, I did terrible things to me, I was terrible for me." He began pressing the beer can between his hands; I watched the metal begin to give. It glittered, as he played with it, like a knife, and I was afraid he would cut himself, but I said nothing. "Oh, well. I can never tell you. I was all by myself at the bottom of something, stinking and sweating and crying and shaking, and I smelled it, you know? my stink, and I thought I'd die if I couldn't get away from it and yet, all the same, I knew that everything I was doing was just locking me in with it. And I didn't know," he paused, still flattening the beer can. "I didn't know, I still don't know, something kept telling me that maybe it was good to smell your own stink, but I didn't think that that was what I'd been trying to do—and—who can stand it?" and he abruptly dropped the ruined beer can, looking at me with a small, still smile, and then rose, walking to the window as though it were a lodestone. I watched his face, he watched the avenue. "I couldn't tell you when Mama died—but the reason I wanted to leave Harlem so bad was to get away from drugs. And then, when I ran away, that's what I was running from—really. When I came back, nothing had changed, I hadn't changed, I was just— older." And he stopped, drumming with his fingers on the windowpane. The sun had vanished, soon darkness would fall. I watched his face. "It can come again," he said, almost as though speaking to himself. Then he turned to me. "It can come again," he repeated. "I just want you to know that."

"All right," I said, at last. "So it can come again. All right."

He smiled, but the smile was sorrowful. "I had to try to tell you," he said.

"Yes," I said. "I understand that."

"You're my brother," he said, looking straight at me, and not smiling at all.

"Yes," I repeated, "yes, I understand that."

He turned back to the window, looking out. "All that hatred down there," he said, "all that hatred and misery and love. It's a wonder it doesn't blow the avenue apart."

We went to the only nightclub on a short, dark street, downtown. We squeezed through the narrow, chattering, jam-packed bar to the entrance of the big room, where the bandstand was. And we stood there for a moment, for the lights were very dim in this room and we couldn't see. Then, "Hello, boy," said a voice, and an enormous black man, much older than Sonny or myself, erupted out of all that atmospheric lighting and put an arm around Sonny's shoulder. "I been sitting right here," he said, "waiting for you."

He had a big voice, too, and heads in the darkness turned toward us.

Sonny grinned and pulled a little away, and said, "Creole, this is my brother. I told you about him."

Creole shook my hand. "I'm glad to meet you, son," he said, and it was clear that he was glad to meet me there, for Sonny's sake. And he smiled, "You got a real musician in your family," and he took his arm from Sonny's shoulder and slapped him, lightly, affectionately, with the back of his hand.

"Well. Now I've heard it all," said a voice behind us. This was another musician, and a friend of Sonny's, a coal-black, cheerful-looking man, built close to the ground. He immediately began confiding to me, at the top of his lungs, the most terrible things about Sonny, his teeth gleaming like a lighthouse and his laugh coming up out of him like the beginning of an earthquake. And it turned out that everyone at the bar knew Sonny, or almost everyone; some were musicians, working there, or nearby, or not working, some were simply hangers-on, and some were there to hear Sonny play. I was introduced to all of them and they were all very polite to me. Yet, it was clear that, for them, I was only Sonny's brother. Here, I was in Sonny's world. Or, rather: his kingdom. Here, it was not even a question that his veins bore royal blood.

They were going to play soon and Creole installed me, by myself, at a table in a dark corner. Then I watched them, Creole, and the little black man, and Sonny, and the others, while they horsed around, standing just below the bandstand. The light from the bandstand spilled just a little short of them and, watching them laughing and gesturing and moving about, I had the feeling that they, nevertheless, were being most careful not to step into that circle of light too suddenly: that if they moved into the light too suddenly, without thinking, they would perish in flame. Then, while I watched, one of them, the small, black man, moved into the light and crossed the bandstand and started fooling around with his drums. Then—being funny and being, also, extremely ceremonious —Creole took Sonny by the arm and led him to the piano. A woman's voice called Sonny's name and a few hands started clapping. And Sonny, also being funny and ceremonious, and so touched, I think, that he could have cried, but neither hiding it nor showing it, riding it like a man, grinned, and put both hands to his heart and bowed from the waist.

Creole then went to the bass fiddle, and a lean, very bright-skinned brown man jumped up on the bandstand and picked up his horn. So there they were, and the atmosphere on the bandstand and in the room began to change and tighten. Someone stepped up to the microphone and announced them. Then there were all kinds of murmurs. Some people at the bar shushed others. The waitress ran around, frantically getting in the last orders, guys and chicks got closer to each other, and the lights on the bandstand, on the quartet, turned to a kind of indigo. Then they all looked different there. Creole looked about him for the last time, as though he were making certain that all his chickens were in the coop, and then he—jumped and struck the fiddle. And there they were.

All I know about music is that not many people ever really hear it. And even then, on the rare occasions when something opens within, and the music enters, what we mainly hear, or hear corroborated, are personal, private, vanishing evocations. But the man who creates the music is hearing something else, is dealing with the roar rising from the void and imposing order on it as it hits the air. What is evoked in him, then, is of another order, more terrible because it has no words, and triumphant, too, for that same reason. And his triumph, when he triumphs, is ours. I just watched Sonny's face. His face was troubled, he was working hard, but he wasn't with it. And I had the feeling that, in a way, everyone on the bandstand was waiting for him, both waiting for him and pushing him along. But as I began to watch Creole, I realized that it was Creole who held them all back. He had them on a short rein. Up there, keeping the beat with his whole body, wailing on the fiddle, with his eyes half closed, he was listening to everything, but he was listening to Sonny. He was having a dialogue with Sonny. He wanted Sonny to leave the shoreline and strike out for the deep water. He was Sonny's witness that deep water and drowning were not the same thing—he had been there, and he knew. And he wanted Sonny to know. He was waiting for Sonny to do the things on the keys which would let Creole know that Sonny was in the water.

And, while Creole listened, Sonny moved deep within, exactly like someone in torment. I had never before thought of how awful the relationship must be between the musician and his instrument. He has to fill it, this instrument, with the breath of life, his own. He has to make it do what he wants it to do. And a piano is just a piano. It's made out of so much wood and wires and little hammers and big ones, and ivory. While there's only so much you can do with it, the only way to find this out is to try to make it do everything.

And Sonny hadn't been near a piano for over a year. And he wasn't on much better terms with his life, not the life that stretched before him now. He and the piano stammered, started one way, got scared, stopped; started another way, panicked, marked time, started again; then seemed to have found a direction, panicked again, got stuck. And the face I saw on Sonny I'd never seen before. Everything had been burned out of it, and, at the same time, things usually hidden were being burned in, by the fire and fury of the battle which was occurring in him up there.

Yet, watching Creole's face as they neared the end of the first set, I had the feeling that something had happened, something I hadn't heard. Then they finished, there was scattered applause, and then, without an instant's warning, Creole started into something else; it was almost sardonic, it was "Am I Blue." And, as though he commanded, Sonny began to play. Something began to happen. And Creole let out the reins. The dry, low, black man said something awful on the drums; Creole answered, and the drums talked back. Then the horn insisted, sweet and high, slightly detached perhaps, and Creole listened, commenting now and then, dry, and driving, beautiful and calm and old. Then they all came together again, and Sonny was part of the family again. I could tell this from his face. He seemed to have found, right there beneath his fingers, a damn brand-new piano. It seemed that he couldn't get over it. Then, for awhile, just being happy with Sonny, they seemed to be agreeing with him that brand-new pianos certainly were a gas.

Then Creole stepped forward to remind them that what they were playing was the blues. He hit something in all of them, he hit something in me, myself, and the music tightened and deepened, apprehension began to beat the air. Creole began to tell us what the blues were all about. They were not about anything very new. He and his boys up there were keeping it new, at the risk of ruin, destruction, madness, and death, in order to find new ways to make us listen. For, while the tale of how we suffer, and how we are delighted, and how we may triumph is never new, it always must be heard. There isn't any other tale to tell, it's the only light we've got in all this darkness.

And this tale, according to that face, that body, those strong hands on those strings, has another aspect in every country, and a new depth in every generation. Listen, Creole seemed to be saying, listen. Now these are Sonny's blues. He made the little black man on the drums know it, and the bright, brown man on the horn, Creole wasn't trying any longer to get Sonny in the water. He was wishing him Godspeed. Then he stepped back, very slowly, filling the air with the immense suggestion that Sonny speak for himself.

Then they all gathered around Sonny and Sonny played. Every now and again one of them seemed to say, Amen. Sonny's fingers filled the air with life, his life. But that life contained so many others. And Sonny went all the way back, he really began with the spare, flat statement of the opening phrase of the song. Then he began to make it his. It was very beautiful because it wasn't hurried and it was no longer a lament. I seemed to hear with what burning he had made it his, with what burning we had yet to make it ours, how we could cease lamenting. Freedom lurked around us and I understood, at last, that he could help us to be free if we would listen, that he would never be free until we did. Yet, there was no battle in his face now. I heard what he had gone through, and would continue to go through until he came to rest in earth. He had made it his; that long line, of which we knew only Mama and Daddy. And he was giving it back, as everything must be given back, so that, passing through death, it can live forever. I saw my mother's face again, and felt, for the first time, how the stones of the road she had walked on must have bruised her feet. I saw the moonlit road where my father's brother died. And it brought something else back to me, and carried me past it; I saw my little girl again and felt Isabel's tears again, and I felt my own tears begin to rise. And I was yet aware that this was only a moment, that the world waited outside, as hungry as a tiger, and that trouble stretched above us, longer than the sky.

Then it was over. Creole and Sonny let out their breath, both soaking wet, and grinning. There was a lot of applause and some of it was real. In the dark, the girl came by and I asked her to take drinks to the bandstand. There was a long pause, while they talked up there in the indigo light, and after awhile, I saw the girl put a Scotch and milk on top of the piano for Sonny. He didn't seem to notice it, but just before they started playing again, he sipped from it and looked toward me, and nodded. Then he put it back on top of the piano. For me, then, as they began to play again, it glowed and shook above my brother's head like the very cup of trembling.

JOSEF SKVORECKY

EINE KLEINE JAZZMUSIK

TRANSLATED BY ALICE DENESOVÁ

IT ALL BEGAN WHEN Paddy—at that time he was still Pavel Nakonec—got his old man to buy him a jazz trumpet.

The fathers of us other boys soon had to follow suit. At a meeting in the Nakonec Villa, we mapped out everybody's job and decided that for a start we needed one of each jazz instrument. We did not then dream that we were laying the foundations of a band that has lasted till today and bears the name of its first and finest trumpet player and leader in undying memory: Paddy's Dixielanders.

But our fathers withstood the initial onslaught. And so, for the first rehearsal in Paddy's room, there gathered a most unlikely band composed of what had been to hand. There was Paddy's horn, a piano and a bass, but round that sound jazz core was grouped a tambour-like outfit of two violins, a mandolin, a Turkish drum, relic of a former castle band, which Franta Rozkosny, the caretaker's son, had discovered in the junk room of the local chateau; and, lastly, a brand-new xylophone, the outcome of my saxophone campaign, which I tried to pass off to myself as a vibraphone.

My father, referring to my weak lungs, had come out flat against a saxophone. But as my mummy could not bear the thought of any of my wishes being denied, they bought me the xylophone.

Well, then, those were our beginnings. The noise that floated from the Nakonec Villa was a dreadful, caterwauling xylophone music, punctuated by artless kicks of Paddy's trumpet. The caterwauling was especially due to the distinctive violin duo which tried (unsuccessfully) to breathe the lightness of swing into the not quite mastered technique of the Malát school of violin playing. Their drawn-out squealing was interspersed with thundering bangs on the Turkish drum, the stubborn plucking of the mandolin, and my helpless and chaotic rappings on the xylophone. The result was absolutely inimitable.

It goes without saying that all this was a far cry from any kind of music, let alone jazz. It was a monotonous mezzoforte jam of noise which enraptured us and drove the neighbors insane. It was not jazz. But somewhere in that hotbed there germinated a seed which survived the atrocity of Paddy's xylophone band.

By late 1940 it had been transformed into the shining miracle of a big swing band with five saxophones, three trumpets, a trio of trombones, a complete rhythm section and the vocalist Suzy Braun.

This last-named piece of the inventory had been acquired for the orchestra by Paddy Nakonec. Suzy was an orphan girl whose parents had disappeared in Oranienburg concentration camp early in 1940. Neither Jewish nor German, she was a Czech in spite of her name. Mr. Nakonec had brought her to K. Her father had been a foreman on construction jobs projected by the Nakonec design office. Until that time Suzy had lived in Prague. The minute she appeared in K. she was an immediate hit. A large number of types from the grammar school and elsewhere began to grovel before her, but the one who grovelled closest was Paddy himself. He was, of course, at an advantage because Suzy had moved in with the Nakonec family and worked as a junior draughtsman in the office of Paddy's father.

Now it must be pointed out that Paddy was not an Aryan, or at best only half a one. His late mother's maiden name had been Sommernitz, and her twenty years younger brother Harry Sommernitz was at present active beyond the frontiers of the Thousand Years Reich as a fighter pilot. From his father Paddy had inherited the Czech name, from his mother his Mosaic facial features. After they had kicked him out of the grammar school on account of this, he worked as a draughtsman in the office of his father's competitor Mojmír Ströbinger and lived in that odd condition in which persons of problematic racial origin existed at that time.

The more he doted on his jazz trumpet, the closer he was drawn to Suzy. And Suzy, our sweet Suzy, was in turn drawn closer to the band and discovered within herself a pleasant, agreeably husky contralto voice and a genius for rhythm and syncopation.

And so she sang, dressed in a black schoolgirl dress with a little white collar, swinging her hips, rotating her arms, and in her eyes sparkled the wicked, savage and sweet soul of jazz:

My heart beats to a syncopated beat,
must sing to feel I'm whole.
Thrills run from my head right down to my feet,
swing, that devil has taken my soul. . . .

The town, at least its younger and, in exceptional cases, even its older inhabitants, was gripped by the music fever. In the Victorian café in the square one could hear names like Chick Webb, Andy Kirk, Duke Ellington, Mary Lou Williams, Count Basie, Bob Crosby, Zuttie Singleton, along with patently non-Aryan names, such as Benny Goodman, and first and foremost, of course, the name of Louis Satchmo Armstrong. Nights at the radio vibrated with syncopated gusts from Stockholm, where in those days of Aryan strains they rendered particular service to the spread of the poison that to us, if I may say so, meant life.

To us life, to "them" death. That is why our music got on their nerves and why we persevered the harder in playing it. Paddy entered into personal relations with the king of the Czech provinces, a man whose fame was based on the fact that even with a bandaged thumb he had served "a machine gun-like piano at a monster concert in Prague's Lucerna Hall" (to quote the impressionistic jazz critics of those days), and whose name was Kamil Ludovít. The late Fritz Schwarz, Kamil's first alto-saxophonist and tune arranger, wrote a special arrangement of the "St. Louis Blues" for us which was to be the highlight of our first band concert at the Municipal Theatre in K.

But it seemed that if this concert would not take place, even though eventually it did.

It so happened that all the powers of the old set conspired against us: the headmaster of the grammar school and the chairman of the parent-teacher association, *Regierungskommissär* Kühl, and the district leader of the "Vlajka" (a fascist organization), and the correspondent of the *Aryan Struggle*, Mr. Bronzoryp. But the special scourge of our movement among that group was Headmaster Cermák, who later spelled his name Czermack, of the State grammar school, an enthusiastic admirer of the Apostolic person of Emanuel Moravec (pro-German Minister of Education in the "Protectorate" government) and a strict man of the new order. This energetic educator not only gave the Aryan raised arm salute when entering class, demanding the fast-as-lighting response of all present, if possible accentuated by heel-clicking, but he even made the Reverend Mr. Melon give the Aryan salute before scripture lessons. The Reverend, who was not as stupid as his name might lead one to believe, deftly expanded the Aryan gesture into a wide-armed Papal cross, each time putting on such an unworldly holy mien that not even the militant spirit of the incisive Czecho-German could raise a protest.

His neo-European efforts did not meet with any success in his institutions of learning. Legendary in this respect was the collection of scrap iron and non-ferous metal from which arms were to be forged against the Bolshevik hordes in the East, as the headmaster put it in his broadcast over the school address system. The collectors optimistically appointed in each class turned up a balance of absolute nil at the end of the first week, a circumstance which obliged the headmaster to make the rounds of the classes in person, with hand raised in the Aryan salute and accompanied by the school porter who was carrying a bucket for the non-ferrous metal. And at that a disgraceful incident occurred in the Upper Sixth. After an urgent appeal by the head educator, which was a mixture of bland fanaticism, Hieronymus-Bosch-like fantasy, veiled threats and crystal-clear rubbish, Franta Jungwirth, our band pianist, got up and with loud sobs wrenched a thickly encrusted nib from his penholder, dropping it into the porter's proffered bucket, presumably to contribute to the forging of arms against the Bolshevik cutthroats. Whereupon the headmaster was seized with a fit of rage which, luckily for Franta Jungwirth, led to nothing worse than a fortnight in the school lockup.

Headmaster Czermack took particular exception to the orchestra because he guessed vaguely (and accurately) that its members were at the bottom of the unpleasant surprises periodically put in his way. One morning, for instance, he had the fright of his life when awaking from a night's alternately greater-German dreams (in which his dearest wish came true: he was awarded the St. Wenceslaus Eagle) and collaborationist dreams (in which he used to swing), to see against the cold autumn sky outside his window a shaggy gorilla watching him with mean, little eyes and apparently about to break the window and fling itself upon his bed. This outrage had indeed been committed by the orchestra: the gorilla was part of the inventory of the natural science class and had been lowered by a clothes line from the window of the fourth form during the night.

Headmaster Czermack had a model son, an Aryan lad distinguished in German, Latin and tuft-hunting. He had an unpleasant experience of a different kind. A promising functionary of the *Kurzatorium* (fascist Youth Organisation), he was strolling in the park one day, enjoying an illustrated account in the magazine *Signal* entitled "Das Ende eines bolschewistischen Panzers." In the midst of his enjoyment, he was suddenly attacked by a band of masked men. A gag was thrust into his mouth and, in the bushes behind the statue of Karel Hynek Mácha, he was deprived of all bodily growth of hair in places visible and invisible. Afterwards he was bound to a tree and left to his fate; a large kitchen mirror had been fixed to the opposite tree. Two hours of looking at himself in this disfigured state filled the headmaster's son with such despair that as soon as he managed to cast off his bonds he did not hesitate to use the rope that had bound him for an attempt at suicide by hanging. But he selected an insufficiently strong branch which broke under his weight. This experience made him think better of it; he decided to live, instead, and crept off to the grammar school under the cover of twilight. Soon after, the theatre barber Kavánek could be seen hurrying into the schoolhouse with a bulky satchel under his arm. The next day Adolf Czermack appeared in a curly wig. Christina Hubálková, pretending to admire his curls, drove her inquisitive fingers into his wig and brought about his downfall. Adolf Czermack, leading light of the *Kuratorium*, headmaster's son and model scholar, was forced to feign a month's illness before the state of his head allowed him to surface again among his classmates.

So it was not surprising that shortly before the concert a circular went round the classes prohibiting all pupils from taking part in any theatrical, concert or other public performance after seven p.m., except on express permission from the headmaster. Headmaster Czermack was closing in on us for the kill.

But storm clouds were also gathering over the planned concert from other quarters. The journal *Reichszeit-Schrift für Volkstanzmusik* published an order by the *Reichsmusikführer* concerning popular and dance music. "In recent months," the document said (I am quoting from memory and cannot guarantee the exact wording, but I do guarantee the authenticity of the unmistakably Aryan spirit of the piece), "in places of entertainment in some areas of the Reich, the spread of music pervaded by the Jewish-Bolshevik-plutocratic infection of nigger jazz has been noticeable." The *Herr Reichsmusikführer* proceeded to list the names of several unfortunate Teutonic bandleaders (for whom this honor probably meant a free ticket to a concentration camp) whose anti-State cacophonic musical activity he contrasted unfavorably with the exemplary, race-conscious, melodic efforts of Peter Kreuder. He finally decreed with the utmost strictness:

1) in the repertoire of light orchestras and dance bands, pieces in fox-trot rhythm (so-called swing) are not to exceed 20%;

2) in the repertoire of this so-called jazz type, preference is to be given to compositions in a major key and to lyrics expressing joy in life (*Kraft durch Freude*), rather than Jewishly gloomy lyrics;

3) as to the tempo, too, preference is to be given to brisk compositions as opposed to slow ones (so-called blues); however, the pace must not exceed a certain degree of allegro commensurate with the Aryan sense for discipline and moderation. On no account will negroid excesses in tempo (so-called hot jazz) be permitted, or in solo performances (so-called breaks);

4) so-called jazz compositions may contain at the most 10% syncopation; the remainder must form a natural legato movement devoid of hysterical rhythmic reverses characteristic of the music of the barbarian races and conducive to dark instincts alien to the German people (so-called *riffs*);

5) strictly forbidden is the use of instruments alien to the German spirit (e.g., so-called cowbells, flex-á-tone, brushes, etc.) as well as all mutes which turn the noble sound of wind-brass instruments into a Jewish-Freemasonric yell (so-called wa-wa, in hat, etc.);

6) prohibited are so-called drum breaks longer than half a bar in four quarter beat (except in stylized military marches);

7) the double bass must be played solely with the bow in so-called jazz compositions; plucking of strings is prohibited, since it is damaging to the instrument and detrimental to Aryan musicality. If a so-called pizzicato effect is absolutely desirable for the character of the composition, let strict care be taken lest the string is allowed to patter on the sordine, which is henceforth forbidden;

8) provocative rising to one's feet during solo performances is forbidden;

9) musicians are likewise forbidden to make vocal improvisations (so-called scat); and

10) all light orchestras and dance bands are advised to restrict the use of saxophones of all keys and to substitute for them violon-celli, violas, or possibly a suitable folk instrument.

Signed: Baldur von Blödheim,
Reichsmusikführer und Oberscharführer SS.

In this situation we turned for help to our patron Kamil Ludovít, and in his Prague abode a plan was hatched.

Soon bills appeared on the boardings of K., announcing that the popular orchestra of the Masked Rhythm Bandits of Prague would present a Program of Joyful Melodies from All Over the World to the local population. In answer to his inquiry, which was not slow in coming, Headmaster Czermack was informed that the Masked Rhythm Bandits was a musical body dispensing light music under contract to bandmaster Kamil Ludovít of Prague-Zizkov, that he was therefore obliged to shut up.

But *Regierungskommissär* Kühl now took a hand. The *Kapellmeister der Maskierten Banditen des Rythmus* received a letter in German on notepaper bearing the letterhead of the *Regierungskommissär* in K., in which the signatory and representative of the *Reich* called on him to submit within five days a complete list of compositions to be presented at the forthcoming concert, including detailed information on tempi, keys, percentage of syncopation, distribution of instruments, as well as nationality and race of the composers performed. In case of failure to comply, the drawing of unspecified but easily imagined conclusions was threatened.

Another séance in Ludovít's flat yielded a program which—at least the way it looked on paper—would not offend even the most Aryan feelings of the Führer and Reichs Chancellor of the Greater German Reich himself.

The show was to open with a number entitled "Curtain-raiser Schottische," followed by creations by a certain Josef Patocka, Prantisek Cechácek and Günther Fürnwald, bearing such titles as "No Tears, my Darling" (*Keine Tränen, mein Liebling*), slow tune; "Our Bull Took Fright" (*Unser Stier wurde aufgescheucht*), quickstep; "In the Swimming Pool" (*In der Schwimmanstalt*), character piece; and "Evening Prayer" (*Gebet um Abend*), song.

On the program figured one or two slow-foxes and two fox-trots by well-known, tolerated music makers, as well as the "Song of Rzeshetova Lhota" (*Lied über die Rzeschetive Lhota*), which was listed as a novelty of the Prague season. Josef Patocka, Frantisek Cechácek and Günther Fürnwald were described as Aryans, in the first two instances Czech, in the third as greater-German Aryan (*grossdeutsch*). According to the program, the distribution of instruments was as follows: three trombones (in C), three horns (in B), six clarinets (in B), alternating in some of the mood compositions with five Sachs soundhorns. On what a Sachs soundhorn was supposed to be the program did not elaborate, judging accurately that the *Herr Regierungsrat* would not inquire for fear of appearing ignorant.

The submitted program was approved without any changes. Only in the "Song of Joy in Life" (*Das Kraft durch-Freude Lied*), Mr. Kühl noted in his own hand: *5% Synkopen auslassen* (omit 5% syncopes)!

However, Paddy Nakonec voiced apprehension as to the effectiveness of the disguises. He was afraid they would hardly protect us from the sleuthing capacity of Headmaster Czermack and insisted that this intruder No. 1 be rendered harmless by more drastic methods.

The headmaster's definite blockade was eventually brought about by Suzy Braun. Her feminine cunning unearthed one important detail, namely, that the day of the concert happened to be the day of an all-Protectorate Session of the *Kuratorium* of the Education of Youth in the Protectorate *Böhmen und Mähren*, at which the best organizational workers of all regions were to be decorated with the Shield of Honor of the St. Wenceslaus Eagle. With the aid of her girlish charms, to which a certain Herbert Starecek—an official of the *Kuratorium* Secretariat—was by no means blind, she got hold of some rubber-stamped *Kuratorium* notepaper and put it to good use in our cause.

And so it happened that the headmaster denied himself the pleasure of exposing the Masked Rhythm Bandits as pupils of his school. The letter that arrived from the Central Secretariat of the *Kuratorium* for the Education of Youth in the Protectorate *Böhmen und Mähren* informed him that in recognition of his services in the realm of fostering the Aryan Idea and the New Order within the Greater German Reich, it had been decided by the leadership of the *Kuratorium* for the Education of Youth in the Protectorate *Böhmen und Mähren* to bestow on him the Shield of Honor of the St. Wenceslaus Eagle, which would be presented at the ceremonial session of the *Kuratorium* for the Education of Youth in the Protectorate *Böhmen und Mähren* on Friday . . . at the Smetana Hall of the *Reprezentacní* Palace in the Royal Capital Prague.

That Friday was the day of the Concert of Joyous Melodies by the Masked Rhythm Bandits in K.

Headmaster Czermack obeyed the Aryan call of the all-Protectorate session of Aryans and departed on the afternoon train to Prague.

That same evening the Masked Rhythm Bandits opened their program in the Municipal Theatre in K. with the composition "Curtain-raiser Schottische" (*Wir fangen an mit dem Hopstanz*). Present connoisseurs had no trouble in recognizing in the schottische the "Casa Loma Stemp" which they rewarded with nerve-frazzling applause. The *Herr Regierungskommissär*, who was vainly trying to keep count of the percentage of syncopes in his box, began to scowl. He was beset by forebodings that the Aryan character of the joyous melodies might be violated. However, in the circle, filled to the last seat with members of a local *Wehrmacht* unit who had bought up every circle ticket in the advance booking by virtue of their superior race, pleasant excitement reigned.

Just then, as if elevated by the caressing rhythm of the syncopated tune, Suzy Braun rose to her feet in her black dress with the little white collar and a black lace mask over her eyes. Swinging her hips and moving her hands in gestures faithfully and naturally copied from every blues singer, seen and unseen, she began in her sweet and provocatively husky little voice:

> Black shadows are falling
> on the white man's city
> train whistles are calling
> life ain't got no pity.
> Oh—ooooh—oh—ooh,
> Give it everything you've got
> C'me on, boys, play it hot!

At the last word, included also in the *Reichsmusikführer's* list of offensive musical nomenclature, *Herr Regierungs-kommissär* turned pale and made up his mind to intervene. But a schizophrenic outburst of Paddy's horn which hit the eardrums of the breathless connoisseurs the following instant, cut the singer short and produced an enraptured sigh among the ranks of the *Infanterieregiment*. The singer continued in her melodic voice:

> Manhattan glows
> in a glare of light.
> Nobody knows
> that you don't treat me right

The *Regierungsrat* rose but was so startled the next instant that he sat down again. In a unisono blast the brass gave forth a fortissimo bellow as if straight at his person. Everything went black before his eyes, and in the blackness sprung up another terrible word from the *Reichsmusikführer's* decree: riff.

And Suzy Braun, transported by the squeal of the clarinets and roused by the sharp barking of Paddy's horn (so-called mute), raised her sweet, husky voice in the triumphant last chorus:

> I'll shake off my sorrow
> and forget my grief.
> There may be no tomorrow
> life is so brief.

> Oh—ooooh—oh—ooh,
> Give it everything you've got
> C'me on, boys play it hot!

There rose a storm of barbarous rapture, especially in the circle where the sexually starved members of the superior race, led astray by the spirit of the negroid music and the charm of the racially inferior singer, forgot their sense of Aryan moderation and called for an encore by stamping of feet and lusty Teutonic shouts.

The *Regierungskommissär*, in view of the situation, decided not to intervene.

Meanwhile, thrilled with sweet anticipation, Headmaster Czermack sat in the half-empty Smetana Hall and listened attentively to a speech on the necessity and glory of the fight against Asiatic Bolshevism and on the historic destination of the Czech nation in the Greater German Reich.

The speech was given by a gentleman with a head like a well-polished billiard ball.

After the speech the session passed on to the granting of distinctions to deserving Aryans.

Meanwhile, the concert of the Masked Rhythm Bandits progressed exactly according to the advance program. That the character piece "In the Swimming Pool," by Josef Patocka, was in fact "Riverside Blues" by the nigger King Oliver and that the quickstep "Our Bull Took Fright," by Günther Fürnwald, was practically indistinguishable from the Jewish-negroid Tiger Rag was known only to the initiated part of the audience who were none the worse for it. But the overwhelming majority of the uninitiated were none the worse for it either, particularly those in the circle, with the exception of Counsellor Prudivy who recognized on the feet of one of the Rhythm Bandits the new shoes of his son Horymír whom he was wont to urge into playing excerpts from Smetana's operas on the piano, and whom he had just imprudently sent to the local Sexton for a lesson in bagpipe playing.

And we went on playing. God Almighty, who has created jazz and all the beauties of this world, only you know how we played!

It seemed to me that the theatre in K. had disappeared, disappeared along with *Regierungskommissär Kühl* and everything, and that there was nothing but the music. It seemed to me that I had escaped the paper score and was playing something that had never been written down and never might be. The sobs of the saxophones were like the sobs of angels or of a man in anguish. The horns wailed like Olympian choirs singing a hymn to the persecuted. And when Paddy rose and started on the great improvised solo in "Matters of the Heart," which was none other than Dippermouth's "Heartbreak Blues," I all at once seemed to hear the imploring and morally anguished voice of Mr. Katz, the teacher, calling, crying out and pleading. . . .

Headmaster Czermack was meanwhile following with impatience and rising nervousness as a gaunt, middle-aged youth in *Kuratorium* uniform called out the names of those about to be decorated on the podium with the Honor Shield of the St. Wenceslaus Eagle.

He waited to hear his own name called.

He waited, but that evening he waited in vain.

At the moment when he ascertained this distressing fact, the concert of the Masked Rhythm Bandits was coming to its climax with the novelty of the season, the "Song of Rzeshetova Lhota."

> Rzeshetova Lhota
> is my home.
> I'm on my way
> to see my Aryan folks. . . .

sang Suzy Braun to the music of the Negroid Jew or

possibly Jewish Negroid, W. C. Handy, known beyond the jurisdictional territory of the Greater German *Reich* (but also inside that territory, and even in the town of K.) under the title of "St. Louis Blues."

The Aryans of the Infantry did not understand the lyrics but applauded wildly all the same. But the connoisseurs in the stalls understood all right. Into the clapping and cheers mingled knowing guffaws.

And at that instant, somewhere in the darkened hall the indignant Aryan Mr. Bronzoryp stood up, for he had perceived that the race of which he was proud (though he had never asked himself whether his race was also proud of him) was being made the butt of ridicule. He pushed his way through to the wings. And we breezed into the last number of the evening until the eardrums burst, until words lost their meaning and it ceased to matter whether they were poetic and witty or lame and banal; only the music had meaning, only the score, the heart, the immortal soul of that provocative, soaring storm of music.

That brings me to the end of the happy part of the story. What is left to tell is the unhappy part.

In the rapture that enveloped us after the concert, for a long time we did not recognize among the shining faces of the connoisseurs who poured into the dressing room the fury-contorted Aryan features of Mr. Bronzoryp.

The no less fury-contorted Headmaster Czermack, whom the puzzled committee of the *Kuratorium* for the Education of Youth in the Protectorate *Böhmen und Mähren* had finally managed to convince that there had been no mistake but an inexplicable hoax, was getting into the night train from Prague to K., blood and murder in his soul.

The consequences of both these events were not long in coming.

If it had only been for us, it would not have mattered. Benny Prema got a severe reprimand and our guitarist

Zábrana was suspended from the grammar school in K. but not barred from finishing his studies elsewhere. Myself and our pianist Jungwirth, the son of a railway official, were similarly afflicted, although in my case the verdict was later changed to debarment from all institutions of learning in the Protectorate *Böhmen und Mähren*, because in the meantime they had sent my father off to Belsen. This and similar measures resulted in the decimation and ruin of the historic swing band of the grammar school in K.

Paddy Nakonec, half-Aryan, half-Jew, paid for that little prank with his life. Mr. Bronzoryp, outraged in his Aryan-most feelings, denounced that half-Jew—who carried on like ten pedigree Jews, as the Aryan put it—as the instigator of the provocation.

Halbjude Nakonec was found guilty of violating the Aryan honor of the town of K., just as he had feared.

He was treated accordingly.

But that is not yet the end of the story. There was still Suzy, sweet Suzy Braun, the unofficial wife of the head trumpeter and shining light of our band, whom we all honored and secretly loved.

Then came the news in a note smuggled out of Pankrác Prison in Prague, that Paddy had been shot. And Suzy broke down.

But after a time she suddenly seemed to have got over it. She was seen in company one would have expected least, in the company of the Aryan Mr. Bronzoryp.

Word even had it that she was his mistress.

Naturally, the town condemned her.

On account of Paddy, the band condemned her too.

Nobody bothered to find out what was going on inside Suzy Braun, the sweet Suzy who was now absolutely alone in the world.

What an ass one sometimes is!

* * *

But that is not the whole story. Like Paddy, Mr. Bronzoryp did not live to see the end of the Protectorate *Böhmen und Mähren* either. One foggy morning he was found in his well-furnished, divorced man's quarters with a bullet in his skull. Beside the bed on which he had died, lay Suzy Braun, her hand holding a Browning, a weapon reliable Aryans were permitted to carry by special license of the *Sicherheitsdienst*. She had shot herself through the mouth.

So she did, poor, dear Suzy, and her lovely mouth will never sing again in her husky little voice. Swing, that devil, has taken my soul. Because her soul was taken away by the angels. And her sweet body was laid to rest in the eternal hospitable soil.

So she died. Died, like Paddy Nakonec and Suzy's parents, like my father and Horst Hüsse and Mr. Katz, the teacher, like Dr. Strass, Mifinka and Bod, the Killer. So they are all dead, and we are living on.

Poor sweet Suzy. When I sit behind the music stand under the neonlit bandstand shell in the Park and play my tenor-sax part in compositions that Suzy no longer knew and never will, I remember her, dear, lovely Suzy Braun, and all the others who are gone. Her sweetly husky voice seems to mingle with the song of the saxophone, and she sings again. And in tears, in sadness and joy over this life of ours, I sing with her:

> Rain or sunshine, come what may
> I'll keep my word until my dying day. . . .

Sleep well, sweet Suzy!

TERRY SOUTHERN

YOU'RE TOO HIP, BABY

THE SORBORNNE, WHERE MURRAY was enrolled for a doc-
torate, required little of his time; class attendance was
not compulsory and there were no scheduled examina-
tions. Having received faculty approval on the subject of
his thesis—"The Influence of Mallarmé on the English
Novel Since 1940"—Murray was now engaged in research
in the libraries, developing his thesis, writing it, and
preparing himself to defend it at some future date of his
own convenience. Naturally he could attend any lectures
at the University which he considered pertinent to his
work, and he did attend them from time to time—usually
those of illustrious guest speakers, like Cocteau, Camus,
and Sartre, or Marcel Raymond, author of *From Baudelaire
to Surrealism*. But for the most part, Murray devoted
himself to less formal pursuits; he knew every Negro jazz
musician in every club in Paris.

At night he made the rounds. If there was someone
really great in town he would sit at the same bar all
evening and listen to him; otherwise he made the rounds,
one club after another, not drinking much, just listening
to the music and talking to the musicians. Then, toward

morning, he would go with them to eat—down the street
to the Brasserie Civet or halfway across Paris to a place
in Montmartre that served spareribs and barbecued
chicken.

What was best though was to hang around the bar of
his own hotel, the Noir et Blanc, in the late afternoon
during a rehearsal or a closed session. At these times
everyone was very relaxed, telling funny stories, drinking Pernod, and even turning on a bit of hashish or
marijuana, passing it around quite openly, commenting
on its quality. Murray derived a security from these
scenes—the hushed camaraderie and the inside jokes.
Later, in the evening, when the place was jumping, Murray kept himself slightly apart from the rest of the crowd—
the tourists, the students, the professional beats, and the
French *de bonne famille*—who all came to listen to the
great new music. And always during the evening there
would be at least one incident, like the famous tenor-
man's casually bumming a cigarette from him, which
would prove Murray's intimacy with the group to those
who observed. Old acquaintances from Yale, who happened in, found Murray changed; they detected in his
attitude toward them, their plans, and their expressed or
implied values a sort of bemused tolerance—as though
he were in possession of a secret knowledge. And then
there would be the inevitable occasion when he was
required to introduce them to one of the musicians, and
that obvious moment when the musician would look to
Murray for his judgment of the stranger as in the question: "Well, man, who *is* that cat? Is he *with* it?" None of
this lessened Murray's attractiveness, nor his mystery,
no less to others, presumably, than to himself; but he
was never too hard on his old friends—because he was
swinging.

When the Negro pianist Buddy Talbott was hired, along
with a French drummer and bass, to play the Noir et

Blanc, he and his wife had been in Paris for only three days. It was their first time out of the States, and except for a few band jobs upstate, it was their first time out of New York City.

Toward the end of the evening, during a break, Murray went into the men's room. Buddy Talbott was there alone, in front of the mirror, straightening his tie. Their eyes fixed for an instant in the glass as Murray entered and walked over to the urinal; the disinfectant did not obscure a thin smell of hashish recently smoked in the room. Murray nodded his head in the direction of the bandstand beyond the wall. "Great sound you got there, man," he said, his voice flat, almost weary in its objectiveness. Buddy Talbott had a dark and delicate face which turned slowly, reluctantly it seemed, from the glass to Murray, smiling, and he spoke now in soft and precisely measured tones: "Glad you like it."

And, for the moment, no more was said, Murray knowing better than that.

Although Murray smoked hashish whenever it was offered, he seldom took the trouble to go over to the Arab quarter and buy any himself; but he always knew where to get the best. And the next evening, when Buddy Talbott came into the men's room, Murray was already there.

They exchanged nods, and Murray wordlessly handed him the smoking stick, scarcely looking at him as he did, walking past to the basin—as though to spare him witness to even the merest glimpse of hesitancy, of apprehension, calculation, and finally, of course, of perfect trust.

"I've got a box, man," Murray said after a minute, by which he meant record player, "and some new Monk—you know, if you ever want to fall by. . . ." He dried his hands carefully, looking at the towel. "Upstairs here," he said, "in number eight. My name is on the door—'Murray.' "

The other nodded, savoring the taste, holding it. "I'd like to very much," he said finally, and added with an unguarded smile, "*Murray*." At which Murray smiled too, and touching his arm lightly said: "Later, man." And left.

The hash seemed to have a nice effect on Buddy's playing. Certainly it did on Murray's listening—every note and nuance came straight to him, through the clatter of service at the bar and the muttered talk nearby, as though he were wearing earphones wired to the piano. He heard subtleties he had missed before, intricate structures of sound, each supporting the next, first from one side, then from another, and all being skillfully laced together with a dreamlike fabric of comment and insinuation; the runs did not sound either vertical or horizontal, but circular ascensions, darting arabesques and figurines; and it was clear to Murray that the player was constructing something there on the stand . . . something splendid and grandiose, but perfectly scaled to fit inside this room, to sit, in fact, alongside the piano itself. It seemed, in the beginning, that what was being erected before him was a castle, a marvelous castle of sound . . . but then, with one dramatic minor—just as the master builder might at last reveal the nature of his edifice in adding a single stone—Murray saw it was not a castle being built, but a cathedral. "*Yeah, man,*" he said, nodding and smiling. A cathedral—and, at the same time, around it the builder was weaving a strange and beautiful tapestry, covering the entire structure. At first the image was too bizarre, but then Murray smiled again as he saw that the tapestry was, of course, being woven *inside* the cathedral, over its interior surface, only it was so rich and strong that it sometimes seemed to come right through the walls. And then Murray suddenly realized—and this was the greatest of all, because he was absolutely certain that only he and Buddy knew— that the fantastic tapestry was being woven, quite deliberately, face against the wall. And he laughed aloud at this, shaking his head, "*Yeah, man,*" the last magnificent irony, and Buddy looked up at the sound, and laughed too.

After the set, Buddy came over and asked Murray if he wanted a drink. "Let's take a table," he said. "My old lady's coming to catch the last set."

"Solid," said Murray, so soft and without effort that none would have heard.

They sat down at a table in the corner.

"Man, that sure is fine gage," Buddy said.

Murray shrugged.

"Glad you like it," he said then, a tone with an edge of mock haughtiness, just faintly mimicking that used by Buddy when they had met; and they both laughed, and Buddy signaled the waiter.

"I was wondering," said Buddy after the waiter had left, "if you could put me onto some of that."

Murray yawned. "Why don't you meet me tomorrow," he said quietly. "I could take you over to the café and, you know, introduce you to the guy."

Buddy nodded, and smiled. "Solid," he said.

Buddy's wife, Jackie, was a tall Negro girl, sort of lank, with great eyes, legs, and a lovely smile.

"What we'd like to do," she said, "is to make it here—you know, like *live* here—at least for a couple of years anyway."

"It's the place for living all right," said Murray.

Murray was helpful in much more than introducing them to a good hash connection. Right away he found them a better and cheaper room, and nearer the Noir et Blanc. He showed Jackie how to shop in the quarter, where to get the best croissants, and what was the cheap wine to buy. He taught them some French and introduced them to the good inexpensive restaurants. He took them to see "L'Âge d'Or" at the Cinémathèque, to the catacombs, to the rib joint in Montmartre, to hear Marcel Raymond speak at the Sorbonne, to the Flea Market, to the Musée Guimet, Musée de l'Homme, to the evening exhibitions at the Louvre. . . . Sometimes Murray would have a girl with him, sometimes not; or on some Sundays when the weather was fine he would get someone with a car, or borrow it himself, and they would all drive out to the Bois de Boulogne and have a picnic, or to Versailles at night. Then again, on certain nights early, or when Buddy wasn't playing, they might have dinner in Buddy and Jackie's room, listening to records, smoking a piece of hash now and then, eating the red beans and rice, the fish, ribs, and chicken that Jackie cooked. The most comfortable place in the small room was the bed, and after a while the three of them were usually lying or half reclining across it, except when one of them would get up to put on more records, get a drink, or go to the bathroom, everything very relaxed, not much talk, occasionally someone saying something funny or relating a strange thing they had seen or heard, and frequently, too, just dozing off.

Once Murray bought a pheasant, had it cooked, and brought it up to their room, along with a couple of bottles of chilled Liebfraumilch, some wild rice, asparagus, and strawberries and cream.

Jackie was quite excited, opening the packages. "You're too much, baby," she said, giving Murray a kiss on the cheek.

"What's the grand occasion, man?" asked Buddy, beaming at him.

Murray shrugged. "I guess we'll have to dream one up," he said.

"I guess we will," said Buddy smiling, and he started slicing up a piece of hash.

Afterward they lay across the bed, smoking and listening to music.

"It's funny, isn't it," said Murray, while they were

listening to Billie, "that there aren't any great ofay singers."

The others seemed to consider it.

"Anita O'Day is all right," said Jackie.

"Yeah, but I mean you wouldn't compare her with Billie, would you," said Murray.

"Some of the French chicks swing," said Buddy absently, ". . . Piaf . . . and what's that other chick's name. . . ."

"Yeah, but I mean like that's something else, isn't it," said Murray.

Buddy shrugged, passing the cigarette, "Yeah, I guess so," he said, sounding half asleep; but his eyes were open, and for several minutes he lay simply staring at Murray with an expression of mild curiosity on his face.

"Murray," he asked finally, "did you want to learn piano . . . or what?" Then he laughed, as though he might not have meant it to sound exactly like that, and he got up to get some wine.

Jackie laughed too. "Maybe he just *likes* you baby—ever think of that?"

"Yeah, that's right," said Buddy, making a joke of it now, pouring the wine, "that ought to be considered." He was still smiling, almost sheepishly. "Well, here's to friendship then," he said, taking a sip.

"You're making me cry," said Murray in his flat, weary voice, and they all laughed.

Then it was time for Buddy to go to the club.

"I'll make it over with you, man," said Murray, slowly raising himself up on the bed.

"Stick around," said Buddy, putting on his tie. "Nothing's happening there yet—you can come over later with Jackie."

"That seems like a good idea," said Jackie.

Murray sat there, staring at nothing.

"It's cool, man," said Buddy smiling and giving Murray an elaborate wink of conspiracy, "it's cool. I mean, you know—make it."

"Solid," said Murray, after a minute, and he lay back across the bed again.

"See you cats," said Buddy, opening the door to leave.

"Later," said Murray.

"Later, baby," said Jackie, getting up and going to the door and locking it. Then she went over to the basin and began brushing her teeth.

"That was a funny thing for him to say, wasn't it," said Murray after a minute, "I mean about did I want 'to learn piano, or *what*?' "

Jackie moved the brush in a slow, languorous motion, looking at Murray in the mirror. "Well, it's very simple really. . . . I mean, he *digs* you, you know—and I guess he would like to do something for you, that sort of thing." She rinsed her mouth and held the brush under the water. "I thought he made that part of it pretty clear," she said, then looking directly at him. She crossed over to the dressing table and stood in front of it, straightening her dress; it was a cream-colored jersey which clung without tightness to all of her. She stood in front of the glass, her feet slightly apart, and touched at her hair. He watched the back of her brown legs, the softly rounded calves, tracing them up past the cream-colored hem behind her knees into their full lean contours above—lines which were not merely suggested, but, because of the clinging jersey and the way she stood, convincingly apparent.

"That's a groovy thread," said Murray, sitting up and taking the glass of wine Buddy had left on the night table.

"Oh?" She looked down at the dress reflexively and again at the mirror. "Madame what's-her-name made it—you know, that seamstress you put me onto." She sat down on a chair by the mirror and carefully wiped the lipstick from her mouth with a Kleenex.

"Yeah, it's crazy," said Murray.

"Glad you like it, Murray." The phrase had become an occasional joke between the three of them.

"I was by the Soleil du Maroc this afternoon," he began then, taking a small packet out of his shirt pocket, unwrapping it as he leaned toward the light at the night table, "I just thought I would twist up a few to take to the club." He looked up at her and paused. "I mean, you know, if there's time."

Jackie's head was cocked to one side as she dabbed perfume behind an ear and watched Murray in the mirror. "Oh there's *time*, baby," she said with a smile, ". . . make no mistake about that."

When Murray had twisted one, he lit it and, after a couple of drags, sat it smoking on the tray, continuing to roll them carefully, placing them in a neat row on the night table.

Jackie finished at the mirror, put another record on, and came over to the bed. As she sat down, Murray passed the cigarette to her, and she lay back with it, head slightly raised on a pillow against the wall, listening to "Blue Monk."

When Murray had rolled several, he put the packet of hash away and stashed the cigarettes in with his Gauloises. Then he leaned back, resting his head on Jackie's lap, or rather on what would have been her lap had she been sitting instead of half lying across the bed; she passed the cigarette to Murray.

"Has a good taste, hasn't it," said Murray.

Jackie smiled. "Yes, indeed," she said.

"Hadj says it's from the Middle Congo," said Murray with a laugh, " *'C'est du vrai congolais!'* " he went on, giving it the Arab's voice.

"That's just how it tastes," said Jackie.

With his face turned toward her, Murray's cheek pressed firmly against the softness of her stomach which just perceptibly rose and fell with breathing, and through the

fine jersey he could feel the taut sheen of her pants
beneath it, and the warmth. There was nothing lank
about her now.

"Yeah," said Murray after a minute, "that's right, isn't
it, that's just how it tastes."

They finished the cigarette, and for a while, even after
the record had ended, they lay there in silence, Jackie
idly curling a finger in Murray's hair. For a long time
Murray didn't move.

"Well," he finally said instead, "I guess we'd better
make it—over to the club, I mean."

Jackie looked at him for a minute, then gave a gentle
tug on the lock of his hair, shrugged, and laughed softly.

"Anything you say, Murray."

That Sunday was a fine day, and Murray borrowed a
car for them to go out to the Bois. Jackie had fried some
chicken the night before and prepared a basket of food,
but now she complained of a cold and decided not to go.
She insisted though that Murray and Buddy go.

"It's a shame to waste the car and this great weather.
You ought to make it."

So they went without her.

They drove up the Champs through a magnificent afternoon, the boulevard in full verdure and the great
cafés sprawled in the sun like patches of huge flowers.
Just past the Étoile they noticed a charcuterie which was
open and they stopped and bought some more to put in
the basket—céleri rémoulade, artichoke hearts, and cheese
covered with grape seeds. At a café next door Murray
was able to get a bottle of cognac.

At the Bois they drove around for a while, then parked
the car and walked into the depth of the woods. They
thought they might discover a new place—and they did,
finally, a grove of poplars which led to the edge of a
small pond; and there, where it met the pond and the
wooded thicket to each side, it formed a picture-book

alcove, all fern, pine and poplar. There was no one else to
be seen on the pond, and they had passed no one in the
grove. It was a pleasing discovery.

Together they carefully spread the checkered tablecloth the way Jackie always did, and then laid out the
food. Buddy had brought along a portable phonograph,
which he opened up now while Murray uncorked the
wine.

"What'll it be," Buddy asked with a laugh, after looking at the records for several minutes, "Bird or Bartók?"

"Bartók, man," said Murray, and added dreamily, "where
do you go after Bird?"

"Crazy," said Buddy, and he put on "The Miraculous
Mandarin."

Murray lay propped on his elbow, and Buddy sat opposite, crosslegged, as they ate and drank in silence, hungry but with deliberation, sampling each dish, occasionally
grunting an appreciative comment.

"Dig that bridge, man," said Buddy once, turning to
the phonograph and moving the needle back a couple of
grooves, "like that's what you might call an 'augmented
oh-so-slightly.'" He laughed. "Cat's too much," he said,
as he leaned forward to touch a piece of chicken to the
mayonnaise.

Murray nodded. "Swings," he said.

They lay on the grass, smoking and drinking the cognac, closing their eyes or shading them against the
slanting sun. They were closer together now, since once
Buddy had gotten up to stretch and then, in giving Murray a cigarette, had sat down beside him to get a light.

After a while Buddy seemed to half doze off, and then
he sleepily turned over on his stomach. As he did, his
knee touched Murray's leg, and Murray moved lightly as
if to break the contact—but then, as if wondering why he
had reacted like that, let his leg ease back to where it

had been, and almost at once dropped into a light sleep,
his glass of cognac still in his hand, resting on his chest.

When Murray awoke, perhaps only seconds later, the
pressure of Buddy's leg on his own was quite strong.
Without looking at Buddy, he slowly sat up, raising his
legs as he did, sitting now with knees under his folded
arms. He looked at the glass of cognac still in his hand,
and finished it off.

"That sort of thing," said Buddy quietly, "doesn't interest you either." It was not put as a question, but as a
statement which required confirmation.

Murray turned, an expression of bland annoyance on
his face, while Buddy lay there looking at him pretty
much the same as always.

"No, man," said Murray, then almost apologetically: "I
mean, like I don't put it down—but it's just not a scene I
make. You know?"

Buddy dropped his eyes to a blade of grass he was
toying with; he smiled. "Well, anyway," he said with a
little laugh, "no offense."

Murray laughed, too. "None taken, man," he said
seriously.

Murray had risen at his more or less usual hour, and
the clock at Cluny was just striking eleven when he
emerged from the hotel stairway, into the street and the
summer morning. He blinked his eyes at the momentary
brightness and paused to lean against the side of the
building, gazing out into the pleasantly active boulevard.

When the clock finished striking he pushed himself
out from the wall and started towards the Royale, where
he often met Buddy and Jackie for breakfast. About
halfway along Boulevard Saint-Germain he turned in at
a small café to get some cigarettes. Three or four people
were coming out the door as Murray reached it, and he
had to wait momentarily to let them pass. As he did he
was surprised to notice, at a table near the side, Buddy

and Jackie, eating breakfast. Buddy was wearing dark
glasses, and Murray instinctively reached for his own as
he came through the door, but discovered he had left
them in his room. He raised his hand in a laconic greet-
ing to them and paused at the bar to get the cigarettes.
Buddy nodded, but Jackie had already gotten up from
the table and was walking toward the girls' room. Murray sauntered over, smiling, and sat down.

"What are you doing here, man?" he asked. "I didn't
know you ever came here."

Buddy shrugged. "Thought we'd give it a try," he said
seriously examining a dab of butter on the end of his
knife. Then he looked up at Murray and added with a
laugh, "You know—new places, new faces."

Murray laughed, too, and picked at a piece of an unfin-
ished croissant. "That's pretty good," he said. "What's
the other one? You know, the one about—oh yeah, 'Old
friends are the best friends.' Ever hear that one?"

"I have heard that one," said Buddy nodding, "yes, I
have heard that one." His smile was no longer a real one.
"Listen, Murray," he said, wiping his hands and sitting
back, putting his head to one side, "let me ask you
something. Just what is it you want?"

Murray frowned down at where his own hands slowly
dissected the piece of croissant as though he were shred-
ding a paper napkin.

"What are you talking about, man?"

"You *don't* want to play music," Buddy began as though
he were taking an inventory, "and you *don't* want . . . I
mean just what have we *got* that interests you?"

Murray looked at him briefly, and then looked away in
exasperation. He noticed that Jackie was talking to the
patron who was standing near the door. "Well, what do
you think, man?" he demanded, turning back to Buddy.
"I dig the *scene*, that's all. I dig the *scene* and the *sounds*."

Buddy stood up, putting some money on the table. He
looked down at Murray, who sat there glowering, and

shook his head. "You're too hip, baby. That's right. You're a *hippy*." He laughed. "In fact, you're what we might call a kind of professional *nigger lover*." He touched Murray's shoulder as he moved to leave. "And I'm not putting you down for it, understand, but, uh, like the man said, 'It's just not a scene I make.'" His dark face set for an instant beneath the smoky glass and he spoke, urgent and imploring, in a flash of white teeth, almost a hiss, "I mean *not when I can help it*, Murray, *not when I can help it*." And he left. And the waiter arrived, picking up the money.

"*Monsieur désire?*"

Still scowling, staring straight ahead, Murray half raised his hand as to dismiss the waiter, but then let it drop to the table. "*Café*," he muttered.

"*Noir, monsieur?*" asked the waiter in a suggestively rising inflection.

Murray looked up abruptly at the man, but the waiter was oblivious, counting the money in his hand.

Murray sighed. "*Oui*," he said softly, "*noir*."

RICHARD YATES

A REALLY GOOD JAZZ PIANO

BECAUSE OF THE MIDNIGHT noise on both ends of the line there was some confusion at Harry's New York Bar when the call came through. All the bartender could tell at first was that it was a long-distance call from Cannes, evidently from some kind of nightclub, and the operator's frantic voice made it sound like an emergency. Then at last, by plugging his free ear and shouting questions into the phone, he learned that it was only Ken Platt, calling up to have an aimless chat with his friend Carson Wyler, and this made him shake his head in exasperation as he set the phone on the bar beside Carson's glass of Pernod.

"Here," he said. "It's for you, for God's sake. It's your buddy." Like a number of other Paris bartenders he knew them both pretty well: Carson was the handsome one, the one with the slim, witty face and the English-sounding accent; Ken was the fat one who laughed all the time and tagged along. They were both three years out of Yale and trying to get all the fun they could out of living in Europe.

"Carson?" said Ken's eager voice, vibrating painfully

in the receiver. "This is Ken—I knew I'd find you there. Listen, when you coming down, anyway?"

Carson puckered his well-shaped brow at the phone. "You know when I'm coming down," he said. "I wired you, I'm coming down Saturday. What's the matter with you?"

"Hell, nothing's the matter with me—maybe a little drunk, is all. No, but listen, what I really called up about, there's a man here named Sid plays a really good jazz piano, and I want you to hear him. He's a friend of mine. Listen, wait a minute, I'll get the phone over close so you can hear. Listen to this, now. Wait a minute."

There were some blurred scraping sounds and the sound of Ken laughing and somebody else laughing, and then the piano came through. It sounded tinny in the telephone, but Carson could tell it was good. It was "Sweet Lorraine," done in a rich traditional style with nothing commercial about it, and this surprised him, for Ken was ordinarily a poor judge of music. After a minute he handed the phone to a stranger he had been drinking with, a farm machinery salesman from Philadelphia. "Listen to this," he said. "This is first-rate."

The farm machinery salesman held his ear to the phone with a puzzled look. "What is it?"

" 'Sweet Lorraine.' "

"No, but I mean what's the deal? Where's it coming from?"

"Cannes. Somebody Ken turned up down there. You've met Ken, haven't you?"

"No, I haven't," the salesman said, frowning into the phone. "Here, it's stopped now and somebody's talking. You better take it."

"Hello? Hello?" Ken's voice was saying. "Carson?"

"Yes, Ken. I'm right here."

"Where'd you go? Who was that other guy?"

"That was a gentleman from Philadelphia named—" he looked up questioningly.

"Baldinger," said the salesman, straightening his coat. "Named Mr. Baldinger. He's here at the bar with me."

"Oh. Well listen, how'd you like Sid's playing?"

"Fine, Ken. Tell him I said it was first-rate."

"You want to talk to him? He's right here, wait a minute."

There were some more obscure sounds and then a deep middle-aged voice said, "Hello there."

"How do you do, Sid. My name's Carson Wyler, and I enjoyed your playing very much."

"Well," the voice said. "Thank you, thank you a lot. I appreciate it." It could have been either a colored or a white man's voice, but Carson assumed he was colored, mostly from the slight edge of self-consciousness or pride in the way Ken had said, "He's a friend of mine."

"I'm coming down to Cannes this weekend, Sid," Carson said, "and I'll be looking forward to—"

But Sid had evidently given back the phone, for Ken's voice cut in. "Carson?"

"What?"

"Listen, what time you coming Saturday? I mean what train and everything?" They had originally planned to go to Cannes together, but Carson had become involved with a girl in Paris, and Ken had gone on alone, with the understanding that Carson would join him in a week. Now it had been nearly a month.

"I don't know the exact train," Carson said, with some impatience. "It doesn't matter, does it? I'll see you at the hotel sometime Saturday."

"Okay. Oh and wait, listen, the other reason I called, I want to sponsor Sid here for the IBF, okay?"

"Right. Good idea. Put him back on." And while he was waiting he got out his fountain pen and asked the bartender for the IBF membership book.

"Hello again," Sid's voice said. "What's this I'm supposed to be joining here?"

"The IBF," Carson said. "That stands for International

Bar Flies, something they started here at Harry's back in— I don't know. Long time ago. Kind of a club."

"Very good," Sid said, chuckling.

"Now, what it amounts to is this," Carson began, and even the bartender, for whom the IBF was a bore and a nuisance, had to smile with pleasure at the serious, painstaking way he told about it—how each member received a lapel button bearing the insignia of a fly, together with a printed booklet that contained the club rules and a listing of all other IBF bars in the world; how the cardinal rule was that when two members met they were expected to greet one another by brushing the fingers of their right hands on each other's shoulders and saying, *"Bzz-z-z, bzz-z-z!"*

This was one of Carson's special talents, the ability to find and convey an unashamed enjoyment in trivial things. Many people could not have described the IBF to a jazz musician without breaking off in an apologetic laugh to explain that it was, of course, a sort of sad little game for lonely tourists, a square's thing really, and that its very lack of sophistication was what made it fun; Carson told it straight. In much the same way he had once made it fashionable among some of the more literary undergraduates at Yale to spend Sunday mornings respectfully absorbed in the funny papers of the *New York Mirror*; more recently the same trait had rapidly endeared him to many chance acquaintances, notably to his current girl, the young Swedish art student for whom he had stayed in Paris. "You have beautiful taste in everything," she had told him on their first memorable night together. "You have a truly educated, truly original mind."

"Got that?" he said into the phone, and paused to sip his Pernod. "Right. Now if you'll give me your full name and address, Sid, I'll get everything organized on this end." Sid spelled it out and Carson lettered it carefully into the membership book, with his own name and Ken's as co-sponsors, while Mr. Baldinger watched. When they were finished Ken's voice came back to say a reluctant goodbye, and they hung up.

"That must've been a pretty expensive telephone call," Mr. Baldinger said, impressed.

"You're right," Carson said. "I guess it was."

"What's the deal on this membership book, anyway? All this barfly business?"

"Oh, aren't you a member, Mr. Baldinger? I thought you were a member. Here, I'll sponsor you, if you like."

Mr. Baldinger got what he later described as an enormous kick out of it: far into the early morning he was still sidling up to everyone at the bar, one after another, and buzzing them.

Carson didn't get to Cannes on Saturday, for it took him longer than he'd planned to çonclude his affair with the Swedish girl. He had expected a tearful scene, or at least a brave exchange of tender promises and smiles, but instead she was surprisingly casual about his leaving— even abstracted, as if already concentrating on her next truly educated, truly original mind—and this forced him into several uneasy delays that accomplished nothing except to fill her with impatience and him with a sense of being dispossessed. He didn't get to Cannes until the following Tuesday afternoon, after further telephone talks with Ken, and then, when he eased himself onto the station platform, stiff and sour with hangover, he was damned if he knew why he'd come at all. The sun assaulted him, burning deep into his gritty scalp and raising a quick sweat inside his rumpled suit; it struck blinding glints off the chromework of parked cars and motor scooters and made sickly blue vapors of exhaust rise up against pink buildings; it played garishly among the swarm of tourists who jostled him, showing him all their pores, all the tension of their store-new sports clothes, their clutched suitcases and slung cameras, all the anxiety of their smiling, shouting mouths. Cannes would be like any

other resort town in the world, all hurry and disappointment, and why hadn't he stayed where he belonged, in a
high cool room with a long-legged girl? Why the hell had
he let himself be coaxed and wheedled into coming here?

But then he saw Ken's happy face bobbing in the
crowd—"Carson!"—and there he came, running in his
overgrown fat boy's thigh-chafing way, clumsy with welcome. "Taxi's over here, take your bag—boy, do you look
beat! Get you a shower and a drink first, okay? How the
hell are you?"

And riding light on the taxi cushions as they swung
onto the Croisette, with its spectacular blaze of blue and
gold and its blood-quickening rush of sea air, Carson
began to relax. Look at the girls! There were acres of
them; and besides, it was good to be with old Ken again.
It was easy to see, now, that the thing in Paris could only
have gotten worse if he'd stayed. He had left just in time.

Ken couldn't stop talking. Pacing in and out of the
bathroom while Carson took his shower, jingling a pock-
etful of coins, he talked in the laughing, full-throated joy
of a man who has gone for weeks without hearing his
own voice. The truth was that Ken never really had a
good time away from Carson. They were each other's
best friends, but it had never been an equal friendship,
and they both knew it. At Yale Ken would probably have
been left out of everything if it hadn't been for his status
as Carson's dull but inseparable companion, and this was
a pattern that nothing in Europe had changed. What *was*
it about Ken that put people off? Carson had pondered
this question for years. Was it just that he was fat and
physically awkward, or that he could be strident and
silly in his eagerness to be liked? But weren't these
essentially likable qualities? No, Carson guessed the closest he could come to a real explanation was the fact that
when Ken smiled his upper lip slid back to reveal a
small moist inner lip that trembled against his gum.
Many people with this kind of mouth may find it no

great handicap—Carson was willing to admit that—but it did seem to be the thing everyone remembered most vividly about Ken Platt, whatever more substantial-sounding reasons one might give for avoiding him; in any case it was what Carson himself was always most aware of, in moments of irritation. Right now, for example, in the simple business of trying to dry himself and comb his hair and put on fresh clothes, this wide, moving, double-lipped smile kept getting in his way. It was everywhere, blocking his reach for the towel rack, hovering too close over his jumbled suitcase, swimming in the mirror to eclipse the tying of his tie, until Carson had to clamp his jaws tight to keep from yelling, "All *right*, Ken—shut *up* now!"

But a few minutes later they were able to compose themselves in the shaded silence of the hotel bar. The bartender was peeling a lemon, neatly pinching and pulling back a strip of its bright flesh between thumb and knife blade, and the fine citric smell of it, combining with the scent of gin in the faint smoke of crushed ice, gave flavor to a full restoration of their ease. A couple of cold martinis drowned the last of Carson's pique, and by the time they were out of the place and swinging down the sidewalk on their way to dinner he felt strong again with a sense of the old camaraderie, the familiar, buoyant wealth of Ken's admiration. It was a feeling touched with sadness, too, for Ken would soon have to go back to the States. His father in Denver, the author of sarcastic weekly letters on business stationery, was holding open a junior partnership for him, and Ken, having long since completed the Sorbonne courses that were his ostensible reason for coming to France, had no further excuse for staying. Carson, luckier in this as in everything else, had no need of an excuse: he had an adequate private income and no family ties; he could afford to browse around Europe for years, if he felt like it, looking for things that pleased him.

"You're still white as a sheet," he told Ken across their restaurant table. "Haven't you been going to the beach?"

"Sure." Ken looked quickly at his plate. "I've been to the beach a few times. The weather hasn't been too good for it lately, is all."

But Carson guessed the real reason, that Ken was embarrassed to display his body, so he changed the subject. "Oh, by the way," he said. "I brought along the IBF stuff, for that piano player friend of yours."

"Oh, swell." Ken looked up in genuine relief. "I'll take you over there soon as we're finished eating, okay?" And as if to hurry this prospect along he forked a dripping load of salad into his mouth and tore off too big a bite of bread to chew with it, using the remaining stump of bread to mop at the oil and vinegar in his plate. "You'll like him, Carson," he said soberly around his chewing. "He's a great guy. I really admire him a lot." He swallowed with effort and hurried on: "I mean hell, with talent like that he could go back to the States tomorrow and make a fortune, but he likes it here. One thing, of course, he's got a girl here, this really lovely French girl, and I guess he couldn't very well take her back with him—no, but really, it's more than that. People accept him here. As an artist, I mean, as well as a man. Nobody condescends to him, nobody tries to interfere with his music, and that's all he wants out of life. Oh, I mean he doesn't tell you all this—probably be a bore if he did—it's just a thing you sense about him. Comes out in everything he says, his whole mental attitude." He popped the soaked bread into his mouth and chewed it with authority. "I mean the guy's got *authentic* integrity," he said. "Wonderful thing."

"Did sound like a damn good piano," Carson said, reaching for the wine bottle, "what little I heard of it."

"Wait'll you really hear it, though. Wait'll he really gets going."

They both enjoyed the fact that this was Ken's discovery. Always before it had been Carson who led the way, who found the girls and learned the idioms and knew how best to spend each hour; it was Carson who had tracked down all the really colorful places in Paris where you never saw Americans, and who then, just when Ken was learning to find places of his own, had paradoxically made Harry's Bar become the most colorful place of all. Through all this, Ken had been glad enough to follow, shaking his grateful head in wonderment; but it was no small thing to have turned up an incorruptible jazz talent in the back streets of a foreign city, all alone. It proved that Ken's dependence could be less than total after all, and this reflected credit on them both.

The place where Sid played was more of an expensive bar than a nightclub, a small carpeted basement several streets back from the sea. It was still early, and they found him having a drink alone at the bar.

"Well," he said when he saw Ken. "Hello there." He was stocky and well-tailored, a very dark Negro with a pleasant smile full of strong white teeth.

"Sid, I'd like you to meet Carson Wyler. You talked to him on the phone that time, remember?"

"Oh yes," Sid said, shaking hands. "Oh yes. Very pleased to meet you, Carson. What're you gentlemen drinking?"

They made a little ceremony of buttoning the IBF insignia into the lapel of Sid's tan garbardine, of buzzing his shoulder and offering the shoulders of their own identical seersucker jackets to be buzzed in turn. "Well, this is fine," Sid said, chuckling and leafing through the booklet. "Very good." Then he put the booklet in his pocket, finished his drink and slid off the barstool. "And now if you'll excuse me, I got to go to work."

"Not much of an audience yet," Ken said.

Sid shrugged. "Place like this, I'd just as soon have it that way. You get a big crowd, you always get some square asking for 'Deep in the Heart of Texas,' or some damn thing."

Ken laughed and winked at Carson, and they both
turned to watch Sid take his place at the piano, which
stood on a low spotlighted dais across the room. He fingered the keys idly for a while to make stray phrases and
chords, a craftsman fondling his tools, and then he settled down. The compelling beat emerged, and out of the
climb and waver of the melody, an arrangement of "Baby,
Won't You Please Come Home."

They stayed for hours, listening to Sid play and buying
him drinks whenever he took a break, to the obvious
envy of other customers. Sid's girl came in, tall and
brown-haired, with a bright, startled-looking face that
was almost beautiful, and Ken introduced her with a
small uncontrollable flourish: "This is Jaqueline." She
whispered something about not speaking English very
well, and when it was time for Sid's next break—the
place was filling up now and there was considerable
applause when he finished—the four of them took a table
together.

Ken let Carson do most of the talking now; he was
more than content just to sit there, smiling around this
tableful of friends with all the serenity of a well-fed
young priest. It was the happiest evening of his life in
Europe, to a degree that even Carson would never have
guessed. In the space of a few hours it filled all the
emptiness of his past month, the time that had begun
with Carson's saying "Go, then. Can't you go to Cannes
by yourself?" It atoned for all the hot miles walked up
and down the Croisette on blistered feet to peek like a
fool at girls who lay incredibly near naked in the sand;
for the cramped, boring bus rides to Nice and Monte
Carlo and St. Paul-de-Vence; for the day he had paid a
sinister druggist three times too much for a pair of sunglasses only to find, on catching sight of his own image
in the gleam of a passing shop window, that they made
him look like a great blind fish; for the terrible daily,
nightly sense of being young and rich and free on the

Riviera—the Riviera!—and of having nothing to do. Once in the first week he had gone with a prostitute whose canny smile, whose shrill insistence on a high price and whose facial flicker of distaste at the sight of his body had frightened him into an agony of impotence; most other nights he had gotten drunk or sick from bar to bar, afraid of prostitutes and of rebuffs from other girls, afraid even of striking up conversations with men lest they mistake him for a fairy. He had spent a whole afternoon in the French equivalent of a dime store, feigning a shopper's interest in padlocks and shaving cream and cheap tin toys, moving through the bright stale air of the place with a throatful of longing for home. Five nights in a row he had hidden himself in the protective darkness of American movies, just as he'd done years ago in Denver to get away from boys who called him Lard-Ass Platt, and after the last of these entertainments, back in the hotel with the taste of chocolate creams still cloying his mouth, he had cried himself to sleep. But all this was dissolving now under the fine reckless grace of Sid's piano, under the spell of Carson's intelligent smile and the way Carson raised his hands to clap each time the music stopped.

Sometime after midnight, when everyone but Sid had drunk too much, Carson asked him how long he had been away from the States. "Since the war," he said. "I came over in the Army and I never did go back."

Ken, coated with a film of sweat and happiness, thrust his glass high in the air for a toast. "And by God, here's hoping you never have to, Sid."

"Why is that, 'have to'?" Jaqueline said. Her face looked harsh and sober in the dim light. "Why do you say that?"

Ken blinked at her. "Well, I just mean—you know— that he never has to sell out, or anything. He never would, of course."

"What does this mean, 'sell out'?" There was an uneasy silence until Sid laughed in his deep, rumbling way.

"Take it easy, honey," he said, and turned to Ken. "We don't look at it that way, you see. Matter of fact, I'm working on angles all the time to get back to the States, make some money there. We both feel that way about it."

"Well, but you're doing all right here, aren't you?" Ken said, almost pleading with him. "You're making enough money and everything, aren't you?"

Sid smiled patiently. "I don't mean a job like this, though, you see. I mean real money."

"You know who is Murray Diamond?" Jacqueline inquired, holding her eyebrows high. "The owner of nightclubs in Las Vegas?"

But Sid was shaking his head and laughing. "Honey, wait a minute—I keep telling you, that's nothing to count on. Murray Diamond happened to be in here the other night, you see," he explained. "Didn't have much time, but he said he'd try to drop around again some night this week. Be a big break for me. 'Course, like I say, that's nothing to count on."

"Well but *Jesus*, Sid—" Ken shook his head in bafflement; then, letting his face tighten into a look of outrage, he thumped the table with a bouncing fist. "Why prostitute yourself?" he demanded. "I mean damn it, you *know* they'll make you prostitute yourself in the States!"

Sid was still smiling, but his eyes had narrowed slightly. "I guess it's all in the way you look at it," he said.

And the worst part of it, for Ken, was that Carson came so quickly to his rescue. "Oh, I'm sure Ken doesn't mean that the way it *sounds*," he said, and while Ken was babbling quick apologies of his own ("No, of course not, all I meant was—*you* know . . .") he went on to say other things, light nimble things that only Carson could say, until the awkwardness was gone. When the time came to say goodnight there were handshakes and smiles and promises to see each other soon.

But the minute they were out on the street, Carson

turned on Ken. "Why did you have to get so damned sophomoric about that? Couldn't you see how embarrassing it was?"

"I know," Ken said, hurrying to keep pace with Carson's long legs, "I know. But hell, I *was* disappointed in him, Carson. The point is I never heard him *talk* like that before." What he omitted here, of course, was that he had never really heard him talk at all, except in the one shy conversation that had led to the calling-up of Harry's Bar that other night, after which Ken had fled back to the hotel in fear of overstaying his welcome.

"Well, but even so," Carson said. "Don't you think it's the man's own business what he wants to do with his life?"

"Okay," Ken said, "*okay*. I *told* him I was sorry, didn't I?" He felt so humble now that it took him some minutes to realize that, in a sense, he hadn't come off too badly. After all, Carson's only triumph tonight had been that of the diplomat, the soother of feelings; it was he, Ken, who had done the more dramatic thing. Sophomoric or not, impulsive or not, wasn't there a certain dignity in having spoken his mind that way? Now, licking his lips and glancing at Carson's profile as they walked, he squared his shoulders and tried to make his walk less of a waddle and more of a headlong, manly stride. "It's just that I can't help how I feel, that's all," he said with conviction. "When I'm disappointed in a person I show it, that's all."

"All right. Let's forget it."

And Ken was almost sure, though he hardly dared believe it, that he could detect a grudging respect in Carson's voice.

Everything went wrong the next day. The fading light of afternoon found the two of them slumped and staring in a bleak workingman's café near the railroad station, barely speaking to each other. It was a day that had started out unusually well, too—that was the trouble.

They had slept till noon and gone to the beach after lunch, for Ken didn't mind the beach when he wasn't there alone, and before long they had picked up two American girls in the easy, graceful way that Carson always managed such things. One minute the girls were sullen strangers, wiping scented oil on their bodies and looking as if any intrusion would mean a call for the police, the next minute they were weak with laughter at the things Carson was saying, moving aside their bottles and their zippered blue TWA satchels to make room for unexpected guests. There was a tall one for Carson with long firm thighs, intelligent eyes and a way of tossing back her hair that gave her a look of real beauty, and a small one for Ken—a cute, freckled good-sport of a girl whose every cheerful glance and gesture showed she was used to taking second best. Ken, bellying deep into the sand with his chin on two stacked fists, smiling up very close to her warm legs, felt almost none of the conversational tension that normally hampered him at times like this. Even when Carson and the tall girl got up to run splashing into the water he was able to hold her interest: she said several times that the Sorbonne "must have been fascinating," and she sympathized with his having to go back to Denver, though she said it was "probably the best thing."

"And your friend's just going to stay over here indefinitely, then?" she asked. "Is it really true what he said? I mean that he isn't studying or working or anything? Just sort of floating around?"

"Well—yeah, that's right." Ken tried a squinty smile like Carson's own. "Why?"

"It's interesting, that's all. I don't think I've ever met a person like that before."

That was when Ken began to realize what the laughter and the scanty French bathing suits had disguised about these girls, that they were girls of a kind neither he nor Carson had dealt with for a long time—suburban, middle-class girls who had dutifully won their parents' blessing for this guided tour; girls who said "golly Moses," whose campus-shop clothes and hockey-field strides would have instantly betrayed them on the street. They were the very kind of girls who had gathered at the punch bowl to murmur "Ugh!" at the way he looked in his first tuxedo, whose ignorant, maddeningly bland little stares of rejection had poisoned all his aching years in Denver and New Haven. They were squares. And the remarkable thing was that he felt so good. Rolling his weight to one elbow, clutching up slow, hot handfuls of sand and emptying them, again and again, he found his flow of words coming quick and smooth:

". . . no, really, there's a lot to see in Paris; shame you couldn't spend more time there; actually most of the places I like best are more or less off the beaten track; of course I was lucky in having a fairly good grasp of the language, and then I met so many congenial. . . ."

He was holding his own; he was making out. He hardly even noticed when Carson and the tall girl came trotting back from their swim, as lithe and handsome as a couple in a travel poster, to drop beside them in a bustle of towels and cigarettes and shuddering jokes about how cold the water was. His only mounting worry was that Carson, who must by now have made his own discovery about these girls, would decide they weren't worth bothering with. But a single glance at Carson's subtly smiling, talking face reassured him: sitting tense at the tall girl's feet while she stood to towel her back in a way that made her breasts sway delightfully, Carson was plainly determined to follow through. "Look," he said. "Why don't we all have dinner together? Then afterwards we might—"

Both girls began chattering their regrets: they were afraid not, thanks anyway, they were meeting friends at the hotel for dinner and actually ought to be starting back now, much as they hated to—"God, look at the time!" And they really did sound sorry, so sorry that Ken, gathering all his courage, reached out and held the warm, fine-boned hand that swung at the small girl's thigh as the four of them plodded back toward the bathhouses. She even squeezed his heavy fingers, and smiled at him.

"Some other night, then?" Carson was saying. "Before you leave?"

"Well, actually," the tall girl said, "our evenings do seem to be pretty well booked up. Probably run into you on the beach again though. It's been fun."

"God damn little snot-nosed New Rochelle bitch," Carson said when they were alone in the men's bathhouse.

"*Sh-h-h!* Keep your *voice* down, Carson. They can *hear* you in there."

"Oh, don't be an idiot." Carson flung his trunks on the duckboards with a sandy slap. "I hope they do hear me—what the hell's the matter with you?" He looked at Ken as if he hated him. "Pair of God damn teasing little professional virgins. *Christ*, why didn't I stay in Paris?"

And now here they were, Carson glowering, Ken sulking at the sunset through flyspecked windows while a pushing, garlic-smelling bunch of laborers laughed and shouted over the pinball machine. They went on drinking until long past the dinner hour; then they ate a late, unpleasant meal together in a restaurant where the wine was corky and there was too much grease on the fried potatoes. When the messy plates were cleared away Carson lit a cigarette. "What do you want to do tonight?" he said.

There was a faint shine of grease around Ken's mouth and cheeks. "I don't know," he said. "Lot of good places to go, I guess."

"I suppose it would offend your artistic sensibilities to go and hear Sid's piano again?"

Ken gave him a weak, rather testy smile. "You still harping on that?" he said. "Sure I'd like to go."

"Even though he may prostitute himself?"

"Why don't you lay off that, Carson?"

They could hear the piano from the street, even before they walked into the square of light that poured up from the doorway of Sid's place. On the stairs the sound of it grew stronger and richer, mixed now with the sound of a man's hoarse singing, but only when they were down in the room, squinting through the blue smoke, did they realize the singer was Sid himself. Eyes half closed, head turned to smile along his shoulder into the crowd, he was singing as he swayed and worked at the keys.

"Man, she got a pair of eyes. . . ."

The blue spotlight struck winking stars in the moisture of his teeth and the faint thread of sweat that striped his temple.

"I mean they're brighter than the summer skies
And when you see them you gunna realize
Just why I love my sweet Lorraine. . . ."

"Damn place is packed," Carson said. There were no vacancies at the bar, but they stood uncertainly near it for a while, watching Sid perform, until Carson found that one of the girls on the barstools directly behind him was Jaqueline. "Oh," he said, 'Hi. Pretty good crowd tonight."

She smiled and nodded and then craned past him to watch Sid.

"I didn't know he sang too," Carson said. "This something new?"

Her smile gave way to an impatient little frown and she put a forefinger against her lips. Rebuffed, he turned back and moved heavily from one foot to the other. Then he nudged Ken. "You want to go or stay? If you want to stay let's at least sit down."

"*Sh-h-h!*" Several people turned in their chairs to frown at him. "*Sh-h-h!*"

"Come on, then," he said, and he led Ken sidling and stumbling through the ranks of listeners to the only vacant table in the room, a small one down in front, too close to the music and wet with spilled drink, that had been pushed aside to make room for larger parties. Settled there, they could see now that Sid wasn't looking into the crowd at large. He was singing directly to a bored-looking couple in evening clothes who sat a few tables away, a silver-blonde girl who could have been a movie starlet and a small, chubby bald man with a deep tan, a man so obviously Murray Diamond that a casting director might have sent him here to play the part. Sometimes Sid's large eyes would stray to other parts of the room or to the smoke-hung ceiling, but they seemed to come into focus only when he looked at these two people. Even when the song ended and the piano took off alone on a long, intricate variation, even when he kept glancing up to see if they were watching. When he finished, to a small thunderclap of applause, the bald man lifted his face, closed it around an amber cigarette holder and clapped his hands a few times.

"Very nice, Sam," he said.

"My name's Sid, Mr. Diamond," Sid said, "but I thank you a lot just the same. Glad y'enjoyed it, sir." He was leaning back, grinning along his shoulder while his fingers toyed with the keys. "Anything special you'd like to hear, Mr. Diamond? Something old-time? Some more of that real old Dixieland? Maybe a little boogie, maybe something a little on the sweet side, what we call a commercial number? Got all kind of tunes here, waitin' to be played."

"Anything at all, uh, Sid," Murray Diamond said, and then the blonde leaned close and whispered something in his ear. "How about 'Stardust,' there, Sid?" he said. "Can you play 'Stardust'?"

"Well, now, Mr. Diamond. If I couldn't play 'Stardust' I don't guess I'd be in business very long, France or any other country." His grin turned into a deep false laugh and his hands slid into the opening chords of the song.

That was when Carson made his first friendly gesture in hours, sending a warm blush of gratitude into Ken's face. He hitched his chair up close to Ken's and began to speak in a voice so soft that no one could have accused him of making a disturbance. "You know something?" he said. "This is disgusting. My God, *I* don't care if he wants to go to Las Vegas. I don't even care if he wants to suck *around* for it. This is something else. This is something that turns my stomach." He paused, frowning at the floor, and Ken watched the small wormlike vein moving in his temple. "Putting on this phony accent," Carson said. "All this big phony Uncle Remus routine." And then he went into a little popeyed, head-tossing, hissing parody of Sid. "Yassuh, Mr. Dahmon' suh. Wudg'all lak t'heah, Mr. Dahmon' suh? Got awl *kine* a toons heah, jes' waitin' to be played, and yok, yok, yok, and shet ma mouf!" He finished his drink and set the glass down hard. "You know damn well he doesn't have to talk that way. You know damn well he's a perfectly bright, educated guy. My God, on the phone I couldn't even tell he was colored."

"Well, yeah," Ken said. "It is sort of depressing."

"Depressing? It's degrading." Carson curled his lip. "It's degenerate."

"I know," Ken said. "I guess that may be partly what I meant about prostituting himself."

"You were certainly right, then. This is damn near enough to make you lose faith in the Negro race."

Being told he was right was always a tonic to Ken, and it was uncommonly bracing after a day like this. He knocked back his drink, straightened his spine and wiped the light mustache of sweat from his upper lip, pressing his mouth into a soft frown to show that his faith, too, in the Negro race was badly shaken. "Boy," he said. "I sure had him figured wrong."

"No," Carson assured him, "you couldn't have known."

"Listen, let's go, then, Carson. The hell with him." And Ken's mind was already full of plans: they would stroll in the cool of the Croisette for a long, serious talk on the meaning of integrity, on how rare it was and how easily counterfeited, how its pursuit was the only struggle worthy of a man's life, until all the discord of the day was erased.

But Carson moved his chair back, smiling and frowning at the same time. "Go?" he said. "What's the matter with you? Don't you want to stay and watch the spectacle? I do. Doesn't it hold a certain horrible fascination for you?" He held up his glass and signaled for two more cognacs.

"Stardust" came to a graceful conclusion and Sid stood up, bathed in applause, to take his break. He loomed directly over their table as he came forward and stepped down off the dais, his big face shining with sweat; he brushed past them, looking toward Diamond's table, and paused there to say, "Thank you, sir," though Diamond hadn't spoken to him, before he made his way back to the bar.

"I suppose he thinks he didn't see us," Carson said.

"Probably just as well," Ken said. "I wouldn't know what to say to him."

"Wouldn't you? I think I would."

The room was stifling, and Ken's cognac had taken on a faintly repellent look and smell in his hand. He loosened his collar and tie with moist fingers. "Come on, Carson," he said. "Let's get out of here. Let's get some air."

Carson ignored him, watching what went on at the bar. Sid drank something Jaqueline offered and then disappeared into the men's room. When he came out a few minutes later, his face dried and composed, Carson turned back and studied his glass. "Here he comes. I think we're going to get the big hello, now, for Diamond's benefit. Watch."

An instant later Sid's fingers brushed the cloth of Carson's shoulder. *"Bzz-z-z, bzz-z-z!"* he said. "How're you tonight?"

Very slowly, Carson turned his head. With heavy eyelids he met Sid's smile for a split second, the way a man might look at a waiter who had accidentally touched him. Then he turned back to his drink.

"Oh-oh," Sid said. "Maybe I didn't do that right. Maybe I got the wrong shoulder here. I'm not too familiar with the rules and regulations yet." Murray Diamond and the blonde were watching, and Sid winked at them, thumbing out the IBF button in his lapel as he moved in sidling steps around the back of Carson's chair. "This here's a club we belong to, Mr. Diamond," he said. "Barflies club. Only trouble is, I'm not very familiar with the rules and regulations yet." He held the attention of nearly everyone in the room as he touched Carson's other shoulder. *"Bzz-z-z, bzz-z-z!"* This time Carson winced and drew his jacket away, glancing at Ken with a perplexed little shrug as if to say, Do you know what this man wants?

Ken didn't know whether to giggle or vomit; both desires were suddenly strong in him, though his face held straight. For a long time afterwards he would remember how the swabbed black plastic of the table looked between his two unmoving hands, how it seemed the only steady surface in the world.

"Say," Sid said, backing away toward the piano with a glazed smile. "What *is* this here? Some kinda conspiracy here?"

Carson allowed a heavy silence to develop. Then with an air of sudden, mild remembrance, seeming to say, Oh yes, of course, he rose and walked over to Sid, who backed up confusedly into the spotlight. Facing him, he extended one limp finger and touched him on the shoulder. "Buzz," he said. "Does that take care of it?" He turned and walked back to his seat.

Ken prayed for someone to laugh—anyone—but no one did. There was no movement in the room but the dying of Sid's smile as he looked at Carson and at Ken, the slow fleshy enclosing of his teeth and the widening of his eyes.

Murray Diamond looked at them too, briefly—a tough, tan little face—then he cleared his throat and said, "How about 'Hold Me,' there, Sid? Can you play 'Hold Me'?" And Sid sat down and began to play, looking at nothing.

With dignity, Carson nodded for the check and laid the right number of thousand- and hundred-franc notes on the saucer. It seemed to take him no time at all to get out of the place, sliding expertly between the tables and out to the stairs, but it took Ken much longer. Lurching, swaying in the smoke like a great imprisoned bear, he was caught and held by Jaqueline's eyes even before he had cleared the last of the tables. They stared relentlessly at the flabby quaver of his smile, they drilled into his back and sent him falling upstairs. And as soon as the sobering night air hit him, as soon as he saw Carson's erect white suit retreating several doors away, he knew what he wanted to do. He wanted to run up and hit him with all his strength between the shoulder blades, one great chopping blow that would drop him to the street, and then he would hit him again, or kick him— yes, kick him—and he'd say, God damn you! God damn you, Carson! The words were already in his mouth and he was ready to swing when Carson stopped and turned to face him under a streetlamp.

"What's the trouble, Ken?" he said. "Don't you think that was funny?"

It wasn't what he said that mattered—for a minute it seemed that nothing Carson said would ever matter again—it was that his face was stricken with the uncannily familiar look of his own heart, the very face he himself, Lard-Ass Platt, had shown all his life to others:

haunted and vulnerable and terribly dependent, trying to smile, a look that said Please don't leave me alone.

Ken hung his head, either in mercy or shame. "Hell, I don't know, Carson," he said. "Let's forget it. Let's get some coffee somewhere."

"Right." And they were together again. The only problem now was that they had started out in the wrong direction: in order to get to the Croisette they would have to walk back past the lighted doorway of Sid's place. It was like walking through fire, but they did it quickly and with what anyone would have said was perfect composure, heads up, eyes front, so that the piano only came up loud for a second or two before it diminished and died behind them under the rhythm of their heels.

WILLARD MARSH

MENDING WALL

SAN FRANCISCO, THE ALTERNATE home of Miguel Flores, was a small, neat village with eroded adobe walls symmetrical around an elevated plaza that was shadowed by the spire of Saint Francis on clement days. Even through the steady drizzle of a mid-June dusk it gave a welcome lift to his spirits. He got off the bus with the two knapsacked Americans who had failed to make a transfer and accompanied them to the waiting room. There he learned that the next bus for their destination, a rowdy foreign colony on the upper edge of Lake Chapala, would not be due till nine-fifteen.

"Oh, man, that's sad news," said Harry, the lean, good-looking taller of the two. "Where's someplace swinging we can sweat out all that time, Mike?"

Miguel smiled at the idioms, hoping to remember them. Swinging, surely from swing music. "There's a pleasant little restaurant where you can sweat yourselves in comfort." He pointed it out. "I think you will not find it swinging, but it is agreeable."

"Grease him, daddy, grease him," Harry's stocky friend Sidecar murmured.

"Have a drink and keep us company a little longer, amigo," Harry urged. "Think of us out here in the cold among alien faces, while you're in that far-out castle of yours, curled up with a warm broad and a bottle."

Again Miguel smiled (because of their broader, child-bearing hips?), hesitating. The family seldom used the villa in the rainy season. On occasional weekends such as this one, Miguel would come out to romp with the dog, play his worn old jazz records while the rain conspired with what he recognized was Weltschmerz (although recognition didn't lesson it), and try his hand at a love poem. "Very well, I will be pleased to join you."

Leading them to a crowded cantina that smelled of wet wool cloaks and stale dried fish, he had a beer while they each tossed off a pair of double tequilas. They were about nineteen, a year or so older than himself, and by a happy coincidence were also prelaw students at Stanford University in California. Furthermore, they were working their way through school as professional jazz musicians, Harry on piano and Sidecar with what Harry had praised as "the funkiest trumpet west of Salt Lake City."

"Well, how does our Frisco compare to yours?" Miguel asked. "I think you will find it lacks your fogs." He began humming a tricky eight-bar opening, slapping his palms in counter-tempo on the bar. Then he laughed, having caught them once again.

A slow, tantalized grin spread over Harry's face. "What the *hell* is the name of that thing?"

"I will give you a hint. They also recorded 'Margie' back in the thirties."

Sidecar began whistling "Margie" thoughtfully.

"Yes, that! That is the trombone solo of 'Margie'!" Miguel said in excitement. "Jimmy Lunceford, of course. And this I am doing now is his 'Frisco Fog.' Remember?"

"Remember it?" Harry said. "I don't think I could forget it if they brainwashed me."

Sidecar's eyes were half-lidded in nostalgia. "They broke the mold."

Pleased, Miguel extended his hand in farewell. "And now I must go home. Thank you for the drink and for the conversation."

"Oh no, Mike, why end it?" Harry said quickly. "Let's have some more of both—here or anywhere you say."

Miguel was touched by their naked loneliness. There was only the caretaker on the grounds, old Rafael, and his ailing wife and little daughter who managed for them. When the family came they always brought the servants from the town house. But even with a skeleton staff, provisions of some sort could be made for guests, he supposed.

"If you would like to wait at the villa, you would be welcome," he told them. "We could play some records, and there is probably beer in the refrigerator. We could have a little lunch of some kind, whatever is in the kitchen." He remembered the perfect expression. "Potluck."

"Crazy! Potluck sounds like great luck."

"Wild, man."

"A real lifesaver, Mike. That's very generous of you."

And buoyed by their appreciation, Miguel took them the kilometer walk across town to Casa Flores, a compact house that lay behind high walls on a short cliff that overhung the lake. Looking through the spiked iron gate onto the lawned terraces that old Rafael kept immaculate, Harry whistled in awe. Miguel wondered how they would react if they could see the opulent neighboring estates. Now he too whistled, a piercing octave drop.

The silence lasted for perhaps two seconds, and then there was an outburst of convulsively ecstatic barking from the direction of the caretaker's cottage. The arthritic collie, Corazón, came out of the woodshed as fast as her legs could bear her, followed by Rafael with his brass key ring. They were about the same age proportionately. Miguel let the collie bathe him with her tongue between the bars, jerking handfuls of her skin the way she liked.

"*Alma mía.* Oh you good girl," he said.

And when Rafael admitted them Miguel embraced him and said, "These two are friends who stay for a brief meal."

"They are welcome," Rafael said and they smiled back, although they didn't understand him. On the flagstoned path to the house, escorted by the bounding collie, they exchanged questions about their families. Finally excusing himself, Rafael said, "I shall send Louisa for your needs."

"Yes, please do so."

With an affectionate spank, Miguel sent the collie back to her lair. Her muddy paws and hair were prohibited from contact with his mother's furniture, and she could have his full attention all tomorrow morning. Then he led Harry and Sidecar down the tiled hall to his rear quarters, where his drums squatted across the room from a pair of angled speakers connected to his turntable. There was a fire laid in the hearth. Lighting it, Miguel pointed out the shelf of loosely stacked records.

"Choose your listening pleasure, *señores*, while I investigate the condition of the department of beer."

He left them eagerly writhing out of their knapsacks and returned up the hall to the kitchen, where young Louisa was chopping cabbage while tortillas simmered in a pan. Again he went through the ritual of comparing the health and fortunes of her scattered family and his own as he opened three chilled bottles of Corona and told her to put the rest of the case in the refrigerator.

Halfway back to his room he heard Art Tatum's "Sweet Lorraine" flare up, and he entered to find Harry and

Sidecar squatting in solemn respect before the speakers. Silently handing them their bottles, Miguel sat on the window ledge and watched Harry's face reflect the dizzying velocity of the blind Negro's right hand, knowing that whatever he himself got from it, a professional pianist would be hearing so much more.

They all sighed at the conclusion of the record, and Sidecar said, "I believe that cat covers just a little more keyboard than you do, daddy."

Harry grinned. "Well, wait till I'm his age."

Laughing, Miguel said, "Now it is the turn to play one for the trumpet man." And selecting Buck Clayton's "Royal Garden Blues," he put it on and watched Sidecar shaking his head in disbelief at the hoarse golden agony and saying *too much, too much*. Harry pointed at the drums in invitation.

"Oh no, I could not," Miguel said quickly, at the same time hoping that they would insist, because this was one of his favorite recordings to play behind. But they let it go, and when the record was over Miguel said,

"And now, shall we have 'Frisco Fog'?"

"Great." Harry absently tilted up his empty bottle.

Embarrassed at being too neglectful a host to realize that they had finished their beers, Miguel went to the door and called Louisa. When she appeared at the head of the hall he ordered three more and hurriedly finished his own. It wasn't until after "Frisco Fog" was done that they were aware she had been shyly knocking at the door.

"Pass, girl, pass!" Miguel called.

The door opened and Louisa slipped in with a tray containing bottles, glasses, and a bowl of radishes.

"Get a load of those splendid little knockers," Harry told Sidecar.

"Oh man, the tenderest meat in town."

Louisa flushed and lowered her eyes under the inten-

sity of their gaze. Miguel was embarrassed at being made
to see that she was no longer a child.

Removing the contents of the tray, Harry said in clumsy
Spanish, "Good morning, beautiful. To dance? To dance?"
He put one hand on his chest and extended his arm,
weaving his torso sensuously. "Slap something on that
gramophone, paisano," he called over his shoulder.

Miguel stepped forward. "No, that is not done here.
She has never in her life danced with a man." Then he
thanked Louisa and dismissed her.

They put another record on, and after awhile the incident had passed. But from then on, whenever Harry and
Sidecar were in need of fresh beers, Miguel went for
them himself.

There was only one bottle remaining from the case by
the time Louisa announced the meal, and Miguel divided
it between the musicians.

"*Buen provecho*, as we say," he said, while they seated
themselves around the heavy walnut dining table and
Louisa brought in a cauldron of chicken broth. "Good
appetite."

"No danger not," Harry said eagerly, ladling himself a
bowl. "You got a dandy stack of platters back there,
Mike. Some real collector's items."

"All that fine listening," Sidecar nodded. "And not
being able to join in, that's what drags me. Man, I wish I
had the old axe with me."

"The old axe?" Miguel smiled.

"My horn, dad."

"I see," he laughed, and then an idea struck him.
"Excuse me for a moment, please."

In the kitchen, he told Louisa to ask Rafael to see if he
could borrow a trumpet or cornet from one of the bands-
men in the village. She returned from the errand in time
to clear the soup bowls and serve them with refried
beans, salad, and rice with bits of roast pork. The food

had more abundance than variety, and they filled themselves at leisure. When they were finishing coffee, Miguel said,

"I wish I could offer you some brandy, but my father keeps it under lock."

"Where is it?" Harry asked, and Miguel uneasily pointed to the glassed liquor cabinet. "Hell, a screwdriver can take care of that."

Miguel tried to laugh it off. "This I think my father would not quite appreciate."

But just then, to ease the awkwardness, Rafael signaled from the kitchen archway. Excusing himself, Miguel hurried over to see that, through some confusion of Louisa's or his own, the old man had got hold of a valve trombone. Miguel thanked him, brought it in and presented it to Sidecar with an elaborate flourish.

"What in hell is *that*?"

"An axe, poor as it is," Miguel said. "I thought we could take my drums to the *sala* where the piano is and make some noise. Just to pass the time."

"Man, if that's a trumpet I'm an ape's pizzaz."

"Come on, clown, don't drag the party," Harry said. "It's got valves, hasn't it? I think that's a real creative suggestion, Mike. Let's all go blow up a storm."

And with Sidecar testing the valve action in amused reluctance, they returned to Miguel's room for the drums.

They arranged themselves in the dimly lit, high-ceilinged living room, Miguel behind his snare and bass with the sizzle cymbal attached to it, next to the grand piano, with Sidecar lounging sardonically in a wing chair. Harry opened the piano, made a little show of blowing imaginary dust from the keyboard and slid his hand down it skeptically.

"Oh, no. When's the last time this thing was tuned?"

"It has been a little while," Miguel admitted.

Harry began striking notes at random, shaking his head in misery. "Terrible, terrible. It's bound to cramp my style."

"It's got keys, hasn't it?" Sidecar called. "Don't drag the party."

Harry gave him an obscene gesture. "You want to tune up?"

"Gimme an A."

Harry struck a key and Sidecar put the trombone to his lips, pushed the first valve down and produced a harsh tone with more breath than timbre.

"You're flat, but it's close enough for jazz," Harry said cheerfully. "OK, brass section, what'll we wail on?"

"Help yourself, Daddy."

"How about 'The Bird on Nelly's Hat'?"

"What key?"

"Help yourself, daddy."

"How about B flat?"

"Oh man, if you'd said *A* flat it would make some sense. But *B* flat?"

Sidecar laughed insultingly. "Make it A flat, then. And give us an up-beat intro."

"With pleasure." Harry settled himself on the bench, serious now, and said quietly, "Leave us swing, gentlemen."

He began with the brisk, two-fingered waltz that nonpianists play at parties, and thoroughly enjoying the wit, Miguel gave him an appropriate backing.

Finishing, Harry called, "Take it, Mike!"

Miguel rolled into four-four, knocking out an eight-bar chorus. He used his snare as a tom-tom, making rim shots with a crossed stick, and at the end he gave them the re-entry riff on his cymbal and bass.

"Take it, Sidecar!" he called happily.

Sidecar brought the horn to his mouth, pushed all three valves down and produced the same strangled noise he'd made when he was tuning up. Then he stopped and stared in total disbelief at Harry, who was still playing "Chopsticks" in syncopated form.

"You son of a bitch, you're in B flat!"

"Of course I'm in B flat, you horse's pratt! Isn't that what we said?"

Then, in their slack-mouthed laughter, Miguel was able to see how far ahead of him they were in drinking. He hoped it had been merely drunkenness, or even contempt for his own performance, that had caused this display. It would be preferable to a deliberate abuse of his confidence.

Miguel glanced at his watch and got up from the drums. "Well, it helped to pass the time, correct? Your bus will come soon," he said. "Perhaps it will come ahead of schedule."

"I guess we're all a little better at law than music," Harry said nonchalantly. And then, to Miguel's amazement at their inability to read social signals, he said, "So listen, why don't we put on a trial? You know, defense attorney, prosecuting attorney—the whole bit."

"Whom do you propose to try?" Miguel asked coldly.

"Oh, we'll figure that out. You know, moot court stuff. Let's go hear some more records. Where's the head?"

"The what?"

"The can, man. The *escusado*."

"Oh. I will show you."

Reconciled to being stuck with them until bus time, less than two hours from now, Miguel pointed out the bathroom on the way back to his room. Perhaps it wasn't too much to hope that Harry would have sense and grace enough to vomit himself into sobriety.

Since he and Sidecar had nothing to communicate to one another, Miguel put a record on to fill the silence. After a while Harry came in with a brandy bottle.

Waving it in grinning apology, he said, "Looking for a

little drink of water in the kitchen. Slipped and broke a panel of the cabinet. Bad show. Thought I'd salvage it with a vintage bottle for the vintage records."

Incapable of further surprise, Miguel found himself thinking *They must be simply savages.* This observation enabled him to remain sitting on the bed like a research anthropologist, dividing his attention between them and his wristwatch.

Harry had passed the bottle to Sidecar and was flipping through the records. Finding one to his liking, he replaced the one that was going on the turntable. The familiar sounds of "Nelly Grey," by Louis Armstrong and the Mills Brothers, came drifting lazily from the speakers.

Harry and Sidecar looked at each other and began laughing in what seemed near hysteria.

"Oh, no, those cats *got* to go. The title alone does it. The bird on darling Nelly Grey's hat." Harry wiped his eyes and took another drink of brandy, coughing a little. "All right, I'll present the case for the plaintiff." He removed the record and waved it in the air. "We contend that this monstrosity does grave mischief to the ear of anyone who was born after 1922. We submit that it is Grade A horsecrap, fresh from the furrows. The plaintiff rests. Take it, Mike."

"Oh, then I am the defense? Very well," Miguel said. "The defense is willing to stipulate that this recording is older than some of the others. The defense further suggests that taste is impossible to define, and that no one forced you to listen to this or any other record."

"Does the defense rest?"

"Yes."

"Take it, paisano. You're the jury."

"We find the defendant guilty as charged," Sidecar said.

"And the jury brings in a verdict of mandatory death," Harry chanted.

He smashed the record against a corner of the shelf. Then as Miguel rose from the bed, he stepped quickly to the door and folded his arms.

"Play it cool, amigo," he cautioned.

"Real cool," Sidecar agreed.

Their faces, slack with liquor, wore a look of wary readiness. Miguel realized he was alone in the house with them, and in the caretaker's cottage there were a feeble old man and two females, one bedridden. He sat back down.

"That's better. Call the next defendant," Harry said, remaining at the door.

Sidecar glanced at a label or two. "That Art Tatum thing?"

"No, that's not too bad. Look for something really spooky."

"Earl Father Hines?"

"Father *who*? Well, hand it over and we'll find out."

"Do you propose to break that record also?" Miguel asked, surprised at the steadiness of his voice. He had been able to find only one Hines recording, their theme song, "Deep Forest."

"Why, Mike, are you suggesting we'd commit a breach of professional ethics?" Harry asked in astonishment. "There is no presentencing here. A defendant is allowed his chance before the bar of justice."

"Sure, what do you think we're running," Sidecar said, "a kangaroo court or something?"

And now Miguel began coughing from the thick smell of their cigarettes. "Can't we have some fresh air?"

"Christ yes. Don't you ever wash your feet, paisan'?"

Harry put the Hines record on, keeping a close eye on Miguel, while Sidecar struggled with the window. Damp new air surged in, along with the somber, deep chorale of Father Hines. The ex-musicians listened to it for a while in only mild amusement before Harry took the record off and weighed it in his hand, considering.

"Well, it's old-timey enough, God knows. Great-grand-father Hines would be more like it. But it doesn't rape your ear lobes. Tell you what, Mike. Make a good, spirited defense and maybe you'll persuade the prosecution to withdraw charges."

Miguel forced himself to casually whistle a few bars of the opening. Then he whistled an octave drop. "I am not sure that it is worth defending." He whistled the octave drop, louder.

"Well, now, *look*, amigo," Harry said in an ugly voice, "that's not professional ethics, abandoning your client to the big drop."

Miguel continued whistling idly.

"You don't want to cooperate?" Harry turned to Sidecar. "I do believe old Mike is dragging the party."

"That'll never do. Guess we have to coax him back into the jolly spirit."

"Looks like he's forcing us. Are you listening, amigo? I'm going to count to three, and if you aren't making a case for it, the record goes. One."

Miguel kept whistling.

"Two. . . ."

Miguel whistled the octave drop, in good volume.

"Three? All right, you asked for it."

In the instant that the record shattered the collie set up her barking from the woodshed. The sound approached rapidly.

"Novak, get that window!" Harry yelled.

"The what?"

"The window, stupid!"

As Sidecar leaped to the window to begin wrestling it shut, Corazón's head appeared in it, her front paws braced on the sill. She resumed barking at the commotion, her tail thrashing in rapture.

"Freeze!" Miguel shouted.

Sidecar froze.

"Now move very slowly, unless you want to lose that entire hand up to the elbow," Miguel told him. "Move backward."

When he was far enough from the window Miguel halted him, went to the ledge and hoisted the collie inside.

"Throw yourself!" he said, and she obediently sprawled at his feet, executing just about the only command he'd ever succeeded in teaching her.

"Guard them closely," he told her in Spanish, her tail thumping the floor contentedly. "Rip their pasty guts out if they even sneeze," he said, in the joy of cold fury that he would have felt had she been able to do such a thing. "I have just told her," he announced, "to go for the throat if either of you move one muscle. Wait here, exactly where you are."

Stepping out of the room, he hurried to his parents' bedroom. There in his mother's night table, as he'd remembered it, was her .25 pistol. It had never been fired, to his knowledge, and after all these years of disuse quite possibly would misfire, assuming it was loaded. But its small heft was welcome to his hand. He raced back in time to see Harry edging cautiously out into the hall.

"Get back in there or you're a dead man!" Miguel called, leveling the pistol at him.

Harry slowly elevated his arms and moved back inside. Joining them, Miguel ordered them both to stand against the wall while he stacked all his records on the floor.

"You must understand that I will not hesitate to kill you if you give me an excuse," he told them sincerely. "Death is a matter of small import in Mexico. Especially the death of a pair of vagabonds, who break into the grounds of a family of influence with intent to rob. No one in this village will challenge my interpretation of events." The collie stretched sleepily. "And now, shall we recommence the trial?" Miguel picked up the first record. "Art Tatum, on 'Sweet Lorraine.' This time you will be the defense, Harry, if that is your name." He thrust the pistol toward him. "Plead."

Harry smiled, or tried to. "Jesus, Mike, it's a beautiful record, I never said it wasn't."

"I am not Mike to you, *puto*. I am señor Flores. And you are wrong. It cannot be a beautiful record. It has been dirtied by your ears."

Miguel smashed it against the shelf and kicked the pieces from him.

"My God, amigo, what are you doing?"

Miguel looked at him. "If you call me amigo one more time, I will put a bullet through your heart." He bent to pick up the next record. It was "Frisco Fog." He set it aside and selected another. "Benny Goodman, 'Sing, Sing, Sing,' Part II. Can it be defended?"

"Look, Mike—I mean, señor. We were drunk clean out of our skulls. Give us a break and let us out of here."

Miguel struck the Goodman record clean in half. "All these records are contaminated by your presence, and by my tolerance of it. They will have to be purified."

Jimmy Lunceford's "Margie" went next, followed by the Teddy Wilson quartet, while the two looked on in fearful silence. By the time Miguel had broken Chick Webb, there was no emotion to it any more. It was an unseeing, mechanical process, during which they could have attacked him or fled and he wouldn't have known or cared.

Finally he was done, the floor littered with Fats Waller, Fletcher Henderson, the King Cole trio, the entire useless past. He met their dazed expressions with his own.

"Put on your packs and leave through the window," he said. "Get over the gate whatever way you can. Do it before I change my mind."

He sat back in utter fatigue, watching them ready themselves and climb quickly out the window. Then they were running down the terraces to the tall iron gate and laboring over it, and then they were gone.

They are simply savages, he found himself repeating, and now he realized whom he meant by *they*. It was all of them, all their stolen land and wealth and power. How could he have ever seen them otherwise? Oh, he would continue to use their language, because it was the language that best functioned on financial levels. But he was forever finished with their quaint Negro artists, their customs, their enthusiasms, their mere sight in any other than a duty situation.

Corazón whimpered, nudging him with her nose. He discovered that "Frisco Fog" was still intact. He swung it listlessly against the turntable until it cracked, perhaps with the sound of an opening egg shell.

C. W. SMITH

THE PLANTATION CLUB

CURTIS "STOOGIE" GOODMAN STEPPED off the bus in our town with an alto sax and a suitcase of uniform remnants from a band which had collapsed in El Paso. Like our Chicano-migrants-turned-residents and redneck roustabouts, he stopped to recoup the means to move on and never made it. Mornings he washed dishes at the Winslow Café. Three nights a week he played at The Plantation, a nightclub in our small black ghetto.

Windowless but for the portholes head-high along the front, the club had the air of a steamboat long since drydocked and crumbling. A plantation scene embellished the expanse of stucco above the portholes—a cotton patch with an Aunt Jemima at its border, a veranda where a colonel with a cigar chatted with a brace of belles whose parasols formed pastel nimbuses behind their curls. The street in front of the club was washboard sand littered with shards of glass—here black whores meandered along the shoulders. We junior classmen cruised this block with only a driver visible and three or four others huddled on the floorboards.

"Hey, wheah you goin' boy?"

"Lookin' for some poontang!"

"You lookin' right at it!"

"How much?"

"They's different kinds!"

"I like it hot and greasy, mama!"

"Lawd! You don't look that rich!"

Then we'd all spring upright, cackle yah-yah-yah, and leave a wash of sand spray to flap her skirt as we sped away, victors again, but over what we never knew. Cute, huh? After they started calling us "Cig-uh-RET Pee-tuhs" we didn't harass them as much.

Maybe that's why we didn't hear Stoogie until the summer before our senior year in 1957 when Terry and I decided a little banter could liven up the night. With two of us the game was limited to an exchange that stalemated when we had to put up or shut up, but it beat going into orbit around the Sonic Dog, and we had already spent an hour on the main drag looking for that mythical nymphomaniac we dreamed would pull up in her Caddy convertible and bare her tits.

Drifting slowly by The Plantation, we heard an alto rise into melancholy flight on the opening bars of "Round Midnight." Confused, I thought I was hearing a record, but even that would have been a marvel: my gods—"The Bird," John Coltrane, Sonny Stitt, Sonny Rollins, Stan Getz, Cannonball Adderly—were so obscure in my town that to ask for an album by one at the music store was like asking for the latest from The Outer Mongolian Preschool Rhythm Band and Chorus in Concert. We had stumbled onto jazz via "Moonglow with Martin" on WWL in New Orleans, and we had spent countless nights since riding in our parents' cars listening to music such as we had never dreamed existed broadcast from some twelve hundred miles away by crow-fly and a century or so by cultural disposition to our remote corner of New Mexico. Barely a decade out of its boom, our overgrown crossroad had a ragged, honky-tonk energy, but it was cowboy country, and we had begun to feel misplaced in it, practitioners of an alien religion.

Terry stopped the car. We heard the opening phrase repeated with a minor variation in the fifth bar, the sound not exactly angry but anguished; midnight was a dark sponge soaking up every man's hope and illusion. Maybe that's too heavy, but we were stunned.

"You boys lookin' for somethin'?"

"No thanks," Terry said. He hooked a thumb toward the club. "Say, who's playing in there?"

"Buncha niggers, I'd say," the woman cracked over her shoulder as she strolled off.

Buncha niggers. We parked across the street and listened to that alto do its tricks on "C-Jam Blues" (a flimsy excuse to take a dozen choruses), "How High the Moon," "A-Train," "Blackbird," and three boogie-shuffle blues each in a different key. Now and then a black face poked its way into our vision, but we made no offers, asked no questions, and sat for an hour astonished that such a sound existed so far from either coast.

A long silence, then four men came out a side door at the rear of the building. Guessing them to be the group, we decided to brave asking if we could listen inside. As we walked toward the club, we got nervous. Our town was relatively peaceful; our schools had integrated soon after the Brown decision without much flap save a plethora of hysterical sermons delivered on the eve of the Apocalypse by our good Baptist brethren, but this wasn't our turf. The uncharted territory around the building hid conspirators whose razors flashed at the corners of my eyes. But—hell!—wasn't I safe? Hadn't I once shocked my Tennessee relatives by shaking hands with a waiter at their country club? Justice always saw that the purehearted were protected and that bigots got their due. . . .

We came up to the men at the door. In the dimness they were only vague shapes, but soon features emerged which I'd come to know well over the year: R.B., the

huge, affable drummer who worked days loading blocks
of ice onto waiting trucks and who had been a Golden
Gloves heavyweight champ; Candy, the piano man, a
small Mescalero-Apache with a cataract on his left eye;
Scratchmo, the eldest, with a thicket of wiry gray hair
around his face, who spat tobacco into a coffee can perched
atop the amplifier of his guitar, who always wore a red
woolen shirt (hence the name) under faded denim overalls, and who displayed a perpetual half-smirk so ambiv-
alent that even a year later I hadn't learned to decipher
it; and Stoogie, a caramel-colored man whose baggy eyelids drooped as though he was forever on the verge of
sleep—and who now lounged against the building with
one sole flat against the wall, his cigarette an orange arc
as he raised it to his lips.

"Hey, you guys are really good!" Terry declared. "We've
been out in the car digging your jazz!"

Scratchmo turned and spat a gob of Beechnut juice
onto the sand behind him. "Hear that, Stoogie? These
boys been digging our jazz."

Stoogie didn't straighten from his slump; only a flicker
of his drooping eyelids suggested he was conscious of us.

"It's in the air," he muttered. He pushed away from
the wall and headed back inside the building, followed
by Candy and Scratchmo. R.B. hung back.

"Ya'll not old enough to drink, are you?"

"No sir," I mumbled.

"Haw!" He ducked his head toward the door and winked.
"Anybody ask, you say you're with R.B., hear?"

Grateful, we scurried in behind him. The interior of
the club smelled of beer and stale smoke; the crowd filled
the intermission lull with loud talk and laughter. Trying
not to lollygag, we aped the pose of jaded nightlife connoisseurs as we threaded our way through the occupied
tables. Sitting just before the bandstand with our backs
to the dance floor, we watched Stoogie ease down into a
metal folding chair and pull his alto out of its open case.

It was silver; I knew it had to be a Strad of saxes—a jazz counterpart to Jascha Heifetz would need a "fine" instrument—but soon I found out it was a crappy axe, one of the worst. The soft metal keys were always bending, which kept the pads from seating properly on their holes, and it was so out of tune with itself that Stoogie had to adjust each note with his ear and embouchure as he played. It was his tenth horn in as many years—he was broke so often that hocking them was his only resort; he could never keep one very long, though his metal Otto Link mouthpiece had been carried from one to the next.

Sagging in his chair like a sack of grain, Stoogie swung the sax on the pivot of his thumb with the Otto Link homing on his mouth; he waited, then at the last millisecond he parted his lips, snapped the mouthpiece in his jaws, and clamped his lips around it, a gesture faintly reminiscent of the end of conflict between a cobra and a mongoose. As he descended into "Summertime," a reedy edge serrated the contours of his voice, and he cut into the melody as if easing a knife into the jugular of a drowsy hog. The "high cotton" and "easy livin'" in the lyrics would seem to call for waltz-time on a banjo, but the melody contains more than a whiff of danger and despair, and Stoogie's first chorus ripped that disparity completely apart—his "summertime" was a stoop where junkies nodded, an alley where dark promises were kept.

Mouth agape, I gawked while phrases blossomed from the bell of his horn; but he might have been asleep, he was so still except for his hands. We sat five feet away, feeling faint huffs of breath from the horn, the strain of melody and improvised line as tangible as a string of sausages in the air before us. He began to sweat and his cheeks bellowed as he finished his fourth chorus and began working seriously to sign his name across the face of the tune. The dancers were warming up too, waving and whooping "Yaah!" as though his solo was the last-lap turn in an evangelical sermon. Had I looked around, I might have recognized them as the minor actors in the dramas played out by the oil-rich whites in town—janitors, maids, junkmen, yard boys, shine boys, dishwashers, and short order cooks—but I was too dazed to notice.

On the fifth chorus the line began to rise, and the tinge of bitterness which had colored his voice turned lighter as he explored the changes. Stoogie had, to backtrack on a metaphor, worked his way up from those fetid stoops, through the tenement and onto the roof, where he could lie on his back to watch winking lights of planes glide by like comets, silent, the engines lost in the muffled thrum from the street below, and beyond those arcing pinpoints a haze of stars appeared dimly through a scrim of reflected city light. Escape. For the moment.

When he was through, Scratchmo broke into laughter. "That's all right, man! All *right!*"

Stoogie acknowledged all the clapping and whistles from the audience with a nod but gave no sign he was pleased with himself.

"Man, I gotta get on the elevator," he said to Scratchmo. He got up, slowly, trudged off the stand and out the side door. The trio went into "Rock Me, Baby, All Night Long," with Scratchmo doing a passable imitation of Big Joe Williams.

After the gig, the quartet went separate ways, but before the club closed we bought R.B. a beer and pumped him for information. Stoogie had grown up on Chicago's South Side, dropped out of the eighth grade to make a temporary flight from the ghetto with a rhythm-and-blues band, married at eighteen, lost his wife to a pimp and gave up their child for adoption, took up with another woman who O.D.'d on heroin, spent a hitch in the navy, then drifted along the California coast playing in clubs and working menial day jobs; he hit the bigtime briefly as a sideman with Billy Eckstine's band, but in New York he was swamped by squalor and bad luck—busted, he served a two-year sentence for possession of marijuana. Man! I thought. Stoogie's really paid some dues! Terry and I were unscathed by divorce, disfigurement, or poverty; our mothers made sure we got fresh vegetables and clean underwear, and our fathers had taught us how to shake hands and use hammers, pull triggers and paddle canoes. Our greatest living enemy was neither want nor oppression but the rampant rashes of acne which came with the chocolate orgies we indulged in and which we tried to banish with soaps and creams and a half-hour spent harvesting the night's crop at the mirror before dashing off to school feeling like living exhibitions of open, running sores. My greatest sorrow to date was having lost my first love to another at age fifteen.

Sooner or later I'd be in luck and some tragedy would really scar me. In the meantime, I'd have to settle for working on technique. We showed up at The Plantation every weekend night, and after a while we talked the group into letting us bring our horns. We would scrunch down against the back wall of the bandstand and try to hit the vein with the needle as the quarter roared away, creating a very soft but discordant clarinet-and-trumpet duet under them which must have sounded like an untuned radio to anyone out front. Now and then Stoogie'd lean back in his chair and say, "Go watch Candy's hand," and we'd tiptoe across to peer over Candy's shoulder as his left hand graphed out the changes to the tune. Or he'd say, "Harmony!" telling us to play a series of whole notes with the changes. It never occurred to me then, but this suggestion often came before one of his solos, so not only would our harmony give him support, it also kept him from having to contend with a lot of gobbling going on behind his back. Sometimes during Scratchmo's or Candy's solos, he'd lean over and play a simple riff and nod his head to get us to pick up that line, then he'd break into another parallel to it and nod again for one of us to imitate the second, so that when he soloed, he'd have a rocking good chorus of two lines behind him.

But I hated clarinet. I'd begun on it in the fifth grade, used it during my brief Dixieland phase, and had endured the agonies of marching and concert band with it, but I'd resolved six months before meeting Stoogie that I had to have a sax, the axe my heroes played. My parents had agreed to provide a matching grant. I had saved my wages from working after school and on Saturdays delivering pianos, earning a well-deserved reputation as a cheapskate date, and once in a while Terry and I had played dances in schools around the area. The horn had been on order for a month after I had been going to the club, and I had driven the owner of the store nuts asking about it daily.

When it came, my alto was a brilliant gold hookah asleep in a red velvet pouf. A gen-yew-ine Selmer Mark VI, axe of the gods—*Downbeat* said so! With it I'd wail my way into Birdland with Kenton or Maynard or Art Blakey; I'd be on Ed Sullivan wailing away with my own Big Band and the girl who'd left me would eat her goddamn heart out! Move over, Sonny Rollins! Bite the dust, John Coltrane! A new star had risen!

When I fingered the keys, a soft *poomp* said they seated perfectly on their holes, the pristine leather pads the color of sand. The horn smelled of polish and oil and cork grease, and I gave it a good going over with beady eyes not so much to inspect it but to lay claim on it. I found a deep scratch in the lacquer under the low C key which wouldn't disappear when I rubbed it, so I decided to ignore it.

I was dying to show it off. But driving alone to the club—Terry had the flu—I began feeling as uneasy as I had felt excited. The worst player in town had a Selmer Mark VI, the best player had a Brand X nickel-plated monster. I kept assuring myself that I had worked like

hell to scrape up half the cost and tried to forget that my
parents had coughed up the other $200.

Looking it over, Stoogie didn't seem to begrudge my
owning it. He advised exchanging the "legitimate" mouthpiece which had come with the horn for something like
his Otto Link, which he slipped from his horn and se-
cured onto the bit of mine after I had invited him to try
it out. When he blew a few scales, I heard the Stoogie-
sound with a new perimeter—rounder, more solid, its
circumference laced with a fretwork of brass.

"Wow!" He shook his head. "Been a long time, man!"
He blew a few more licks, pleased at how his phrases
took to the air without much drag. "It's sure easy." He
played to low Bb and above high F for notes I didn't
know existed on the saxophone. "Man," he breathed,
"this is a nice axe."

"Go ahead and play it," I offered quickly when he
started to hand it back.

When the first set began, his solos contained new dimensions, but I was too lost in my skull to study them.
He was playing MY horn, and MY horn sounded fantastic! Great music was being made on my horn and that
gave me hope, as though his improvised lines would stick
to the lining of the horn to be unpeeled by my breath. As
they played on, I felt that after Stoogie had sort of primed
the horn like a handpump on a waterwell, all I had to do
was stick it in my mouth, take a breath, and—zoom—out
would come phrases as rich, juicy, and evocative as
Stoogie's! (No matter that in my bedroom I had gotten
nothing but squawks, even though the fingering was
similar to my clarinet's.) I got itchy to try it out.

But Stoogie wasn't in a hurry to turn it over. One tune
led to another; a half-hour went by, then an hour—
Stoogie's enjoyment spread to the others, and they
began playing into break-time with no desire at all
to quit.

What if he couldn't stop playing it? Refused to? On the dance floor, Friday night's drunks were whooping and hollering, and I looked too long at them—wow! I was the only white person there! Although a veil was actually descending over the scene, I could have sworn one was lifting, one composed of my delusion that we were all asshole buddies of the blue note. The hoisted veil revealed all these ... niggers rocking and jumping, and one named Curtis Goodman was going to steal my goddamned brand-new Selmer Mark VI! I just knew that when they finished the set and I asked for the horn, he'd give me a dumb, droopy-eyed look and say, *Huh? You shoah talkin' some trash, white boy!* I'd treat it like a joke and say, Aw shit, Stoogie! Come on, man, let me try it out! *Hey Scratchmo! Who the fuck's this white boy callin' me Stoogie and jivin' about my axe, huh?* And Scratchmo would guffaw, slap his knee, then turn his sinister gaze to within an inch of my face and say, *Hey, boy! You'd best scat before I cut you three ways—wide, deep and quite frequently!* God! How could I prove the horn was mine? That scratch under the C key?

Miserable, I missed what was probably Stoogie's finest work in years, to judge by how everyone carried on when they broke after the set.

"Whew! That's a fine, fine horn," Stoogie said when he handed it to me. "You better learn how to blow it." Humbled, I accepted the compliment to the horn and the proverbial boot from teacher to student with a nod. But when I took the horn and slipped the hook of the neckstrap through the holding hole, the horn hung from my neck like a gaudy brass albatross, so heavy I could hardly stand.

I begged off and slunk away. Driving home, I could feel my ears burning. How could I ever do justice to this horn that lay on the backseat of my parents' Ford like hot loot from a burglary? Only by practice could I earn the right to play it. And in return for those unofficial lessons I had taken for granted from Stoogie, I'd . . . save him. It wasn't fair that this black Paganini had to wash dishes at the Winslow Café. I'd talk the city fathers into making him an Honorary Mayor or an Artist in Residence! I'd find him a good gig where nobody would be allowed to request "San Antonio Rose" or "Anniversary Waltz." I'd get all the young musicians in town to chip in to buy him a Mark VI; I'd find a way to get the group on record. . . .

Every morning thereafter my horn reached my mouth when my feet hit the floor, much to my family's dismay. I bought an Otto Link. I got to school early enough to have a half-hour warmup before band, then I'd sneak away from study hall to the bandroom and remain there during lunch hour. I took the horn to work after school so that between deliveries I could play in the stockroom. After work, I'd play before supper, then until bedtime I blew scales, riffs I had learned from Stoogie, arpeggios from my Universal-Prescott book, improvisation exercises with my Music Minus One records, hot licks from my *Jimmy Dorsey One Hundred Hot Licks* book until, with a pair of chops hanging on my mouth like the limp fingers of rubber gloves, I'd put the horn up for the day.

At last I got to solo. A Saturday night and, as they used to say, the joint was jumping. The band had condescended to do "The Hucklebuck," and the air was charged with lascivious electricity as people buckled their buckles. R.B. started hammering out a stripper's beat with cymbal and bass drum crashes on 2 and 4; Stoogie, just returned from taking the elevator, was grinning so hard he could only play greasy honks. He looked back at us and jerked his head toward the mike: Get on up here, one of you!

Heart thudding, my hands suddenly slick and my armpits spewing out a deluge, I stumbled toward the mike while the quartet vamped changes. My brain whirled to map out my melodic strategy, trying to recall the notes in those three simple chords—going about soloing like building a gun rack from a plan in *Popular Mechanics*. I reached the mike, stuck the mouthpiece between my quivering jaws, blew an A in the upper register and held it. Somebody on the dance floor said, "Yeah!" Though I'm sure now it was in reply to something like "Ain't he awful?" which mercifully, I hadn't heard, I dreamed that my A was really turning them on; I thanked my lucky stars for finding it and hung onto it, pausing only for breath. Along about bar eleven, I saw that I couldn't get away with taking another chorus with that A—it was weird, if not monotonous, and Scratchmo would jibe me all night about my two-chorus whole note. Something stunning in contrast was called for, a Yin to the first chorus's Yang, and the solution came in a flash—if I played enough notes, I was bound to get some right ones in; people would hear those and pick out their own melodic line from the heap of assorted phrases I would toss onto the air like articles on a clearance table in a bargain basement. And if I played fast enough, the clinkers would pass undetected.

It's a blessing no one was cruel enough to have taped that second chorus; I believe I played through the entire Universal-Prescott book in those twelve bars. I left enough "melodies" tangled in the air that an academy of musicologists could have devoted a lifetime to unballing them and still couldn't see through the skein of noise above the bandstand. But I had lost my musical cherry; I could survive that stretch of sound-time, and though I was terrible, I knew I couldn't get worse.

We had come to know the players in a western swing band at a local honky tonk and found that they too were jazz buffs, though their axes wouldn't have suggested it. Gradually I was getting a picture—musicians were poor

outcasts given to fits of insanity; they had vices ranging
from perversions to narcotics to alcohol; they were—in a
word—outlaws. We tried to develop the Outlaw Outlook
as a means of shedding our old skins. We began to imagine that The Plantation was our club and that we were
inconspicuous there, though how we thought two white
children in sunglasses and berets could have gone unnoticed among two hundred blacks is a testament to our
innocence. At school, Terry and I went about laden with
props—cigarette holders a la Dizzy Gillespie, *Downbeat*
tucked under our arms. We jived along in a slouch, eyelids drooping, talking hiptalk, feeling more and more
alienated from our classmates' concern for ball games
and proms. We gave each other skin, we snapped our
fingers and sang complicated scat riffs in those syllables
the uninitiated find so strange. We quickly became in-
sufferable, and that only ossified our belief that we were
cool. I took to calling everyone, even my mother, "man."
These were years when moustaches adorned only the
upper lips of black pimps, Mexican revolutionaries, Italian
barbers, and jazz musicians, and we were the only two
persons in our school to sport them, save for Glenneta
Price. Mine was probably no thicker or darker than hers
and occasionally I had to sneak my mother's eyeliner to
give those fine brown hairs a blacking. Terry was also
working on a goatee, seven or eight hairs about two
inches long which stuck out from his chin and curled into
springs.

Part of the myth of Jazz Star required that we be out
of our skulls as much as possible, so during the spring
months we drank a good deal more than we really wanted
to. We downed innumerable cases of beer and fifths of
bourbon before settling down to the wine of the people,
Thunderbird. Once when Woody Herman played a one-
nighter in town, Terry and I each drank a quart of
Listerine—definitely not recommended!—and wound up

spraying the restroom with medicinal-smelling puke. How were we going to play jazz without paying any dues?

Inevitably we got more curious about Stoogie's dope. We saw it as a must for every Jazz Star's prop locker. Besides washing dishes and playing at The Plantation to keep his household—a Chicana and her four children—together, Stoogie also watered greens at the golf course on weeknights. He was growing his own stuff in a nearby pasture and was looking forward to a bountiful harvest come the fall. He worked out of a shed on a far boundary of the grounds, and sometimes we'd go out there, perch on fertilizer sacks, and listen to "Moonglow" on a portable radio while he made his rounds changing sprinklers. Stoogie had never offered us any of his homegrown. But neither had he forbidden it, so once when he was out on the course we smoked a joint. When he found us collapsed on the floor, giggling, he said, "You just best be sure when you walkin' on clouds you don't trip over the Man." Point made—we sobered some and ended up at the Sonic Dog ordering triple-decker banana splits, tripping on the lights, and smothering the sillies with sleeves pressed against our mouths. Just your ordinary goofy high-school high.

We had few delusions about the effect of cannabis on our playing; we had heard Stoogie play stoned and the only difference I could tell was that he preferred ballads because they gave him time to think, and occasionally we'd heard him unable to quit grinning. Naturally, we had to try it, and we badgered Stoogie into letting us take the elevator with him at the club. While my notes felt good when they entered the warm, furry hollows of my ears, I lost track of the court, the meter, the changes, and the number of choruses. The distinct possibility was that I sounded very, very bad, which Scratchmo confirmed when I finished a solo and asked him how many choruses I had played—thinking about three—and he snorted, "How many fleas on a coon dog's ass?"

But it did wonders for our self-esteem. We became walking Hip Happenings:

> A beatnik is standing on a streetcorner when all at once there's a terrific crash as a bus and a truck collide. In the aftermath, people are lying in the street wailing and moaning. A little old lady runs up to the beatnik: "You've got to do something, young man!" Beatnik, snapping his fingers: "I am, man—I'm humming the changes."

Not one of our peers understood that the beatnik was stoned. By August, as we got ready to attend the Berkeley School of Music, we had become unspeakably With It. One night Terry and I got stoned at his crib while we were digging some sides, and when I had to split, the mirror showed me two swollen orbs with a reddish wash against a yellow background. I'd walked over there and I'd have to walk home. Very cleverly, I decided to carry an empty beer can. As I floated home, I smirked—six months prior to this I would've been peeing my pants to think that the Man would catch me with illegal booze, and now here I was—practically a junkie no less!—using it as a decoy. Too much! Buoyant with self-discovery, I bopped along, humming the changes.

The crash came one night later. Caught red-handed (green-handed?) by two white patrolmen outside the back door of the club after the gig, Stoogie and I and Terry were whisked to the station and separated for questioning before we could gather our wits.

"That colored boy sell you those two sticks of marijuana?"

"No sir!"

Sgt. Cheney was seated behind the Chief's desk. He peeled off the wrapper on a Snicker and bit into it.

"How'd they come to be in your shirt pocket?"

"Nobody sold them to me, I swear!"

The Snicker disappeared like a square turd returning to its point of origin.

"Thadwuddenwhhusss."

"Sir?"

He crushed the wrapper into a ball and pleased himself by scoring in the trash can.

"That wasn't what I asked."

My noncommunication games were having a short shelf life. Though Sgt. Cheney had proved himself to be a boor over the previous twenty minutes, he knew a nonanswer when he heard one. But the primary rule of antiaircraft gunnery is to keep throwing flak until you hit.

"Well, sir, we'd never tried any and we were just curious about it, you know, so we only smoked a little bit and decided we didn't want any more of it, and I really didn't like it much to tell the truth, and I don't think I'd ever do it again." As I squirmed in the hard wooden chair, the beret wadded in my hip pocket pressed into my left ham. The instant we had been busted, I had slipped my sunglasses into my shirt pocket; I had lost my cigarette holder in the patrol car, and, props gone, I could feel an older self rising to the surface—the youth whose classmates had elected him City Manager for a Day; the Boy Scout of some distinction; the son of decent, tax-paying citizens and church members; the promising debater and the best civics student Miss Hall ever had. I kept blinking—man, this couldn't be happening! We had meant harm to none, our destinies as Jazz Stars had already been mapped out and the supplies laid by—it would be grossly injust to have all that interrupted for such a stupid reason as having two joints in my shirt pocket. But Sgt. Cheney's glare was very real, and I had visions of my brilliant career being cut short, my parents disgraced, my teachers despairing, and my unfaithful girl friend secretly exultant that she'd managed to avoid being tied down to a convict.

"Something wrong with your hearing, son?"

"No, sir."

"Then where'd you get the stuff?"

"Found it."

"Aw-huh." He nodded. "Where?"

"Uh . . . it was on the parking lot, you know, out at the Sonic Dog."

"Were you by yourself?"

Haw! I thought. No witnesses, no contradictions.

"Yes, sir."

He smiled. "Maybe they had little tags that said, 'Smoke Me, I'm a Marijuana Cigarette'?"

"Uh . . ." Did that require an answer? "No, sir."

"Then how'd you know what they were?"

"They just looked . . . funny, you know. Not like regular cigarettes. And they smelled like mari . . . smelled weird, you know? So we just guessed."

"We?"

I flushed. "I mean after I'd already showed it to them."

"Uh-huh. And I reckon you gave some to that colored boy because he wanted to try a little too."

I nodded.

Sgt. Cheney sighed, rose and paced about the room, then eased a haunch onto the desk. He gave me a benign and fatherly look. "Now, I can tell you aren't a dope addict. I can see how a couple kids out for a lark decided out of curiosity to try the stuff, you see? Maybe you didn't know you can get hooked and start craving the stuff."

I wagged my head to encourage this line of thought. Innocence was my best guise and my spotless record the evidence to give it credibility. He had already asked my name and address and whether I had been in trouble before, to which I had given truthful answers, and it looked as though the end might be in sight. I covered my mouth with my hand as though to massage the muscles in my cheeks and let my insides go lax. Apparently Sgt. Cheney was going to give me Monster Drug Lecture #17 and let me off with a warning, and I prepared to tune him out. The Chief appeared annually in an all-school assembly to peddle the same propaganda, though with what I'd have to admit was a dramatic flair—he'd hold a heap of grass in his open palm and say, "I want anybody who wants some of this to come right down here and I'll give it to them for nothing." Then he'd pull his pistol from his holster. "But he might as well take *this* too because he'll be needing something to put him out of his misery!"

"So you smoked a little marijuana—is that any reason to spend a lot of your young life in jail?" Sgt. Cheney was saying. "I know you don't think so. We ain't out to wreck any lives here. Boys will be boys, we know that."

My head was bobbing madly in agreement: Yessir, two tadpoles curious as coons, that's us, sir, no kidding!

"And you say you found it?"

"Yessir."

"At the Sonic Dog."

I nodded.

"Then why's that other boy say you got it in Juarez?"

Had Terry said that? What did Stoogie say? The accused's right to one phone call popped to mind, but not only would my parents learn where I was, it was a definite sign of non-cooperation, and I still hoped I'd be able to talk my way out of the station.

"Well, I didn't. He was just guessing."

"He said ya'll both got it there."

All I could do was shrug to suggest that life was full of peculiar circumstances that defied credulity.

He eased his haunch off the desk. "Son, you're starting to piss me off!" He pulled a key chain from his pocket and jangled the keys as he moved behind the desk. They made a steady *clink* like a stack of coins passed through the fingers. My mouth was dry; I swallowed with difficulty. Were those keys to the cells? I shivered. He wasn't buying my story.

"You come in here and start talking like a straight shooter, then you bullshit me when I'm trying my best to appreciate your situation—you think I'm dumb?"

"No, sir."

"I don't have to give you the benefit of the doubt. I can lock you up and charge you with possession right now, you understand? It don't make a damn if it fell out of the sky, you got it! For all I know, you been peddling the stuff—maybe you gave it to them, maybe you sold it!"

"Oh no, sir!"

"I don't have any use at all for a slimy creep that'd get other people hooked just to line his pockets! We can put you up for twenty years for dealing in it—you want that?"

"I swear I wasn't doing that!"

"How about finding it—you swear to that too?"

I hesitated. "Yes," I said finally, with less conviction.

He threw up his hands in exasperation. "Well, if you don't beat all!" He strode to the door and grabbed the knob. "You're not even trying to help me! I got the dope and I'm going to put somebody in jail for it! I'd sooner have it be the pusher you got it from, but if I can't find him, you're the next best thing, you see?"

I did. With an icy clarity. Every crime had to have a criminal. It kept the books neat. Naïvely, I had assumed that everybody would get off if I could convince Sgt. Cheney of our innocent intentions, but the full implications of my choice grew terribly apparent as I sat looking up at him while he waited for me to make up my mind, hand on the doorknob. It was hard for me to believe there wasn't an alternative to telling the truth. His glare of contempt chilled my spine; I couldn't meet his gaze.

"Well come on, son! You still claim you found it?" he

huffed. "You gonna sit there and tell me a white kid supplied a nigger musician with dope he'd never seen before?"

He kept staring at me. My jaw dropped a bit and my teeth parted as though I were about to speak, but what I'd say even I didn't know. My chin trembled; I shut my jaws and swallowed hard. I shivered again and let it stand as a shrug.

"Lord love a duck!" he spat and opened the door. "Bud?" he yelled down the hall. There was a distinct "Yeah?" then Cheney roared, "Come get this silly sumbitch out of my sight, will you? Lock him up!"

He left the door ajar and strode back to the desk, refusing to look at me. He yanked the top drawer open and tossed a pad and pencil into it, then straightened out the objects on the desktop: everything was final. Wait! God! What'd they want to know? That Terry and I had asked Stoogie for a few joints to tide us over for the long drive to Boston in a couple of days? That Stoogie had given it to us? But those facts were no more the truth than Marilyn Monroe's circulatory system was a sex symbol—they'd believe that Stoogie had passed out free samples to get us hooked. Stoogie was a poverty-stricken black musician who'd paid heavy dues and who could play alto in a way that could make your heart sing! He wasn't a dope peddler! Was he? How could I be sure enough that I'd gamble twenty years of my life on it?

Bud's footsteps had grown to monstrous explosions in the hallway. When it came time to sign on the bottom line, how could I lie? Wasn't that perjury? Didn't lies always get caught in the courtroom, even ones told with good intentions? And wouldn't I just be piling trouble on trouble to keep on lying? I started shaking violently. I didn't want to go to jail! God! All my dreams . . . Bud's shadow fell across me when he walked through the door, and I blurted out that I hadn't found the stuff.

Later, I waited on one of the wooden benches outside the doors to the Magistrate Courtroom. My father wasn't thrilled to be awakened in the middle of the night to be told his son had been experimenting with narcotics and was at the police station where he could be released to his custody without charges filed. I dreaded the ride home. But I was more relieved than anything else, and I could take his anger as easy payment for my guilt. I'd told them not only the facts, which they were happy to hear, but also the truth, which they weren't concerned about. They didn't care that I had *asked* Stoogie for the stuff, that he hadn't offered it. I kept insisting that we were *all* innocent in the sense that Stoogie and I and Terry were three musicians, friends, fellow craftsmen sharing a pursuit, engaged in making jazz, and there was nothing sinister in our smoking the joints any more than if "Bud" shared a beer with Sgt. Cheney in his living room. They agreed that I was at least naïve, if not innocent.

I hadn't told them about Stoogie's stash at the golf course, narrowing my confession to what happened earlier in the night. I didn't know that Terry had told the same story more or less; I didn't know that Stoogie had clammed up, that in time they'd run a check and discover his first offense jail term. I only knew I was off the hook; even if I had to come back for a hearing or a trial, I wouldn't go to jail—my age, my parents, and my white skin had spared me that. With our horns, our high-school diplomas, and our tuition fees, Terry and I could proceed as planned to become players of and at jazz, props and accouterments intact, while Stoogie would serve another sentence, this one longer than the first; he'd be stripped of everything he needed to play except the only thing they couldn't take from him, the thing they'd unintentionally given him—the suffering, the soul, the reason for the blues.

The beret in my pocket pressed like a fist into the

cheek of my ass. I pulled it out and absently brushed out
the wrinkles in the black felt and was about to put it on
my head when my arms failed me and I dropped it to the
bench. Directly across the hall the varnished courtroom
doors gave off a dull gleam. My eyes were drawn to the
ceiling light, then to the figure in bronze relief it illumi-
nated just above the doorway: it was the same image my
eyes had idly skimmed day after day on the textbook
cover of the civics course I had shown such promise
in—Lady Justice in her robe, her arm extended to hold
her scales, the platform leveled, weighing nothing, and
for the first time I could see that she was blindfolded.

MAYA ANGELOU

THE REUNION

NOBODY COULD HAVE TOLD me that she'd be out with a black man; out, like going out. But there she was, in 1958, sitting up in the Blue Palm Café, when I played the Sunday matinee with Cal Callen's band.

Here's how it was. After we got on the stage, the place was packed, first Cal led us into "D. B. Blues." Of course I know just like everybody else that Cal's got a thing for Lester Young. Maybe because Cal plays the tenor sax, or maybe because he's about as red as Lester Young, or maybe just cause Lester is the Prez. Anybody that's played with Cal knows that the kickoff tune is gotta be "D. B. Blues." So I was ready. We romped.

I'd played with some of those guys, but never all together, but we took off on that tune like we were headed for Birdland in New York City. The audience liked it. Applauded as much as black audiences ever applaud. Black folks act like they are sure that with a little bit of study they could do whatever you're doing on the stage as well as you do it. If not better. So they clap for your luck. Lucky for you that they're not up there to show you where it's really at.

Anyway, after the applause, Cal started to introduce the band. That's his style. Everybody knows that too. After he's through introducing everybody, he's not going to say anything else till the next set, it doesn't matter how many times we play. So he's got a little comedy worked into the introduction patter. He started with Olly, the trumpet man.... "And here we have a real Chicagoan ... by way of Atlanta, Georgia ... bringing soul to Soulville ... Mr. Olly Martin."

He went on. I looked out into the audience. People sitting, not listening, or better, listening with one side of their ears and talking with both sides of their mouths. Some couples were making a little love ... and some whites were there trying hard to act natural ... like they come to the South Side of Chicago every day or maybe like they live there ... then I saw her. Saw Miss Beth Ann Baker, sitting up with her blond self with a big black man ... pretty black man. What? White girls, when they look alike, can look so much alike, I thought maybe it wasn't Beth. I looked again. It was her. I remember too well the turn of her cheek. The sliding way her jaw goes up to her hair. That was her. I might have missed a few notes, I might have in fact missed the whole interlude music.

What was she doing in Chicago? On the South Side. And with a black man? Beth Ann Baker of the Baker Cotton Gin. Miss Cotton Queen Baker of Georgia ...

Then I heard Cal get round to me. He saved me for the last. Mainly cause I'm female and he can get a little rise out of the audience if he says, as he did say, "And our piano man is a lady. And what a lady. A cooker and a looker. Ladies and Gentlemen, I'd like to introduce to you Miss Philomena Jenkins. Folks call her Meanie." I noticed some applause, but mainly I was watching Beth. She heard my name and she looked right into my eyes. Her blue ones got as big as my black ones. She recognized me, in fact in a second we tipped eyelids at each other. Not winking. Just squinting, to see better. There was something that I couldn't recognize. Something I'd never seen in all those years in Baker, Georgia. Not panic, and it wasn't fear. Whatever was in that face seemed familiar, but before I could really read it, Cal announced our next number. "Round 'bout Midnight."

That used to be my song, for so many reasons. In Baker, the only time I could practice jazz, in the church, was round 'bout midnight. When the best chord changes came to me it was generally round 'bout midnight. When my first lover held me in his arms, it was round 'bout midnight. Usually when it's time to play that tune I dig right in it. But this time, I was too busy thinking about Beth and her family ... and what she was doing in Chicago, on the South Side, escorted by the grooviest looking cat I'd seen in a long time. I was really trying to figure it out, then Cal's saxophone pushed it's way into my figurings. Forced me to remember "Round 'bout Midnight." Reminded me of the years of loneliness, the doing-without days, the C.M.E. church, and the old ladies with hands like men and the round 'bout midnight dreams of crossing over Jordan. Then I took thirty-two bars. My fingers found the places between the keys where the blues and the truth lay hiding. I dug out the story of a woman without a man, and a man without hope. I tried to wedge myself in and lay down in the groove between B-flat and B-natural. I must of gotten close to it, because the audience brought me out with their clapping. Even Cal said, "Yeah baby, that's it." I nodded to him then to the audience and looked around for Beth.

How did she like them apples? What did she think of little Philomena that used to shake the farts out of her sheets, wash her dirty drawers, pick up after her slovenly mama? What did she think now? Did she know that I was still aching from the hurt Georgia put on me? But Beth was gone. So was her boyfriend.

I had lived with my parents until I was thirteen, in the

servants' quarters. A house behind the Baker main house. Daddy was the butler, my mother was the cook, and I went to a segregated school on the other side of town where the other kids called me the Baker Nigger. Momma's nimble fingers were never able to sew away the truth of Beth's hand-me-down and thrown away clothing. I had a lot to say to Beth, and she was gone.

That was a bring-down. I guess what I wanted was to rub her face in "See now, you thought all I would ever be was you and your mama's flunky." And "See now, how folks, even you, pay to listen to me" and "See now, I'm saying something nobody else can say. Not the way I say it, anyway." But her table was empty.

We did the rest of the set. Some of my favorite tunes, "Sophisticated Lady," "Misty," and "Cool Blues." I admit that I never got back into the groove until we did "When Your Lover Has Gone."

After the closing tune, "Lester Leaps In," which Cal set at a tempo like he was trying to catch the last train to Mobile, was over, the audience gave us their usual thank-you, and we were off for a twenty-minute intermission.

Some of the guys went out to turn on and a couple went to tables where they had ladies waiting for them. But I went to the back of the dark smoky bar where even the occasional sunlight from the front door made no difference. My blood was still fluttering in my fingertips, throbbing. If she was listed in the phone directory I would call her. Hello Miss Beth . . . this is Philomena . . . who was your maid, whose whole family worked for you. Or could I say, Hello Beth. Is this Beth? Well, this is Miss Jenkins. I saw you yesterday at the Blue Palm Café. I used to know your parents. In fact your mother said my mother was a gem, and my father was a treasure. I used to laugh 'cause your mother drank so much whiskey, but my Momma said, "Judge not, that ye be not judged." Then I found out that your father had three

children down in our part of town and they all looked
just like you, only prettier. Oh Beth, now ... now ...
shouldn't have a chip ... mustn't be bitter ... She of
course would hang up.

Just imagining what I would have said to her cheered
me up. I ordered a drink from the bartender and settled
back into my reverie.... Hello Beth ... this is a friend
from Baker. What were you doing with that black man
Sunday? ...

"Philomena? Remember me?" She stood before me ab-
sorbing the light. The drawl was still there. The soft
accent rich white girls practice in Georgia to show that
they had breeding. I couldn't think of anything to say.
Did I remember her? There was no way I could answer
the question.

"I asked Willard to wait for me in the car. I wanted to
talk to you."

I sipped my drink and looked in the mirror over the
bar and wondered what she really wanted. Her reflection
wasn't threatening at all.

"I told him that we grew up ... in the same town."

I was relieved that she hadn't said we grew up together. By the time I was ten, I knew growing up meant
going to work. She smiled and I held my drink.

"I'm engaged to Willard and very happy."

I'm proud of my face. It didn't jump up and walk the
bar.

She gave a practiced nod to the bartender and ordered
a drink. "He teaches high school here on the South Side."
Her drink came and she lifted the glass and our eyes met
in the mirror. "I met him two years ago in Canada. We
are very happy."

Why the hell was she telling me her fairy story? We
weren't kin. So she had a black man. Did she think like
most whites in mixed marriages that she had done the
whole race a favor?

"My parents ..." her voice became small, whispery.

"My parents don't understand. They think I'm with Willard just to spite them. They ... When's the last time you went home, Mena?" She didn't wait for my answer.

"They hate him. So much, they say they will disown me." Disbelief made her voice strong again. "They said I could never set foot in Baker again." She tried to catch my eyes in the mirror but I looked down at my drink. "I know there's a lot wrong with Baker, but it's my home." The drawl was turning into a whine. "Mother said, now mind you, she has never laid eyes on Willard, she said, if she had dreamed when I was a baby that I would grow up to marry a nig . . . a black man, she'd have choked me to death on her breast. That's a cruel thing for a mother to say. I told her so."

She bent forward and I shifted to see her expression, but her profile was hidden by the blond hair. "He doesn't understand, and me either. He didn't grow up in the South." I thought, no matter where he grew up, he wasn't white and rich and spoiled. "I just wanted to talk to somebody who knew me. Knew Baker. You know, a person can get lonely. . . . I don't see any of my friends, anymore. Do you understand, Mena? My parents gave me everything."

Well, they owned everything.

"Willard is the first thing I ever got for myself. And I'm not going to give him up."

We faced each other for the first time. She sounded like her mother and looked like a ten-year-old just before a tantrum.

"He's mine. He belongs to me."

The musicians were tuning up on the bandstand. I drained my glass and stood.

"Mena, I really enjoyed seeing you again, and talking about old times. I live in New York, but I come to Chicago every other weekend. Say, will you come to our wedding? We haven't set the date yet. Please come. It's going to be here . . . in a black church . . . somewhere."

"Good-bye Beth. Tell your parents I said go to hell and take you with them, just for company."

I sat down at the piano. She still had everything. Her mother would understand the stubbornness and send her off to Paris or the Moon. Her father couldn't deny that black skin was beautiful. She had money and a wonderful-looking man to play with. If she stopped wanting him she could always walk away. She'd still be white.

The band was halfway into the "D. B. Blues" release before I thought, she had the money, but I had the music. She and her parents had had the power to hurt me when I was young, but look, the stuff in me lifted me up high above them. No matter how bad times became, I would always be the song struggling to be heard.

The piano keys were slippery with tears. I know, I sure as hell wasn't crying for myself.

AL YOUNG

CHICKEN HAWK'S DREAM

CHICKEN HAWK STAYED HIGH pretty much all the time and he was nineteen years old limping down academic corridors trying to make it to twelfth grade.

Unlike his good sidekick Wine, whose big reason for putting up with school was to please his mother, Chicken Hawk just loved the public school system and all the advantages that came with it. He could go on boarding at home, didnt have to work, and could mess over a whole year and not feel he'd lost anything.

He sat behind me in Homeroom Study Hall, sport shirt, creased pants, shiny black pointy-toed stetsons, jacket, processed hair. He'd look around him on lean days and say, "Say, man, why dont you buy this joint off me so I can be straight for lunch, I'd really appreciate it."

One morning he showed up acting funnier than usual. Turns out he was half-smashed and half-drunk because he'd smoked some dope when he got up that morning, then on the way to school he'd met up with Wine, so the two of them did up a fifth of Nature Boy, a brand of sweet wine well known around Detroit. Wine wasnt called Wine for nothing. Between the Thunderbird and Nature

Boy he didnt know what to do with himself. He was a
jokey kind of lad who drank heavily as a matter of
form—his form. "I like to juice on general principle," is
the way he put it.

That morning Chicken Hawk eased up to me during a
class break. "Man, I had this dream, the grooviest dream
I had in a long time, you wanna know how it went?"

By that time I thought I could anticipate anything
Chicken Hawk would come up with, but for him to relate
a private dream was something else, something new.
"What you dream, man?"

"Dreamed I was walkin round New York, you know,
walkin round all the places where Bird walked and seen
all the shit he seen and all thru this dream I'm playin
the background music to my own dream, dig, and it's on
alto sax, man, and I'm cookin away somethin terrible
and what surprise me is I can do the fingerin and all that
jive—I can blow that horn, I know I can blow it in real
life, I *know* I can! You know somebody got a horn I can
borrow, I'll show everybody what I can do."

"Drew's got an alto and he live up the street from me.
Maybe you could get your chops together on his horn. It
dont belong to him tho, it's his brother's and Drew dont
hardly touch it, he too busy woodsheddin his drums. I'll
ask him if you can come over after school and play
some."

"Aw, baby, yeah, nice, that's beautiful, Al, that sure
would be beautiful if you could arrange all that. Think
maybe Drew'd lemme borrow it for a few days?"

"Well, I don't know about all that, you could ask him."

"Yeah, unh-hunh, know what tune I wanna blow first?
Listen to this . . ."—and he broke off into whistling
something off a very old LP.

Wellsir—Drew said OK, to bring Chicken Hawk on
over and we'd see what he could do. "But if you ask me
the dude aint nothin but another pot head with a lotta
nerve. On the other hand he might just sit up and shake
all of us up."

Six of us, mostly from band, went over to Drew's house after school to find out what Chicken Hawk could do with a saxophone. As we went stomping thru the snow, old Wine was passing the bottle—"Just a little taste, fellas, to brace ourself against the cold, dig it?"

Drew's mother, a gym teacher, took one look at us at the front door and said, "Now I know all you hoodlums is friendsa Drew's but you are not comin up in here trackin mud all over my nice rugs, so go on round the back way and wipe your feet before you go down in the basement, and I mean wipe em good!"

We got down there where Drew had his drums set up and Drew got out his brother's old horn. "Be careful with it, Chicken Hawk, it aint mine and Bruh gon need it when he get back from out the Service."

We all sat around to watch.

Chicken Hawk, tall, cool, took the horn and said, "Uh, show me how you hold this thing, just show me that, show me how you hold it and I'll do the rest."

"Show him how to hold it, Butter."

One of the reed players, a lightskin fellow named Butter, leaned over Chicken Hawk and showed him where to place his fingers on the keys. Chicken Hawk looked at Butter as tho he were insane. "Look here, gimme a little credit for knowin somethin about the thing will you, you aint got to treat me like I'm some little baby."

"Then go ahead and blow it, baby!"

"Damn, I shoulda turned on first, I'd do more better if I was high. Anybody got a joint they can lay on me?"

Everybody started getting mad and restless. Drew said, "Mister Chicken Hawk, sir, please blow somethin on the instrument and shut up!"

"Shit, you dudes dont think I can blow this thing but I mo show you."

"Then kindly show us."

Poor Chicken Hawk, he finally took a deep breath and huffed and puffed but not a sound could he make. "You sure this old raggedy horn work?"

"Dont worry about that, man," Drew told him, "just go head and play somethin. You know—*play?*"

Chicken Hawk slobbered all over the mouthpiece and blew on it and worked the keys until we could all hear them clicking but still no sound. He wiped his lips on his coat sleeve and called his boy Wine over. "Now, Wine, you see me playin on this thing, dont you?"

"Yes, I am quite aware of that, C.H."

"You see me scufflin with it and it still dont make a sound?"

"Yes, I aint heard anything, C.H., my man."

"Then, Wine, would you say—would you say just offhand that it could be that Drew's brother's horn aint no damn good?"

Old Wine looked around the room at each of us and rubbed his hands together and grinned. "Well, uh, now I'd say it's a possibility, but I dont know about that. Would you care for a little taste to loosen you up?"

Chicken Hawk screwed his face up, blew into the instrument and pumped keys until he turned colors but all that came out were some feeble little squeaks and pitiful honks. "Well, gentlemen," he announced, "I've had it with this axe. It dont work. It's too beat-up to work. It just aint no more good. I can blow it all right. O yeah—I could play music on it all right but how you expect me to get into anything on a jive horn?"

Drew took the saxophone and carefully packed it back inside its case. Wine passed Chicken Hawk the Nature Boy and we all started talking about something else. There were no jokes about what had just happened, no See-Now-What-I-Tell-You.

Drew got to showing us new things he'd worked out on drums for a Rock & Roll dance he'd be playing that weekend. He loved to think up new beats. After everyone got absorbed in what Drew was doing, Chicken Hawk and Wine, well-juiced, eased quietly up the back steps.

*   *   *

I saw Chicken Hawk on 12th Street in Detroit. He was out of his mind standing smack on the corner in the wind watching the light turn green, yellow, red, back to green, scratching his chin, and he smiled at me.

"Hey, Chicken Hawk!"

"Hey now, what's goin on?"

"You got it."

"And dont I know it, I'm takin off for New York next week."

"What you gon do in New York?"

"See if I can get me a band together and cut some albums and stuff."

"Well—well, that's great, man, I hope you make it. Keep pushin."

"Gotta go get my instrument out of the pawnshop first, mmmm—you know how it is."

"Yeah, well, all right, take care yourself, man."

DONALD BARTHELME

THE KING OF JAZZ

WELL I'M THE KING of jazz now, thought Hokie Mokie to himself as he oiled the slide on his trombone. Hasn't been a 'bone man been king of jazz for many years. But now that Spicy MacLammermoor, the old king, is dead, I guess I'm it. Maybe I better play a few notes out of this window here, to reassure myself.

"Wow!" said somebody standing on the sidewalk. "Did you hear that?"

"I did," said his companion.

"Can you distinguish our great homemade American jazz performers, each from the other?"

"Used to could."

"Then who was that playing?"

"Sounds like Hokie Mokie to me. Those few but perfectly selected notes have the real epiphanic glow."

"The what?"

"The real epiphanic glow, such as is obtained only by artists of the caliber of Hokie Mokie, who's from Pass Christian, Mississippi. He's the king of jazz, now that Spicy MacLammermoor is gone."

Hokie Mokie put his trombone in its trombone case

and went to a gig. At the gig everyone fell back before him, bowing.

"Hi Bucky! Hi Zoot! Hi Freddie! Hi George! Hi Thad! Hi Roy! Hi Dexter! Hi Jo! Hi Willie! Hi Greens!"

"What we gonna play, Hokie? You the king of jazz now, you gotta decide."

"How 'bout 'Smoke'?"

"Wow!" everybody said. "Did you hear that? Hokie Mokie can just knock a fella out, just the way he pronounces a word. What a intonation on that boy! God Almighty!"

"I don't want to play 'Smoke,' " somebody said.

"Would you repeat that, stranger?"

"I don't want to play 'Smoke.' 'Smoke' is dull. I don't like the changes. I refuse to play 'Smoke.' "

"He refuses to play 'Smoke'! But Hokie Mokie is the king of jazz and he says 'Smoke'!"

"Man, you from outa town or something? What do you mean you refuse to play 'Smoke'? How'd you get on this gig anyhow? Who hired you?"

"I am Hideo Yamaguchi, from Tokyo, Japan."

"Oh, you're one of those Japanese cats, eh?"

"Yes I'm the top trombone man in all of Japan."

"Well you're welcome here until we hear you play. Tell me, is the Tennessee Tea Room still the top jazz place in Tokyo?"

"No, the top jazz place in Tokyo is the Square Box now."

"That's nice. OK, now we gonna play 'Smoke' just like Hokie said. You ready, Hokie? OK, give you four for nothin'. One! Two! Three! Four!"

The two men who had been standing under Hokie's window had followed him into the club. Now they said:

"Good God!"

"Yes, that's Hokie's famous 'English sunrise' way of playing. Playing with lots of rays coming out of it, some red rays, some blue rays, some green rays, some green stemming from a violet center, some olive stemming from a tan center—"

"That young Japanese fellow is pretty good, too."

"Yes, he is pretty good. And he holds his horn in a peculiar way. That's frequently the mark of a superior player."

Bent over like that with his head between his knees—good God, he's sensational!"

He's sensational, Hokie thought. Maybe I ought to kill him.

But at that moment somebody came in the door pushing in front of him a four-and-one-half-octave marimba. Yes, it was Fat Man Jones, and he began to play even before he was fully in the door.

"What're we playing?"

" 'Billie's Bounce.' "

"That's what I thought it was. What're we in?"

"F."

"That's what I thought we were in. Didn't you use to play with Maynard?"

"Yeah I was on that band for a while until I was in the hospital."

"What for?"

"I was tired."

"What can we add to Hokie's fantastic playing?"

"How 'bout some rain or stars?"

"Maybe that's presumptuous?"

"Ask him if he'd mind."

"You ask him, I'm scared. You don't fool around with the king of jazz. That young Japanese guy's pretty good, too."

"He's sensational."

"You think he's playing in Japanese?"

"Well I don't think it's English."

This trombone's been makin' my neck green for thirty-five years, Hokie thought. How come I got to stand up to yet another challenge, this late in life?

"Well, Hideo—"

"Yes, Mr. Mokie?"

"You did well on both 'Smoke' and 'Billie's Bounce.' You're just about as good as me, I regret to say. In fact, I've decided you're *better* than me. It's a hideous thing to contemplate, but there it is. I have only been the king of jazz for twenty-four hours, but the unforgiving logic of this art demands we bow to Truth, when we hear it."

"Maybe you're mistaken?"

"No, I got ears. I'm not mistaken. Hideo Yamaguchi is the new king of jazz."

"You want to be king emeritus?"

"No, I'm just going to fold up my horn and steal away. This gig is yours, Hideo. You can pick the next tune."

"How 'about 'Cream'?"

"OK, you heard what Hideo said, it's 'Cream.' You ready, Hideo?"

"Hokie, you don't have to leave. You can play too. Just move a little over to the side there—"

"Thank you, Hideo, that's very gracious of you. I guess I will play a little, since I'm still here. Sotto voce, of course."

"Hideo is wonderful on 'Cream'!"

"Yes, I imagine it's his best tune."

"What's that sound coming in from the side there?"

"Which side?"

"The left."

"You mean that sound that sounds like the cutting edge of life? That sounds like polar bears crossing Arctic ice pans? That sounds like herd of musk ox in full flight? That sounds like male walruses diving to the bottom of the sea? That sounds like fumaroles smoking on the slopes of Mt. Katmai? That sounds like the wild turkey walking through the deep, soft forest? That sounds like beavers chewing trees in an Appalachian marsh? That sounds like an oyster fungus growing on an aspen trunk? That sounds like a mule deer wandering a montane of the Sierra Nevada? That sounds like prairie dogs kissing? That sounds like witchgrass tumbling or a river meandering? That sounds like manatees munching seaweed at Cape Sable? That sounds like coatimundis moving in packs across the face of Arkansas? That sounds like—"

"Good God, it's Hokie! Even with a cup mute on, he's blowing Hideo right off the stand!"

"Hideo's playing on his knees now! Good God, he's reaching into his belt for a large steel sword— Stop him!"

"Wow! That was the most exciting 'Cream' ever played! Is Hideo all right?"

"Yes, somebody is getting him a glass of water."

"You're my man, Hokie! That was the dadblangedest thing I ever saw!"

"You're the king of jazz once again!"

"Hokie Mokie is the most happening thing there is!"

"Yes, Mr. Hokie sir, I have to admit it, you blew me right off the stand. I see I have many years of work and study before me still."

"That's OK, son. Don't think a thing about it. It happens to the best of us. Or it almost happens to the best of us. Now I want everybody to have a good time because we're gonna play 'Flats.' 'Flats' is next."

"With your permission, sir, I will return to my hotel and pack. I am most grateful for everything I have learned here."

"That's OK, Hideo. Have a nice day. He-he. Now, 'Flats.' "

MEDLEY

I COULD TELL THE minute I got in the door and dropped my bag, I wasn't staying. Dishes piled sky-high in the sink looking like some circus act. Glasses all ghosty on the counter. Busted tea bags, curling canteloupe rinds, white cartons from the Chinamen, green sacks from the deli, and that damn dog creeping up on me for me to wrassle his head or kick him in the ribs one. No, I definitely wasn't staying. Couldn't even figure why I'd come. But picked my way to the hallway anyway till the laundry-stuffed pillowcases stopped me. Larry's bass blocking the view to the bedroom.

"That you, Sweet Pea?"

"No, man, ain't me at all," I say, working my way back to the suitcase and shoving that damn dog out of the way. "See ya round," I holler, the door slamming behind me, cutting off the words abrupt.

Quite naturally sitting cross-legged at the club, I embroider a little on the homecoming tale, what with an audience of two crazy women and a fresh bottle of Jack Daniels. Got so I could actually see shonuff toadstools

growing in the sink. Canteloupe seeds sprouting in the
muck. A goddamn compost heap breeding near the stove,
garbage gardens on the grill.

"Sweet Pea, you oughta hush, cause you can't possibly
keep on lying so," Pot Limit's screaming, tears popping
from her eyes. "Lawd hold my legs, cause this liar bout
to kill me off."

"Never mind about Larry's housekeeping, girl," Sylvia's soothing me, sloshing perfectly good bourbon all
over the table. "You can come and stay with me till your
house comes through. It'll be like old times at Aunt
Merriam's."

I ease back into the booth to wait for the next set. The
drummer's fooling with the equipment, tapping the mikes,
hoping he's watched, so I watch him. But feeling worried
in my mind about Larry, cause I've been through days
like that myself. Cold cream caked on my face from the
day before, hair matted, bathrobe funky, not a clean pair
of drawers to my name. Even the emergency ones, the
draggy cotton numbers stuffed way in the back of the
drawer under the scented paper gone. And no clean sil-
verware in the box and the last of the paper cups gone,
too. Icebox empty cept for a rock of cheese and the lone
water jug that ain't even half full that's how anyhow the
thing's gone on. And not a clue as to the next step. But
then Pot Limit'll come bamming on the door to say So-
and-so's in town and can she have the card table for a
game. Or Sylvia'll send a funny card inviting herself to
dinner and even giving me the menu. Then I zoom
through that house like a manic work brigade till me
and the place ready for white-glove inspection. But what
if somebody or other don't intervene for Larry, I'm
thinking.

The drummer's messin round on the cymbals, head
cocked to the side, rings sparkling. The other dudes are
stepping out from behind the curtain. The piano man
playing with the wah-wah doing splashy, breathy science

fiction stuff. Sylvia checking me out to make sure I ain't too blue. Blue got hold to me, but I lean forward out of the shadows and babble something about how off the bourbon tastes these days. Hate worryin Sylvia, who is the kind of friend who bleeds at the eyes with your pain. I drain my glass and hum along with the opening riff of the guitar and I keep my eyes strictly off the bass player, whoever he is.

Larry Landers looked more like a bass player than ole Mingus himself. Got these long arms that drape down over the bass like they were grown special for that purpose. Fine, strong hands with long fingers and muscular knuckles, the dimples deep black at the joints. His calluses so other-colored and hard, looked like Larry had swiped his grandmother's tarnished thimbles to play with. He'd move in on that bass like he was going to hump it or something, slide up behind it as he lifted it from the rug, all slinky. He'd become one with the wood. Head dipped down sideways bobbing out the rhythm, feet tapping, legs jiggling, he'd look good. Thing about it, though, ole Larry couldn't play for shit. Couldn't never find the right placement of the notes. Never plucking with enough strength, despite the perfectly capable hands. Either you didn't hear him at all or what you heard was off. The man couldn't play for nuthin is what I'm saying. But Larry Landers was baad in the shower, though.

He'd soap me up and down with them great, fine hands, doing a deep bass walking in the back of his mouth. And I'd just have to sing, though I can't sing to save my life. But we'd have one hellafyin musical time in the shower, lemme tell you. "Green Dolphin Street" never sounded like nuthin till Larry bopped out them changes and actually made me sound good. On "My Funny Valentine" he'd do a whizzing sounding bow thing that made his throat vibrate real sexy and I'd cutesy up the introduction, which is, come to think of it, my favorite part. But the main number when the hot water started running out was "I Feel Like Making Love." That was usually the wind up of our repertoire cause you can imagine what that song can do to you in the shower and all.

Got so we spent a helluva lotta time in the shower. Just as well, cause didn't nobody call Larry for gigs. He a nice man, considerate, generous, baad in the shower, and good taste in music. But he just wasn't nobody's bass player. Knew all the stances, though, the postures, the facial expressions, had the choreography down. And right in the middle of supper he'd get some Ron Carter thing going in his head and hop up from the table to go get the bass. Haul that sucker right in the kitchen and do a number in dumb show, all the playing in his throat, the acting with his hands. But that ain't nuthin. I mean that can't get it. I can impersonate Betty Carter if it comes to that. The arms crooked just so, the fingers popping, the body working, the cap and all, the teeth, authentic. But I got sense enough to know I ain't nobody's singer. Actually, I am a mother, though I'm only just now getting it together. And too, I'm an A-1 manicurist.

Me and my cousin Sinbad come North working our show in cathouses at first. Set up a salon right smack in the middle of Miz Maybry's Saturday traffic. But that wasn't no kind of life to be bringing my daughter into. So I parked her at a boarding school till I could make some other kind of life. Wasn't no kind of life for Sinbad either, so we quit.

Our first shop was a three-chair affair on Austin. Had a student barber who could do anything—blow-outs, do's, corn rows, weird cuts, afros, press and curl, whatever you wanted. Plus he din't gab you to death. And he always brought his sides and didn't blast em neither. He went on to New York and opened his own shop. Was a boot-black too then, an old dude named James Noughton, had a crooked back and worked at the post office at night, and knew everything about everything, read all the time.

"Whatcha want to know about Marcus Garvey, Sweet Pea?"

If it wasn't Garvey, it was the rackets or the trucking industry or the flora and fauna of Greenland or the planets or how the special effects in the disaster movies were done. One Saturday I asked him to tell me about the war, cause my nephew'd been drafted and it all seemed so wrong to me, our men over there in Nam fighting folks who fighting for the same things we are, to get that blood-sucker off our backs.

Well, what I say that for. Old dude gave us a deep knee bend, straight up eight-credit dissertation on World Wars I and II—the archduke getting offed, Africa cut up like so much cake, Churchill and his cigars, Gabriel Heatter on the radio, Hitler at the Olympics igging Owens, Red Cross doing Bloods dirty refusing donuts and bandages, A. Philip Randolph scaring the white folks to death, Mary McLeod Bethune at the White House, Liberty Bond drives, the Russian front, frostbite of the feet, the Jew stiffs, the gypsies no one mourned ... the whole johnson. Talked straight through the day, Miz Mary's fish dinner growing cold on the radiator, his one and only customer walking off with one dull shoe. Fell out exhausted, his shoe rag limp in his lap, one arm draped over the left foot platform, the other clutching his heart. Took Sinbad and our cousin Pepper to get the old man home. I stayed with him all night with the ice pack and a fifth of Old Crow. He liked to die.

After while trade picked up and with a better class of folk too. Then me and Sinbad moved to North and Gaylord and called the shop Chez Sinbad. No more winos stumbling in or deadbeats wasting my time talking raunchy shit. The paperboy, the numbers man, the dudes with classier hot stuff coming in on Tuesday mornings only. We did up the place nice. Light globes from a New Orleans whorehouse, Sinbad likes to lie. Brown-and-black-and-silver-striped wallpaper. Lots of mirrors and hanging plants. Them old barber chairs spruced up and called antiques and damn if someone didn't buy one off us for eight hundred, cracked me up.

I cut my schedule down to ten hours in the shop so I could do private sessions with the gamblers and other business men and women who don't like sitting around the shop even though it's comfy, specially my part. Got me a cigar showcase with a marble top for serving coffee in clear glass mugs with heatproof handles too. My ten hours in the shop are spent leisurely. And my twenty hours out are making me a mint. Takes dust to be a mother, don't you know.

It was a perfect schedule once Larry Landers came into my life. He part-timed at a record shop and bartended at Topp's on the days and nights I worked at the shops. That gave us most of Monday and Wednesdays to listen to sides and hit the clubs. Gave me Fridays all to myself to study in the library and wade through them college bulletins and get to the museum and generally chart out a routine for when Debbie and me are a team. Sundays I always drive to Delaware to see her, and Larry detours to D.C. to see his sons. My bankbook started telling me I was soon going to be a full-time mama again and a college girl to boot, if I can ever talk myself into doing a school thing again, old as I am.

Life with Larry was cool. Not just cause he wouldn't hear about me going halves on the bills. But cause he was an easy man to be easy with. He liked talking softly and listening to music. And he liked having folks over for dinner and cards. Larry a real nice man and I liked him a lot. And I liked his friend Hector, who lived in the back of the apartment. Ole moon-face Hector went to school with Larry years ago and is some kind of kin. And they once failed in the funeral business together and I guess those stories of them times kinda keep them friends.

The time they had to put Larry's brother away is their

best story, Hector's story really, since Larry got to play a little grief music round the edges. They decided to pass up a church service, since Bam was such a treacherous desperado wouldn't nobody want to preach over his body and wouldn't nobody want to come to hear no lies about the dearly departed untimely ripped or cut down or whatever. So Hector and Larry set up some kind of pop stand awning right at the gravesite, expecting close blood only. But seems the whole town turned out to make sure old evil, hell-raising Bam was truly dead. Dudes straight from the barber chair, the striped ponchos blowing like wings, fuzz and foam on they face and all, lumbering up the hill to the hole taking bets and talking shit, relating how Ole Crazy Bam had shot up the town, shot up the jail, shot up the hospital pursuing some bootlegger who'd come up one keg short of the order. Women from all around come to demand the lid be lifted so they could check for themselves and be sure that Bam was stone cold. No matter how I tried I couldn't think of nobody bad enough to think on when they told the story of the man I'd never met.

Larry and Hector so bent over laughing bout the funeral, I couldn't hardly put the events in proper sequence. But I could surely picture some neighbor lady calling on Larry and Bam's mama reporting how the whole town had turned out for the burying. And the mama snatching up the first black thing she could find to wrap around herself and make an appearance. No use passing up a scene like that. And Larry prancing round the kitchen being his mama. And I'm too stunned to laugh, not at somebody's mama, and somebody's brother dead. But him and Hector laughing to beat the band and I can't help myself.

Thing about it, though, the funeral business stories are Hector's stories and he's not what you'd call a good storyteller. He never gives you the names, so you got all these he's and she's floating around. And he don't believe in giving details, so you got to scramble to paint your own pictures. Toward the end of that particular tale of Bam, all I could picture was the townspeople driving a stake through the dead man's heart, then hurling that coffin into the hole right quick. There was also something in that story about the civil rights workers wanting to make a case cause a white cop had cut Bam down. But looked like Hector didn't have a hold to that part of the story, so I just don't know.

Stories are not Hector's long suit. But he's an absolute artist on windows. Ole Moon-face can wash some windows and make you cry about it too. Makes these smooth little turns out there on that little bitty sill just like he wasn't four stories up without a belt. I'd park myself at the breakfast counter and thread the new curtains on the rods while Hector mixed up the vinegar solution real chef-like. Wring out the rags just so, scrunch up the newspapers into soft wads that make you think of cat's paws. Hector was a cat himself out there on the sill, making these marvelous circles in the glass, rubbing the hardhead spots with a strip of steel wool he had pinned to his overalls.

Hector offered to do my car once. But I put a stop to that after that first time. My windshield so clear and sparkling felt like I was in an accident and heading over the hood, no glass there. But it was a pleasure to have coffee and watch Hector. After while, though, Larry started hinting that the apartment wasn't big enough for four. I agreed, thinking he meant Earl had to go. Come to find Larry meant Hector, which was a real drag. I love to be around people who do whatever it is they do with style and care.

Larry's dog's named Earl P. Jessup Bowers, if you can get ready for that. And I should mention straightaway that I do not like dogs one bit, which is why I was glad when Larry said somebody had to go. Cats are bad enough. Horses are a total drag. By the age of nine I was fed up with all that noble horse this and noble horse that. They got good PR, horses. But I really can't use em. Was a fire once when I was little and some dumb horse almost burnt my daddy up messin around, twisting, snorting, bouncing, rearing up, doing everything but comin on out the barn like even the chickens had sense enough to do. I told my daddy to let that horse's ass burn. Horses be as dumb as cows. Cows just don't have good press agents is all.

I used to like cows when I was real little and needed to hug me something bigger than a goldfish. But don't let it rain, the dumbbells'll fall right in a ditch and you break a plow and shout yourself hoarse trying to get them fools to come up out the ditch. Chipmunks I don't mind when I'm at the breakfast counter with my tea and they're on their side of the glass doing Disney things in the yard. Blue jays are law-and-order birds, thoroughly despicable. And there's one prize fool in my Aunt Merriam's yard I will one day surely kill. He tries to "whip whip whip-poorwill" like the Indians do in the Fort This or That movies when they're signaling to each other closing in on George Montgomery but don't never get around to wiping that sucker out. But dogs are one of my favorite hatreds. All the time woofing, bolting down their food, slopping water on the newly waxed linoleum, messin with you when you trying to read, chewin on the slippers.

Earl P. Jessup Bowers was an especial drag. But I could put up with Earl when Hector was around. Once Hector was gone and them windows got cloudy and gritty, I was through. Kicked that dog every chance I got. And after thinking what it meant, how the deal went down, place too small for four and it was Hector not Earl—I started moving up my calendar so I could get out of there. I ain't the kind of lady to press no ultimatum on no man. Like "Chose, me or the dog." That's unattractive. Kicking Hector out was too. An insult to me, once I got to thinking on it. Especially since I got one item on my agenda, making a home for me and my kid. So if anybody should've been given walking papers, should've been me.

Anyway. One day Moody comes waltzing into Chez Sinbad's and tips his hat. He glances at his nails and glances at me. And I figure here is my house in a green corduroy suit. Pot Limit had just read my cards and the jack of diamonds kept coming up on my resource side. Sylvia and me put our heads together and figure it got to be some gambler or hustler who wants his nails done. What other jacks do I know to make my fortune? I'm so positive about Moody, I whip out a postcard from the drawer where I keep the emeries and write my daughter to start packing.

"How much you make a day, Miss Lady?"

"Thursdays are always good for fifty," I lie.

He hands me fifty and glances over at Sinbad, who nods that it's cool. "I'd like my nails done at four-thirty. My place."

"Got a customer at that time, Mr. Moody, and I like to stay reliable. How about five-twenty?"

He smiles a slow smile and glances at Sinbad, who nods again, everything's cool. "Fine," he says. "And do you think you can manage a shave without cutting a person's throat?"

"Mr. Moody, I don't know you well enough to have just cause. And none of your friends have gotten to me yet with that particular proposition. Can't say what I'm prepared to do in the future, but for now I can surely shave you real careful-like."

Moody smiles again, then turns to Sinbad, who says it's cool and he'll give me the address. This look-nod dialogue burns my ass. That's like when you take a dude to lunch and pay the check and the waiter's standing there with *your* money in his paws asking *the dude* was everything all right and later for *you*. Shit. But I take down Moody's address and let the rest roll off me like so much steaming lava. I start packing up my little alligator case—buffer, batteries, clippers, emeries, massager, sifter, arrowroot and cornstarch, clear sealer, magnifying glass, and my own mixture of green and purple pigments.

"Five-twenty ain't five-twenty-one, is it, Miss Lady?"

"Not in my book," I say, swinging my appointment book around so he can see how full it is and how neatly the times are printed in. Course I always fill in phony names case some creep starts pressing me for a session.

For six Thursdays running and two Monday nights, I'm at Moody's bending over them nails with a miner's light strapped to my forehead, the magnifying glass in its stand, nicking just enough of the nails at the sides, tinting just enough with the color so he can mark them cards as he shuffles. Takes an hour to do it proper. Then I sift my talc concoction and brush his hands till they're smooth. Them cards move around so fast in his hands, he can actually tell me he's about to deal from the bottom in the next three moves and I miss it and I'm not new to this. I been a gambler's manicurist for more years than I care to mention. Ten times he'll cut and each time the same fifteen cards in the top cut and each time in exactly the same order. Incredible.

Now, I've known hands. My first husband, for instance. To see them hands work their show in the grandstands, at a circus, in a parade, the pari-mutuels—artistry in action. We met on the train. As a matter of fact, he was trying to burgle my bag. Some story to tell the grandchildren, hunh? I had to get him straight about robbing from folks. I don't play that. Ya gonna steal, hell, steal back some of them millions we got in escrow is my opinion. We spent three good years on the circuit. Then credit cards moved in. Then choke-and-grab muggers killed the whole tradition. He was reduced to a mere shell of his former self, as they say, and took to putting them hands on me. I try not to think on when things went sour. Try not to think about them big slapping hands, only of them working hands. Moody's working hands were something like that, but even better. So I'm impressed and he's impressed. And he pays me fifty and tips me fifty and shuts up when I shave him and keeps his hands off my lovely person.

I'm so excited counting up my bread, moving up the calendar, making impulsive calls to Delaware and the two of us squealing over the wire like a coupla fools, that what Larry got to say about all these goings-on just rolls off my back like so much molten lead.

"Well, who be up there while he got his head in your lap and you squeezing his goddamn blackheads?"

"I don't squeeze his goddamn blackheads, Larry, on account of he don't have no goddamn blackheads. I give him a shave, a steam, and an egg-white face mask. And when I'm through, his face is as smooth as his hands."

"I'll bet," Larry says. That makes me mad cause I expect some kind of respect for my work, which is better than just good.

"And he doesn't have his head in my lap. He's got a whole barbershop set up on his solarium."

"His what?" Larry squinting at me, raising the wooden spoon he stirring the spaghetti with, and I raise the knife I'm chopping the onions with. Thing about it, though, he don't laugh. It's funny as hell to me, but Larry got no sense of humor sometimes, which is too bad cause he's a lotta fun when he's laughing and joking.

"It's not a bedroom. He's got this screened-in sun porch where he raises African violets and—"

"Please, Sweet Pea. Why don't you quit? You think I'm dumb?"

"I'm serious. I'm serious and I'm mad cause I ain't got no reason to lie to you whatever was going on, Larry." He turns back to the pot and I continue working on the sauce and I'm pissed off cause this is silly. "He sits in the barber chair and I shave him and give him a manicure."

"What else you be giving him? A man don't be paying a good-looking woman to come to his house and all and don't—"

"Larry, if you had the dough and felt like it, wouldn't you pay Pot Limit to come read your cards? And couldn't you keep your hands to yourself and she a good-looking woman? And couldn't you see yourself paying Sylvia to come and cook for you and no funny stuff, and she's one of the best-looking women in town?"

Larry cooled out fast. My next shot was to bring up the fact that he was insulting my work. Do I go around saying the women who pass up Bill the bartender and come to him are after his joint? No, cause I respect the fact that Larry Landers mixes the best piña coladas this side of Barbados. And he's flashy with the blender and the glasses and the whole show. He's good and I respect that. But he cooled out so fast I didn't have to bring it up. I don't believe in overkill, besides I like to keep some things in reserve. He cooled out so fast I realized he wasn't really jealous. He was just going through one of them obligatory male numbers, all symbolic, no depth.

Like the time this dude came into the shop to talk some trash and Sinbad got his ass on his shoulders, talking about the dude showed no respect for him cause for all he knew I could be Sinbad's woman. And he arguing that since that ain't the case, what's the deal? I mean why get hot over what if if what if ain't. Men are crazy. Now there is Sinbad, my blood cousin who grew up right in the same house like a brother damn near, putting me through simple-ass changes like that. Who's got time for grand opera and comic strips, I'm trying to make a life for me and my kid. But men are like that. Gorillas, if you know what I mean.

Like at Topp's sometimes. I'll drop in to have a drink with Larry when he's on the bar and then I leave. And maybe some dude'll take it in his head to walk me to the car. That's cool. I lay it out right quick that me and Larry are a we and then we take it from there, just two people gassing in the summer breeze and that's just fine. But don't let some other dude holler over something like "Hey, man, can you handle all that? Why don't you step aside, junior, and let a man . . ." and blah-de-da-de-dah. They can be the best of friends or total strangers just kidding around, but right away they two gorillas pounding on their chest, pounding on their chest and talking over my head, yelling over the tops of cars just like I'm not a person with some say-so in the matter. It's a man-to-man ritual that ain't got nothing to do with me. So I just get in my car and take off and leave them to get it on if they've a mind to. They got it.

But if one of the gorillas is a relative, or a friend of mine, or a nice kinda man I got in mind for one of my friends, I will stick around long enough to shout em down and point out that they are some ugly gorillas and are showing no respect for me and therefore owe me an apology. But if they don't fit into one of them categories, I figure it ain't my place to try to develop them so they can make the leap from gorilla to human. If their own mamas and daddies didn't care whether they turned out to be amoebas or catfish or whatever, it ain't my weight. I got my own weight. I'm a mother. So they got it.

Like I use to tell my daughter's daddy, the key to getting along and living with other folks is to keep clear whose weight is whose. His drinking, for instance, was not my weight. And him waking me up in the night for them long, rambling, ninety-proof monologues bout how the whole world's made up of victims, rescuers, and executioners and I'm the dirty bitch cause I ain't rescuing him fast enough to suit him. Then got so I was the executioner, to hear him tell it. I don't say nuthin cause my philosophy of life and death is this—I'll go when the wagon comes, but I ain't going out behind somebody else's shit. I arranged my priorities long ago when I jumped into my woman stride. Some things I'll go off on. Some things I'll hold my silence and wait it out. Some things I just bump off, cause the best solution to some problems is to just abandon them.

But I struggled with Mac, Debbie's daddy. Talked to his family, his church, AA, hid the bottles, threatened the liquor man, left a good job to play nurse, mistress, kitten, buddy. But then he stopped calling me Dahlin and started calling me Mama. I don't play that. I'm my daughter's mama. So I split. Did my best to sweeten them last few months, but I'd been leaving for a long time.

The silliest thing about all of Larry's grumblings back then was Moody had no eyes for me and vice versa. I just like the money. And I like watching him mess around with the cards. He's exquisite, dazzling, stunning shuffling, cutting, marking, dealing from the bottom, the middle, the near top. I ain't never seen nothing like it, and I seen a whole lot. The thing that made me mad, though, and made me know Larry Landers wasn't ready to deal with no woman full grown was the way he kept bringing it up, always talking about what he figured was on Moody's mind, like what's on my mind don't count. So I finally did have to use up my reserves and point out to Larry that he was insulting my work and that I would never dream of accusing him of not being a good bartender, of just being another pretty face, like they say.

"You can't tell me he don't have eyes," he kept saying.

"What about my eyes? Don't my eyes count?" I gave it up after a coupla tries. All I know is, Moody wasn't even thinking about me. I was impressed with his work and needed the trade and vice versa.

One time, for instance, I was doing his hands on the solarium and thought I saw a glint of metal up under his jacket. I rearranged myself in the chair so I could work my elbow in there to see if he was carrying heat. I thought I was being cool about it.

"How about keeping your tits on your side of the table, Miss Lady."

I would rather he think anything but that. I would rather he think I was clumsy in my work even. "Wasn't about tits, Moody. I was just trying to see if you had a holster on and was too lazy to ask."

"Would have expected you to. You a straight-up, di-rect kind of person." He opened his jacket away with the heel of his hand, being careful with his nails. I liked that.

"It's not about you," he said quietly, jerking his chin in the direction of the revolver. "Had to transport some money today and forgot to take it off. Sorry."

I gave myself two demerits. One for the tits, the other for setting up a situation where he wound up telling me something about his comings and goings. I'm too old to be making mistakes like that. So I apologized. Then gave myself two stars. He had a good opinion of me and my work. I did an extra-fine job on his hands that day.

Then the house happened. I had been reading the rental ads and For Sale columns for months and looking at some awful, tacky places. Then one Monday me and Sylvia lucked up on this cute little white-brick job up on a hill away from the street. Lots of light and enough room and not too much yard to kill me off. I paid my money down and rushed them papers through. Got back to Larry's place all excited and found him with his mouth all poked out.

Half grumbling, half proposing, he hinted around that we all should live at his place like a family. Only he didn't quite lay it out plain in case of rejection. And I'll tell you something, I wouldn't want to be no man. Must be hard on the heart always having to get out there, setting yourself up to be possibly shot down, approaching the lady, calling, the invitation, the rap. I don't think I could handle it myself unless everybody was just straight up at all times from day one till the end. I didn't answer Larry's nonproposed proposal cause it didn't come clear to me till after dinner. So I just let my silence carry whatever meaning it will. Ain't nuthin too much changed from the first day he came to get me from my Aunt Merriam's place. My agenda is still to make a home for my girl. Marriage just ain't one of the things on my mind no more, not after two. Got no regrets or bad feelings about them husbands neither. Like the poem says, when you're handed a lemon, make lemonade, honey, make lemonade. That's Gwen Brook's motto, that's mine too. You get a lemon, well, just make lemonade.

"Going on the road next week," Moody announces one day through the steam towel. "Like you to travel with me, keep my hands in shape. Keep the women off my neck. Check the dudes at my back. Ain't asking you to carry heat or money or put yourself in no danger. But I could use your help." He pauses and I ease my buns into the chair, staring at the steam curling from the towel.

"Wicked schedule though—Mobile, Birmingham, Sarasota Springs, Jacksonville, then Puerto Rico and back. Can pay you two thousand and expenses. You're good, Miss Lady. You're good and you got good sense. And while I don't believe in nothing but my skill and chance, I gotta say you've brought me luck. You a lucky lady, Miss Lady."

He raises his hands and cracks his knuckles and it's like the talking towel has eyes as well cause damn if he ain't checking his cuticles.

"I'll call you later, Moody," I manage to say, mind reeling. With two thousand I can get my stuff out of storage, and buy Debbie a real nice bedroom set, pay tuition at the college too and start my three-credit-at-a-time grind.

Course I never dreamed the week would be so unnerv-

ing, exhausting, constantly on my feet, serving drinks,
woofing sisters, trying to distract dudes, keeping track of
fifty-leven umpteen goings on. Did have to carry the heat
on three occasions and had to do helluva lotta driving.
Plus was most of the time holed up in the hotel room
close to the phone. I had pictured myself lazying on the
beach in Florida dreaming up cruises around the world
with two matching steamer trunks with the drawers and
hangers and stuff. I'd pictured traipsing through the
casinos in Puerto Rico ordering chicken salad and coffee
liqueur and tipping the croupiers with blue chips. Shit
no. Was work. And I sure as hell learned how Moody got
his name. Got so we didn't even speak, but I kept those
hands in shape and his face smooth and placid. And
whether he won, lost, broke even, or got wiped out, I don't
even know. He gave me my money and took off for New
Orleans. That trip liked to kill me.

"You never did say nothing interesting about Moody,"
Pot Limit says insinuatingly, swinging her legs in from
the aisle cause ain't nobody there to snatch so she might
as well sit comfortable.

"Yeah, she thought she'd put us off the trail with a
rip-roaring tale about Larry's housekeeping."

They slapping five and hunching each other and making a whole lotta noise, spilling Jack Daniels on my
turquoise T-straps from Puerto Rico.

"Come on, fess up, Sweet Pea," they crooning. "Did you
give him some?"

"Ahhh, yawl bitches are tiresome, you know that?"

"Naaw, naaw," say Sylvia, grabbing my arm. "You can
tell us. We wantta know all about the trip, specially the
nights." She winks at Pot Limit.

"Tell us about this Moody man and his wonderful hands
one more time, cept we want to hear how the hands feeel
on the flesh, honey." Pot Limit doing a bump and grind

in the chair that almost makes me join in the fun, except I'm worried in my mind about Larry Landers.

Just then the piano player comes by and leans over Sylvia, blowing in her ear. And me and Pot Limit mimic the confectionary goings-on. And just as well, cause there's nothin to tell about Moody. It wasn't a movie after all. And in real life the good-looking gambler's got cards on his mind. Just like I got my child on my mind. Onliest thing to say about the trip is I'm five pounds lighter, not a shade darker, but two thousand closer toward my goal.

"Ease up," Sylvia says, interrupting the piano player to fuss over me. Then the drummer comes by and eases in on Pot Limit. And I ease back into the shadows of the booth to think Larry over.

I'm staring at the entrance half expecting Larry to come into Topps, but it's not his night. Then, too, the thing is ended if I'd only know it. Larry the kind of man you're either living with him or you're out. I for one would've liked us to continue, me and Debbie in our place, him and Earl at his. But he got so grumpy the time I said that, I sure wasn't gonna bring it up again. Got grumpy in the shower, too, got so he didn't want to wash my back.

But that last night fore I left for Birmingham, we had us one crazy musical time in the shower. I kept trying to lure him into "Maiden Voyage," which I really can't do without back-up, cause I can't sing all them changes. After while he come out from behind his sulk and did a Jon Lucien combination on vocal and bass, alternating the sections, eight bars of singing words, eight bars of singing bass. It was baad. Then he insisted on doing "I Love You More Today Than Yesterday." And we like to break our arches, stomping out the beat against the shower mat.

The bathroom was all steamy and we had the curtains open so we could see the plants and and watch the candles burning. I had bought us a big fat cake of sandal-

wood soap and it was matching them candles scent for
scent. Must've been two o'clock in the morning and looked
like the hot water would last forever and ever and ever.
Larry finally let go of the love songs, which were making
me feel kinda funny cause I thought it was understood
that I was splitting, just like he'd always made it clear
either I was there or nowhere.

Then we hit on a tune I don't even know the name of
cept I like to scat and do my thing Larry calls Swahili
wailing. He laid down the most intricate weaving, walking, bopping, strutting bottom to my singing I ever heard.
It inspired me. Took that melody and went right on out
that shower, them candles bout used up, the fatty soap
long since abandoned in the dish, our bodies barely visible in the steamed-up mirrors walling his bathroom.
Took that melody right on out the room and out of doors
and somewhere out this world. Larry changing instruments fast as I'm changing moods, colors. Took an alto
solo and gave me a rest, worked an intro up on the piano
playing the chords across my back, drove me all up into
the high register while he weaved in and out around my
head on a flute sounding like them chilly pipes of the
Andes. And I was Yma Sumac for one minute there, up
there breathing some rare air and losing my mind, I was
so high on just sheer music. Music and water, the health-
iest things in the world. And that hot water pounding
like it was part of the group with a union card and all.
And I could tell that if that bass could've fit in the tub,
Larry would've dragged that bad boy in there and played
the hell out of them soggy strings once and for all.

I dipped way down and reached way back for snatches
of Jelly Roll Morton's "Deep Creek Blues" and Larry so
painful, so stinging on the bass, could make you cry.
Then I'm racing fast through Bessie and all the other
Smith singers, Mildred Bailey, Billie and imitators, Betty
Roche, Nat King Cole vintage 46, a little Joe Carroll,
King Pleasure, some Babs. Found myself pulling lines

out of songs I don't even like, but ransacked songs just for the meaningful lines or two cause I realized we were doing more than just making music together, and it had to be said just how things stood.

Then I was off again and lost Larry somewhere down there doing scales, sound like. And he went back to that first supporting line that had drove me up into the Andes. And he stayed there waiting for me to return and do some more Swahili wailing. But I was elsewhere and liked it out there and ignored the fact that he was aiming for a wind-up of "I Love You More Today Than Yesterday." I sang myself out till all I could ever have left in life was "Brown Baby" to sing to my little girl. Larry stayed on the ground with the same supporting line, and the hot water started getting funny and I knew my time was up. So I came crashing down, jarring the song out of shape, diving back into the melody line and somehow, not even knowing what song each other was doing, we finished up together just as the water turned cold.

LEROI JONES

THE SCREAMERS

LYNN HOPE ADJUSTS HIS turban under the swishing red
green yellow shadow lights. Dots. Suede heaven raining,
windows yawning cool summer air, and his musicians
watch him grinning, quietly, or high with wine blotches
on four-dollar shirts. A yellow girl will not dance with
me, nor will Teddy's people, in line to the left of the
stage, readying their *Routines*. Haroldeen, the most beautiful, in her pitiful dead sweater. Make it yellow, wish it
whole. Lights. Teddy, Sonny Boy, Kenny & Calvin, Scram,
a few of Nat's boys jamming long washed handkerchiefs
in breast pockets, pushing shirts into homemade cum-
merbunds, shuffling lightly for any audience.

"The Cross-Over,"
Deen laughing at us all. And they perform in solemn
unison a social tract of love. (With no music till Lynn
finishes "macking" with any biglipped Esther screws across
the stage. White and green plaid jackets his men wear,
and that twisted badge, black turban/on red string conked
hair. (OPPRESSORS!) A greasy hip-ness, down-ness, nobody in our camp believed (having social-worker mothers
and postman fathers; or living squeezed in lightskinned

projects with adulterers and proud skinny ladies with soft voices). The theory, the spectrum, this sound baked inside their heads, and still rub sweaty against those lesser lights. Those niggers. Laundromat workers, beauticians, pregnant short-haired jail bait separated all ways from "us," but in this vat we sweated gladly for each other. And rubbed. And Lynn could be a common hero, from whatever side we saw him. Knowing that energy, and its response. That drained silence we had to make with our hands, leaving actual love to Nat or Al or Scram.

He stomped his foot, and waved one hand. The other hung loosely on his horn. And their turbans wove in among those shadows. Lynn's tighter, neater, and bright gorgeous yellow stuck with a green stone. Also, those green sparkling cubes dancing off his pinkies. A-boomp bahba bahba, A-boomp bahba bahba, A-boomp bahba bahba, A-boomp bahba bahba, the turbans sway behind him. And he grins before he lifts the horn, at Deen or drunk Becky, and we search the dark for girls.

Who would I get? (Not anyone who would understand this.) Some light girl who had fallen into bad times and ill-repute for dating Bubbles. And he fixed her later with his child, now she walks Orange St. wiping chocolate from its face. A disgraced white girl who learned to calypso in vocational school. Hence, behind halting speech, a humanity as paltry as her cotton dress. (And the big hats made a line behind her, stroking their elections, hoping for photographs to take down south.) Lynn would oblige. He would make the most perverted hopes sensual and possible. Chanting at that dark crowd. Or some girl, a wino's daughter, with carefully vaselined bow legs would drape her filthy angora against the cardboard corinthian, eyeing past any greediness a white man knows, my soft tyrolean hat, pressed corduroy suit, and "B" sweater. Whatever they meant, finally, to her, valuable shadows barely visible.

Some stuck-up boy with "good" hair. And as a naked display of America, for I meant to her that same oppression. A stunted head of greased glass feathers, orange lips, brown pasted edge to the collar of her dying blouse. The secret perfume of poverty and ignorant desire. Arrogant too, at my disorder, which calls her smile mysterious. Turning to be eaten by the crowd. That mingled foliage of sweat and shadows: "Night Train" was what they swayed to. And smelled each other in The Grind, The Rub, The Slow Drag. From side to side, slow or jerked staccato as their wedding dictated. Big hats bent tight skirts, and some light girls' hair swept the resin on the floor. Respectable ladies put stiff arms on your waist to keep some light between, looking nervously at an ugly friend forever at the music's edge.

I wanted girls like Erselle, whose father sang on television, but my hair was not straight enough, and my father never learned how to drink. Our house sat lonely and large on a half-Italian street, filled with important Negroes. (Though it is rumored they had a son, thin with big eyes, they killed because he was crazy.) Surrounded by the haughty daughters of depressed economic groups. They plotted in their projects for mediocrity, and the neighborhood smelled of their despair. And only the wild or the very poor thrived in Graham's or could be roused by Lynn's histories and rhythms. America had choked the rest, who could sit still for hours under popular songs, or be readied for citizenship by slightly bohemian social workers. They rivaled pure emotion with wind-up record players that pumped Jo Stafford into Home Economics rooms. And these carefully scrubbed children of my parents' friends fattened on their rhythms until they could join the Urban League or Household Finance and hound the poor for their honesty.

I was too quiet to become a murderer, and too used to extravagance for their skinny lyrics. They mentioned neither cocaine nor Bach, which was my reading, and the flaw of that society. I disappeared into the slums, and fell in love with violence, and invented for myself a mysterious economy of need. Hence, I shambled anonymously thru Lloyd's, The Nitecap, The Hi-Spot, and Graham's desiring everything I felt. In a new English overcoat and green hat, scouring that town for my peers. And they were old pinch-faced whores full of snuff and weak dope, celebrity fags with radio programs, mute bass players who loved me, and built the myth of my intelligence. You see, I left America on the first fast boat.

This was Sunday night, and the Baptists were still praying in their "fabulous" churches. Though my father sat listening to the radio, or reading pulp cowboy magazines, which I take in part to be the truest legacy of my spirit. God never had a chance. And I would be walking slowly toward The Graham, not even knowing how to smoke. Willing for any experience, any image, any further separation from where my good grades were sure to lead. Frightened of post offices, lawyer's offices, doctor's cars, the deaths of clean politicians. Or of the imaginary fat man, advertising cemeteries to his "good colored friends." Lynn's screams erased them all, and I thought myself intrepid white commando from the West. Plunged into noise and flesh, and their form become an ethic.

Now Lynn wheeled and hunched himself for another tune. Fast dancers fanned themselves. Couples who practiced during the week talked over their steps. Deen and her dancing clubs readied *avant-garde* routines. Now it was "Harlem Nocturne," which I whistled loudly one Saturday in a laundromat, and the girl who stuffed in my khakis and stiff underwear asked was I a musician. I met her at Graham's that night and we waved, and I suppose she knew I loved her.

"Nocturne" was slow and heavy and the serious dancers loosened their ties. The slowly twisting lights made specks of human shadows, the darkness seemed to float around the hall. Any meat you clung to was yours those few minutes without interruption. The length of the music was the only form. And the idea was to press against each other hard, to rub, to shove the hips tight, and gasp at whatever passion. Professionals wore jocks against embarrassment. Amateurs, like myself, after the music stopped, put our hands quickly into our pockets, and retreated into the shadows. It was as meaningful as anything else we knew.

All extremes were popular with that crowd. The singers shouted, the musicians stomped and howled. The dancers ground each other past passion or moved so fast it blurred intelligence. We hated the popular song, and any freedman could tell you if you asked that white people danced jerkily, and were slower than our champions. One style, which developed as Italians showed up with pegs, and our own grace moved toward bellbottom pants to further complicate the cipher, was the honk. The repeated rhythmic figure, a screamed riff, pushed in its insistence past music. It was hatred and frustration, secrecy and despair. It spurted out of the diphthong culture, and reinforced the black cults of emotion. There was no compromise, no dreary sophistication, only the elegance of something that is too ugly to be described, and is diluted only at the agent's peril. All the saxophonists of that world were honkers, Illinois, Gator, Big Jay, Jug, the great sounds of our day. Ethnic historians, actors, priests of the unconscious. That stance spread like fire thru the cabarets and joints of the black cities, so that the sound itself became a basis for thought, and the innovators searched for uglier modes. Illinois would leap and twist his head, scream when he wasn't playing. Gator would strut up and down the stage, dancing for emphasis, shaking his long gassed hair in his face and coolly mopping it back. Jug, the beautiful horn, would wave back and forth so high we all envied him his connection, or he'd stomp softly to the edge of the stage whispering those raucous threats. Jay first turned the mark around, opened the way further for the completely nihilistic act. McNeeley, the first Dada coon of the age, jumped and stomped and yowled and finally sensed the only other space that form allowed. He fell first on his knees, never releasing the horn, and walked that way across the stage. We hunched together drowning any sound, relying on Jay's contorted face for evidence that there was still music, though none of us needed it now. And then he fell backwards, flat on his back, with both feet stuck up high in the air, and he kicked and thrashed and the horn spat enraged sociologies.

That was the night Hip Charlie, the Baxter Terrace Romeo, got wasted right in front of the place. Snake and four friends mashed him up and left him for the ofays to identify. Also the night I had the gray bells and sat in the Chinese restaurant all night to show them off. Jay had set a social form for the poor, just as Bird and Dizzy proposed it for the middle class. On his back screaming was the Mona Lisa with the mustache, as crude and simple. Jo Stafford could not do it. Bird took the language, and we woke up one Saturday whispering *Ornithology*. Blank verse.

And Newark always had a bad reputation, I mean, everybody could pop their fingers. Was hip. Had walks. Knew all about The Apple. So I suppose when the word got to Lynn what Big Jay had done, he knew all the little down cats were waiting to see him in this town. He knew he had to cook. And he blasted all night, crawled and leaped, then stood at the side of the stand, and watched us while he fixed his sky, wiped his face. Watched us to see how far he'd gone, but he was tired and we weren't, which was not where it was. The girls rocked slowly against the silence of the horns, and big hats pushed each other or made plans for murder. We had not completely come. All sufficiently eaten by Jay's memory, "on his back, kicking his feet in the air, Go-ud Damn!" So he moved cautiously to the edge of the stage, and the gritty Muslims he played with gathered close. It was some mean honking blues, and he made no attempt to hide his intentions. He was breaking bad. "Okay, baby," we all thought. "Go for yourself." I was standing at the back of the hall with one arm behind my back, so the overcoat could hang over in that casual gesture of fashion. Lynn was moving, and the camel walkers were moving in the corners. The fast dancers and practicers making the whole hall dangerous. "Off my suedes, motherfucker." Lynn was trying to move us, and even I did the one step I knew, safe at the back of the hall. The hippies ran for girls. Ugly girls danced with each other. Skippy, who ran the lights, made them move faster in that circle on the ceiling, and darkness raced around the hall. Then Lynn got his riff, that rhythmic figure we knew he would repeat, the honked note that would be his personal evaluation of the world. And he screamed it so the veins in his face stood out like neon. "Uhh, yeh, Uhh, yeh, Uhh, yeh," we all screamed to push him further. So he opened his eyes for a second, and really made his move. He looked over his shoulder at the other turbans, then marched in time with his riff, on his toes across the stage. They followed; he marched across to the other side, repeated, then finally he descended, still screaming, into the crowd, and as the sidemen followed, we made a path for them around the hall. They were strutting, and all their horns held very high, and they were only playing that one scary note. They moved near the back of the hall, chanting and swaying, and passed right in front of me. I had a little cup full of wine a murderer friend of mine made me drink, so I drank it and tossed the cup in the air, then fell in line behind the last wild horn man, strutting like the rest of them. Bubbles and Rogie followed me, and four-eyed Moselle Boyd. And we strutted back and forth pumping our arms, repeating with Lynn Hope, "Yeh, Uhh, Yeh, Uhh." Then everybody fell in behind us, yelling still. There was confusion and stumbling, but there were no real fights. The thing they wanted was right there and easily accessible. No one could stop you from getting in that line. "It's too crowded. It's too many people on the line!" some people yelled. So Lynn thought further, and made to destroy the ghetto. We went out into the lobby and in perfect rhythm down the marble steps. Some musicians laughed, but Lynn and some others kept the note, till the others fell back in. Five or six hundred hopped-up woogies tumbled out into Belmont Avenue. Lynn marched right in the center of the street. Sunday night traffic stopped, and honked. Big Red yelled at a bus driver, "Hey, baby, honk that horn in time or shut it off!" The bus driver cooled it. We screamed and screamed at the clear image of ourselves as we should always be. Ecstatic, completed, involved in a secret communal expression. It would be the form of the sweetest revolution, to hucklebuck into the fallen capital, and let the oppressors lindy hop out. We marched all the way to Spruce, weaving among the stalled cars, laughing at the dazed white men who sat behind the wheels. Then Lynn turned and we strutted back toward the hall. The late show at the National was turning out, and all the big hats there jumped right in our line.

Then the Nabs came, and with them, the fire engines. What was it, a labor riot? Anarchists? A nigger strike? The paddy wagons and cruisers pulled in from both sides, and sticks and billies started flying, heavy streams of water splattering the marchers up and down the street. America's responsible immigrants were doing her light work again. The knives came out, the razors, all the Biggers who would not be bent, counterattacked or came up behind the civil servants smashing at them with coke bottles and aerials. Belmont writhed under the dead economy and splivs floated in the gutters, disappearing under cars. But for a while, before the war had reached its peak, Lynn and his musicians, a few other fools, and I, still marched, screaming thru the maddened crowd. Onto the sidewalk, into the lobby, halfway up the stairs, then we all broke our different ways, to save whatever it was each of us thought we loved.

JULIO CORTÁZAR

THE PURSUER

In memoriam Ch. P.

Be thou faithful unto death
APOCALYPSE 2:10

O make me a mask
DYLAN THOMAS

DÉDÉE HAD CALLED ME in the afternoon saying that Johnny wasn't very well, and I'd gone to the hotel right away. Johnny and Dédée have been living in a hotel in the rue Lagrange for a few days now, they have a room on the fourth floor. All I have to do is see the door to the room to realize that Johnny's in worse shape than usual; the window opens onto an almost black courtyard, and at one in the afternoon you have to keep the light on if you want to read the newspaper or see someone else's face. It's not that cold out, but I found Johnny wrapped up in a blanket, and squeezed into a raunchy chair that's shedding yellowed hunks of old burlap all over the place. Dédée's gotten older, and the red dress doesn't suit her at

all: it's a dress for working under spotlights; in that
hotel room it turns into a repulsive kind of coagulation.

"Faithful old buddy Bruno, regular as bad breath,"
Johnny said by way of hello, bringing his knees up until
his chin was resting on them. Dédée reached me a chair
and I pulled out a pack of Gauloises. I'd brought a bottle
of rum too, had it in the overcoat pocket, but I didn't
want to bring it out until I had some idea of how things
were going. I think the lightbulb was the worst irritation, its eye pulled out and hanging suspended from a
long cord dirtied by flies. After looking at it once or
twice, and putting my hand up to shade my eyes, I asked
Dédée if we couldn't put out the damned light and wouldn't
the light from the window be okay. Johnny followed my
words and gestures with a large, distracted attention,
like a cat who is looking fixedly, but you know it's something else completely; that it is something else. Finally
Dédée got up and turned off the light. Under what was
left, some mishmosh of black and gray, we recognized
one another better. Johnny had pulled one of his big
hands out from under the blanket and I felt the limber
warmth of his skin. Then Dédée said she'd make us some
Nescafé. I was happy to know that at least they had a tin
of Nescafé. I always know, whatever the score is, when
somebody has a can of Nescafé it's not fatal yet; they can
still hold out.

"We haven't seen one another for a while," I said to
Johnny. "It's been a month at least."

"You got nothin' to do but tell time," he answered. He
was in a bad mood. "The first, the two, the three, the
twenty-one. You, you put a number on everything. An'
that's cool. You wanna know why she's sore? 'Cause I
lost the horn. She's right, after all."

"Lost it, but how could you lose it?" I asked, realizing
at the same moment that that was just what you couldn't
ask Johnny.

"In the metro," Johnny said. "I shoved it under the

seat so it'd be safe. It was great to ride that way, know-ing I had it good and safe down there between my legs."

"He finally missed it when he was coming up the stairs in the hotel," Dédée said, her voice a little hoarse. "And I had to go running out like a nut to report it to the metro lost-and-found and to the police." By the silence that followed I figured out that it'd been a waste of time. But Johnny began to laugh like his old self, a deep laugh back of the lips and teeth.

"Some poor devil's probably trying to get some sound out of it," he said. "It was one of the worst horns I ever had; you know that Doc Rodriguez played it? Blew all the soul out of it. As an instrument, it wasn't awful, but Rodriguez could ruin a Stradivarius just by tuning it."

"And you can't get ahold of another?"

"That's what we're trying to find out," Dédée said. "It might be Rory Friend has one. The awful thing is that Johnny's contract . . ."

"The contract," Johnny mimicked. "What's this with the contract? I gotta play and that's it, and I haven't got a horn or any bread to buy one with, and the boys are in the same shape I am."

This last was not the truth, and the three of us knew it. Nobody would risk lending Johnny an instrument, because he lost it or ruined it right off. He lost Louis Rolling's sax in Bordeaux, the sax Dédée bought him when he had that contract for a tour in England he broke into three pieces, whacking it against a wall and tram-pling on it. Nobody knew how many instruments had already been lost, pawned, or smashed up. And on all of them he played like I imagine only a god can play an alto sax, given that they quit using lyres and flutes.

"When do you start, Johnny?"

"I dunno. Today, I think, huh, De?"

"No, day after tomorrow."

"Everybody knows the dates except me," Johnny grum-bled, covering himself up to the ears in his blanket.

"I'd've sworn it was tonight, and this afternoon we had to go in to rehearse."

"It amounts to the same thing," Dédée said. "The thing is that you haven't got a horn."

"What do you mean, the same thing? It isn't the same thing. Day after tomorrow is the day after tomorrow, and tomorrow is much later than today. And today is later than right now, because here we are yakking with our old buddy Bruno, and I'd feel a lot better if I could forget about time and have something hot to drink."

"I'll boil some water, hold on for a little."

"I was not referring to boiling water," Johnny said. So I pulled out the bottle of rum, and it was as though we'd turned the light on; Johnny opened his mouth wide, astonished, and his teeth shone, until even Dédée had to smile at seeing him, so surprised and happy. Rum and Nescafé isn't really terrible, and all three of us felt a lot better after the second swallow and a cigarette. Then I noticed that Johnny was withdrawing little by little and kept on referring to time, a subject which is a preoccupation of his ever since I've known him. I've seen very few men as occupied as he is with everything having to do with time. It's a mania of his, the worst of his manias, of which he has plenty. But he explains and develops it with a charm hard to resist. I remember a rehearsal before a recording session in Cincinnati, long before he came to Paris, in forty-nine or fifty. Johnny was in great shape in those days and I'd gone to the rehearsal just to talk to him and also to Miles Davis. Everybody wanted to play, they were happy, and well-dressed (this occurs to me maybe by contrast with how Johnny goes around now, dirty and messed up), they were playing for the pleasure of it, without the slightest impatience, and the sound technician was making happy signs from behind his glass window, like a satisfied baboon. And just at that moment when Johnny was like gone in his joy, suddenly he stopped playing and threw a punch at I don't know who and said, "I'm playing this tomorrow," and the boys stopped short, two or three of them went on for a few measures, like a train slowly coming to a halt, and Johnny was hitting himself in the forehead and repeating, "I already played this tomorrow, it's horrible, Miles, I already played this tomorrow," and they couldn't get him out of that, and everything was lousy from then on, Johnny was playing without any spirit and wanted to leave (to shoot up again, the sound technician said, mad as hell), and when I saw him go out, reeling and his face like ashes, I wondered how much longer that business could go on.

"I think I'll call Dr. Bernard," Dédée said, looking at Johnny out of the corner of her eye, he was taking his rum in small sips. "You've got a fever and you're not eating anything."

"Dr. Bernard is a sad-assed idiot," Johnny said, licking his glass. "He's going to give me aspirin and then he'll tell me how very much he digs jazz, for example Ray Noble. Got the idea, Bruno? If I had the horn I'd give him some music that'd send him back down the four flights with his ass bumping on every step."

"It won't do you any harm to take some aspirin in any case," I said, looking out of the corner of my eye at Dédée. "If you want, I'll telephone when I leave so Dédée won't have to go down. But look, this contract . . . If you have to start day after tomorrow, I think something can be done. Also I can try to get a sax from Rory Friend. And at worst . . . The whole thing is you have to take it easier, Johnny."

"Not today," Johnny said, looking at the rum bottle. "Tomorrow, when I have the horn. So don't you talk about that now. Bruno, every time I notice that time . . . I think the music always helps me understand this business a little better. Well, not understand, because the truth of the matter is, I don't understand anything. The only thing I do is notice that there is something. Like those dreams, I'm not sure, where you begin to figure that everything is going to smash up now, and you're a little afraid just to be ready for it; but at the same time nothing's certain, and maybe it'll flip over like a pancake and all of a sudden, there you are, sleeping with a beautiful chick and everything's cool."

Dédée's washing the cups and glasses in one corner of the room. I noticed they don't even have running water in the place; I see a stand with pink flowers, and a washbasin which makes me think of an embalmed animal. And Johnny goes on talking with his mouth half stopped up by the bottle, and he looks stuffed too, with his knees up under his chin and his black smooth face which the rum and the fever are beginning to sweat up a little.

"I read some things about all that, Bruno. It's weird, and really awful complicated . . . I think the music helps, you know. Not to understand, because the truth is I don't understand anything." He knocks on his head with a closed fist. His head sounds like a coconut.

"Got nothing inside here, Bruno, what they call, nothing. It doesn't think and don't understand nothing. I've never missed it, tell you the truth. I begin to understand from the eyes down, and the lower it goes the better I understand. But that's not really understanding, oh, I'm with you there."

"You're going to get your fever up," Dédée muttered from the back of the place.

"Oh, shut up. It's true, Bruno. I never thought of nothing, only all at once I realize what I thought of, but that's not funny, right? How's it funny to realize that you've thought of something? Because it's all the same thing whether you think, or someone else. I am not I, me. I just use what I think, but always afterwards, and that's what I can't stand. Oh it's hard, it's so hard . . . Not even a slug left?"

I'd poured him the last drops of rum just as Dédée

came back to turn on the light; you could hardly see in the place. Johnny's sweating, but keeps wrapped up in the blanket, and from time to time he starts shaking and the chair legs chatter on the floor.

"I remember when I was just a kid, almost as soon as I'd learned to play sax. There was always a helluva fight going on at home, and all they ever talked about was debts and mortgages. You know what a mortgage is? It must be something terrible, because the old lady blew her wig every time the old man mentioned mortgage, and they'd end up in a fistfight. I was thirteen then . . . but you already heard all that."

Damned right I'd heard it; and damned right I'd tried to write it well and truly in my biography of Johnny.

"Because of the way things were at home, time never stopped, dig? From one fistfight to the next, almost not stopping for meals. And to top it all off, religion, aw, you can't imagine. When the boss got me a sax, you'd have laughed yourself to death if you'd seen it, then I think I noticed the thing right off. Music got me out of time, but that's only a way of putting it. If you want to know what I think, really, I believe that music put me *into* time. But then you have to believe that this time had nothing to do with . . . well, with us, as they say."

For some time now I've recognized Johnny's hallucinations, all those that constitute his own life, I listen to him attentively, but without bothering too much about what he's saying. On the other hand, I was wondering where he'd made a connection in Paris. I'd have to ask Dédée, ignoring her possible complicity. Johnny isn't going to be able to stand this much longer. Heroin and poverty just don't get along very well together. I'm thinking of the music being lost, the dozens of sides Johnny would be able to cut, leaving that presence, that astonishing step forward where he had it over any other musician. "I'm playing that tomorrow" suddenly fills me with a very clear sense of it, because Johnny is always blowing tomorrow, and the rest of them are chasing his tail, in this today he just jumps over, effortlessly, with the first notes of his music.

I'm sensitive enough a jazz critic when it comes to understanding my limitations, and I realize that what I'm thinking is on a lower level than where poor Johnny is trying to move forward with his decapitated sentences, his sighs, his impatient angers and his tears. He gives a damn where I think everything ought to go easy, and he's never come on smug that his music is much farther out than his contemporaries are playing. It drags me to think that he's at the beginning of his sax-work, and I'm going along and have to stick it out to the end. He's the mouth and I'm the ear, so as not to say that he's the mouth and I'm the ... Every critic, yeah, is the sad-assed end of something that starts as taste, like the pleasure of biting into something and chewing on it. And the mouth moves again, relishing it, Johnny's big tongue sucks back a little string of saliva from the lips. The hands make a little picture in the air.

"Bruno, maybe someday you'll write ... Not for me, dig, what the hell does it matter to me. But it has to be beautiful, I feel it's gotta be beautiful. I was telling you how when I was a kid learning to play, I noticed that time changed. I told that to Jim once and he said that everybody in the world feels the same way and when he gets lost in it ... He said that, when somebody gets lost in it ... Hell no, I don't get lost when I'm playing. Only the place changes. It's like in an elevator, you're in an elevator talking with people, you don't feel anything strange, meanwhile you've passed the first floor, the tenth, the twenty-first, and the city's down there below you, and you're finishing the sentence you began when you stepped into it, and between the first words and the last ones, there're fifty-two floors. I realized that when I started to play I was stepping into an elevator, but the elevator was time, if I can put it that way. Now realize that I haven't forgotten the mortgage or the religion. Like it's the mortgage and the religion are a suit I'm not wearing at the moment; I know that the suit's in the closet, but at that moment you can't tell me that that suit exists. The suit exists when I put it on, and the mortgage and religion existed when I got finished playing and the old lady came in with her hair, dangling big hunks of hair all over me and complaining I'm busting her ears with that goddamned music."

Dédée had brought another cup of Nescafé, but Johnny was looking with misery at his empty glass.

"This time business is complicated, it grabs me. I'm beginning to notice, little by little, that time is not like a bag that keeps filling up. What I mean is, even though the contents change, in the bag there's never more than a certain amount, and that's it. You see my suitcase, Bruno? It holds two suits and two pairs of shoes. Now, imagine that you empty it, okay? And afterwards you're going to put back the two suits and the two pairs of shoes, and then you realize that only one suit and one pair of shoes fit in there. But that's not the best of it. The best is when you realize you can put a whole store full of suits and shoes in there, in that suitcase, hundreds and hundreds of suits, like I get into the music when I'm blowing sometimes. Music, and what I'm thinking about when I ride the metro."

"When you ride the metro."

"Oh yeah, that, now there's the thing," Johnny said, getting crafty. "The metro is a great invention, Bruno. Riding the metro you notice everything that might end up in the suitcase. Maybe I didn't lose the horn in the metro, maybe . . ."

He breaks into laughter, coughs, and Dédée looks at him uneasily. But he's making gestures, laughing and coughing at the same time, shivering away under the blanket like a chimpanzee. His eyes are running and he's drinking the tears, laughing the whole time.

"Don't confuse the two things," he says after a spell. "I lost it and that's it. But the metro was helpful, it made me notice the suitcase bit. Look, this bit of things being elastic is very weird, I feel it everyplace I go. It's all elastic, baby. Things that look solid have an elasticity . . ."

He's thinking, concentrating.

". . . a sort of delayed stretch," he concludes surprisingly. I make a gesture of admiring approval. Bravo, Johnny. The man who claims he's not capable of thinking. Wow. And now I'm really interested in what he's going to say, and he notices that and looks at me more cunning than ever.

"You think I'll be able to come by another horn so I can play day after tomorrow, Bruno?"

"Sure, but you'll have to take care of it."

"Sure, I'll have to take care of it."

"A month's contract," explains poor Dédée. "Two weeks in Rémy's club, two concerts, and the record dates. We could clean up."

"A month's contract," Johnny imitates her with broad gestures. "Rémy's club, two concerts, and the record dates. Be-bata-bop bop bop, chrrr. What I got is a thirst, a thirst, a thirst. And I feel like smoking, like smoking. More'n anything else, I feel like a smoke."

I offer him my pack of Gauloises, though I know perfectly well that he's thinking of pot. It's already dark out, people are beginning to come and go in the hallway, conversations in Arabic, singing. Dédée's left, probably to buy something to eat for that night. I feel Johnny's hand on my knee.

"She's a good chick, you know? But I've had enough. It's some time now I'm not in love with her, and I can't stand her. She still excites me, she knows how to make love like . . ." he brought his forefinger and middle finger together, Italian-fashion. "But I gotta split, go back to New York. Everything else aside, I gotta get back to New York, Bruno."

"What for? There you were worse off than you are here. I'm not talking about work but about your own life. Here, it looks like you have more friends."

"Sure, there's you, and the marquesa, and the guys at the club . . . Did you ever make love with the marquesa, Bruno?"

"No."

"Well, it's something that . . . But I was talking about the metro, and I don't know, how did we change the subject? The metro is a great invention, Bruno. One day I began to feel something in the metro, then I forgot . . . Then it happened again, two or three days later. And finally I realized. It's easy to explain, you dig, but it's easy because it's not the right answer. The right answer simply can't be explained. You have to take the metro and wait until it happens to you, though it seems to me that that only would happen to me. It's a little like that, see. But honestly, you never made love with the marquesa? You have to ask her to get up on that gilt footstool that she has in the corner of her bedroom, next to that pretty lamp and then . . . Oh shit, she's back already."

Dédée comes in with a package and looks at Johnny.

"Your fever's higher. I telephoned the doctor already, he's going to come at ten. He says you should stay quiet."

"Okay, okay, but first I'm going to tell Bruno about the subway. The other day I noticed what was happening. I started to think about my old lady, then about Lan and the guys, an' whup, it was me walking through my old neighborhood again, and I saw the kids' faces, the ones from then. It wasn't thinking, it seems to me I told you a lot of times, I never think; I'm like standing on a corner watching what I think go by, but I'm not thinking what I see. You dig? Jim says that we're all the same, that in general (as they say) one doesn't think on his own. Let's say that's so, the thing is I'd took the metro at Saint-Michel, and right away I began to think about Lan and the guys, and to see the old neighborhood. I'd hardly sat down and I began to think about them. But at the same time I realized that I was in the metro, and I saw that in a minute or two we had got to Odéon, and that people were getting on and off. Then I went on thinking about Lan, and I saw my old lady when she was coming back from doing the shopping, and I began to see them all around, to be with them in a very beautiful way, I hadn't felt that way in a long time. Memories are always a drag, but this time I liked thinking about the guys and seeing them. If I start telling you everything I saw you're not going to believe it because I would take a long time doing it. And that would be if I economized on details. For example, just to tell you one thing, I saw Lan in a green suit that she wore when she came to Club 33 where I was playing with Hamp. I was seeing the suit with some ribbons, a loop, a sort of trim down the side and a collar ... Not at the same time, though, really, I was walking around Lan's suit and looking at it pretty slow. Then I looked at Lan's face and at the boy's faces, and then I remembered Mike who lived in the next room, and how Mike had told me a story about some wild horses in Colorado, once he worked on a ranch, and talked about the balls it took for cowboys to break wild horses ..."

"Johnny," Dédée said from her far corner.

"Now figure I've told you only a little piece of everything that I was thinking and seeing. How much'll that take, what I'm telling you, this little piece?"

"I don't know, let's say about two minutes?"

"Let's say about two minutes," Johnny mimicked. "Two minutes and I've told you just a little bitty piece, no more. If I were to tell you everything I saw the boys doing, and how Hamp played "Save It Pretty Mama," and listened to every note, you dig, every note, and Hamp's not one of them who gets tired, if I told you I heard an endless harangue of my old lady's, she was saying something about cabbages, if I remember, she was asking pardon for my old man and for me, and was saying something about some heads of cabbage ... Okay, if I told you all that in detail, that'd take more than two minutes, huh, Bruno?"

"If you really heard and saw all that, it'd take a good quarter-hour," I said, laughing to myself.

"It'd take a good quarter-hour, huh, Bruno. Then tell me how it can be that I feel suddenly the metro stop and I come away from my old lady and Lan and all that, and I see that we're at Saint-Germain-des-Prés, which is just a minute and a half from Odéon."

I never pay too much attention to the things Johnny says, but now, with his way of staring at me, I felt cold.

"Hardly a minute and a half in your time, in her time," Johnny said nastily. "And also the metro's time and my watch's, damn them both. Then how could I have been thinking a quarter of an hour, huh, Bruno? How can you think a quarter of an hour in a minute and a half? That day I swear I hadn't smoked even a roach, not a crumb," he finished like a boy excusing himself. "And then it happened to me again, now it's beginning to happen to me everyplace. But," he added astutely, "I can only notice in the metro, because to ride the metro is like being put in a clock. The stations are minutes, dig, it's that time of yours, now's time; but I know there's another, and I've been thinking, thinking ..."

He covers his face with his hands and shakes. I wish I'd gone already, and I don't know how to get out now without Johnny resenting it, he's terribly touchy with his friends. If he goes on this way he's going to make a mess of himself, at least with Dédée he's not going to talk about things like that.

"Bruno, if I could only live all the time like in those moments, or like when I'm playing and the time changes then too ... Now you know what can happen in a minute and a half ... Then a man, not just me but her and you and all the boys, they could live a thousand times faster than we're living because of the damned clocks, that mania for minutes and for the day after tomorrow . . ."

I smile the best I can, understanding fuzzily that he's right, but what he suspects and the hunch I have about what he suspects is going to be deleted as soon as I'm in the street and've gotten back into my everyday life. At that moment I'm sure that what Johnny's saying doesn't just come from his being half-crazy, that he's escaping from reality; I'm sure that, in the exchange, what he thinks leaves him with a kind of parody which he changes into a hope. Everything Johnny says to me at such moments (and it's been five years now Johnny's been saying things like this to me and to people) you can't just listen and promise yourself to think about it later. You hardly get down into the street, the memory of it barely exists and no Johnny repeating the words, everything turns into a potdream, a monotonous gesticulating (because there're others who say things like that, every minute you hear similar testimony) and after the wonder of it's gone you get an irritation, and for me at least it feels as though Johnny's been pulling my leg. But this always happens the next day, not when Johnny's talking to me about it, because then I feel that there's something that I'd like to admit at some point, a light that's looking to be lit, or better yet, as though it were necessary to break something, split it from top to bottom like a log, setting a wedge in and hammering it until the job's done. And Johnny hasn't got the strength to hammer anything in, and me, I don't know where the hammer is to tap in the wedge, which I can't imagine either.

So finally I left the place, but before I left one of those things that have to happen happened—if not that, then something else—and it was when I was saying goodbye to Dédée and had my back turned to Johnny that I felt something was happening, I saw it in Dédée's eyes and swung around quickly (because maybe I'm a little afraid of Johnny, this angel who's like my brother, this brother

who's like my angel) and I saw Johnny had thrown off
the blanket around him in one motion, and I saw him
sitting in the easy-chair completely nude, his legs pulled
up and the knees underneath his chin, shivering but
laughing to himself, naked from top to bottom in that
grimy chair.

"It's beginning to get warm," Johnny said. "Bruno,
look what a pretty scar I got between my ribs."

"Cover yourself," Dédée ordered him, embarrassed and
not knowing what to say. We know one another well
enough and a naked man is a naked man, that's all, but
anyway Dédée was scandalized and I didn't know how to
not give the impression that what Johnny was doing had
shocked me. And he knew it and laughed uproariously,
mouth wide open, obscenely keeping his legs up so that
his prick hung down over the edge of the chair like a
monkey in a zoo, and the skin of his thighs had some
weird blemishes which disgusted me completely. Then
Dédée grabbed the blanket and wrapped it tightly around
him, while Johnny was laughing and seemed very cheerful. I said goodbye hesitatingly, promised to come back
the next day, and Dédée accompanied me to the landing,
closing the door so Johnny couldn't hear what she was
going to say to me.

"He's been like this since we got back from the Belgian
tour. He'd played very well everyplace, and I was so
happy."

"I wonder where he got the heroin from," I said, looking her right in the eye.

"Don't know. He'd been drinking wine and cognac almost constantly. He's been shooting up too, but less than
there . . ."

There was Baltimore and New York, three months in
Bellevue psychiatric, and a long stretch in Camarillo.

"Did Johnny play really well in Belgium, Dédée?"

"Yes, Bruno, better than ever, seems to me. The people
went off their heads, and the guys in the band told me so,

too, a number of times. Then all at once some weird things were happening, like always with Johnny, but luckily never in front of an audience. I thought . . . but you see now, he's worse than ever."

"Worse than in New York? You didn't know him those years."

Dédée's not stupid, but no woman likes you to talk about her man before she knew him, aside from the fact that now she has to put up with him and whatever "before" was is just words. I don't know how to say it to her, I don't even trust her fully, but finally I decide.

"I guess you're short of cash."

"We've got that contract beginning day after tomorrow," said Dédée.

"You think he's going to be able to record and do the gig with an audience too?"

"Oh, sure." Dédée seemed a bit surprised. "Johnny can play better than ever if Dr. Bernard can get rid of that flu. The problem is the horn."

"I'll take care of that. Here, take this, Dédée. Only . . . Maybe better Johnny doesn't know about it."

"Bruno . . ."

I made a motion with my hand and began to go down the stairway, I'd cut off the predictable words, the hopeless gratitude. Separated from her by four or five steps, made it easier for me to say it to her.

"He can't shoot up before the first concert, not for anything in the world. You can let him smoke a little, but no money for the other thing."

Dédée didn't answer at all, though I saw how her hands were twisting and twisting the bills as though she were trying to make them disappear. At least I was sure that Dédée wasn't on drugs. If she went along with it, it was only out of love or fear. If Johnny gets down on his knees, like I saw once in Chicago, and begs her with tears . . . But that's a chance, like everything else with Johnny, and for the moment they'd have enough money to eat, and for medicines. In the street I turned up the collar on my raincoat because it was beginning to drizzle, and took a breath so deep that my lungs hurt; Paris smelled clean, like fresh bread. Only then I noticed how Johnny's place had smelled, of Johnny's body sweating under the blanket. I went into a café for a shot of cognac and to wash my mouth out, maybe also the memory that insisted and insisted in Johnny's words, his stories, his way of seeing what I didn't see and, at bottom, didn't want to see. I began to think of the day after tomorrow and it was like tranquillity descending, like a bridge stretching beautifully from the zinc counter into the future.

When one is not too sure of anything, the best thing to do is to make obligations for oneself that'll act as pontoons. Two or three days later I thought that I had an obligation to find out if the marquesa was helping Johnny Carter score for heroin, and I went to her studio down in Montparnasse. The marquesa is really a marquesa, she's got mountains of money from the marquis, though it's been some time they've been divorced because of dope and other, similar, reasons. Her friendship with Johnny dates from New York, probably from the year when Johnny got famous overnight simply because someone had given him the chance to get four or five guys together who dug his style, and Johnny could work comfortably for the first time, and what he blew left everyone in a state of shock. This is not the place to be a jazz critic, and anyone who's interested can read my book on Johnny and the new postwar style, but I can say that forty-eight— let's say until fifty—was like an explosion in music, but a cold, silent explosion, an explosion where everything remained in its place and there were no screams or debris flying, but the crust of habit splintered into a million pieces until its defenders (in the bands and among the public) made hipness a question of self-esteem over something which didn't feel to them as it had before.

Because after Johnny's step with the alto sax you couldn't keep on listening to earlier musicians and think that they were the end; one must submit and apply that sort of disguised resignation which is called the historical sense, and say that any one of those musicians had been stupendous, and kept on being so, in his moment. Johnny had passed over jazz like a hand turning a page, that was it.

The marquesa had the ears of a greyhound for everything that might be music, she'd always admired Johnny and his friends in the group enormously. I imagine she must have "loaned" them no small amount of dollars in the Club 33 days, when the majority of critics were screaming bloody murder at Johnny's recordings, and were criticizing his jazz by worse-than-rotten criteria. Probably also, in that period, the marquesa began sleeping with Johnny from time to time, and shooting up with him. I saw them together often before recording sessions or during intermissions at concerts, and Johnny seemed enormously happy at the marquesa's side, even though Lan and the kids were waiting for him on another floor or at his house. But Johnny never had the vaguest idea of what it is to wait for anything, he couldn't even imagine that anyone was somewhere waiting for him. Even to his way of dropping Lan, which tells it like it really is with him. I saw the postcard that he sent from Rome after being gone for four months (after climbing onto a plane with two other musicians, Lan knowing nothing about it). The postcard showed Romulus and Remus, which had always been a big joke with Johnny (one of his numbers has that title), said: "Waking alone in a multitude of loves," which is part of a first line of a Dylan Thomas poem, Johnny was reading Dylan all the time then; Johnny's agents in the States agreed to deduct a part of their percentages and give it to Lan, who, for her part, understood quickly enough that it hadn't been such a bad piece of business to have gotten loose from Johnny. Somebody told me that the marquesa had given Lan money too, without Lan knowing where it had come from. Which didn't surprise me at all, because the marquesa was absurdly generous and understood the world, a little like those omelets she makes at her studio when the boys begin to arrive in droves, and which begins to take on the aspect of a kind of permanent omelet that you throw different things into and you go on cutting out hunks and offering them in place of what's really missing.

I found the marquesa with Marcel Gavoty and Art Boucaya, and they happened just at that moment to be talking about the sides Johnny had recorded the previous afternoon. They fell all over me as if I were the archangel himself arriving, the marquesa necked with me until it was beginning to get tedious, and the boys applauded the performance, bassist and baritone sax. I had to take refuge behind an easy chair and stand them off as best I could, all because they'd learned that I'd provided the magnificent sax with which Johnny had cut four or five of the best. The marquesa said immediately that Johnny was a dirty rat, and how they'd had a fight (she didn't say over what) and that the dirty rat knew very well that all he had to do was beg her pardon properly and there would have been a check immediately to buy a new horn. Naturally Johnny hadn't wanted to beg her pardon since his return to Paris—the fight appears to have taken place in London, two months back— and so nobody'd known that he lost his goddamned horn in the metro, etcetera. When the marquesa started yakking you wondered if Dizzy's style hadn't glued up her diction, it was such an interminable series of variations in the most unexpected registers, until the end when the marquesa slapped her thighs mightily, opened her mouth wide and began to laugh as if someone were tickling her to death. Then Art Boucaya took advantage of the break to give me details of the session the day before, which I'd missed on account of my wife having pneumonia.

"Tica can tell you," Art said, pointing to the marquesa who was still squirming about with laughter. "Bruno, you can't imagine what it was like until you hear the discs. If God was anywhere yesterday, I think it was in that damned recording studio where it was as hot as ten thousand devils, by the way. You remember "Willow Tree," Marcel?"

"Sure, I remember," Marcel said. "The fuck's asking me if I remember. I'm tattooed from head to foot with 'Willow Tree.' "

Tica brought us highballs and we got ourselves comfortable to chat. Actually we talked very little about the recording session, because any musician knows you can't talk about things like that, but what little they did say restored my hope and I thought maybe my horn would bring Johnny some good luck. Anyway, there was no lack of anecdotes which stomped that hope a bit, for example, Johnny had taken his shoes off between one cutting and the next and walked around the studio barefoot. On the other hand, he'd made up with the marquesa and promised to come to her place to have a drink before the concert tonight.

"Do you know the girl Johnny has now?" Tica wanted to know. I gave the most succinct possible description of the French girl, but Marcel filled it in with all sorts of nuances and allusions which amused the marquesa very much. There was not the slightest reference to drugs, though I'm so uptight that it seemed to me I could smell pot in Tica's studio, besides which Tica laughed in a way I've noted in Johnny at times, and in Art, which gives the teahead away. I wondered how Johnny would have gotten heroin, though, if he'd had a fight with the marquesa; my confidence in Dédée hit the ground floor, if really I'd ever had any confidence in her. They're all the same, at bottom.

I was a little envious of the equality that brought them closer together, which turned them into accomplices so easily; from my puritanical world—I don't need to admit it, anyone who knows me knows that I'm horrified by vice—I see them as sick angels, irritating in their irresponsibility, but ultimately valuable to the community because of, say, Johnny's records, the marquesa's generosity. But I'm not telling it all and I want to force myself to say it out: I envy them, I envy Johnny, that Johnny on the other side, even though nobody knows exactly what that is, the other side. I envy everything except his anguish, something no one can fail to understand, but even in his pain he's got to have some kind of in to things that's denied me. I envy Johnny and at the same time I get sore as hell watching him destroy himself, misusing his gifts, and the stupid accumulation of nonsense the pressure of his life requires. I think that if Johnny could straighten out his life, not even sacrificing anything, not even heroin, if he could pilot that plane he's been flying blind for the last five years better, maybe he'd end up worse, maybe go crazy altogether, or die, but not without having played it to the depth, what he's looking for in those sad *a posteriori* monologues, in his retelling of great, fascinating experiences which, however, stop right there, in the middle of the road. And all this I back up with my own cowardice, and maybe basically I want Johnny to wind up all at once like a nova that explodes into a thousand pieces and turns astronomers into idiots for a whole week, and then one can go off to sleep and tomorrow is another day.

It felt as though Johnny had surmised everything I'd been thinking, because he gave me a big hello when he came in, and almost immediately came over and sat beside me, after kissing the marquesa and whirling her around in the air, and exchanging with Art and her a complicated onomatopoetic ritual which made everybody feel great.

"Bruno," Johnny said, settling down on the best sofa, "that's a beautiful piece of equipment, and they tell me I was dragging it up out of my balls yesterday. Tica was crying electric-light bulbs, and I don't think it was because she owed bread to her dressmaker, huh, Tica?"

I wanted to know more about the session, but Johnny was satisfied with this bit of braggadocio. Almost immediately he turned to Marcel and started coming on about that night's program and how well both of them looked in their brand-new gray suits in which they were going to appear at the theater. Johnny was really in great shape, and you could see he hadn't used a needle overmuch in days; he has to take exactly the right amount to put him in the mood to play. And just as I was thinking that, Johnny dropped his hand on my shoulder and leaned over:

"Dédée told me I was very rough with you the other afternoon."

"Aw, you don't even remember."

"Sure. I remember very well. You want my opinion, actually I was terrific. You ought to have been happy I put on that act with you; I don't do that with anybody, believe me. It just shows how much I appreciate you. We have to go someplace soon where we can talk over a pile of things. Here . . ." He stuck out his lower lip contemptuously, laughed, shrugged his shoulders, it looked like he was dancing on the couch. "Good old Bruno. Dédée told me I acted very bad, honestly."

"You had the flu. You better now?"

"It wasn't flu. The doc arrived and right away began telling me how he liked jazz enormously, and that one night I'd have to come to his house and listen to records. Dédée told me that you gave her money."

"So you could get through all right until you get paid. How do you feel about tonight?"

"Good, shit, I feel like playing, I'd play right now if I had the horn, but Dédée insisted she'd bring it to the theater herself. It's a great horn, yesterday it felt like I was making love when I was playing it. You should have seen Tica's face when I finished. Were you jealous, Tica?"

They began to laugh like hell again, and Johnny thought it an opportune moment to race across the studio with great leaps of happiness, and between him and Art they started dancing without the music, raising and lowering their eyebrows to set the beat. It's impossible to get impatient with either Johnny or Art; it'd be like getting annoyed with the wind for blowing your hair into a mess. Tica, Marcel and I, in low voices, traded our conceptions of what was going to happen that night. Marcel is certain that Johnny's going to repeat his terrific success of 1951, when he first came to Paris. After yesterday's job, he's sure everything is going to be A-okay. I'd like to feel as confident as he does, but anyway there's nothing I can do except sit in one of the front rows and listen to the concert. At least I have the assurance that Johnny isn't out of it like that night in Baltimore. When I mentioned this to Tica, she grabbed my hand like she was going to fall into the water. Art and Johnny had gone over to the piano, and Art was showing him a new tune, Johnny was moving his head and humming. Both of them in their new gray suits were elegant as hell, although Johnny's shape was spoiled a bit by the fat he'd been laying on these days.

We talked with Tica about that night in Baltimore, when Johnny had his first big crisis. I looked Tica right in the eye as we were talking, because I wanted to be sure she understood what I was talking about, and that she shouldn't give in to him this time. If Johnny managed to drink too much cognac, or smoke some tea, or go off on shit, the concert would flop and everything fall on its ass. Paris isn't a casino in the provinces, and everybody has his eye on Johnny. And while I'm thinking that, I can't help having a bad taste in my mouth, anger, not against Johnny nor the things that happen to him;

rather against the people who hang around him, myself, the marquesa and Marcel, for example. Basically we're a bunch of egotists; under the pretext of watching out for Johnny what we're doing is protecting our idea of him, getting ourselves ready for the pleasure Johnny's going to give us, to reflect the brilliance from the statue we've erected among us all and defend it till the last gasp. If Johnny zonked, it would be bad for my book (the translation into English or Italian was coming out any minute), and part of my concern for Johnny was put together from such things. Art and Marcel needed him to help them earn bread, and the marquesa, well, dig what the marquesa saw in Johnny besides his talent. All this has nothing to do with the other Johnny, and suddenly I realized that maybe that was what Johnny was trying to tell me when he yanked off the blanket and left himself as naked as a worm, Johnny obsessed by something that his intelligence was not equal to comprehending, but which floats slowly into his music, caresses his skin, perhaps is readying for an unpredictable leap which we will never understand.

And when one thinks things out that way, one really ends up with a bad taste in the mouth, and all the sincerity in the world won't equalize the sudden discovery that next to Johnny Carter one is a piss-poor piece of shit, that now he's come to have a drink of cognac and is looking at me from the sofa with an amused expression. Now it's time for us to go to the Pleyel Hall. That the music at least will save the rest of the night, and fulfill basically one of its worst missions, to lay down a good smokescreen in front of the mirror, to clear us off the map for couple of hours.

As is natural, I'll write a review of tonight's concert tomorrow for *Jazz*. But now at intermission, with this shorthand scrawl on my knee, I don't feel exactly like talking like a critic, no comparative criticisms. I know very well that, for me, Johnny has ceased being a jazzman and that his musical genius is a façade, something that everyone can manage to understand eventually and admire, but which conceals something else, and that other thing is the only one I ought to care for, maybe because it's the only thing really important to Johnny himself.

It's easy to say it, while I'm still in Johnny's music. When you cool off . . . Why can't I do like him, why can't I beat my head against the wall? Pickily enough, I prefer the words to the reality that I'm trying to describe, I protect myself, shielded by considerations and conjectures that are nothing other than a stupid dialectic. I think I understand why prayer demands instinctively that one fall on one's knees. The change of position is a symbol of the change in the tone of voice, in what the voice is about to articulate, in the diction itself. When I reach the point of specifying the insight into that change, things which seemed to have been arbitrary a second before are filled with a feeling of depth, simplify themselves in an extraordinary manner and at the same time go still deeper. Neither Marcel nor Art noticed yesterday that Johnny was not crazy to take his shoes off at the recording session. At that moment, Johnny had to touch the floor with his own skin, to fasten himself to the earth so that his music was a reaffirmation, not a flight. Because I feel this also in Johnny, he never runs from anything, he doesn't shoot up to get out of it like most junkies, he doesn't blow horn to squat behind a ditch of music, he doesn't spend weeks in psychiatric clinics to feel protected from the pressures he can't put up with. Even his style, the most authentic thing he has, that style which deserves all the absurd names it's ever gotten, and doesn't need any of them, proves that Johnny's art is neither a substitute nor a finished thing. Johnny abandoned the language of "That Old Fashioned Love" more or less current ten years ago, because that violently erotic language was too passive for him. In his case he preferred desire rather than pleasure and it hung him up, because desire necessitated his advancing, experimenting, denying in advance the easy rushing around of traditional jazz. For that reason, I don't think Johnny was terribly fond of the blues, where masochism and nostalgia ... But I've spoken of all that in my book, showing how the denial of immediate satisfaction led Johnny to elaborate a language which he and other musicians are carrying today to its ultimate possibilities. This jazz cuts across all easy eroticism, all Wagnerian romanticism, so to speak, to settle firmly into what seems to be a very loose level where the music stands in absolute liberty, as when painting got away from the representational, it stayed clear by not being more than painting. But then, being master of a music not designed to facilitate orgasms or nostalgia, of a music which I should like to call metaphysical, Johnny seems to use that to explore himself, to bite into the reality that escapes every day. I see here the ultimate paradox of his style, his aggressive vigor. Incapable of satisfying itself, useful as a continual spur, an infinite construction, the pleasure of which is not in its highest pinnacle but in the exploratory repetitions, in the use of faculties which leave the suddenly human behind without losing humanity. And when Johnny, like tonight, loses himself in the continuous creation of his music, I know best of all that he's not losing himself in anything, nothing escapes him. To go to a date you can't get away from, even though you change the place you're going to meet each time. And as far as what is left behind, can be left, Johnny doesn't know or puts it down supremely. The marquesa, for example, thinks that Johnny's afraid of poverty, without knowing that the only thing Johnny can be afraid of is maybe not finding the pork chop on the end of the fork when it happens he would like to eat it, or not finding a bed when he's sleepy, or a hundred dollars in his wallet when it seems he ought to be the owner of a hundred dollars. Johnny doesn't move in a world of abstractions like we do; the reason for his music, that incredible music I've listened to tonight, has nothing to do with abstractions. But only he can make the inventory of what he's taken in while he was blowing, and more likely, he's already onto something else, losing that already in a new conjecture or a new doubt. His conquests are like a dream, when he wakes up he forgets them, when the applause brings him back from his spin, that man who goes so far out, living his quarter of an hour in a minute and a half.

It would be like living connected to a lightning rod in the middle of a thunderstorm and expecting that nothing's going to happen. Four or five days later I ran into Art Boucaya at the Dupont in the Latin Quarter, and he had no opportunity to make his expression blank as he gave me the bad news. For the first second I felt a kind of satisfaction which I find no other way of qualifying except to call it spiteful, because I knew perfectly well that the calm could not last long; but then I thought of the consequences and my fondness for Johnny, thinking of them, made my stomach churn; then I downed two cognacs while Art was telling me what had happened. In short, it seems that Delaunay called a recording session to put out a new quintet under Johnny's name, with Art, Marcel Gavoty and a pair of very good sidemen from Paris on piano and drums. The thing was supposed to begin at three in the afternoon, and they were counting on having the whole day and part of the night for warm-up and to cut a number of tunes. And what happened? It started when Johnny arrived at five, Delaunay was boiling already, then Johnny sat down on a chair and said he didn't feel very well and that the only reason he came was not to queer the day's work for the boys, but HE didn't feel up to playing.

"Between Marcel and me, we tried to convince him to

lie down for a bit and rest, but he wouldn't do anything but talk about, I don't know, he'd found some fields with urns, and he gave us those goddamned urns for about a quarter of an hour. Finally, he started to haul out piles of leaves that he'd gathered in some park or another and had jammed into his pockets. The floor of the goddamned studio looked like a botanical garden, the studio personnel were tromping around looking as mean as dogs, and all this without laying anything down on the acetate; just imagine the engineer sitting in his booth for three hours smoking, and in Paris that's a helluva lot for an engineer.

"Finally Marcel convinced Johnny it'd be better to try something, the two of them started to play and we moved in after a bit, better that than sitting around getting tired of doing nothing. After a while I noticed that Johnny was having a kind of contraction in his right arm, and when he began to blow it was terrible to watch, I'm not shitting you. His face all gray, you dig, and every once in a while a chill'd shake him; and I didn't catch that moment when it got him on the floor. After a few tries he lets loose with a yell, looks at each of us one by one, slowly, and asks us what the hell we're waiting for, begin 'Amorous.' You know, that tune of Alamo's. Well, Delaunay signals the engineer, we all start out the best possible, and Johnny opens his legs, stands up as though he were going to sleep in a boat rocking away, and lets loose with a sound I swear I'd never heard before or since. That goes on for three minutes, then all of a sudden he lets go with a blast, could of split the fuckin' celestial harmonies, and he goes off into one corner leaving the rest of us blowing away in the middle of the take, which we finish up best we can.

"But now the worst part, when we get finished, the first thing Johnny says was that it was all awful, that it came out like a piece of shit, and that the recording was not worth a damn. Naturally, neither we nor Delaunay paid any attention because, in spite of the defects, Johnny's solo was worth any thousand of what you hear today. Something all by itself, I can't explain it to you . . . You'll hear it, I guess. I don't imagine that either Delaunay or the technicians thought of wiping out the acetate. But Johnny insisted like a nut, he was gonna break the glass in the control booth if they didn't show him that the acetate had been wiped. Finally the engineer showed him something or other and convinced him, and then Johnny suggested we record 'Streptomycin,' which came out much better, and at the same time much worse, I mean it's clean and full, but still it hasn't got that incredible thing Johnny blew on 'Amorous.' "

Breathing hard, Art had finished his beer and looked at me, very depressed. I asked him what Johnny had done after that, and he told me that after boring them all to tears with his stories about the leaves and the fields full of urns, he had refused to play anymore and went stumbling out of the studio. Marcel had taken his horn away from him so that he couldn't lose it or stomp on it again, and between him and one of the French sidemen, they'd gotten him back to the hotel.

What else was there to do except to go see him immediately? But what the hell, I left it for the next day. And the next morning I found Johnny in the Police Notices in *Figaro*, because Johnny'd set fire to the hotel room during the night and had escaped running naked down the halls. Both he and Dédée had gotten out unhurt, but Johnny's in the hospital under observation. I showed the news report to my wife so as to cheer her up in her convalescence, and dashed off immediately to the hospital where my press pass got me exactly nowhere. The most I managed to find out was that Johnny was delirious and had enough junk in him to drive ten people out of their heads. Poor Dédée had not been able to resist him, or to convince him to not shoot up; all Johnny's women ended up his accomplices, and I'm sure as can be that the marquesa was the one who got the junk for him.

Finally I ended up by going immediately to Delaunay's place to ask if I could hear "Amorous" as soon as possible. To see if "Amorous" would turn out to be Johnny's last will and testament. In which case, my professional duty would be . . .

But not yet, no. Five days later Dédée's phoned me saying that Johnny is much better and that he wants to see me. I'd rather not reproach her, first of all because I imagined it'd be a waste of time, and secondly because poor Dédée's voice sounds as though it were coming out of a cracked teakettle. I promised to go immediately, and said that perhaps when Johnny was better, we could organize a tour through the provinces, a lot of cities. I hung up when Dédée started crying into the phone.

Johnny's sitting up in bed, in a semi-private with two other patients who are sleeping, luckily. Before I can say anything to him, he's grabbed my head with both paws and kissed me on the forehead and cheeks numerous times. He's terribly emaciated, although he tells me that he's got a good appetite and that they give him plenty to eat. For the moment the thing that worries him most is whether the boys are bad-mouthing him, if his crisis has hurt anyone, things like that. It's almost useless to answer him, he knows well enough that the concerts have been canceled and that that hurt Art and Marcel and the others; but he asks me like he expected that something good had happened meanwhile, anything that would put things together again. And at the same time he isn't playing me a trick, because back of everything else is his supreme indifference; Johnny doesn't give a good goddamn if everything goes to hell, and I know him too well to pay any attention to his coming on.

"What do you want me to tell you, Johnny? Things

could have worked out better, except you have this talent for fucking up."

"Okay, I don't deny that," Johnny said tiredly. "And all because of the urns."

I remembered Art's account of it and stood there looking at him.

"Fields filled with urns, Bruno. Piles of invisible urns buried in an immense field. I was wandering around there and once in a while I'd stumble across something. You'd say that I'd dreamt it, huh? It was just like that, believe it: every once in a while I'd stumble across an urn, until I realized that the whole field was full of urns, that there were miles and miles of them, and there were a dead man's ashes inside every urn. Then I remember I got down on my knees and began to dig up the ground with my nails until one of the urns appeared. Then I remember thinking, 'This one's going to be empty because it's the one for me.' But no, it was filled with a gray dust like I knew all the others were I hadn't seen yet. Then ... then that was when we began to record 'Amorous', if I remember."

I glanced discreetly at the temperature chart. According to it, reasonably normal. A young intern showed up in the doorway, acknowledging me with a nod, and made a gesture indicating food to Johnny, an almost sporty gesture, a good kid, etc. But when Johnny didn't answer him, when the intern had left, not even entering the door, I saw Johnny's hands were clenched tight.

"They'll never understand," he said. "They're like a monkey with a feather duster, like the chicks in the Kansas City Conservatory who think they're playing Chopin, nothing less. Bruno, in Camarillo they put me in a room with another three people, and in the morning an intern came in all washed up and all rosy, he looked so good. He looked like the son of Tampax out of Kleenex, you believe it. A kind of specimen, an immense idiot that sat down on the edge of the bed and was going to cheer me up, I mean that was when I wanted to kill myself, and I hadn't thought of Lan or of anyone, I mean, forget it. And the worst was, the poor cat was offended because I wasn't paying attention to him. He seemed to think I should sit up in bed en-goddamn-chanted with his white skin and beautifully combed hair and his nails all trimmed, and that way I'd get better like the poor bastards who come to Lourdes and throw away the crutches and leave, really jumping . . .

"Bruno, this cat and all the cats at Camarillo were convinced. You know what I'm saying? What of? I swear I don't know, but they were convinced. Of what they were, I imagine, of what they were worth, of their having a diploma. No, it's not that. Some were modest and didn't think they were infallible. But even the most humble were sure. That made me jumpy, Bruno, *that they felt sure of themselves*. Sure of what, tell me what now, when a poor devil like me with more plagues than the devil under his skin had enough awareness to feel that everything was like a jelly, that everything was very shaky everywhere, you only had to concentrate a little, feel a little, be quiet for a little bit, to find the holes. In the door, in the bed: holes. In the hand, in the newspaper, in time, in the air: everything full of holes, everything spongy, like a colander straining itself . . . But they were American science, Bruno, dig? White coats were protecting them from the holes; didn't see anything, they accepted what had been seen by others, they imagined that they were living. And naturally they couldn't see the holes, and they were very sure of themselves, completely convinced of their prescriptions, their syringes, their goddamned psychoanalysis, their don't smoke and don't drink . . . Ah, the beautiful day when I was able to move my ass out of that place, get on the train, look out the window how everything was moving backward, I don't know, have you seen how the landscape breaks up when you see it moving away from you . . ."

We're smoking Gauloises. They've given Johnny permission to drink a little cognac and smoke eight or ten cigarettes a day. But you can see it's not *him*, just his body that's smoking, and he's somewhere else almost as if he'd refuse to climb out of the mine shaft. I'm wondering what he's seen, what he's felt these last few days. I don't want to get him excited, if he could speak for himself . . . We smoke silently, and occasionally he moves his arm and runs his fingers over my face as though he were indentifying me. Then he plays with his wristwatch, he looks at it tenderly.

"What happens to them is that they get to think of themselves as wise," he said sharply. "They think it's wisdom because they've piled up a lot of books and eaten them. It makes me laugh, because really they're good kids and are really convinced that what they study and what they do are really very difficult and profound things. In the circus, Bruno, it's all the same, and between us it's the same. People figure that some things are the height of difficulty, and so they applaud trapeze artists, or me. I don't know what they're thinking about, do they imagine that you break yourself up to play well, or that the trapeze artist sprains tendons every time he takes a leap? The really difficult things are something else entirely, everything that people think they can do anytime. To look, for instance, or to understand a dog or a cat. Those are the difficult things, the big difficulties. Last night I happened to look in this little mirror, and I swear, it was so terribly difficult I almost threw myself out of bed. Imagine that you're looking at yourself; that alone is enough to freeze you up for half an hour. In reality, this guy's not me, the first second I felt very clearly that he wasn't me. I took it by surprise, obliquely, and I knew it wasn't me. I felt that, and when something like that's felt . . . But it's like at Atlantic City, on top of one wave the second one falls on you, and then another . . . You've hardly felt and already another one comes, the words come ... No, not words, but what's in the words, a kind of glue, that slime. And the slime comes and covers you and convinces you that that's you in the mirror. Sure, but not to realize that the only thing that they accept is the slime, and that's why they think it's easy to look in a mirror. Or cut a hunk of bread with a knife. Have you ever cut a hunk of bread with a knife?"

"I'm in the habit of it," I said, amused.

"And you've stayed all that calm. Not me, Bruno, I can't. One night I shot all of it so far that the knife almost knocked the eye out of a Japanese at the next table. That was in Los Angeles, and there was such a fantastic brawl ... When I explained to them, they dumped me. And it seemed to me so simple to explain it all to them. At that time I knew Dr. Christie. A terrific guy, and you know how I am about doctors ..."

One hand waves through the air, touching it on all sides, laying it down as though marking its time. He smiles. I have the feeling that he's alone, completely alone. I feel hollow beside him. If it had occurred to Johnny to pass his hand through me I would have cut like butter, like smoke. Maybe that's why once in a while he grazes my face with his fingers, cautiously.

"You have the loaf of bread there, on the tablecloth," Johnny says looking down into the air. "It's solid, no denying it, toasted a lovely color, smells beautiful. Something that's not me, something apart, outside me. But if I touch it, if I move my fingers and grasp it, then something changes, don't you think so? The bread is outside me, but I touch it with my fingers, I feel it, I feel that that's the world, but if I can touch it and feel it, then you can't really say it's something else, or do you think you can say it's something else?"

"Oh baby, for thousands of years now, whole armies of graybeards have been beating their heads to solve that problem."

"There's some day in the bread," murmured Johnny,

covering his face. "And I dared to touch it, to cut it in two, to put some in my mouth. Nothing happened, I know; that's what's terrible. Do you realize it's terrible that nothing happened? You cut the bread, you stick the knife into it, and everything goes on as before. I don't understand, Bruno."

Johnny's face was beginning to upset me, his excitement. Every time, it was getting more difficult to get him to talk about jazz, about his memories, his plans, to drag him back to reality. (To reality: I barely get that written down and it disgusts me. Johnny's right, reality can't be this way, it's impossible to be a jazz critic if there's any reality, because then someone's pulling your leg. But at the same time, as for Johnny, you can't go on buying it out of his bag or we'll all end up crazy.)

Then he fell asleep, or at least he's closed his eyes and is pretending to be asleep. Again I realize how difficult it is to tell where Johnny *is* from what he's doing. If he's asleep, if he's pretending to sleep, if he thinks he's asleep. One is much further away from Johnny than from any other friend. No one can be more vulgar, more common, more strung out by the circumstances of a miserable life; apparently accessible on all sides. Apparently, he's no exception. Anyone can be like Johnny if he just resigns himself to being a poor devil, sick, hung up on drugs, and without will power—and full of poetry and talent. Apparently. I, who've gone through life admiring geniuses, the Picassos, the Einsteins, the whole blessed list anyone could make up in a minute (and Gandhi, and Chaplin, and Stravinsky), like everyone else, I tend to think that these exceptions walk in the clouds somewhere, and there's no point in being surprised at anything they do. They're different, there's no other trip to take. On the other hand, the difference with Johnny is secret, irritating by its mystery, because there's no explanation for it. Johnny's no genius, he didn't discover anything, he plays jazz like several thousand other black and white men, though he's better than any of them, and you have to recognize that that depends somewhat on public taste, on the styles, in short, the times. Panassié, for example, has decided that Johnny is outright bad, and although we believe that if anyone's outright bad it's Panassié, in any case there's an area open to controversy. All this goes to prove is that Johnny is not from some other world, but the moment I think that, then I wonder if precisely so there is not in Johnny something of another world (he'd be the first to deny it). Likely he'd laugh his ass off if you told him so. I know fairly well what he thinks, which of these things he lives. I say: which of these things he lives, because Johnny ... But I'm not going that far, what I would like to explain to myself is the distance between Johnny and ourselves that has no easy answer, is not based in explainable differences. And it seems to me that he's the first to pay for the consequences of that, that it affects him as much as it does us. I really feel like saying straight off that Johnny is some kind of angel come among men, until some elementary honesty forces me to swallow the sentence, turn it around nicely and realize that maybe what is really happening is that Johnny is a man among angels, one reality among the unrealities that are the rest of us. Maybe that's why Johnny touches my face with his fingers and makes me feel so unhappy, so transparent, so damned small, in spite of my good health, my house, my wife, my prestige. My prestige above all. Above all, my prestige.

But it turns out the same old way, I leave the hospital and hardly do I hit the street, check the time, remember what all I have to do, the omelet turns smoothly in the air and we're right side up again. Poor Johnny, he's so far out of it. (That's the way it is, the way it is. It's easier for me to believe that that's the way it really is, now I'm in the café and the visit to the hospital was two hours ago, with everything that I wrote up there forcing me,

like a condemned prisoner, to be at least a little decent
with my own self.)

Luckily, the business about the fire got fixed up okay, or
it seemed reasonable to imagine that the marquesa did
her best to see that the fire business would be fixed up
okay. Dédée and Art Boucaya came looking for me at the
paper, and the three of us went over to *Vix* to listen to
the already famous—still secret—recording of "Amorous."
Dédée told me, not much caring to, in the taxi, how the
marquesa had gotten Johnny out of the trouble over the
fire, that anyway there was nothing worse than a scorched
mattress and a terrible scare thrown into all the Algeri-
ans living in the hotel in the rue Lagrange. The fine
(already paid), another hotel (already arranged for by
Tica), and Johnny is convalescing in an enormous bed,
very pretty, drinking milk out of a milkcan and reading
Paris Match and *The New Yorker*, once in a while changing off to his famous (and scroungy) pocket notebook
with Dylan Thomas poems and penciled notations all
through it.

After all this news and a cognac in the corner café, we
settled down in the audition room to listen to "Amorous"
and "Streptomycin." Art had asked them to put out the
lights, and lay down on the floor to hear better. And then
Johnny came in and his music moved over our faces, he
came in there even though he was back in the hotel
propped up in bed, and scuttled us with his music for a
quarter of an hour. I understand why the idea that they
were going to release "Amorous" infuriated him, anyone
could hear its deficiencies, the breathing perfectly audible at the ends of the phrase, and especially the final
savage drop, that short dull note which sounded to me
like a heart being broken, a knife biting into the bread
(and he was speaking about bread a few days back). But
on the other hand, and it would escape Johnny, there
was what seemed to us a terrible beauty, the anxiety

looking for an outlet in an improvisation full of flights in all directions, of interrogation, of desperate gestures. Johnny can't understand (because what for him is a calamity, for us looks like a road, at least a road-sign, a direction) that "Amorous" is going to stand as one of jazz's great moments. The artist inside him is going to blow his stack every time he hears this mockery of his desire, of everything that he'd wanted to say while he was fighting, the saliva running out of his mouth along with the music, more than ever alone up against that he was pursuing, against what was trying to escape him while he was chasing it. That hard. Curious, it had been indispensable to listen to this, even though already everything was converging into this, this solo in "Amorous," so that I realized that Johnny was no victim, not persecuted as everyone thought, as I'd even insisted upon in my biography of him (The English edition has just appeared and is bound to sell like Coca-Cola). I know now that's not the way it is, that Johnny pursues and is not pursued, that all the things happening in his life are the hunter's disasters, not the accidents of the harassed animal. No one can know what Johnny's after, but that's how it is, it's there, in "Amorous," in the junk in his absurd conversations on any subject, in his breakdowns, in the Dylan Thomas notebook, in the whole of the poor sonofabitch that Johnny is, which makes him larger than life, and changes him into a living weirdo, into a hunter with no arms and legs, into a rabbit running past a sleeping tiger's nose. And I find it absolutely necessary to say that, at bottom, "Amorous" made me want to go vomit, as if that might free me of him, of everything in him that was going up against me and against everybody, that shapeless black mass without feet or hands, that crazy chimp that puts his fingers on my face and looks at me tenderly.

Art and Dédée don't see (I think they don't want to see) more than the formal loveliness of "Amorous". Dédée

even liked "Streptomycin" better, where Johnny impro-
vises with his usual ease and freedom, which the audience understands perfectly well and which to me sounds
more like Johnny's distracted, he just lets the music run
itself out, that he's on the other side. When we got into
the street, I asked Dédée what their plans were, and she
said that as soon as Johnny was out of the hotel (for the
moment the police had him under surveillance), a new
record company wanted to have him record anything he
wanted to and it'd pay him very well. Art backed her up,
said Johnny was full of terrific ideas, and that he and
Marcel Gavoty were going to do this new bit with Johnny,
though after the past few weeks you could see that Art
wasn't banking on it, and privately I knew that he'd
been having conservations with his agent about going
back to New York as soon as possible. Something I more
than understood, poor guy.

"Tica's doing very well," Dédée said bitterly. "Of course,
it's easy for her. She always arrives at the last minute
and all she has to do is open her handbag and it's all
fixed up. On the other hand, I . . ."

Art and I looked at one another. What in hell could we
say? Women spend their whole lives circling around
Johnny and people like Johnny. It's not weird, it's not
necessary to be a woman to feel attracted to Johnny.
What's hard is to circle about him and not lose your
distance, like a good satellite, like a good critic. Art
wasn't in Baltimore at that time, but I remember from
the times I knew Johnny when he was living with Lan
and the kids. To look at Lan really hurt. But after dealing with Johnny for a while, after accepting little by
little his music's influence, his dragged-out terrors, his
inconceivable explanations of things that had never happened, his sudden fits of tenderness, then one understood
why Lan wore that face and how it was impossible that
she live with Johnny and have any other face at all.
Tica's something else, she gets out from under by being

promiscuous, by living the dolce vita, and besides she's
got the dollar bill by the short hairs, and that's a better
scene than owning a machine gun, at least if you believe
what Art Boucaya says when he gets pissed off at Tica
or when he's got a hangover.

"Come as soon as you can," Dédée said. "He'd like to
talk with you."

I would have liked to lecture the hell out of him about
the first (the cause of the fire, in which he was most
certainly involved), but it would have been almost as
hopeless to try to convince Johnny that he should become
a useful citizen. For the moment everything's going well
(it makes me uneasy) and it's strange that whenever
everything goes well for Johnny, I feel immensely content. I'm not so innocent as to think this is merely a
friendly reaction. It's more like a truce, a breather. I
don't need to look for explanations when I can feel it as
clearly as the nose on my face. It makes me sore to be the
only person who feels this, who is hung with it the whole
time. It makes me sore that Art Boucaya, Tica or Dédée
don't realize that every time Johnny gets hurt, goes to
jail, wants to kill himself, sets a mattress on fire or runs
naked down the corridors of a hotel, he's paying off something for them, he's killing himself for them. Without
knowing it, and not like he was making great speeches
from the gallows or writing books denouncing the evils of
mankind or playing the piano with the air of someone
washing away the sins of the world. Without knowing it,
poor saxophonist, as ridiculous as that word is, however
little a thing it is, just one among so many other poor
saxophonists.

What's terrible is if I go on like that, I'm going to end
up writing more about myself than about Johnny. I'm
beginning to compare myself to a preacher and that
doesn't give me too big a laugh, I'm telling you. By the
time I got home I was thinking cynically enough to
restore my confidence, that in my book on Johnny I

mention the pathological side of his personality only in passing and very discreetly. It didn't seem necessary to explain to people that Johnny thinks he's walking through fields full of urns, or that pictures move when he looks at them; junk-dreams, finally, which stop with the cure. But one could say that Johnny leaves these phantoms with me in pawns, lays them on me like putting a number of handkerchiefs in a pocket until the time comes to take them back. And I think I'm the only one who can stand them, who lives with them and is scared shitless of them; and nobody knows this, not even Johnny. One can't admit things like that to Johnny, as one might confess them to a really great man, a master before whom we humiliate ourselves so as to obtain some advice in exchange. What is this world I have to cart around like a burden? What kind of preacher am I? There's not the slightest bit of greatness in Johnny, I've known that since I've known him, since I began to admire him. And for a while now this hasn't surprised me, although at the beginning the lack of greatness upset me, perhaps because it's one quality one is not likely to apply to the first comer, and especially to jazzmen. I don't know why (I don't *know* why) I believed at one time that Johnny had a kind of greatness which he contradicts day after day (or which we contradict, it's not the same thing really; because, let's be honest, there is in Johnny the phantom of another who could be, and this other Johnny is very great indeed; one's attention is drawn to the phantom by the lack of that quality which nevertheless he evokes and contains negatively).

I say this because the tries Johnny has made to change his life, from his unsuccessful suicide to using junk, are ones you finally expect from someone with as little greatness as he. I think I admire him all the more for that, because he really is the chimpanzee who wants to learn to read, a poor guy who looks at all the walls around him, can't convince himself, and starts all over again.

Ah, but what if one day the chimp does begin to read, what a crack in the dam, what a commotion, every man for himself, head for the hills, and I first of all. It's terrible to see a man lacking all greatness beat his head against the wall that way. He is the critic of us all with his bones cracking, he tears us to shreds with the opening notes of his music. (Martyrs, heroes, fine, right: one is certain with them. But Johnny!)

Sequences. I don't know how better to say it, it's like an idea of what abruptly brings about terrible or idiotic sequences in a man's life, without his knowing what law outside the categories labeled "law" decides that a certain telephone call is going to be followed immediately by the arrival of one's sister who lives in the Auvergne, or that the milk is going to be upset into the fire, or that from a balcony we're going to see a boy fall under an automobile. As on football teams or boards of directors, it appears that destiny always appoints a few substitutes when those named to the positions fall out as if by themselves. And so it's this morning, when I'm still happy knowing that things are going better and more cheerfully with Johnny Carter, there's an urgent telephone call for me at the paper, and it's Tica calling, and the news is that Bee, Johnny and Lan's youngest daughter, has just died in Chicago, and that naturally Johnny's off his head and it would be good of me to drop by and give his friends a hand.

I was back climbing the hotel stairs—and there have been a lot of them during my friendship with Johnny—to find Tica drinking tea, Dédée soaking a towel, and Art, Delaunay, and Pepe Ramírez talking in low voices about the latest news of Lester Young, Johnny very quiet on the bed, a towel on his forehead, and wearing a perfectly tranquil and almost disdainful air. I immediately put my sympathetic face back into my pocket, restricting myself to squeezing Johnny's hand very hard, lighting a cigarette, and waiting.

"Bruno, I hurt here," Johnny said after a while, touching his chest in the conventional location. "Bruno, she was like a small white stone in my hand. I'm nothing but a pale horse with granulated eyelids whose eyes'll run forever."

All of this said solemnly, almost recited off, and Tica looking at Art, and both of them making gestures of tender forbearance, taking advantage of the fact that Johnny has his face covered with the towel and can't see them. Personally, I dislike cheap sentimentality and its whole vocabulary, but everything that Johnny had just said, aside from the impression that I'd read it somewhere, felt to me like a mask that he'd put on to speak through, that empty, that useless. Dédée had come over with another towel to replace the one plastered on there, and in the interval I caught a glimpse of Johnny's face uncovered and I saw an ashy grayness, the mouth twisted, and the eyes shut so tight they made wrinkles on his forehead. As always with Johnny, things had happened in a way other than what one had expected, and Pepe Ramírez who doesn't know him very well is still flipped out and I think from the scandal, because after a time Johnny sat up in bed and started slowly, chewing every word, and then blew it out like a trumpet solo, insulting everyone connected with recording "Amorous," without looking at anyone but nailing us all down like bugs in a box with just the incredible obscenity of his words, and so for two full minutes he continued cursing everyone on "Amorous," starting with Art and Delaunay, passing over me (but I . . .) and ending with Dédée, Christ omnipotent and the whore who without exception gave birth to us all. And this was profoundly, this and the small white stone, the funeral oration for Bee, dead from pneumonia in Chicago.

*   *   *

Two empty weeks will pass; piles of work, journalism, magazine articles, visits here and there—a good résumé of a critic's life, a man who only lives on borrowed time, borrowed everything, on novelties for the news-hungry and decisions not of one's making. I'm talking about what happened one night Tica, Baby Lennox and I were together in the Café de Flore humming "Out of Nowhere" very contentedly and talking about a piano solo of Bud Powell's which sounded particularly good to all three of us, especially to Baby Lennox who, on top of being otherwise spectacular, had done herself up à la Saint-Germain-des-Prés, and you should have seen how great it looked on her. Baby will see Johnny show up with the rapturous admiration of her twenty years, and Johnny look at her without seeing her and continue wide of us and sit alone at another table, dead drunk or asleep. I'll feel Tica's hand on my knee.

"You see, he started shoving needles in his arm again last night. Or this afternoon. Damn that woman . . ."

I answered grudgingly that Dédée was as guilty as anyone else, starting with her, she'd turned on with Johnny dozens of times and would continue to do so whenever she goddamn well felt like it. I'd feel an overwhelming impulse to go out and be by myself, as always when it's impossible to get close to Johnny, to be with him and beside him. I'll watch him making designs on the table with his finger, sit staring at the waiter who's asking him what he would like to drink, and finally Johnny'll draw a sort of arrow in the air and hold it up with both hands as though it weighed a ton, and people at other tables would begin to be discreetly amused, which is the normal reaction in the Flore. Then Tica will say, "Shit," and go over to Johnny's table, and after placing an order with the waiter, she'll begin to talk into Johnny's ear. Not to mention that Baby will hasten to confide in me her dearest hopes, but then I'll tell her vaguely that she has to leave Johnny alone and that nice girls are supposed to be in bed early, and if possible with a jazz critic. Baby will laugh amiably, her hand stroking my hair, and then we'll sit quietly and watch the chick go by who wears the white-leaded cape up over her face and who has green eyeshadow and green lipstick even. Baby will say it really doesn't look so bad on her, and I'll ask her to sing me very quietly one of those blues that have already made her famous in London and Stockholm. And then we'll go back to "Out of Nowhere," which is following us around tonight like a dog which would also be the chick in the cape and green eyes.

Two of the guys from Johnny's new quintet will also show up, and I'll take advantage of the moment to ask how the gig went tonight; that way I'll find out that Johnny was barely able to play anything, but that what he had been able to play was worth the collected ideas and works of a John Lewis, assuming that the last-named could manage any idea whatsoever, like one of the boys said, the only one he having always close at hand being to push in enough notes to plug the hole, which is not the same thing. Meanwhile I'll wonder how much of this is Johnny going to be able to put up with, not to mention the audience that believes in Johnny. The boys will not sit down and have a beer, Baby and I'll be sitting there alone again, and I'll end up by answering her questions and explain to Baby, who is really worthy of her nickname, why Johnny is so sick and washed up, why the guys in the quintet are getting more fed up every day, why one day the whole shebang is going to blow up, in one of those scenes that had already blown up San Francisco, Baltimore and New York half-a-dozen times.

Other musicians who work in the quarter'll come in, and some'll go to Johnny's table to say hello to him, but he'll look at them from far off like some idiot with wet mild eyes, his mouth unable to keep back the saliva glistening off his lips. It will be interesting to watch the double maneuvers of Tica and Baby, Tica having recourse to her domination of men to keep them away from Johnny, turning them off with a quick explanation and a smile, Baby whispering her admiration of Johnny in my ear and how good it would be to get him off to a sanitorium for a cure, and all because she's jealous and would like to sleep with Johnny tonight even, something impossible furthermore as anyone can see and which pleases me considerably. For ever since I've known her, I've been thinking of how nice it would be to caress, to run my hand over Baby's thighs, and I'll be a step away from suggesting that we leave and have a drink someplace quieter (she won't care to, and at bottom, neither will I, because that other table will hold us there, attached and unhappy) until suddenly, no notice of what's coming, we'll see Johnny get up slowly, looking at us, recognizing us, coming toward us—I should say towards me, Baby doesn't count—and reaching the table he'll bend over a little naturally as if he were about to take a fried potato off the plate, and we'll see him go to his knees just in front of me, with all naturalness he'll get down on his knees in front of me and look me in the eye, and I'll see that he's crying and'll know without any say-so that Johnny is crying for little Bee.

My reaction is that human, I wanted to get Johnny up, keep him from making an ass of himself, and finally I make myself the ass, because there's absolutely nothing more ridiculous than a man trying to move another who is very well off where he is and comfortable and feels perfectly natural in that position, he likes it down there, so that the customers at the Flore, who never get upset over trifles, looked at me in a rather unfriendly fashion, none of them knowing, however, that the Negro on his knees there is Johnny Carter, they all look at me as if they were looking at someone climbing up on the altar to tug Christ down from his cross. Johnny was the first to reproach me, just weeping silently he raised his eyes and looked at me, and between that and the evident disapproval of the customers I was left with the sole option of sitting down again in front of Johnny, feeling worse than he did, wanting to be anywhere else in the world but in that chair face to face with Johnny on his knees.

The rest hadn't been so bad, though it's hard to tell how many centuries passed with no one moving, with the tears coursing down Johnny's face, with his eyes fixed on mine continuously, meanwhile I was trying to offer him a cigarette, to light one for myself, to make an understanding gesture toward Baby who, it seemed to me, was on the point of racing out or of breaking into tears herself. As usual, it was Tica who settled the problem, sitting herself down at our table in all her tranquility, drawing a chair over next to Johnny and putting a hand on his shoulder, not pushing it, until finally Johnny rose a little and changed from that horror into the conventional attitude of a friend sitting down with us, it was a matter only of raising his knees a few centimeters and allowing the honorable comfort of a chair to be edged between his buttocks and the floor (I almost said "and the cross," really this is getting contagious). People had gotten tired of looking at Johnny, he'd gotten tired of crying, and we of sitting around like dogs. I suddenly understood the loving attitude some painters have for chairs, any one of the chairs in the Flore suddenly seemed to me a miraculous object, a flower, a perfume, the perfect instrument of order and uprightness for men in their city.

Johnny pulled out a handkerchief, made his apologies without undue stress, and Tica had a large coffee brought and gave it to him to drink. Baby was marvelous, all at once dropping her stupidity when it came to Johnny, she began to hum "Mamie's Blues" without giving the impression that she was doing it on purpose, and Johnny looked at her and smiled, and it felt to me that Tica and I at the same time thought that Bee's image was fading slowly at the back of Johnny's eyes, and that once again Johnny was willing to return to us for a spell, keep us company until the next flight. As usual, the moment of feeling like a dog had passed, when my superiority to Johnny allowed me to be indulgent, talking a little with everyone without getting into areas rather too personal (it would have been horrible to see Johnny slip off the chair back onto his . . .) and luckily Tica and Baby were both acting like angels and the people at the Flore had been going and coming for at least the length of an hour, being replaced, until the customers at one in the morning didn't even realize that something had just happened, although really it hadn't been a big scene if you think of it rightly. Baby was the first to leave (Baby is a chick full of application, she'll be rehearsing with Fred Callender at nine in the morning for a recording session in the afternoon) and Tica had downed her third cognac and offered to take us home. When Johnny said no, he'd rather stay and bat the breeze with me, Tica thought that was fine and left, not without paying the rounds for us all, as befits a marquesa. And Johnny and I ordered a glass of chartreuse apiece, among friends such weaknesses are forgiven, and we began to walk down Saint-Germain-des-Prés because Johnny had insisted that he could walk fine and I'm not the kind of guy to let a friend drop under such circumstances.

We go down the rue de l'Abbaye as far as the place Furstenberg, which reminds Johnny dangerously of a play-theater which his godfather seems to have given him when he was eight years old. I try to head for the rue Jacob afraid that his memories will get him back onto Bee, but you could say that Johnny had closed that chapter for what was left of the night. He's walking along peacefully, not staggering (at other times I've seen him stumble in the street, and not from being drunk; something in his reflexes that doesn't function) and the night's heat and the silence of the streets makes us both feel good. We're smoking Gauloises, we drift down toward the river, and opposite one of those galvanized iron coffins the booksellers use as stands along the quai de Conti, some memory or another or maybe a student whistling reminds us of a Vivaldi theme, humming it, then the two of us begin to sing it with a great deal of feeling and enthusiasm, and Johnny says that if he had the horn there he'd spend the night playing Vivaldi, I find the suggestion exaggerated.

"Well, okay, I'd also play a little Bach and Charles Ives," Johnny says condescendingly. "I don't know why the French are not interested in Charles Ives. Do you know his songs? The one about the leopard, you have to know the one about the leopard. 'A leopard . . .' "

And in his weak tenor voice he goes on at great length about the leopard, needless to say, many of the phrases he's singing are not absolutely Ives, something Johnny's not very careful about while he's sure that what he's singing is something good. Finally we sit down on the rail opposite the rue Gît-le-Coeur and smoke another cigarette because the night is magnificent and shortly thereafter the taste of the cigarette is forcing us to think of having a beer at a café, just thinking of the taste of it is a pleasure for Johnny and me. I pay almost no attention when he mentions my book the first time, because right away he goes back to talking about Charles Ives and how numerous times he'd enjoyed working Ives's themes into his records, with nobody even noticing (not even Ives, I suppose), but after a bit I get to thinking about the business of the book and try to get him back onto the subject.

"Oh, I've read a few pages," Johnny says. "At Tica's they talk a lot about your book, but I didn't even understand the title. Art brought me the English edition yesterday and then I found out about some things. It's very good, your book."

I adopt the attitude natural in such a situation, an air

of displeased modesty mixed with a certain amount of interest, as if his opinion were about to reveal to me—the author—the truth about my book.

"It's like a mirror," Johnny says. "At first I thought that to read something that'd been written about you would be more or less like looking at yourself and not into a mirror. I admire writers very much, it's incredible the things they say. That whole section about the origins of bebop . . ."

"Well, all I did was transcribe literally what you told me in Baltimore," I say defensively, not knowing what I'm being defensive about.

"Sure, that's all, but in reality it's like in a mirror," Johnny persists stubbornly.

"What more do you want? Mirrors give faithful reflections."

"There're things missing, Bruno," Johnny says. "You're much better informed than I am, but it seems to me like something's missing."

"The things that you've forgotten to tell me," I answer, reasonably annoyed. This uncivilized monkey is capable of . . . (I would have to speak with Delaunay, it would be regrettable if an imprudent statement about a sane, forceful criticism that . . . *For example Lan's red dress,* Johnny is saying. And in any case take advantage of the enlightening details from this evening to put into a new edition; that wouldn't be bad. *It stank like an old washrag,* Johnny's saying, *and that's the only value on the record.* Yes, listen closely and proceed rapidly, because in other people's hands any possible contradiction might have terrible consequences. *And the urn in the middle, full of dust that's almost blue,* Johnny is saying, *and very close to the color of a compact my sister had once.* As long as he wasn't going into hallucinations, the worst that could happen would be that he might contradict the basic ideas, the aesthetic system so many people have praised . . .

And furthermore, cool doesn't mean, even by accident ever, what you've written, Johnny is saying. Attention.)

"How is it not what I've written, Johnny? It's fine that things change, but not six months ago, you . . ."

"Six months ago," Johnny says, getting down from the rail and setting his elbows on it to rest his head between his hands. "Six months ago. Oh Bruno, what I could play now if I had the kids with me . . . And by the way: the way you wrote 'the sax, the sex,' very ingenious, very pretty, that, the word-play. *Six months ago. Six, sax, sex*. Positively lovely. Fuck you, Bruno."

I'm not going to start to say that his mental age does not permit him to understand that this innocent word-play conceals a system of ideas that's rather profound (it seemed perfectly precise to Leonard Feather when I explained it to him in New York) and that the paraeroticism of jazz evolved from the washboard days, etc. As usual, immediately I'm pleased to think that critics are much more necessary than I myself am disposed to recognize (privately, in this that I'm writing) because the creators, from the composer to Johnny, passing through the whole damned gradation, are incapable of extrapolating the dialectical consequences of their work, of postulating the fundamentals and the transcendency of what they're writing down or improvising. I should remember this in moments of depression when I feel dragged that I'm nothing more than a critic. *The name of the star is called Wormwood*, Johnny is saying, and suddenly I hear his other voice, the voice that comes when he's . . . how say this? how describe Johnny when he's beside himself, already out of it, already gone? Uneasy, I get down off the rail and look at him closely. And the name of the star is called Wormwood, nothing you can do for him.

"The name of the star is called Wormwood," says Johnny, using both hands to talk. "And their dead bodies shall lie in the streets of the great city. Six months ago."

Though no one see me, though no one knows I'm there,

I shrug my shoulders at the stars (the star's name is Wormwood). We're back to the old song: "I'm playing this tomorrow." The name of the star if Wormwood and their bodies'll be left lying six months ago. In the streets of the great city. Out, very far out. And I've got blood in my eye just because he hasn't wanted to say any more to me about the book, and truly, I don't know what he thinks of the book, which thousands of fans are reading in two langauges (three pretty soon, and a Spanish edition is being discussed, it seems that they play something besides tangos in Buenos Aires).

"It was a lovely dress," Johnny says. "You do not want to know how beautifully it fit on Lan, but it'll be easier to explain it to you over a whiskey, if you got the money. Dédée sent me out with hardly three hundred francs."

He laughs sarcastically, looking at the Seine. As if he hadn't the vaguest idea of how to get drink or dope when he wanted it. He begins to explain to me that really Dédée is very goodhearted (nothing about the book) and that she does it out of kindness, but luckily there's old buddy Bruno (who's written a book, but who needs it) and it'd be great to go to the Arab quarter and sit in a café, where they always leave you alone if they see that you belong a little to the star called Wormwood (I'm thinking this, and we're going in by the Saint-Séverin side and it's two in the morning, an hour at which my wife is very used to getting up and rehearsing everything she's going to give me at breakfast, along with the cup of coffee, light). So I'm walking with Johnny, so we drink a terrible cognac, very cheap, so we order double shots and feel very content. But nothing about the book, only the compact shaped like a swan, the star, bits and hunks of things, that flow on with hunks of sentences, hunks of looks, hunks of smiles, drops of saliva on the table and dried on the edge of the glass (Johnny's glass). Sure, there are moments when I wish he were already dead. I imagine there are plenty of people who would

think the same if they were in my position. But how can
we resign ourselves to the fact that Johnny would die
carrying with him what he doesn't want to tell me tonight, that from death he'd continue hunting, would continue flipping out (I swear I don't know how to write all
this) though his death would mean peace to me, prestige,
the status incontrovertibly bestowed upon one by un-
beatable theses and efficiently arranged funerals.

Every once in a while Johnny stops his constant drumming on the tabletop, looks over at me, makes an incom-
prehensible face and resumes his drumming. The café
owner knows us from the days when we used to come
there with an Arab guitarist. It's been some time now
that Ben Aifa has wanted to go home and sleep, we're
the last customers in the filthy place that smells of chili
and greasy meat pies. Besides, I'm dropping from sleepi-
ness, but the anger keeps me awake, a dull rage that
isn't directed against Johnny, more like when you've
made love all afternoon and feel like a shower so that the
soap and water will scrub off everything that's beginning
to turn rancid, beginning to show too clearly what, at the
beginning ... And Johnny beats a stubborn rhythm on
the tabletop, and hums once in a while, almost without
seeing me. It could very well happen that he's not going
to make any more comments on the book. Things go on
shifting from one side to another, tomorrow it'll be another woman, another brawl of some sort, a trip. The
wisest thing to do would be to get the English edition
away from him on the sly, speak to Dédée about that,
ask it as a favor in exchange for so many I've done her.
This uneasiness is absurd, it's almost a rage. I can't
expect any enthusiasm on Johnny's part at all; as matter
of fact, it had never occurred to me that he'd read the
book. I know perfectly well that the book doesn't tell the
truth about Johnny (it doesn't lie either), it just limits
itself to Johnny's music. Out of discretion, out of charity,
I've not wanted to show his incurable schizophrenia na-

kedly, the sordid, ultimate depths of his addiction, the promiscuity in that regrettable life. I set out to show the essential lines, emphasizing what really counts, Johnny's incomparable art. What more could anyone say? But maybe it's exactly there that he's expecting something of me, lying in ambush as usual, waiting for something, crouched ready for one of those ridiculous jumps in which all of us get hurt eventually. That's where he's waiting for me, maybe, to deny all the aesthetic bases on which I've built the ultimate structure of his music, the great theory of contemporary jazz which has resulted in such acclaim from everywhere it's appeared so far.

To be honest, what does his life matter to me? The only thing that bothers me is that if he continues to let himself go on living as he has been, a style I'm not capable of following (let's say I don't want to follow it), he'll end up by making lies out of the conclusions I've reached in my book. He might let it drop somewhere that my statements are wrong, that his music's something else.

"Hey, you said a bit back that there were things missing in the book."

(Attention now.)

"Things are missing, Bruno? Oh yeah, I said there were things missing. Look, it's not just Lan's red dress. There're ... Will there really be urns, Bruno? I saw them again last night, an enormous field, but they weren't so buried this time. Some had inscriptions and pictures on them, you could see giants with helmets like in the movies, and monstrous cudgels in their hands. It's terrible to walk around between the urns and know there's no one else, that I'm the only one walking around in them and looking for ... Don't get upset, Bruno, it's not important that you forgot to put all that in. But Bruno," and he lifts a finger that does not shake, "what you forgot to put in is me."

"Come on, Johnny."

"About me, Bruno, about me. And it's not your fault

that you couldn't write what I myself can't blow. When you say there that my true biography is in my records, I know you think that's true and besides it sounds very pretty, but that's not how it is. And if I myself didn't know how to blow it like it should be, blow what I really am . . . you dig, they can't ask you for miracles, Bruno. It's hot inside here, let's go."

I follow him into the street, we wander a few feet off and white cat comes out of an alley and meows at us; Johnny stays there a long time petting it. Well, that does it; I'll find a taxi in the place Saint-Michel, take him back to the hotel and go home myself. It hasn't been so awful after all; for a moment there I was afraid that Johnny had constructed a sort of antitheory to the book's and that he was trying it out on me before spilling it at full speed. Poor Johnny petting a white cat. Basically, the only thing he said was that no one can know anything about anyone, big deal. That's the basic assumption of any biography, then it takes off, what the hell. Let's go, Johnny, let's go home, it's late.

"Don't think that that's all it is," Johnny says, standing up suddenly as if he knew what I was thinking. "It's God, baby. Now that's where you missed out."

"Let's go, Johnny, let's go home, it's late."

"It's what you and people like my buddy Bruno call God. The tube of toothpaste in the morning, they call that God. The garbage can, they call that God. Afraid of kicking the bucket, they call that God. And you have the barefaced nerve to mess me up with that pigsty, you've written that my childhood, and my family, and I don't know what ancestral heritage of the Negro . . . shit. A mountain of rotten eggs and you in the middle of it crowing, very happy with your God. I don't want your God, he's never been mine."

"The only thing I said is that Negro music . . ."

"I don't want your God," Johnny says again. "Why've you made me accept him in your book? I don't know if there's a God, I play my music, I make my God, I don't need your inventions, leave those to Mahalia Jackson and the Pope, and right now you're going to take that part out of your book."

"If you insist," I say, to say something. "In the second edition."

"I'm as alone as that cat, much more alone because I know it and he doesn't. Damn, he's digging his nails into my hand. Bruno, jazz is not only music, I'm not only Johnny Carter."

"Exactly what I was trying to say when I wrote that sometimes you play like . . ."

"Like it's raining up my asshole," Johnny says, and it's the first time all night that I feel he's getting really sore. "A man can't say anything, right away you translate it into your filthy language. If I play and you see angels, that's not my fault. If the others open their fat yaps and say that I've reached perfection, it's not my fault. And that's the worst thing, the thing you really and truly left out of your book, Bruno, and that's that I'm not worth a damn, that what I play and what the people applaud me for is not worth a damn, really not worth a damn."

Truly a very rare modesty at this hour of the morning. This Johnny . . .

"How can I explain it to you?" Johnny yells, putting his hands on my shoulders, jerking me to the right and to the left. (Cut out the noise! they scream from a window.) "It isn't a question of more music or less music, it's something else . . . for example, it's the difference between Bee being dead and being alive. What I'm playing is Bee dead, you dig, while what I want to, what I want to . . . And sometimes because of that I wreck the horn and people think that I'm up to my ears in booze. Really, of course, I'm always smashed when I do it, because after all, a horn costs a lot of bread."

"Let's go this way. I'll get a taxi and drop you at the hotel."

"You're a mother of goodness, Bruno," Johnny sneers.
"Old buddy Bruno writes everything down in his notebook that you say, except the important things. I never
would have believed you could be so wrong until Art
passed that book on to me. At the beginning I thought
you were talking about someone else, about Ronnie or
about Marcel, and then Johnny here and Johnny there, I
mean it was about me and I wondered, but where am I?,
and you dish it out about me in Baltimore, and at
Birdland, and my style ... Listen," he added almost
coldly, "it isn't that I didn't realize that you'd written a
book for the public. That's very fine, and everything you
say about my way of playing and feeling jazz seems
perfectly okay to me. Why are we going on talking about
the book? A piece of garbage floating in the Seine, that
piece of straw floating beside the dock, your book. And
I'm that other straw, and you're that bottle going by
bobbing over there. Bruno, I'm going to die without having found ... without ..."

I catch him under his arms and hold him up, I prop
him against the railing above the pier. He's slipping into
his usual delirium, he mutters parts of words, spits.

"Without having found," he repeats. "Without having
found ..."

"What is it you want to find, brother," I tell him. "You
don't have to ask the impossible, what you have found is
enough for ..."

"For you, I know," Johnny says bitterly. "For Art, for
Dédée, for Lan ... You donno how ... Sure, every once
in a while the door opens a little bit ... Look at the two
straws, they've met, see they're dancing, one in front of
the other ... It's pretty, huh ... It began to open out ...
Time ... I told you, it seems to me that time business
... Bruno, all my life in my music I looked for that door
to open finally. Nothing, a crack ... I remember in New
York one night ... A red dress. Yeah, red, and it fit her
beautifully. Okay, one night we were with Miles and Hal

. . . we were carrying it for about an hour I think, playing the same piece, all by ourselves, happy . . . Miles played something so lovely it almost pulled me out of my chair, then I let loose, I just closed my eyes and I flew. Bruno, I swear I was flying . . . And I was hearing it like from a place very far away, but inside me just the same, beside myself, someone was standing there . . . Not exactly someone . . . Look, the bottle, it's incredible how it bobs along . . . It wasn't anyone, just that you look for comparisons . . . It was the sureness, the meeting, like in some dreams, what do you think?, when everything's resolved, Lan and the chicks waiting for you with a turkey in the oven, you get in the car and never hit a red light, everything running as smooth as a billiard ball. And who I had beside me was like myself but not taking up any space, without being in New York at all, and especially without time, without afterwards . . . without there having to be an afterwards . . . for a while there wasn't anything but always . . . And I didn't know that it was a lie, that that happened because I was lost in the music, and that I hardly finish playing, because after all I had to give Hal his chance to do his thing at the piano, at that same moment my head would fall out, I'd be plunged into myself . . ."

He's crying softly, he rubs his eyes with his filthy hands. Me, I don't know what to do, it's so late, the dampness coming up from the river, we're going to catch cold, both of us.

"It felt like I wanted to swim with no water," Johnny murmurs. "It felt like I wanted to have Lan's red dress but without Lan inside it. And Bee's dead, Bruno. And I think you're right, your book really is very good."

"Let's go, Johnny, I'm not getting offended at what you think's bad about the book."

"It's not that, your book is okay because . . . because it doesn't have urns, Bruno. It's like what Satchmo blows, that clean, that pure. Doesn't it seem to you that what

Satch's playing is like a birthday party or a decent action? We . . . I tell you I felt like I wanted to swim without water. It seemed to me . . . no you have to be an idiot . . . it seemed to me that one day I was going to find something else. I wasn't satisfied, I thought that the good things, Lan's red dress, even Bee, were like rat traps, I don't know how to put it any other way . . . Traps so that you would conform, dig, so that you would say everything's all right, baby. Bruno, I think that Lan and jazz, yeah, even jazz, were like advertisements in a magazine, pretty things so that I would stay conformed like you stay because you've got Paris and your wife and your work . . . I got my sax . . . and my sex, like the good book say. Everything that's missing. Traps, baby . . . because it's impossible there's nothing else, it can't be we're that close to it, that much on the other side of the door . . ."

"The only thing that counts is to give whatever one has that's possible," I say, feeling incredibly stupid.

"And win the poll every year in *Down Beat*, right," Johnny agrees. "Sure, baby. Sure. Sure. Sure. Sure."

I'm moving little by little toward the square. With any luck there'll be a taxi on the corner.

"On top of everything, I don't buy your God," murmured Johnny. "Don't come on to me that way, I won't put up with it. If it's really him on the other side of the door, fuck it. There's no use getting past that door if it's him on the other side opening it. Kick the goddamn thing in, right? Break the mother down with your fist, come all over the door, piss all day long against the door. Right? That time in New York I think I opened the door with my music, until I had to stop and then the sonofabitch closed it in my face only because I hadn't prayed to him ever, because I'm never going to pray to him, because I don't wanna know nothing about that goddamned uniformed doorman, that opener of doors in exchange for a goddamned tip, that . . ."

Poor Johnny, then he complains that you can't put

these things in a book. Three o'clock in the morning, Jesus Christ.

Tica went back to New York, Johnny went back to New York (without Dédée, now happily settled at Louis Perron's, a very promising trombonist). Baby Lennox went back to New York. The season in Paris was very dull and I missed my friends. My book on Johnny was selling very well all over, and naturally Sammy Pretzal was already talking about the possibility of an adaptation for Hollywood; when you think of the relation of the franc rate to the dollar, that's always an interesting proposition. My wife was still furious over my passage with Baby Lennox, nothing too serious overall finally, Baby is promiscuous in a reasonably marked manner and any intelligent woman would have to understand that things like that don't compromise the conjugal equilibrium, aside from which, Baby had already gone back to New York with Johnny, she'd decided that she'd enjoy returning on the same boat with Johnny. She'd already be shooting junk with Johnny, and lost like him, poor doll. And "Amorous" had just been released in Paris, just as the second edition of my book went to press and they were talking about translating it into German. I had thought a great deal about the changes possible in a second edition. To be honest within the limits permitted by the profession, I wondered whether it would not be necessary to show the personality of my subject in another light. I discussed it at different times with Delaunay and with Hodeir, they didn't really know what to advise me because they thought the book terrific and realized that the public liked it the way it was. It seemed I was being warned that they were both afraid of a literary infection, that I would end up by riddling the work with nuances which would have little or nothing to do with Johnny's music, at least as all of us understood it. It appeared to me that the opinion of people in authority (and my own personal decision, it would be dumb to negate that at this level of consideration) justified putting the second edition to bed as was. A close reading of the trade magazines from the States (four stories on Johnny, news of a new suicide attempt, this time with tincture of iodine, stomach pump and three weeks in the hospital, working in Baltimore again as though nothing had happened) calmed me sufficiently, aside from the anguish I felt at these ghastly backslidings. Johnny had not said one compromising word about the book. Example (in *Stomping Around*, a music magazine out of Chicago, Teddy Rogers' interview with Johnny): "Have you read what Bruno V———in Paris wrote about you?" "Yes, it's very good." "Nothing to say about the book?" "Nothing, except that it's fine. Bruno's a great guy." It remained to be seen what Johnny might say if he were walking around drunk or high, but at least there were no rumors of the slightest contradiction from him. I decided not to touch the second edition, to go on putting Johnny forth as he was at bottom: a poor sonofabitch with barely mediocre intelligence, endowed like so many musicians, so many chess players and poets, with the gift of creating incredible things without the slightest consciousness (at most, the pride of a boxer who knows how strong he is) of the dimensions of his work. Everything convinced me to keep, no matter what, this portrait of Johnny; it wasn't worth it to create complications with an audience that was crazy about jazz but cared nothing for either musical or psychological analysis, nothing that wasn't instant satisfaction and clear-cut besides, hands clapping to keep the beat, faces gone beatific and relaxed, the music that was driving through the skin, seeping into the blood and breath, and then finish, to hell with profound motives.

First two telegrams came (one to Delauney, one to me, in the afternoon the newspapers came out with their idiotic comments); twenty days later I had a letter from Baby Lennox, who had not forgotten me. "They treated him wonderfully at Bellevue and I went to fetch him when he got out. We were living in Mike Russolo's apartment, he's gone on tour to Norway. Johnny was in very good shape, and even though he didn't want to play dates, he agreed to record with the boys at Club 28. You I can tell this, really he was pretty weak"—I can imagine what Baby meant by that after our affair in Paris—"and at night he scared me, the way he'd breathe and moan. The only thing that softens it for me," Baby summed it up beautifully, "is that he died happy and without knowing it was coming. He was watching TV and all of a sudden slumped to the floor. They told me it was instantaneous." From which one inferred that Baby had not been present, and the assumption was correct because later we found out that Johnny was living at Tica's place and that he'd been there with her for five days, depressed and preoccupied, talking about quitting jazz, going to live in Mexico and work in the fields (he'd handed that to everybody at some time or other in his life, it's almost boring), and that Tica was taking care of him and doing everything possible to keep him quiet, making him think of the future (this is what Tica said later, as if she or Johnny had ever had the slightest idea of the future). In the middle of a television program which Johnny was enjoying, he started to cough, all at once he slumped down all of a sudden, etc. I'm not all that sure that death was as instantaneous as Tica declared to the police (Johnny's death in her apartment had put her in an unusually tight spot she was trying to get out of, pot was always within reach, and probably a stash of heroin somewhere, poor Tica'd had several other bad scenes there, and the not completely convincing results of the autopsy. One can imagine completely what a doctor would find in Johnny's lungs and liver). "You wouldn't want to know how painful his death is to me, although I could tell you some other things," sweet Baby added gently, "but sometime when I feel better I'll write you or tell you (it looks like Rogers wants to get me contracts in Paris and Berlin) everything you need to know, you were Johnny's best friend." And after a page dedicated to insulting Tica, you'd believe she not only caused Johnny's death but was responsible for the attack on Pearl Harbor and the Black Plague, poor Baby ended up: "Before I forget, one day in Bellevue he asked after you a lot, he was mixed up and thought you were in New York and didn't want to come see him, he was talking all the time about fields full of things, and after he was calling for you, even cussing you out, poor baby. You know what a fever's like. Tica told Bob Carey that Johnny's last words were something like: 'Oh, make me a mask,' but you can imagine how at that moment . . ." I sure could imagine it. "He'd gotten very fat," Baby added at the end of her letter, "and panted out of breath when he walked." These were details you might expect from a person as scrupulous as Baby Lennox.

All this happened at the same time that the second edition of my book was published, but luckily I had time to incorporate an obituary note edited under full steam and inserted, along with a news photo of the funeral in which many famous jazzmen were identifiable. In that format the biography remained, so to speak, intact and finished. Perhaps it's not right that I say this, but naturally I was speaking from a merely aesthetic point of view. They're already talking of a new translation, into Swedish or Norwegian, I think. My wife is delighted at the news.

THE AUTHORS

Some of the following biographical information has been taken from *Current Biography*, *Contemporary Novelists*, *The International Dictionary of 20th Century Biography*, and *Contemporary Authors*.

ANGELOU, MAYA (1928–). Born in St. Louis. Angelou is best known for her volumes of memoirs: *I Know Why the Caged Bird Sings* (1970), *Gather Together in My Name* (1974), *Singin' and Swingin' and Gettin' Merry Like Christmas* (1976), *The Heart of a Woman* (1981), and *All God's Children Need Traveling Shoes* (1986). She has also published several collections of poetry and produced and acted in a number of plays. She is currently Reynolds Professor of American Studies at Wake Forest University in Winston-Salem, North Carolina.

BALDWIN, JAMES (1924–1987). Born in Harlem. James Baldwin is one of America's preeminent black writers. His best-known works include *Go Tell It on the Mountain* (1953), *Giovanni's Room* (1956), *Another Country* (1962), a novel about a jazz drummer, the short story collection *Going to Meet the Man* (1965), and *Tell Me How Long the*

Train's Been Gone (1968). Baldwin was an articulate spokesman for the cause of blacks and homosexuals.

BAMBARA, TONI CADE (1939–). Born in New York City. Bambara has written several collections of short stories. *Gorilla, My Love* (1972) and the *The Sea Birds Are Still Alive* (1977). She has also written a novel *The Salt Eaters* (1980). Like Maya Angelou, she is excellent at capturing the rhythms and humor of black speech.

BARTHELME, DONALD (1931–1989). Born in Philadelphia and raised in Houston. He is a postmodernist, eschewing linear development for a surrealistic, collage-like approach to writing. His stories frequently appeared in *The New Yorker*. He published many collections of short stories including *Unspeakable Practices, Unnatural Acts* (1968), *Sadness* (1973), and *Great Days* (1979). Also the novels *The Dead Father* (1977) and *Paradise* (1986). His style is highly original.

CORTÁZAR, JULIO (1914–1984). Argentine novelist and short story writer who emigrated to France in the 1950s. He was an amateur jazz trumpeter as well. His best-known novels are *The Winners* (1965), *Hopscotch* (1966), a novel filled with jazz references, and *A Manual for Manuel* (1978). His short story collections include *The End of the Game* (1967) and *We Loved Glenda So Much* (1983). A postmodernist, Cortázar was a tireless stylistic experimenter. His collection of short essays and reflective pieces, *Around the Day in Eighty Worlds* (1986), contains a marvelous review of a Thelonious Monk performance.

DE VRIES, PETER (1910–). Born in Chicago. De Vries worked on *Poetry* magazine before joining the staff of *The New Yorker* in 1944. He has published more than twenty novels including *The Mackerel Plaza* (1958), *The Blood of the Lamb* (1962), and *Slouching Towards Kalamazoo* (1983). His fictional world is that of the upper-middle-class. He is a master satirist given to wordplay and literary allusions.

FISHER, RUDOLPH (1897–1934). Born in Washington, D.C. Fisher was a part of the Harlem renaissance of the 1920s. He was one of the first writers to depict urban black society, and he did so with a combination of humor and realism. He wrote the novels *The Walls of Jericho* (1928) and *The Conjure-Man Dies: A Mystery Tale of Dark Harlem* (1932). Aside from "Common Meter," his best known story is "Miss Cynthie."

GARDNER, MARTIN (1914–). Born in Tulsa. Gardner is known for his many books that combine math, science, philosophy, and literature. He is a prolific author. Some of his books are *Fads and Fallacies in the Name of Science* (1957), *The Flight of Peter Fromm* (1973), and his recent collection *The No-Sided Professor* (1987). "The Fall of Flatbush Smith," included in the latter, is another jazz story.

HUGHES, LANGSTON (1902–1967). Born in Joplin, Missouri. Hughes published his first book of poems, *The Weary Blues*, in 1926. Carl Van Vechten dubbed him "the Negro Poet Laureate." Hughes was a major figure of the Harlem renaissance. He wrote novels, stories, songs, speeches, and children's books. His short story collections are *The Ways of White Folks* and *Laughing to Keep From Crying* (1930). He described his life and travels in *The Big Sea* (1940) and *I Wonder as I Wander* (1956). Hughes is one of America's great writers. His work is characterized by its biting irony and humor.

JONES, LEROI (AMIRI BARAKA) (1934–). A controversial poet and playwright, Jones grew up in Newark, NJ, and attended Howard University. In the 1960s he converted to Islam and adopted an African name. He is best known for his plays, *Dutchman* and *The Slave* (1964). He is an important figure on the New York City cultural scene and frequently participates in jazz/poetry events.

MARSH, WILLARD (1922–1970). Born in Oakland, California. Marsh was a musician, playing trumpet and then trombone, before devoting himself full-time to writing. He was a college English teacher and a free-lance writer in Mexico. His works include the novel *Week With No Friday* (1965) and the short story collection *Beachhead in Bohemia* (1970). His story "It Always Comes Out Dixie" is also about jazz.

PETRY, ANN (1908–). Born in Old Saybrook, Connecticut. A graduate of the Connecticut College of Pharmacy, Petry has written books for children and adults. The latter include *The Street* (1947), *Country Place* (1948), and *The Narrows* (1954), all novels. Her biography of Harriet Tubman for young readers is a classic. Her collection of short stories, *Miss Muriel* (1971), demonstrates her range and variety in terms of theme and style. She is a writer of great distinction who deserves to be more widely read.

POWERS, J. F. (1917–). Born in Jacksonville, Illinois. Powers' writing milieu is that of the Midwest. His novels are *Morte d'Urban* (1962) and *Wheat That Springeth Green* (1989), both of which deal with the Roman Catholic clergy. He has written several collections of short stories, including *Prince of Darkness* (1948) and *Look How the Fish Live* (1975).

SKVORECKY, JOSEF (1924–). Born in Nachod, Bohemia, Czechoslovakia. Skvorecky's fiction, beginning with his novel *The End of the Nylon Age* (1956), has been variously censored and banned in his native land. His novels and stories take place in totalitarian regimes, and he employs jazz as a symbol for human freedom and expression. His works include *The Cowards* (1970), *The Bass Saxophone* (1977), *The Engineer of Human Souls* (1984), and his collection of detective stories, *The Mournful Demeanor of Lieutenant Boruvka* (1987).

SMITH, C. W. (1940–). Born in Corpus Christi, Texas. Smith is a college English teacher as well as a writer. His books include the novels *Thin Men of Haddam* (1974) and *Country Music* (1975). His collection of short stories is titled *Letters from the Horse Latitudes*.

SOUTHERN, TERRY (1924–). Born in Alvarado, Texas. Southern has written novels, stories, and screenplays. His novels *Flash and Filigree* (1958) and *Candy* (1968, co-authored with Mason Hoffenberg) were labelled pornographic by the literary establishment. His characters include transvestites, psychotics, and dope-taking Academics. He explores a reality that is decidedly counter-culture. His screenplays, co-authored with others, include *Easy Rider*, *The Loved One*, *The Cincinnati Kid*, and *Barbarella*.

WELTY, EUDORA (1909–). Born in Jackson, Mississippi. Welty won the Pulitzer Prize in 1973 for her novel *The Optimist's Daughter*. Her stories and novels depict life in rural Mississippi. Her short story collections include *A Curtain of Green* (1943), *The Wide Net* (1945) and *The Golden Apples* (1950). Other novels are *Delta Wedding* (1947), *The Ponder Heart* (1954), and *Losing Battles* (1982). *The Eye of the Story* (1978) is a collection of her essays, and *One Writer's Beginnings* (1984) is her best-selling autobiography.

YATES, RICHARD (1926–). Born in Yonkers, New York. Yates' better-known novels include *Revolutionary Road* (1962), *The Easter Parade* (1978), and *A Good School* (1978). His mastery of the short story is displayed in *Eleven Kinds of Loneliness* (1964) and *Liars in Love* (1982). Yates describes the suburban world familiar to readers of John Cheever's and John Updike's fiction with, however, a more melancholy undertone.

YOUNG, AL (1939–). Born in Ocean Springs, Mississippi. Young is primarily a poet and novelist. He has also written what he calls "musical memoirs." These include *Bodies and Soul* (1981), *Kinds of Blue* (1984), and *Things Ain't What They Used to Be* (1987). Along with Ishmael Reed, Young was a founding editor of *Yardbird Reader*. His novels include *Snakes* (1971), *Ask me Now* (1980), and *Seduction by Light* (1988). Forthcoming titles include *Heaven: Poems 1958–1988* and *Mingus/Mingus* (with Janet Coleman).

(The following pages constitute an extension of the copyright page.)

Acknowledgments

For permission to reprint the stories in this collection, grateful acknowledgment is made to the following:

Angelou, Maya, "The Reunion," copyright © 1983 by Maya Angelou. Reprinted from *Confirmation: An Anthology of African-American Women Writers*, edited by Amiri and Amina Baraka, by permission of the author.

Baldwin, James, "Sonny's Blues," copyright © 1957 by James Baldwin. From *Going to Meet the Man* by permission of Doubleday, a division of Bantam Doubleday Dell Publishing Group, Inc.

Bambara, Toni Cade, "Medley," copyright © 1974, 1976, 1977 by Toni Cade Bambara. Reprinted from *The Sea Birds Are Still Alive* by permission of Random House, Inc.

Barthelme, Donald, "The King of Jazz," copyright © 1977, 1979 by Donald Barthelme. Reprinted from *Great Days* by permission of Farrar, Straus & Giroux, Inc.

Cortázar, Julio, "The Pursuer," translated by Paul Blackburn, copyright © 1967 by Random House, Inc. Reprinted from *End of the Game and Other Stories* by permission of Pantheon Books, a division of Random House, Inc.

De Vries, Peter, "Jam Today," copyright © 1950 by Peter De Vries. Reprinted from *No, But I Saw the Movie* by permission of Little, Brown and Company. First appeared in *The New Yorker*.

Fisher, Rudolph, "Common Meter," copyright © 1930 by the *Baltimore Afro-American*. Reprinted from *Black Voices: An Anthology of Afro-American Literature,* edited by Abraham Chapman, by permission of the *Baltimore Afro-American*.

Gardner, Martin, "The Devil and the Trombone," copyright © 1987 by Martin Gardner. Reprinted from *The No-Sided Professor* by permission of Prometheus Books.

Hughes, Langston, "The Blues I'm Playing," copyright © 1934, 1962 by Langston Hughes. Reprinted from *The Ways of White Folks* by permission of Alfred A. Knopf, Inc.

Jones, LeRoi (Amiri Baraka), "The Screamers," copyright © by

338